A ONE WOMAN MAN

"Avid Hunter readers will appreciate [*A One Woman Man*]. New readers will be fond of his edgy style and heartfelt delivery and will probably come back for more. . . . He has the uncanny ability to speak to real life situations." —*Rolling Out*

"Hunter's dialogue is urban contemporary and quick, and the story his characters tell makes one think about the consequences that result from the choices we can make."

—*Black Issues Book Review*

"Another good Hunter novel about family love and sibling respect." —*Booklist*

TROUBLE MAN

"Highly recommended—and y'all know I don't recommend much!"
—ERIC JEROME DICKEY, author of *The Other Woman*

"Once again, Travis Hunter gives us unforgettable characters that move and touch us in a way very few authors have done. *Trouble Man* is full of surprises, and it shows that, with patience, love, and a willingness to look deep within our souls, we all have the capacity to grow and change for the better. This is fabulous work from a writer who has proven once again that he's here to stay."

—MARY J. JONES, PageTurner.net

"Travis Hunter continues to deliver entertaining, funny, true-to-life stories with his latest, *Trouble Man,* a novel about love, war, family, and people struggling to do the right thing. I felt that I knew these people." —MALIK YOBA, actor and playwright

MARRIED BUT STILL LOOKING

"Travis Hunter offers insight into the male psyche in ways that will captivate the reader, with stories that are both entertaining and compelling. There is a truth and boldness to his words that make him a noteworthy force in a new generation of fiction writers."
—LOLITA FILES, bestselling author of *Child of God*

"Despite its title, *Married but Still Looking* is about the sanctity of marriage, accepting responsibility for one's actions and understanding the consequences of bad choices. . . . [Hunter is] a good storyteller. . . . Readers are given solid, positive messages. . . . There's a lifetime of messages in these pages."
—*The Dallas Morning News*

"An honest and multidimensional portrait of a self-centered player and his entourage, framed by the crooked consequences of his own indiscretions . . . a fast and appealing read, thanks in part to the authentic characterization of Genesis . . . His struggle is genuine and familiar, and yet his actions are unpredictable."

—aalbc.com

"The novel brings [Genesis Styles] and a handful of other characters . . . to understand that they can accept responsibility as lovers and parents only when they have worked through the consequences of their parents' failings. Growing up means having the faith, and the conviction, to be better lovers and better parents to the next generation." —*The Washington Post*

"Hunter's writing is fluid and fast, and the dialogue is often raw and gritty yet comical." —*Black Issues Book Review*

THE HEARTS OF MEN

"Entertaining yet enlightening . . . Travis Hunter holds the reader hostage in his thought-provoking debut. Be prepared to laugh and cry as you examine *The Hearts of Men.*"
—E. LYNN HARRIS, author of *A Love of My Own*

"Travis Hunter takes us into the lives, the thoughts, and straight to the hearts of men. His work reflects the voice that is often missing—the voice of a brother who loves, listens, and tells his own truth."—BERTICE BERRY, author of *Jim and Louella's Homemade Heart-Fix Remedy*

"A book I'll share with my sons for years to come."
—CARL WEBER, author of *Baby Momma Drama*

"This moving novel . . . is insightful, sensitive and impressively real. . . ." —*Essence*

"True-to-life debut novel. Tough lessons and father-wit loom large in this story about men staying the course and stumbling along the way." —*Black Issues Book Review*

"Interesting and revealing look into the male psyche."
—*Today's Black Woman*

"Even cynical readers may be won over by his relentless positive message and push for African American communities built on respect and love." —*Publishers Weekly*

"Hunter is a fresh new talent and his book, *The Hearts of Men,* gives us a glimpse into the mysterious void where black men hide their expectations, inspirations, disappointments and dreams—a place they rarely share with anyone."—*The St. Louis American*

SOMETHING
TO DIE FOR

SOMETHING
TO DIE FOR

A NOVEL

Travis Hunter

ONE WORLD

BALLANTINE BOOKS

NEW YORK

A One World Books Trade Paperback Original

Published in the United States by One World Books,
an imprint of The Random House Publishing Group,
a division of Random House, Inc., New York.

ONE WORLD is a registered trademark and
the One World colophon is a trademark
of Random House, Inc.

Library of Congress Cataloging-in-Publication Data

Hunter, Travis.
    Something to die for: a novel / by Travis Hunter.
        p.   cm.
    ISBN 0-345-48167-4
    1. African American men—Fiction.   2. Basketball players—Fiction.   3. False
imprisonment—Fiction.   4. Ex-convicts—Fiction.   5. African American
families—Fiction.   6. City and town life—Fiction.   7. Atlanta (Ga.)—Fiction.
I. Title.

PS3558.U497S66 2006
813'.6—dc22

                                                                    2006040007

Printed in the United States of America

www.oneworldbooks.net

9   8   7   6   5   4   3   2

Book design by Jo Anne Metsch

ACKNOWLEDGMENTS

IT SEEMS like a lifetime since my last novel hit the shelves. For all of you who kept me in your thoughts over the last year or so, I hope that *Something to Die For* is worth the wait. Lots of hard work goes into publishing a book and there are a few people I'd like to acknowledge. First and foremost I have to thank God for His many blessings. I look at my life and realize how fortunate I am to do something I really enjoy and still manage to pay the electric bill every now and then.

Rashaad Hunter, for being God's true gift to me. You are my inspiration, little fella, and I love ya love ya love ya. Linda Hunter for being a great mother and for always being there. Dr. Carolyn Rogers for being the best aunt a guy like me could ask for. Aunt Donna and Uncle Dick, thanks for the smiles. Aunt Necie, I still miss you. Sharon Capers, the greatest cousin/attorney on the planet. Andrea and David Gilmore, thanks for everything. My cousins Lynette, Barry, Ray, Gervane, Amado, Hunter, Ron, Daryl, Shay, Tre, Tyler, Trevor, Brittany, Christina, Aaron, Moses, Dominique, Marla, and Billy. Justin Henderson. Shemika Turner, thanks for making me see people for who they are, not who they were J. Louis Johnson, and my siblings Ahmed, Shani, Ayinde, and Jabodi. Melody Guy, thanks for making the fifth book happen. Sara Camilli, my new agent, I really look forward to working with you. Brian McLendon, Dreu Pennington-McNeil, and all the folks at One World who made this book possible, thanks from the bottom of my heart. Mary and Willard Jones, you guys are the best hosts a guy could ask for. Pam and Ruffus Williams, thanks for everything. Yolanda Cutino, Christy Dennis, Crystal Kennedy, The G.A.A.L. book club, Katrina Leonce and the Sista's Sippin Tea, Circle of Friends, and all the other book clubs out there who read my work, I'm forever grateful. Willie and Schnell Martin. Moe and Dionne Kelly. My friends of the Pen. Eric Jerome Dickey, Jihad, R. M. Johnson, Kim Roby, Timm McCann, Victoria C Murray, Lolita Files, Walter Mosley, Kendra Bellamy, E. Lynn Harris, and anyone else who stepped out on faith and did your thing. The Hearts of Men Foundation, let's keep building strong young men. Finally, to the honest, hardworking kids at the DeKalb County Regional Youth Detention Center, I got nothing but love for ya. It's time to put that self-destructive gangsta rap down. You guys are trying to live out what these guys come up with in their heads, and it's sending you guys off to prison by the busloads.

SOMETHING
TO DIE FOR

GUESS WHO'S BACK?

*N*asir Lassiter pulled into an open spot in front of The "U," the University Homes Apartments, and put the silver Aston Martin in park. He took a deep breath and exhaled. He'd been away for far too long. Nasir looked around and felt a chill roll down his spine. He couldn't count the number of times he had dreamed about this day. It had been five long years since his feet touched these grounds.

With the exception of a few minor adjustments here and there, The "U" hadn't changed much since he'd been gone. The housing department finally paid someone to paint the doors the ugliest blue they could find and a short gate was put up, a blatant barrier constructed to separate the ghettofied residents of The "U" from the good-paying students across Fair

Street who attended Clark Atlanta University, Spelman, and Morehouse College. A knock on Nasir's car window disturbed his survey of the surroundings.

"Ay, man, lemme hold a li'l something?"

"Nah," Nasir said, staring at the projects that raised him.

"Nasir?" the vagrant said, leaning in for a closer look. "Is that you?"

"Yeah." Nasir got out of the car.

"Boy, what you doing back here?"

Nasir smiled. "I know I know you but I forgot your name."

The old man folded his arms, an offended look on his face.

Nasir smiled and tried to place a name with the face. "Man, it escapes me."

"It escapes ya, huh? Well, just think of the best-looking specimen the good Lawd ever created," the man said, closing his eyes and showing what he probably considered his good side, which really wasn't all that good.

"Monroe," Nasir said. He reached out and took the old man's hand and damn near choked on the funk. "Damn, Monroe"—Nasir frowned, holding his breath—"I see you still boycotting the bathtub."

"And I see you still got jokes. I was gonna let you just give me five dollars but since you wanna be Richard Pryor, make it ten. And where you get this fancy ride from?"

Nasir reached into his pocket, pulled out a few dollars, and handed Monroe a five. "Here ya go, handsome."

Monroe quickly snatched the bill and slid it in his pocket, then nodded. "Thank ya, baby boy. Welcome home."

As if the streets could smell the return of their prodigal son, folks started showing up from nowhere and crowding around Nasir. He was backed against his car as little kids and adults alike rushed up to him asking all kinds of questions.

"Hey, Nasir, you remember me?"

"You seen yo momma yet?"

"Damn you fine!"

"You still play basketball?"

Nasir couldn't explain the joy he felt to be back among his people. Someone handed him a baby and told him the boy was named after him.

"Forget LeBron James, you our hero 'round here," the lady who handed him the child said.

A loud scream came from behind the crowd and a large woman ran toward them with a raggedy smile and her hair in pink and yellow rollers.

"Nasirrrrrr," she yelled, stopping her momentum by slamming right into the shiny car he was driving.

"You all right?" Nasir tried to hold back his laughter.

"Get your damn hands offa me and give me a hug. Don't act like you don't remember me."

"Crystal, if I lived to be a hundred and fifty, I couldn't forget you. I've tried, trust me." Nasir smiled and stretched his long arms as wide as they would go for an embrace.

"You still got that smart-ass mouth," Crystal said, hugging Nasir.

"And I see yours is still filthy," Nasir said, stepping back to get a better view of her. "Girl, what have you been eating?"

"People," Monroe said in the rear of the crowd.

"Shut up, Monroe, and go wash. You smell like you dead," Crystal barked.

"Don't pay her no attention, Nasir, she gets like that when she's hungry."

Nasir tried to hold in his laughter.

"What you laughing at?" Crystal snapped.

"Nothing."

"Guess what?"

"What?"

"I got four kids."

"Four? My God, you've been busy," Nasir said, surprised that Crystal was even into men. As long as he'd known her, she dressed and carried herself with more masculinity than most of the men in his neighborhood. If there was ever a woman who could make the argument that people could be born gay it was Crystal.

"Nah. Got quadruplets. You believe that? It ought to be against the law for poor folks to have that many damn kids at one time," Crystal said. "But they my babies. With they bad asses."

"Bad! Those li'l fuckers are possessed," Monroe said. "You might as well take they li'l asses down to the jail right now and save somebody from getting knocked crossed they head. And I don't know how they got like that 'cuz we all know they mammy is a positive role model and all. Smoking, drinking, cussing like Jesus ain't coming back."

"Say one more thing and you gonna wish Jesus was already here," Crystal said.

"Girl, you look good," Nasir said, trying to save Monroe from a guaranteed beat down.

"Don't come back here lying now," Monroe said, shaking in disgust. "You know doggone well ain't nuttin' look good on her big ass."

"Monroe, I already warned you now. I'mma knock them two rotten teeth out of your mouth if you keep on."

"Make your move, Sasquatch," Monroe challenged, getting in his boxer's stance.

Nasir couldn't hold in his laughter. Even Crystal smiled and shook her head at the neighborhood drunk.

Man, it was good to be home.

"What's up, playboy?" a voice called from the street.

Suddenly, everyone got real quiet.

Savion Jackson sat behind the wheel of a navy blue 1964 Impala hitting switches that caused the car to bounce up and down.

Standing there looking at the man who set his life on a collision course with hell sent Nasir's mind back to the night that changed him forever.

❖ ❖ ❖

FIVE YEARS AGO, the rain came down in mothball-like sizes as Nasir hustled his way down Martin Luther King Drive toward his girlfriend Ayana's apartment. When he arrived he found Ayana sitting on the sofa with a sad face.

"Hey," Nasir said as he walked over to her. "Is everything all right?"

"No," Ayana said, shaking her head.

Nasir sat down beside her and placed his arm around her but she pulled away.

"I'm pregnant," she spat.

Shocked, Nasir shook his head to make sure he heard her correctly.

"Say that again?" he asked.

"I'm pregnant and I . . ."

"Hey, that's a good thing. Why do you look so disappointed?" Nasir smiled from ear to ear. He couldn't control his joy.

"Because I don't want a baby."

"Ayana," Nasir said, touching her leg cautiously.

"No! I told you how I felt about this a long time ago. So you can save the sweet talk. It's not happening. I'm getting an abortion."

"Wait a minute. This is my child too."

"But it's my body and therefore it's my choice."

"You gotta be kidding me. How could you be so selfish?"

"Selfish? I was beaten, raped, and treated like I was the scum of this earth for as far back as I can remember just for being born. So you can think what you will but I will not bring a child into this world."

"Baby, I understand all of that but none of those things will happen to our child."

"How do you know?"

"Do I look like some deadbeat to you?"

"Nasir, we're wasting our time. I'm getting an abortion."

"So why did you even bother to tell me about it then? If you already had your mind made up?"

"I just thought you should know."

"Maybe we can talk about it later."

"There's nothing else to say."

"So it's like that, huh?"

"Pretty much."

Nasir stared at his girl in disbelief. He grabbed his book bag and stormed out of the apartment.

He took off running to avoid the pelting rain when a beat-up Chevrolet pulled up beside him.

"Playboy," Savion called.

Nasir stopped. Something told him to keep running but his reputation in The "U" had been taking a hit. Even though he didn't actually live in University Homes, he claimed them and lately some of his people started to accuse him of forgetting where he came from. They were calling him bourgeois and said he preferred the company of those rich white folks at Georgia Tech. So, against his better judgment, he climbed into the backseat of Savion's car. The passenger seat was already taken by a shady-looking character Nasir had never seen before.

"Man, what you doing out in this weather? You gonna fuck

around and catch pneumonia, then how *we* gonna go to the NBA?"

Nasir smiled. For as long as he could remember it was always *we* with Savion. As elementary schoolkids whenever Nasir made some athletic team, Savion would run into Nasir's house screaming, "Mrs. Lassiter, WE made the team."

When Nasir scored fifty-five points against a rival high school, Savion walked around telling anyone who would listen, "We hit them hos up for a double nickel last night," and when Nasir shunned the offers of the University of Maryland, Georgetown, Duke, UNC Chapel Hill, and Wake Forest to shoot threes at the hometown Georgia Tech, Savion had T-shirts printed up for the residents of The "U" saying, *We Staying Home.*

Savion pulled into a gas station off Martin Luther King Drive in the West End section of Atlanta.

"Bring me a Gatorade," Nasir said right before he noticed a beautiful woman pumping gas at a nearby pump. Since his selfish girlfriend Ayana practically sealed their fate as a couple with all of her abortion talk, it was time to start looking for a replacement. And that five-foot-nine, curvy piece of work was just the one to help get the search started.

As soon as the car stopped Nasir hopped out and walked over.

"How you doing?"

The young lady ignored him.

"Hello," he said, waving his hand.

Still no response.

"What's up with the sisters? Does it cost anything to speak?"

For his efforts all he got was teeth sucked and a pair of rolled eyes.

"Well f—" Nasir started.

"Well what? Fuck you, bitch?" the woman challenged.

Nasir stopped and stared at her. "Now was that necessary? I wasn't about to call you out of your name. But I guess that's what you think of yourself if that's the first thing that came to mind."

"No, that's the first thing that comes out y'all ignorant niggas' mouths when you get dissed," she said, hands firmly planted on her hips.

"First of all I'm not a nigga and second, why are you dissing me? Have I done anything to you?"

"Leave me alone," she snapped.

"Gladly," Nasir said, turning to leave. He paused, then stopped and turned back around. "You know you are a very pretty lady but that attitude makes you ugly real quick."

"Whatever," the lady said, then her eyes widened as a hint of recognition crossed her face. "Oh my God. Are you Nasir Lassiter?"

Nasir kept walking.

"Wait a second."

Nasir stopped.

"I am so sorry," she said, putting her hand up over her mouth. "You are like my son's favorite basketball player. You did a camp at his school and you signed a poster for him. He talks about you all the time."

"Tell your son I said hello."

"I will but will you sign something for me? He's not going to believe I met you."

"Let me ask you a question," Nasir said, pissed.

"Okay."

"Where do you see black people ten, twenty years from now? Being that we seem to have plummeted to the point of not even being capable of speaking to one another without some drama?"

"I'm sorry about that," she said, slightly embarrassed. "I was having a bad da—"

POW!

POW!

POW!

"Was that a gun?" she asked.

"All day long," Nasir said, looking in the direction of the blast and ducking down.

"Get in the car! Get in the car!" Savion yelled as he ran from the store with his thug of a friend hot on his heels.

Nasir froze.

"Nasir, get yo ass in this car!" Savion snapped.

Nasir didn't move. He couldn't. Savion frowned and tossed a blood-soaked bottle of Gatorade at him right before he screeched out of the parking lot. Just before the hooptie turned onto the MLK, Nasir saw his book bag fly out of the passenger window.

Nasir found his legs and turned to the woman but she was already in her car and speeding out of the parking lot. He watched as the silver BMW screeched away and burned her license plate into his memory, 1DIVA4U.

Nasir heard the familiar wail of police sirens and although he wanted to wait and explain what happened, his instincts told him to run. He picked up his book bag and ran like his life depended on it. He didn't make it fifty yards before Atlanta's finest had him thrown across the hood of a police car.

After being handcuffed and roughly tossed in the back of the police cruiser, Nasir watched through the pouring rain as a police officer went through his backpack.

Relief coursed through his body. *The only things they could possibly find in that bag are books,* he thought. But then everything changed.

The police officer removed a shiny silver gun from his backpack. The officer walked over to Nasir and opened the car door and got right in his face. "I'm willing to bet you a million dollars to fifty cents that all that blood on your shirt came from those people in that store. And I'll double that bet if Ballistics comes back and says this gun doesn't match those bullets that killed those people," the cop said before slamming the door.

Killed those people? he thought as his heart ached. This cannot be happening.

NASIR SAT in jail for more than three months before his case made it to trial. None of the pro scouts or agents, who had acted like his best friends when they were wooing him to sign with them before his arrest, came to his rescue. He watched as the media portrayed him as another ghettofied ballplayer who thought he was above the law. He became the poster child for what was wrong with African American athletes. But the press neglected to mention that he had never been in trouble a day in his life and that he earned a 3.2 GPA at one of the top colleges in the country. That wasn't the slant they were going for.

Nasir was assigned a public "pretender" fresh out of law school to defend him. He told the man at least ten times to look up the license plate number of the woman he met in the parking lot who could corroborate his story of being outside the gas station during the shooting, but the guy was determined to remain incompetent. His dumb lawyer faced a top-notch, overzealous prosecutor, who wasn't about to let the facts get in the way of winning this high-profile case, which would surely boost his career.

Adding more fuel to Nasir's already hellish nightmare, Savion showed up with his own top-dollar lawyer. Pissed that Nasir ratted him out, Savion retaliated by cooperating with the prosecution to pin the murder and robbery on Nasir. Nasir was sentenced to life in prison without the possibility of parole for the murder of the store clerk and his wife.

Nasir looked around the courtroom as he was handcuffed by the court's bailiff and found it ironic that his entire life was undone by black people. The shooter, the cops, the prosecutor, the public defender, and most of the jury and the judge were all people of color.

Nasir turned and looked at his mother who was being comforted by Ayana and when they made eye contact, he literally saw her will break. Her face was contorted by a pain that ran to the depths of her soul. He couldn't take his eyes off of his mother as she collapsed into Ayana's arms much too weak to cry.

Seeing his mother's pain hurt Nasir more than any life sentence any judge could throw at him.

NOW, FIVE years later, Savion had the nerve to approach Nasir as if he had just returned from vacation instead of hell. "Looks like you hit the lottery or something," Savion said from his car. "What kind of ride is that?"

Nasir steadied his breathing. He couldn't believe the audacity of this fool. At that moment, he'd have given his right foot if he could walk over and choke the life out of Savion without going back to prison.

Savion shut his car off and jumped out. He walked over to the Aston Martin and ran his hand across the hood.

"Looks like life done took a turn for the better. What *we* do, banged the warden's daughter or something? I knew *we* wouldn't be up in there for long," he said extending his hand.

Nasir didn't respond.

Savion pulled his hand back and faced Nasir. "Hey, looka here, homie. I know I went out a little foul on that case you caught but them crackers had me on them papers already and you know they would've thrown my ass under the jail if I didn't get that lawyer. He was the one who told me to worry about me. He said you had a big-time lawyer and you were copping pleas and thangs. But it's all good. You home now," Savion said.

Nasir's hands started shaking and he forced himself to breathe.

"Looks like prison been good to ya. Playboy done got diesel." Savion reached out and touched Nasir's thick bicep.

One touch was all it took. Nasir's fist crashed into the side of Savion's face with the impact of a big rig hitting a cardboard wall. The skinny man's eyes rolled into the back of his head and he was unconscious before he hit the ground. His body crashed to the pavement, and Nasir was all over him.

"What the fuck you mean 'we'?" Nasir said, straddling Savion and punching him in the face. "*We* didn't go to prison."

Smack!

"*We* sold me out to save your own sorry ass."

Smack!

"Now yo ass gotta pay."

Smack! Smack! Smack!

Punches rained down on Savion for every wrong Nasir ever endured in or out of prison and not a single person moved to stop him. That was until Sammy showed up.

"Knock!" Sammy called out Nasir's nickname as he grabbed

his cousin's hand and pulled him off Savion. Nasir stopped and looked at his enemy before standing and removing his shirt, which now had Savion's blood all over it.

Monroe walked over and poured a little beer on Savion.

"Get your ass up. You ain't dead," Monroe said, kicking the man.

Savion came to and struggled to his feet. He looked around trying to figure out what had just happened to him.

"Who jumped me?" he asked, looking around wild-eyed.

Nasir stared at his former friend and wanted nothing more than to finish the job but Sammy had a death grip on him.

Savion wobbled but stayed on his feet. He strained his eyes to make out who was standing before him. "Okay, somebody gonna get fucked up. Whoever it was that jumped me, I'mma tighten that ass up."

"Ain't nobody jumped you," Crystal said.

"No, buddy, what you just experienced was a good ole-fashion ass whipping. Something you young folks don't know nuttin' 'bout. Too busy running to get a gun. Li'l sissies is all ya is," Monroe said.

"You wanna get back at somebody holla at me," Nasir said.

"Knock, don't even sweat him. You fresh out of prison and he ain't worth going back," Sammy said.

Just because you live in the ghetto doesn't mean you have to be ghetto, his mother's words registered as he looked down at his bloody hands.

Those words served him well until he went to prison. There, he learned there was no such thing as taking the high road. But standing on the grounds that raised him, he felt ashamed.

"Oh, it was you who snuck me? You gonna regret the day you left the penitentiary, boy. You were safer inside," Savion said, almost crying as he ran to his car and got in.

"Oh, shut up and get yo raggedy ass up outta here," Monroe yelled at Savion.

"Go to hell, stink man, and since you wanna run off at the mouth I'mma tighten yo ass up too," Savion promised before he took off in his car, his tires screeching all the way up Fair Street.

Nasir calmed down enough to give his cousin a hug.

"When did you get home?" Sammy asked.

"Friday," Nasir said, happy to see the first person from his family other than his grandmother in five years. They embraced. "How you doing, cuz?"

"Friday!" Sammy yelled. "Boy, today is Sunday. Where the hell you been?"

"At Granny's. Just trynna get adjusted to being home."

"You seen your mom yet?"

"Nah, I'm about to go and holla at her right now."

Sammy sighed and seemed like he wanted to tell Nasir something but changed his mind.

"Cuz, I swear that car is off the heazy," Sammy said, walking over to the Aston. "This real pimpish right here, boy."

"Yeah, it's nice."

"This you?"

"Nah, a friend from Tech let me borrow it to get around until I can get on my feet," Nasir said.

Sammy smiled. "I could use a friend like that."

"Tell me about it."

"You always had them on-the-ball-ass friends. That's why I couldn't figure out why you were out slumming with Savion," Sammy said.

"I asked myself that question a million times and still haven't come up with a good answer."

"It's all good. How you get out so soon? You ain't snitching, are ya?"

"Snitching? Man, I would've told on God if it would've gotten me out of there but that's not the case. Some guardian angel came and got me," Nasir said with a smile.

"What?"

"Must've been. I mean one day I'm locked up going through the motions and the next I'm told to pack up. They gave me some papers and said I was free to go."

"No lie?"

"None."

"Well, damn."

"Damn is right. I'm sure I'll find out soon enough. Somebody gonna say something."

"How you doing for money?"

"I'm not. I mean I got a few bucks but I'm going to have to get something going with the quickness."

Sammy reached in his pocket and pulled out a large roll. He peeled off several bills and handed them to his cousin.

"Thanks, cuz. I'll get this back to you when I'm on my feet," Nasir said, wiping the blood from his hands onto his balled-up shirt as he walked over toward the building Sammy grew up in.

Sammy turned around and noticed Crystal peeping into the fancy car his cousin was driving. "Crystal, please don't get in that car. It ain't built to hold all that ass."

Crystal gave Sammy the finger and opened the door of the luxury sports car and plopped down in the driver's seat. The poor car's shocks screamed for mercy.

Nasir and Sammy took a seat on the steps of the building.

"Man, a whole lot has changed since you left." Sammy sighed and pulled a little furry animal from out of his pocket and let it climb onto his shoulder.

"Oh yeah," Nasir said, sitting down beside him. "What's up? Give me the short version," Nasir said, smiling. "You know how long-winded you can get."

Sammy didn't smile. He just shook his head. "Why you cut everybody off?"

Nasir turned away and changed the subject.

"Why you walking around with a squirrel on your shoulder?" Nasir asked.

"This ain't no squirrel, man. It's a ferret."

"Like a weasel?"

"The weasel's cousin. I breed 'em. Got folks buying 'em up like crazy," Sammy said, picking up the long animal. "This my stud right here. Boy, I give 'em a shot of Viagra and he'll break his li'l dick off in some ferret coochie. I'm telling you I got a sweet business here, Knock. I can't keep up with the demand."

"Boy, you're a fool."

"I'm doing big dough, baby. Two bills a pop and I'm selling twenty or so every other week. Cuz, I got cages all over The 'U.' "

"Guess that means you stopped selling drugs?"

"Yeah, I had to let that go," Sammy said. "Too much work. Now I just rob a summabitch if things get tight," Sammy said with a straight face.

"You better let that go too. Being locked up ain't no joke."

"Don't you worry about that. I'm scared of cells."

"Good," Nasir said, then turned to his cousin. "Yo man, I heard about Aunt Kim. I'm sorry."

Sammy stared at his cousin then dropped his head.

"You aight?" Nasir asked.

"When your mother dies, something deep happens to you. Losing a father is different. Shit, half of us lost our daddies on day one, but Momma"—Sammy shook his head—"ain't nothing to prepare you for that."

"I hear ya."

"Yeah," Sammy said, ready to change the subject. "Granny told me you were swole up. What are you, about two hundred and thirty pounds?"

"Cuz, you can do one of three things in prison. Fuck, fight, or check into protective custody. So I made up my mind on day one, I wasn't fucking and I wasn't checking in. So I did what I had to do to keep my manhood."

"Yeah, cuz, they would've had a field day with your pretty ass."

"Wasn't happening."

"Yeah. You know the ghetto ain't nothing but a prison itself. Just a different location. When cats got out they would give me the word that you were in there holding it down."

"Whatever," Nasir said. He didn't want to talk about prison. "What's new?"

Sammy's smile disappeared.

"Man," Sammy sighed. "Your mom."

"What about my mom?"

"She missed you, Knock, and when you wouldn't write her or take her visits that did something to her, man. Why you do that?"

Nasir sighed and stared off into the distance.

"What's going on with her?" he asked.

"Keep it to yourself if you want but that was a dumb-ass move on your part, potna. Not to mention selfish. But I'll tell you what's going on with her. When you got sent up, she flipped out. Started walking around here talking to herself and shit. Then she took the plunge and started putting that shit in her arm. Man, she's walking around here like a damn zombie. I'm trynna keep folks off her and she ain't helping me. I damn near caught three-four cases behind her."

"Wha . . . What?" Nasir said, stunned. He felt like he had just gotten hit by a ton of bricks.

"Yeah. That's real."

"How the hell did that happen?" Nasir said, still confused. His mother was one of the strongest women he'd ever known.

"You know Auntie ain't like us. I love her but . . . Now, no disrespect to you or her but she's one of them cultured suburban black folks. That silver spoon she grew up with didn't help her around here. She ain't built for no adversity."

Nasir closed his eyes and when he opened them they were filled with tears. He jumped up and darted off toward his house across the street from Sammy's building.

"Wait up, Knock," Sammy said, snatching up his stud of a ferret and running along beside his cousin. "Don't go in there going off, man. She missed you and this was just her way of dealing with it." Sammy grabbed Nasir's arm to stop him. "Remember, only God can judge us," Sammy said.

Nasir nodded. He and Sammy gave each other brotherly hugs.

"Glad you home, cuz."

"I'mma holla at you later."

"I'll be around."

Nasir ran across the street to the house he grew up in. He took in its condition and surmised that it could use a total overhaul. The gable edges were falling down, bars over the windows were rusting, and the paint had all but evaporated.

He knocked on the door and a cute little girl answered. He leaned back and checked the number on the door.

"Is this Marcy Lassiter's house?"

"Yes," answered the little girl, who looked to be about four or five years old.

"She's not here right now," the little girl said, standing behind the door as if her fifty pounds could stop an intruder.

"What's your name?" he asked.

"Brandy."

"It's nice to meet you, Brandy. Are you Mrs. Marcy's little friend?"

The little girl looked him up and down.

"She's my grandmother."

Nasir smiled. Kids in the ghetto were always claiming other people's parents.

"What's your mother's name?"

"Ayana."

Ayana? That's when his heart hit the floor.

2

LIFE

andstone subdivision's million-dollar estates were home to many of Atlanta's well-to-do African American athletes, entertainers, prominent attorneys, and anyone else who was long on cash.

Ayana Zion sat on the terrace off of her bedroom overlooking a beautifully manicured lawn and watched the ducks swim in the lake on her property. The house she shared with her boyfriend Alonzo could be described as nothing short of fabulous. Six bedrooms with nine-foot ceilings, six bathrooms, a four-car garage, a theater room, an entertainment room with full-size arcade games, and many more bells and whistles. She always dreamed of living in a house like this and now that she did, she could only think of how it felt more like a gilded cage than a home.

For Ayana, the best part about living in Sandstone wasn't all the unnecessary extras, which they hardly ever used, it was the life it provided for her daughter, Brandy.

She had just returned home from dropping Brandy off with her grandmother for her weekly Sunday visit and now she was thoroughly enjoying some much needed quiet time.

The song "Heaven Must Be Like This" danced in her head as she lay back and enjoyed the beautiful Sunday morning.

The phone rang breaking the peacefulness of the moment. She reluctantly picked it up.

"Hello?" she said.

"Oh, you still in my house?" a venomous voice snapped. "I'mma kill you, you conniving bitch . . ."

Ayana placed the handset down in its cradle and closed her eyes again.

Alonzo's ex-girlfriend was the caller. Every two or three months the woman would get drunk and start with the harassing phone calls. Ayana wished the woman would just come to grips with the fact that her days were done *and move on.* Ayana closed her eyes again. She felt a twinge of guilt for her role in the woman's misery because God knew Alonzo wasn't her type but at the time he was her only choice.

The phone rang again a few minutes later and Ayana checked the caller ID: the ex again. She stared at the phone and felt bad. She felt bad for the woman on the other end of the line and she felt bad for herself. Alonzo wasn't really her man and this wasn't really her house. The man she really loved didn't want anything to do with her, and if she was honest with herself, she was just as homeless as she had been when she was born.

Ayana tried to clear her mind. Just as she sat back to reclaim her solitude she heard the chime of the front door.

That could only mean one of three things. Someone was breaking in, Alonzo was home, or his ex-girlfriend had somehow jimmied the lock. She closed her eyes and prayed for a burglar.

Ayana jumped up and hurried toward the master bathroom, anything for a few more minutes of serenity. Alonzo rushed into their bedroom, which was on the main level, and stopped in his tracks when he caught sight of her walking into the bathroom.

"Hey, hey! Where you running off to?" he asked.

"I'm not running off anywhere. I'm going to the bathroom," Ayana snapped. "Is that allowed?"

"You can't speak?" Alonzo said, eyeing her suspiciously.

"Can you?"

Alonzo narrowed his eyes at her, tilted his head back, and took a whiff of the air, trying to sense if anyone else had been in the house.

"How are you, Alonzo?" Ayana said, shaking her head at the paranoid nutcase in front of her.

"Fine now that I see you," Alonzo said, loosening his tie, lustfully eyeing Ayana. "Why don't you turn the Jacuzzi on while you're in there and I'll join you?"

"I'm really not feeling well," Ayana lied, rubbing her stomach.

Alonzo narrowed his one good eye and cocked his head to the side.

"What's wrong with you?" he asked.

"Cramps."

"Cramps?" he asked, confused. "It's not time for your cycle," he said, rushing over to his nightstand for the calendar.

"Alonzo," Ayana said, not believing what had just come out of this man's mouth. "Have you completely lost your damn mind? You don't know everything that goes on with my body."

"Oh yes I do and if you cuss one more time in my house I'mma choke the shit outta you." Alonzo stormed toward Ayana. He lunged toward her as if he was about to hit her.

She didn't even flinch.

"I think I might've been gone just a little too long. You done forgot who pays the cost to be the boss up in here."

Alonzo owned a string of travel agencies, catering to Atlanta's wealthy African American population, that often kept him away from home, and that suited Ayana all too well.

Alonzo refused to tell Ayana when he was leaving or when he would return. That way he could catch her "in the act," if she was indeed acting up. Ayana knew where Alonzo's insecurities stemmed from: his five-foot-two-inch frame. Plus, he wasn't the most attractive man in the world. He wasn't quite ugly but he was beating on its door. And like most short men, Alonzo over-compensated by acting tough. The smallest issue would send him scurrying for his gun.

Alonzo had never been with a woman as beautiful as Ayana. She was five feet eight inches tall, with more curves than a Magic City stripper. She usually wore her long, silky hair in a bun. Her skin, smooth as milk and dark as night, was accentuated by a pair of hazel eyes that had the hypnotic powers of a voodoo priestess. And Alonzo was indeed hypnotized. Never in his wildest dreams did he think he would end up with a woman like her on his arm, and he didn't have a problem letting anyone know what extreme measures he'd take in order to keep her.

Ayana had gotten used to his lack of height and wayward left eye (the poor thing had a mind all of its own), but there was no getting used to that jealousy. His mood swings were amazing. There were times when he would move heaven and earth just to make her smile, then other times he would be ready to join the Taliban and bomb a whole city at the mere thought of her being with another man. Whether he was home or not, at least three times a week he'd go off on a tangent about her cheating on him, and his covetous rages made it very difficult to like him.

A glass left on his nightstand had to mean someone else had been in bed with her. An extra towel in the hamper would set off a windstorm of accusations. Someone calling the house and hanging up could send him on a two-day rampage. But even worse than all of that was the sex. It was pure torture. Ayana was never the type to have frivolous sex, so every time he crawled on top of her she simply closed her eyes and prayed that it would be over soon. She told herself that it was a small price to pay for what she got in return, and what she got in return was security for her daughter.

Rough would be an understatement in describing how Ayana grew up, and she told herself the day her daughter was born, she would do whatever it took to keep her away from any of the foolishness that plagued her own childhood. All she wanted was the best for her child, and Alonzo made sure Brandy had the best of everything. So if Ayana had to sacrifice her own happiness in order to give it to her then so be it. At least that's what she kept telling herself, yet whenever Alonzo was around she felt trapped and she could literally feel her life being sucked right out of her.

Alonzo turned and walked into Ayana's bathroom. He emptied the contents of her wastebasket on the marble floor.

"Where they at?"

"Where is what at?"

"Your little pads," Alonzo demanded. "See that's what I'm talking about. Lies. You don't have to lie to me. If you don't wanna be with me then say so."

I don't want to be with you! she thought but kept it to herself.

"Maybe I emptied the trash, Alonzo. Ever thought of that?"

"Yo lazy ass ain't emptied a trash can since you been here. Now all of a sudden you wanna get all domesticated. I'm not buying it." Alonzo stormed out of the room and into the kitchen. He snatched open the pantry door and kicked over the trash can. Empty. He threw open the door leading to the garage and headed for the big trash can. He snatched the top off and picked through the waste like a homeless man. Then he found a thick pink ball, wrapped in toilet paper. He removed the pink tissue paper, and at the first sight of red, he visibly relaxed. Satisfied with his findings, he tossed it back into the trash can and cleaned up his mess, a guilty smirk on his face.

Ayana stood at the doorway shaking her head.

"Yeah, well that still doesn't give you no cause to be acting all snotty. I've been gone for almost a month and this is the treatment I get? Hell, somebody must've been over here tapping that thing for you." Alonzo tilted his nose up and took a few more whiffs of the air.

"Why does it always have to be somebody else? Why can't I just have cramps?"

"Whatever, Ayana," Alonzo said, still looking at her with that crooked eye. "Don't get smart."

"Alonzo, anything I say to you would be getting smart."

"What?"

Ayana turned and walked away. She went into her bathroom and sat down in front of her vanity mirror. Her fingers traced the edges of a framed picture of her daughter Brandy, as she thought about the events that led her to live in the house with this crazy man.

FIVE YEARS earlier, it was Christmastime at Georgia Tech and folks were running around making plans to be with their families for the holidays.

Ayana worked in the registrar's office, and her mind drifted as she contemplated another lonely holiday season.

"Hey," a handsome young man said to her, smiling from ear to ear. "How you doing?"

Ayana was surprised that one of the most popular guys at the university was talking to her. She was a nobody who didn't fit in with anybody. She didn't wear the best clothes, didn't hang out at the popular sports bars, and she was dark-skinned with funny-looking eyes that made people question her nationality on a daily basis. Nasir Lassiter was the guy everyone said could be the next Yellow Jacket to play professional basketball.

"I'm fine," she said nervously but maintaining her poise.

"Don't look so sad. It's Christmastime," he said, walking over to her. He leaned over the counter and smiled a smile that melted her like wax. "Nasir Lassiter," he said, extending his hand.

Ayana nodded and took his hand.

"Ayana Zion," she said, grabbing a stack of financial aid paperwork to keep busy.

"It's nice to meet you, Ayana. Where's home?" Nasir asked, attempting to draw her into a conversation.

Ayana shook her head. She hated when people asked her that question.

Ayana had been born to a mother who loved her so much she left her behind a Dumpster. She was found by a homeless man, who just happened to be searching for a quiet place to end his own life. They saved each other. The homeless man gave her to a policeman who took her to a foster care center and they shipped her to a group home. From day one, she was unwanted and unloved. Throughout her childhood Ayana was shipped around from one group home to another, and then she hit her teens. Becoming a teenager in the foster care world was like a death sentence. Potential parents were almost always looking for newborns. Most figured if you went that long without being adopted something had to be wrong with you. And Ayana felt like something was wrong with her, she felt cursed. After all, why else had she been beaten, neglected, and, worst of all, sexually assaulted at various foster homes? All for no other reason than being born.

"Where are you from?" Nasir tried again.

"Here and there," she replied.

"Here and there? Are you trying to blow me off?"

"No." Ayana smiled to disarm him. "I'm from nowhere."

"Nowhere, U.S.A., or Nowhere, some other country?"

"Just nowhere."

"Okay. I can take a hint. I didn't mean to pry," he said, walking away.

"You're not prying," she said, stopping him for a reason she didn't quite understand. "It's a long story. One I don't care to revisit, but if you must know, I grew up in a bunch of different foster houses, but none that I would call a home."

"I see. Well, you're very pretty."

That was a first. Most guys didn't find beauty in her hue.

"What about you?" she asked, even though she already knew his bio.

"Nasir Lassiter from University Homes in West End."

Ayana smiled. It felt good talking to him.

"So where are you going for the holidays?"

"Nowhere special."

"What's that mean?"

"It means, I'll be here. Studying."

"Here? I thought the school was closed for the holidays."

"They let me stay," Ayana said.

"Okay, this is going to sound crazy considering we just met like two minutes ago, but why don't you come home with me? My mom can't cook a lick but we make do."

Ayana laughed. Nasir didn't.

"I'm serious."

"I can't do that. You don't even know me. For all you know I could be a mass murderer."

"True but I'm weird like that."

"No, I don't need your charity."

"It's not charity. I'm just asking a pretty lady to join me for dinner."

"Were you the kid who always brought home the stray cat?"

"Yeah, I tried that for real when I was six or seven and the little buster bit me. Look, I believe in fate. I've seen you a trillion times but for some reason today I found the nerve to say something." Nasir looked at his watch and frowned. "But I'm running late. My coach just sent me over here to get some papers for the team and he's waiting. So whadda ya say?"

"About what?"

"Come on now. You know what I'm talking about."

"But you don't know me."

"So, we'll get to know each other. If you don't like me, the school is only a hop, skip, and a jump from my house. I'll bring you right back."

"That's a kind offer but I can't accept."

"Sure you can."

"No I can't."

"Why?"

"Because the holidays are for spending time with your family and we're not family. We're not even friends."

"The only thing that's stopping us from being friends is you. Come on, live a little."

Ayana read his face for signs of game. She knew how athletes were. Everything was a joke to half of them and the other half were looking for a quick piece of booty just so they could say they had it. She wasn't interested in either.

She set the stack down.

"Are you serious?"

"As a heart attack," Nasir said with sincere eyes.

"What are your parents going to say?"

"Hey, baby, you hungry?" Nasir said, mimicking his mother. "But you better say no or you'll spend your holidays in the hospital with ptomaine poisoning."

Ayana laughed. He was charming and fine as the day was long.

"I'm sure her cooking can't be that bad."

"Okay, but you've been warned."

AND SHE went home with him, and from that day on they were practically inseparable. But then it was as if someone sent a memo to God informing Him that Ayana was enjoying life because after one full year of Nasir's company, her entire world came shattering down. She cursed God for allowing her life to be what it was and then teasing her with happiness. Her entire life was one loveless long day yet all that changed when Nasir walked into that registrar's office. She went from being a nobody to being Nasir's girl. And he loved her with everything he had and she knew it. But it seemed her bad luck rubbed off on Nasir. One day he was shooting hoops on television, and the next day he was on the news in handcuffs being shipped off to prison. That turn of events sent her into a spiral of depression. She found herself sitting in the wrong classes at school and wandering around the yard as if she was lost in a daze. It wasn't long before she just stopped going to school altogether.

Nasir's mother suggested that she come and live with her and that was her first mistake. Two women staying in the same house, grieving the loss of the same man, was a recipe for disaster.

There would be times when the misery would be so thick it could be felt the moment you walked in the door.

When she lost Nasir, Ayana had felt she hit her lowest point. She didn't know that the worst was yet to come.

Ayana found herself staying out more and more. That's when she met Lucky. He told her he was a scout for a modeling agency, but she didn't really care what he did. He was good to her and always took her out to nice places, which was what she needed more than anything.

Staying away from the house helped keep her mind off of the man she loved, which helped her remain sane. Before long, Ayana notified Nasir's mom that she was moving out.

"Ayana, that man is no good for you. Now, I may not be privy to the ins and outs of the streets, but I know a pimp when I see one."

"He's not a pimp," Ayana protested.

"Well, what is he then?"

"He's a modeling agent," Ayana said.

"A modeling agent? Is that what they are calling pimps these days? Sometimes you're about as naive as a newborn. Get your head out of the dirt for a few seconds so you can see that flea for what he is: a parasite who preys on vulnerable young girls like you."

"Whatever, Mom," Ayana said with a sigh. She loved calling Marcy "Mom," and deep inside she was happy that the woman even cared enough about her to chastise her.

"Okay, but you mark my words. If you keep hanging around him he'll have you walking up and down Metropolitan Avenue selling more than favors."

"I know what this is about. It's about your son. But he's gone. He didn't want me at the trial, won't accept my visits, and won't answer my letters. What would you have me do, stay around here and die of old age? I still have a life to live."

"This has nothing to do with Nasir. This is about you and that pimp. I wouldn't trust that man any more than I would a stray dog. Now I know how this seems but you're like a daughter to me and I don't want to lose another child."

"I appreciate that," Ayana said as she walked over and hugged the only mother she had ever known. "I really do but I have to get out of here. Every day in this house, I lose a little bit more of my mind than I did the day before."

Ayana could see tears in Marcy's eyes, which caused her own to form. She turned and walked back to her room and started packing.

"Ayana, I know you think I'm being a little out of touch right now but this guy is not who you think he is," Marcy kept on. Her voice broke as she followed Ayana into her bedroom. She wasn't going to lose this battle without a fight.

"It's not about what he does, Mom. It's about me moving on. Besides, he's not what you think."

"Oh really?"

"Yes really."

"Well, I think he's a fraud. He isn't educated enough to know that men don't have perms in their hair? Walks around with his pants hanging off his butt. Gold teeth. He's just a mess. Ask yourself what reputable modeling company is going to hire someone looking like that to represent them?"

"Times have changed, Mom. But I'm not going to try to convince you. The bottom line is that it's time for me to leave."

"So that's it?"

"No, it's not it. I'll still be around. It's not like I'm moving to the moon. I'll be three blocks from here." Ayana rubbed her ever-growing tummy.

"This is not going to turn out good for you, Ayana. Why don't you stay at least until the baby is born? That's not good that you are carrying my son's child and laying up with some other man."

Ayana stared at Marcy and sighed.

"We will not be laying up. We're just friends. No more than roommates."

"Oh my God. Do I look stupid? Even if that's true, how long do you think that will last? I don't know what I've done for God to keep punishing me like this. First my husband is murdered, then my son is sent off to prison for something even Jesus Christ knows he didn't do, and now you are leaving me," Marcy said on the verge of breaking down.

Ayana felt bad but staying with Marcy would only delay the inevitable. It was time to step out on her own, accept that what she and Nasir had was over, and see what life had to offer.

"Mom, I have to go."

"Then get out," Marcy yelled. "And when you see him for what he really is, don't you dare call me."

Ayana moved in with Lucky and soon the truth of Marcy's words revealed itself.

One month after she was there the telephone rang. It was three o'clock in the morning, and when she lifted the receiver she heard an automated voice: *"You have a collect call from 'Lucky' at the Atlanta City Jail. Press one to accept, two to reject."*

Ayana pressed the one button and waited. A few seconds later Lucky's voice came across the line.

"Babygirl I need you to come get me."

"What's going on?"

"I'm in jail."

"I can see that. But for what?"

Lucky was silent.

"I'm waiting."

"They got me on some ol' bullshit. False charges and I'mma sue this whole city when I get out of here."

"What are the false charges?"

A long silence, followed by the clearing of his throat before blurting out, "Pimping. But it's a setup. Come on and get me and I'll get this thing straight tomorrow."

Pimping? Had she heard him right?

Ayana's first inclination was to hang up the phone and run for the hills, but where would she go? Marcy wasn't talking to her and she didn't have any money saved. So she bit the bullet and went and got him out. She did a little snooping through the paperwork in the house and found out that Lucky had sixteen girls working for him on an Internet site, *onenight hoochies.com.*

Ayana was livid and she confronted him with her findings, and to her surprise, he admitted it. But he assured her that he had never even considered asking her to be a part of that life.

Ayana wasn't too happy about her discovery, but as long as he never tried anything crazy with her, she could deal with it. After all, he wasn't her man.

But things changed after Lucky's admission. He stopped hiding his girls and started bringing them into the home they shared. Ayana found herself trying to talk girls out of the life Lucky was trying to pull them into. Sometimes she succeeded but most of the time she failed.

Just as Ayana moved into the final trimester of her pregnancy, she started having complications and the doctors put her on bed rest. That's when the real devil surfaced.

Lucky knocked on her bedroom door and told her he had recruited a few more girls and they needed her room. She sat on the side of the bed and shook her head.

How in the hell did I get myself here? she wondered.

Ayana got up and walked out into the living room and stopped dead in her tracks. A little girl who reminded her so much of herself when she was ten years old sat on the floor eating a bowl of cereal.

"Lucky, tell me this is your daughter?"

"I guess you can call her that," he said.

"How old are you?" Ayana asked the little girl.

"Old enough," was her reply.

"Old enough for what?"

"Old enough to make my daddy proud." She smiled at Lucky.

Ayana looked at Lucky and frowned. Ayana picked up a glass that was sitting on the counter and threw it at Lucky. He ducked and was on her before she could think twice. He grabbed her around her neck and threw her down on the floor.

"I'm sick of your highfalutin ass trynna destroy my business," Lucky said as he punched her in the face. He hit her repeatedly until her face was a puffy mess.

Ayana got up and made her way to the bathroom. Calling the police was out of the question. All they would do was put her in some battered-women's shelter and she would rather die than spend one night in another shelter. So she decided to nurse her own injuries and bide her time until the baby was born and then she would leave.

She wasn't allowed that luxury. Two days after the beating Lucky came in the house, high out of his mind, with another man.

"Babygirl," he called. "Come on out here for a minute."

Ayana wobbled out into the living room eight months pregnant.

"Take this here fella in the back and hook him up."

Ayana shook her head to clear her hearing because she could not have heard what she thought she had heard.

"What do you mean 'hook him up'?" Ayana spat.

"Suck 'em, fuck 'em, do whatever he wants. He say he got a thing for pregnant women and . . . well, you know. You're the only pregnant woman I got on my staff," Lucky said as nonchalantly as if he were asking her to feed the dog.

Your staff! Negro, you must be on something stronger than crack.

Ayana's eyes bulged out of her head and her heart wouldn't stop racing. She couldn't believe what she was hearing. She could deal with drinking, the weed smoke, and the ménage à trois in the living room and even the underage girls. But this level of disrespect was where she drew the line.

"Are you crazy?" she asked.

"Are you?"

"No," Ayana said. "And no I'm not doing that! Who do you think I am?"

"Did you just tell me no?"

"You heard me. I'm not some naive little girl."

"What you trynna say?"

"I'm not having sex with that man."

"Well, just suck his dick then," Lucky said as if he was making some major concession.

"I'm not doing that either."

Lucky walked over to her and reared back.

Slap!

Slap!

"Bitch, you'll do what I tell you to do. Did you think you was just gonna lay your fat ass up here for free? Now you better get in that back room and earn your keep. You ain't my kin and after you tried to ruin my business we ain't even friends."

Ayana held her face. The slap stung but it was nothing like the beating she took two days ago. She knew she couldn't beat him, especially in her condition. She had to be smart. As horrible as her childhood was it didn't come close to preparing her for this.

She looked at the man for help, hoping he would see that she wasn't a willing participant and call this thing off, but all he did was blow her a kiss and rub his crotch.

"Okay," she eased out through tears. "Just give me a second to freshen up."

"That's better," Lucky breathed a sigh of relief. "I don't know why you be making me put my hands on you. You know I don't like being that kind of player. Now when you're done, I'll take you to Red Lobster or something and you can order whatever you want," Lucky said as he plopped down on the sofa and re-moved his shoes.

"Sorry 'bout that, homeboy, sometimes these hos get outta hand and you gotta discipline 'em," Lucky said to the man. "Ain't that what Snoop Dogg say? You gotta check these hos from they head to they toes," Lucky sang.

Ayana walked back to the bedroom on shaky legs. She closed the door behind her and locked it. She rested her back against the door and heard Marcy's words loud and clear.

He'll have you selling more than favors.

Why didn't she listen? She wasn't about to be a whore, she would rather die.

Ayana snapped out of her pity party as a bright idea popped into her head. She walked out of her bedroom across the hall to Lucky's bedroom. She had noticed he kept a pistol under the mattress during one of her snooping expeditions. She walked over and lifted the mattress. There it was. She picked up the shiny piece of steel and took a deep breath, mentally preparing herself for what the next few minutes would bring.

After checking to make sure the gun was loaded, she stormed out of the bedroom.

"I'm leaving and you better not try to stop me," Ayana said sternly, pointing the gun at Lucky.

Startled, Lucky narrowed his eyes, then stood.

"Bitch, if you don't put that gun down, I'mma put it someplace it ain't s'pose to go," Lucky said.

"You take another step toward me and I'll bury you," Ayana said, trying to hold the gun steady. She was done with being the victim.

Lucky looked at the customer and then back at Ayana.

He was perplexed.

None of his hos had ever crossed him before. The ones that

did got right back in line after he smacked them around a few times but this, this was something new.

"What you gonna do, shoot me and go to prison with ya boyfriend? Who's gonna raise ya baby? You gonna throw your life away just 'cause you don't wanna suck a dick? Come on, Ayana, be reasonable. Put the gun down," Lucky said, using his best pimp's psychology.

"Be reasonable? Okay, I'll tell you what," Ayana said, turning the gun on the customer who was now easing toward the door.

"Where do you think you're going?"

"Hey I—I—I don't want no part of this," the man stuttered.

"Didn't you come here to get hooked up?" Ayana said. "Well, I'm going to make sure you get what you came for." She turned and pointed the gun back to Lucky. "Get on your knees."

"Hey, I ain't into no gay stuff," the man said, waving his hands.

"But you're into rape. You saw that I wasn't interested in your little ignorant episode but you're still here. So you was gonna take advantage of me, so now I'll take advantage of you."

"I'm sorry. I—I—" the man said.

"Shut up. Both of you are some sick bastards."

"Bitch, you getting outta order," Lucky said, walking toward Ayana. "You think I'm scared of that . . ."

POW! The bullet exploded out of the gun and sent Lucky flying back down onto the sofa.

"Aughhh. Aughhh. Aughhh," Lucky screamed in a high-pitched voice as he rolled around holding his arm. "God, come get this crazy bitch. She done shot me. Aughhh."

The man covered his face and the front of his pants told a liquid story.

"Get up," Ayana said, standing over Lucky.

"Okay, okay, okay," Lucky said, holding his shoulder and grimacing in pain. "Oh, please, baby. Don't shoot me no more."

"Now you get over here," Ayana said to the man. "Unzip 'em."

"Baby, please don't do this," Lucky pleaded, still holding on to his arm and rocking back and forth in agonizing pain. "I love you."

"I can't believe you had the nerve to try and pimp me. Well, if you can dish it out, you should be able to take it. Get on your knees," she screamed.

Lucky looked at her, swallowed hard, and eased down onto the floor.

"Okay, you"—Ayana motioned to the man—"get over there and unzip 'em."

The man hesitated.

"I'm not asking you again."

The man looked like he wanted to cry as he walked over to Lucky and unzipped his pants.

"How does it feel to be used?"

"Come on, Ayana. Baby, look at all I've done for you. I took you in knowing you were carrying another man's child."

"And now I see why. You had a plan but it's not going to work with me."

"Come on, baby. You know what? I meant to tell you I got a modeling call today for you," Lucky stuttered. "But I—I—I told them you were pregnant. That's why I couldn't send you to New York. New York, baby. We going big-time."

Ayana laughed. "Shut up, Lucky. I'm tired of your lying ass. You're nothing but a pimp. A low-life parasite."

"Baby, please listen to me," Lucky pleaded, real tears running down his face. "I'm just doing that to get the money to send you places. It's all about you, baby. Hell, you the one who's pimping me," he said, laughing nervously, "I should be mad at you but, baby, I believe in you."

Ayana cocked the hammer back on the gun.

"You just don't stop, do you? But I don't wanna hear it. All I want right now is for you to give your customer what he came for. Hook him up," she said, blowing the man a kiss.

"Ayana . . ."

"One more word and I'll blow your brains out. Now suck his dick!" she screamed.

Ayana eased back toward the front door as Lucky opened up and literally got a taste of his own medicine.

Ayana opened the door and ran from the apartment like she was following Harriet Tubman. All she had were the clothes on her back. She ran into the street and was almost run over by a big black Mercedes-Benz. The car skidded to a halt and a man jumped out and ran over to her.

"Are you all right?" he asked.

"No," Ayana said, dropping the gun and stepping away from it.

"I could give you a ride somewhere," he said, walking over and picking up the gun from the pavement.

"My name is Alonzo. You're in good hands now. Nobody's gonna hurt you."

Ayana had the man take her over to Marcy's house but she wasn't home or maybe she just wasn't answering her door.

And when you see him for what he really is, don't you dare ring my phone.

Standing on Marcy's porch Ayana had never felt so alone in her life. Alonzo generously offered to put her up in a hotel for a few weeks, then he hired her to watch his home while he traveled for business. They developed an easy friendship and then one day he came home and said he wanted more. He wanted a family with her and Brandy. He was good to her and her daughter, and more out of gratitude than any real feelings for Alonzo, she took him up on his offer.

THE PHONE rang and Alonzo ran from the closet and literally dived over the bed to grab the phone before Ayana could take a step out of the bathroom.

Ayana couldn't hold in her laughter.

"Hello," he snapped into the receiver, hoping to catch some unsuspecting man who didn't know he was home.

"Hey, Alonzo," Alonzo's cousin Lorraine said.

"Aw damn," Alonzo said, tossing the phone down without even acknowledging the greeting.

"Hey, girl," Ayana said, still laughing at Alonzo.

"You tell that little cockeyed bastard I said to learn some telephone etiquette."

"I'm not in it," Ayana said, not in the mood to get into it with those two. They hated each other.

"Let's do lunch."

"Sure," Ayana said, anxious to get out of the house now that Alonzo was back. "Let me throw on some clothes and I'll meet you at your place."

Ayana quickly dressed and headed out to the garage.

"Where you going?" Alonzo asked, standing in the kitchen.

"Over to Lorraine's for a few."

"I thought you didn't feel well."

"And?"

"Come here."

Ayana walked over to Alonzo and looked down at him.

"What?"

"You screwing somebody else?"

"Alonzo," Ayana said in a low and seductive voice. She always knew how to end an argument with Alonzo and now was a good time for her to do it. "The only man I'm screwing is you. Stop worrying and think of what you want for dinner. I'll be back shortly."

Satisfied, Alonzo smiled and wrapped his arms around her waist.

"How much longer before your little visitor goes away?"

"Any day now," she said, air-kissing him as she walked out the door.

3

FLESH OF MY FLESH

asir stared at the little girl, and the longer he looked the more he saw his own features in her pretty brown face. She had his light eyes and high cheekbones but the rest of her belonged to Ayana.

"What did you say your mother's name was?"

"Ayana," she said, as if she was already tired of repeating herself.

Nasir couldn't believe what he was hearing.

"May I come in?"

"No, my grandmother will be mad at me."

Nasir looked around and sighed. This was too much, too soon.

"You know what? I've known your grandmother for a very long time and I promise you she'll be happy to see me," he coaxed.

Brandy wasn't going for it. She shook her head.

"Okay, you win," Nasir said, peering over Brandy to see a photo of himself on top of the television set. "I'll tell you what. You go over and grab that picture that's sitting on the TV and I'll wait right here."

Brandy closed and locked the door while she did as she was told. A few seconds later the locks clicked open and Brandy handed Nasir the picture.

"Okay, take a look at this guy," he said, pointing to the picture. "Then look at me."

Brandy took the picture. She looked at it, then did a double take. "This is my daddy on this picture."

"I know," Nasir said, his eyes watering. He dropped down to one knee so she could get a better look at him but Brandy was still confused.

"Do you know my daddy?" Brandy asked, frowning.

"Brandy"—Nasir paused, then cleared his throat—"take a closer look at that picture."

Brandy looked at the picture again and then back at the man kneeling in front of her.

She backed away and closed the door. Inside she ran over to the shelf where her grandma Marcy kept all of her father's trophies and photos. She snatched up a picture of Nasir wearing one of his basketball uniforms. He was skinny and his face wasn't as full as the man who was down on his knees with tears in his eyes but they sure did look alike.

One more inspection and she dropped the picture, smashing

glass all over the hard tile floor, and opened the door to leap into her father's arms.

"Daddy," she screamed.

Nasir lifted up his daughter and she wrapped her little arms around his neck.

Nasir took a deep breath, inhaling the very essence of his child, and he didn't bother to wipe away the tears that streamed down his face. What he felt at that moment was beyond explanation.

As he stood there enjoying the best moment of his life, he heard his mother's voice.

"I see you've met my grandchild," Marcy said, standing by the door.

Nasir looked up at the woman who raised him with nothing but a hope and a dream. The woman who died right in front of his eyes when that judge and jury ignored the facts and sentenced him to life in prison. The woman he loved more than anything was now a shadow of the woman he knew before life had beat the life out of her. He couldn't believe his eyes.

Marcy's once smooth caramel-colored skin was now riddled with dark acne scars. Her hair that was once full and healthy was nothing but greasy strings which barely covered her skull. Her eyes seemed to have wanted a reprieve from the horrors they'd witnessed and sank a little farther back into her head, and she was rail thin.

Nasir stood with Brandy in his arms and stared at his mother.

Marcy tried to smile but she stopped halfway and dropped her head, ashamed of what she knew her son saw when he looked at her.

"Hi, Mom," Nasir said softly.

"When did they let you out?" Marcy said. "Of the army," she added, quickly looking at Brandy.

"Friday," Nasir said, setting his daughter down on the sofa. He walked over to his mother and gently lifted her head.

"Friday? But today is Sunday. Where you been?"

"At Granny's. Just had to get my mind right before I could come here."

Marcy frowned but she nodded her head as if she understood.

"It's good to see you, Mom," he said, smiling. He was careful to act as if he didn't notice the changes he saw.

Marcy tried to speak but nothing came out. She wrapped her arms around her son and buried her head into his shoulder sobbing. "I missed you so much," she cried.

"I missed you too," Nasir said, holding on to his fragile mother.

"I'm sorry, Nasir. I'm so sorry."

"There's nothing for you to be sorry about," Nasir said. "Everything's going to be all right."

Brandy stood and grabbed her father's leg and they stayed in that position until the phone rang.

Marcy pulled herself away from her son and ran into her bedroom.

Nasir picked his daughter up again and walked over to answer the phone.

"Hello?"

"Hello, this is the Atlanta Gas Company. May I speak to Mrs. Lassiter or anyone responsible for the bills of the house?"

"What can I do for you?"

"I'm calling about your June, July, and August bills. They are all past due and the service is scheduled to be disconnected on Tuesday. Can you at least pay the past due portion of the bill?"

"Man, you guys call on Sundays?"

"Yes, sir. Bills are past due on Sundays too."

"Don't get smart, homie. How much are we talking about?"

"To get completely caught up, it'll be six hundred dollars, but we can keep the services running if you pay the past due amount which is . . . three hundred and sixty-seven dollars and thirty-nine cents."

Nasir wanted to pay the entire bill for his mother but the only money he had was the eight hundred dollars his cousin had just given him.

"I can pay the past due amount and get the rest taken care of within the next few days. Is that okay?"

"Sure. If you'll give me your credit card or a checking account number we can get this taken care of."

"Can I just go somewhere and pay it?"

"Sure."

Nasir took down the information and hung up the phone.

"Was that a bill collected man?" Brandy asked.

"Yes, that was a bill collected man." Nasir tickled his daughter and scooped her up again. He never wanted to put her down and she didn't ask to leave his arms.

"They always call Grandma Marcy. My mommy pays them to stop calling but they still call."

"Is that right," Nasir said, happy that Ayana was taking care of his mother. "I'm going to make it so that they don't call ever again."

Brandy giggled and snuggled up with her father.

"Daddy, I'm hungry."

Daddy!

Nasir had never heard a sweeter-sounding word and he had to take a moment to let it sink in. He'd always dreamed of being a father, and he felt bad that he had missed so much of her life already.

"Why don't you go and get Grandma and I'll take you guys out to any restaurant you want," Nasir said, wiping his eyes.

"Daddy," Brandy asked, "are you sad?"

Nasir wiped his eyes. "No, sweetie. Daddy's happy."

"Then why are you crying?"

"A bug got in my eye," he said, smiling.

Brandy giggled and that made Nasir happy. Her laughter was just what the doctor ordered.

"Can we go to Dave and Buster's? My mommy takes me there when I'm a good girl."

"And I bet that's all the time," Nasir said, taking a seat on the arm of the sofa.

He thought back to the altercations he had in prison and how he went toe-to-toe with men who stood well over six feet and never took a back step yet here he was knocked out completely by a little girl who wasn't even tall enough to ride a roller coaster.

Nasir stood in awe as he watched his little girl run down the same hallway he tore up as a child and felt joy for the first time in five years.

Brandy went to her grandmother's door and tried to open it but it was locked.

"Grandma's taking her medicine right now," she said, walking back toward her father with a sad face.

"Why don't you go and watch TV for a few minutes. Okay?" Nasir told his daughter.

"I don't like when Grandma takes her medicine; she's always sleepy-looking."

Nasir nodded and walked over to his mother's bedroom door and turned the knob.

It was locked.

He placed his ear to the door and could hear the faint sound of his mother weeping. He tapped on the door.

"Just a second," Marcy said. A few seconds later the door opened. She walked back to her bed and sat on the edge. In her hand was an old picture. She patted a spot next to her for Nasir to sit.

"Your father would be so proud of you." Marcy smiled at a long-ago memory. "He used to walk around here with you attached to his hip all day long. It was a beautiful sight to see."

In the photo Marcy sat in a lawn chair holding three-year-old Nasir on her lap while her husband stood behind them proudly.

"Your father loved his family," Marcy said, staring at the picture. "And he loved you more than anything."

"I know he did," Nasir said, wrapping his arm around his mother.

"The funny thing is, we were never supposed to meet. We couldn't have been more different from each other."

MARCIA GOLD always played to her own fiddle. Born into black wealth and privilege, her father came from a long line of doctors and was one of Atlanta's finest neurological surgeons and her mother was a partner in a prominent law practice. Her parents belonged to the shining set of the African American upper class and gave their only child every advantage—summers at the Vineyard, dance classes, travel abroad, membership in Jack and Jill—yet there was always something pulling Marcia toward those less fortunate.

When she got her driver's license at sixteen, she would often find herself driving through Atlanta's inner-city neighborhoods just so she could get an up close look at poverty.

After being accepted to Georgia Tech, Marcy stunned her parents with the news that she would not be reporting to freshman orientation. She had decided she would take a year off to map out her future. Much to the dismay of her father, who had dreams of her continuing the family's tradition in medicine. They allowed her a year to cool her heels but fully expected her to be sitting in a freshman class somewhere come the following fall. But one night while hanging out with her friends she met the man who would change her life forever.

Marcy couldn't take her eyes off of a tall, charismatic specimen who kept sneaking peeks at her too. Instead of playing the lookie-look game all night, Marcy surprised her friends when she stood and walked over to him.

"Hi. My name is Marcia Gold. I'm sorry to be so forward but . . ."

"No need for apologies. Moses Lassiter. It's nice to meet you, Marcy."

Normally, Marcia would correct anyone who changed her name but for some reason she didn't mind when Moses did it.

They spent the next few days talking on the phone and found they had a lot in common. He was interested in helping poor black people overcome the rut they seemed to be stuck in and she was interested in why they seemed to be stuck there. Moses was impressed with her interest in folks who had the same skin color as her but didn't have the same background. It didn't take long before they fell in love and jumped headfirst into the struggle.

She helped him out with his community outreach program,

which was housed in the basement of an old boys and girls club building located in the West End section of Atlanta.

Marcy's parents were outraged when she told them she was moving out of their million-dollar home into a shabby house in the middle of the ghetto. They did everything they could to get her to leave "those people" to their own self-destruction.

"Why do you want to help people who don't even want to help themselves?" her father asked, dumbfounded.

"If I can help them get to the point where they can provide for themselves, then maybe I can keep a gun out of your face!" Marcy screamed.

"*My* face?"

"Yes, you or anybody else. A lot of these people turn to crime because they weren't given opportunities to make their own way."

"Oh please. Those ghetto people turn to crime because they are lazy. Marcia, you're young and full of energy but there is no way you can fix these people. This is a slave mentality that one little girl, no matter how noble, can't even begin to penetrate."

"That's your opinion, and you're wrong."

"Don't you think you could help them more by becoming a doctor? God knows they shoot each other enough. Just think about how many real lives you could save."

Marcy gave up trying to convince her father that his views of lower-class blacks were well off base. She believed in the faces she saw every day at the community center and she celebrated in their progress. And the joy she felt when a transformation was made outweighed any other feeling she had ever experienced in a biology class.

The Golds' devastation showed when they gave her an ultimatum. "It's him or us," her father said. "There is no way we can sit back and watch you throw your life away."

"Do you feel this way too, Mom?"

"Marcy, your father is right. Now I know you're young and optimistic but you just have to trust us on this one. But if you choose to go out there and throw your life away then yes, I'm with him one hundred percent."

Marcy grabbed a few of her things and walked out.

She hated being estranged from her family but she was young and in love. Besides, being a doctor was her parents' idea, it was never hers. She prayed they would come around, but knowing how much her father disliked the folks he often referred to as niggers, she didn't hold out much hope they would.

Then, three years later on New Year's night, Marcy heard a loud explosion followed by the sound of breaking glass.

"Moses!" she screamed out to the man who was now her husband.

Moses appeared in the doorway wearing only his boxers and holding a shotgun.

"Stay down, baby," he said and hurried out of the house.

Marcy ran over and snatched her three-year-old son out of his crib and held him close.

Moses came back in the house and peeped in on his family.

"Y'all okay?" he asked.

"Who was that?" Marcy asked.

"I don't know," Moses said in his usual calm manner. He sat on the side of the bed and ran his fingers through his thinning hair. "There's something I need to tell you."

Marcy's heart tightened up.

"I was always told that love could always overrule hate but I'm not so sure that's true."

"What are you talking about, Moses?" Marcy said, staring up at him with loving eyes.

Moses walked over to the closet and pulled out a bunch of scraps of paper.

You're a dead man.

Your days are numbered, nigger.

You are not worthy.

I told you to leave.

"I've been getting these for a minute now," Moses said but stopped.

Marcy could feel her blood boil. She hated racism in the worst way. To her it was the worst kind of ignorance.

"No matter what happens to me, you make sure my son gets a good education. That's all I ask."

"Wait a minute. What are you talking about, Moses? What do you mean 'if something happens to you'?"

"I just feel something bad is about to happen. Whoever is

sending this stuff isn't going away. Just promise me you'll make sure my son gets what he deserves."

Marcy started to cry. Her husband was talking like he would die any minute.

"How long have you been getting these notes?" she asked. "Talk to me!"

"As long as I can remember. But now it's a little more serious than just these notes," Moses said, shaking his head. "Somebody wants me dead."

"But who? And why?" Marcy said.

Moses just shook his head. "I have no idea. I don't owe anybody any money. I don't do people wrong. I have no idea."

"So what is it?"

Marcy knew there was something he wasn't telling her but she also knew he would never tell.

"Have you talked to the police about this?"

"The police! Please. I don't know how many times I have to tell you, that's your first call, not mine. Baby, this is the ghetto, not Dunwoody where you grew up. The police have never been our friends," Moses said, tossing the notes in the trash.

"So what are you gonna do, just sit back and wait for something bad to happen?"

"Just make sure my son is taken care of," he said, then walked out of the room.

The conversation was over and that night would end up being the last one they would spend together. One week later Marcy was paid a visit by two plainclothes detectives.

They showed her a picture of Moses sitting in a chair in what appeared to be some sleazy hotel with a hypodermic needle protruding from his massive arm.

"THAT WAS the beginning of the end in a way. I was pregnant at the time, and I miscarried. Things were never the same after that," Marcy sighed. "I tried to hang on in there at the community center but my heart wasn't in it anymore. I wanted to move but your father loved this house so much. His father built it with his own hands, you know. But seeing how things turned out maybe staying was a mistake. Maybe my father was right after all. I mean what kind of people would sit up and allow a good boy like you to go to prison?"

"When is the last time you spoke with your parents?" Nasir asked.

Marcy stared off into the distance and her eyes watered again.

"I spoke to my mother when you first got arrested. I asked her for her help but she said she was too busy. They sort of wrote me off. And my dad, well . . . he meant what he said. I haven't spoken with him in I don't know how many years," Marcy said. "You know after your father died I stopped by so they could see you but my father stood on the porch and told me to take my ghetto child back where we came from." Marcy looked down at her hands. "But that didn't really bother me because I didn't expect any more than that from him. What hurt me the most was seeing my mother and not being allowed to touch her. She sat in the window upstairs. I could see the tears in her eyes."

"Why'd you wait so long to tell me this?" Nasir asked.

"I don't know. I guess I wanted to forget them like they wanted to forget me. I still miss them though." Marcy shook her head.

Nasir pulled his mother close.

"Mom, I know you're going through a lot right now, but try not to stress yourself out."

Marcy smiled. "You sound like your father."

"You know, when I was in prison I would lie on my bed and think back to those days when all we had to eat was one can of ravioli and you'd give it all to me. I never heard you complain.

"I would think of the times when I would stand in front of the oven trying to stay warm while you boiled water for my bath. Never heard you complain."

Marcy grimaced at the thought.

"I need to boil some now. That bill is sky high and I can't pay it."

"It's taken care of," Nasir said. And it felt really good for him to say that.

"You paid it?"

"It's taken care of."

"I should get a check on Monday and I'll pay you for . . ."

"Mom," Nasir said, holding up a hand. "I don't want your money. It's the least I can do."

"You know I could never keep a job. Losing your father and the baby at the same time did a number on me. Nobody was going to keep me around crying all the time. I mean, I've been laid off or fired more times than I can count on both my hands and my feet," Marcy said with a chuckle. "I could never get it together. I guess I fell in love with the misery, but looking back I see now I should've been stronger for you. I'm sorry, Nasir."

"You were strong enough and you don't have to apologize for anything. I wouldn't trade you or my childhood for the world."

"That's nice of you to say but we both know that it's not true."

"It is true. Yeah, we may not have had all the material possessions in the world and we had more than our fair share of hungry nights, but the love was always there and that's more important than anything you could've ever given me."

Marcy grunted and shook her head. "I'm sure the choices I made had a lot to do with you turning me away when I came to visit you or why you never returned any of my letters."

"Nothing is further from the truth. I never blamed you for anything. Never crossed my mind," Nasir said. "My reason for alienating everyone was—"

"Hey," Marcy said, cutting him off. "What's done is done. You are a man now and you don't need to explain your actions to me. I'm just glad you're home."

Nasir nodded. Something wasn't right. She seemed to be tired of talking all of a sudden. It was as if something came over her.

"Brandy said she was hungry. Why don't you get dressed and go out with us?"

"Oh no. You go on and spend some time with your daughter. I'll be right here."

Nasir stared at his mother for a moment, then leaned down

and kissed her forehead. When he stood he noticed what looked like the stem of a needle sticking out from under a pillow. He reached down and picked it up. He stared at his mother.

"Oh, throw that thing away. I found it outside on the ground and I didn't want Brandy or any of them other kids to find it. Somebody needs to clean this place up."

Nasir had been around drug addicts all of his life and he knew one when he saw one. The hardest thing in the world for him to do was accept the fact that his mother had become one.

4

GIRL TALK

"You know that man I live with is getting crazier and crazier by the second," Ayana said as she walked into Lorraine's house. Lorraine lived two streets over from Ayana and was her closest friend, even though she also happened to be Alonzo's cousin.

"It's the same old thing every time he comes home," Ayana said, her heels clicking across the marble floor. " 'Who's been in my bed? Let me smell your panties.' One day I'm going to take them off and shove 'em down his throat."

"He might like that," Lorraine said, giving her friend a hug.

"You're right," Ayana said, kissing both of Lorraine's cheeks. "Maybe I'll stick 'em up his butt."

"He might like that too."

"You need help," Ayana said, laughing.

"I don't see how you do it," Lorraine said. "Life is too short for all that unnecessary drama."

Ayana flopped down onto the living-room sofa.

"Unnecessary drama is the story of my life but what the hell, it's all about Brandy."

"Honey, I understand you want the best for your child, but you still have a life to live yourself."

"I know," Ayana said.

"Well, get out and live it. I wish I were your age. I'd be running wild and free."

"You're twice my age and you're still running wild and free."

"Hey, I still look good."

"You sure do," Ayana said with a wide smile.

"Damn right," Lorraine said, rolling her neck for emphasis. "I got boys your age trynna get my attention. I'm tempted to take one of 'em up on their offer since George's old ass can't hang for more than two minutes. And, girl, it's a slow two minutes at that. Damn."

George was the closest thing Lorraine had to a man. He was married to someone else and that suited her just fine. In fact, she said it was part of the attraction. "At the end of the day he has to take his black ass home," she would always say.

"So how long has mini-me been home?" said Lorraine.

"He just got there so that's why I knew it was time to leave."

"Normally I can't pay your boring butt to come out of that house."

"That's not true."

"Girl, please. But I don't blame you. Who in their right mind would voluntarily stay around Alonzo unless they had to?" Lorraine said.

"Do you know he had the nerve to come in the house accusing me of being a ho, then had the audacity to turn around and try to get him some?"

Lorraine made an ugly face as if the thought alone turned her stomach.

"No he didn't?"

"Yes he did."

"I hope you're using protection. You know he's probably sticking his ugly little wiener in some hooker while he's out there on the road."

"Yeah, I use protection. It's called, 'Hell no, you can't have none.'"

"I hear ya, but as much as I can't stand my midget of a cousin, you got to get you some. I'm not one of those abstinence preachers. I believe a good screwing will change your outlook on life. You know what you need?"

"What?"

"An emergency dick in a glass—for those lonely nights when the vibrator just won't do."

"Please. That's the last thing on my mind. I'm already dealing with one man I can't stand and here you are trying to add another one to the mix."

"I didn't say fall in love. Hell, I'm only trying to add a little spice to your life. You're pitiful. All you do is sit around the house all day reading trashy novels and waiting on Brandy to come home."

"I'mma get it together."

"When?" Lorraine said, frowning.

"Soon."

"But for now you're okay with playing wifey?"

"No." Ayana stood up and walked into the kitchen. "Do you want some wine?"

"Yeah, I already had a bottle earlier but bring another one."

Ayana returned with a bottle of red wine and two goblets.

"Ayana, on a serious note," Lorraine said, "what will you do if Alonzo gets tired of you and asks you to leave?"

"He's not going to do that."

"Don't be so sure. I've known him all my life and he's tossed out more than his share. First of all I don't know how his ugly ass keeps getting women to throw out in the first place. Must be the money. Got to be the money."

"It's not about the money. I don't want his money. Trust me when I say it's all about Brandy."

"You keep saying that but tell me this: how do you think Brandy would feel if she came home from school one day and all of your things were tossed out in the street? Just because he got

a wild hair up his butt. I mean he really doesn't owe you anything."

Ayana poured the wine and sat back down. That scenario had
crossed her mind a million times but for whatever reason she
wasn't able to put a plan B in motion.

"I don't mean to be all up in your business." Lorraine sipped
her wine. "I'm lying. I don't give a damn about being in your
business."

"I know."

"But it troubles me to see you just existing. I want to see you
living," Lorraine said. "And let me tell you this: nothing in this
life is free. One day all debts become due."

Ayana grunted at the truth she was hearing.

"Damn, girl," Lorraine said, taking a gulp of wine. "You have
so much to offer this world and you're sitting here looking pitiful. I'm going to find you a man today. And I'm going to hold you
down and let him fuck some sense in your head."

Ayana laughed and playfully poked Lorraine.

"I've thought about hooking up but the truth is, I'm not interested. Besides, if anything gets me put out it'll be that. The
minute Alonzo finds out I'm out with some man is the minute
I'm tossed out in the streets."

"Key words, 'find out.' Why does he have to find out?"

"He'll find out because he's naturally suspicious, and I can't
lie. It'll show up on my face. Then what will I tell Brandy?"
Ayana grabbed a pillow from the sofa and stared at it. " 'Brandy,

I know you love that private school you attend but you won't be going back there anymore.'

" 'Why, Mommy?'

" 'Well, sweetie, it's a long story but the short version is . . . Mommy's a ho.' "

"Very funny," Lorraine said. "But it's not going to happen. Alonzo is nothing but hot air, with his diminutive ass."

"I wouldn't be surprised if he had a private investigator watching my every move."

"Girl, that's old news. Alonzo had you tailed when you first moved in."

"Are you kidding me?" Ayana asked, shocked.

"Nope. But all that snooping got him was a few pictures of you sitting in the park feeding the pigeons and a nice little bill from that private investigator. If you ask me, that's all the more reason for you to go out and get your freak on."

Ayana shook her head. Alonzo needed to get a life, and if the truth was to be told, so did she. Ever since Nasir was sent away her life had taken one bad turn after another, especially when it came to men.

The phone rang and Lorraine held up a finger and stumbled over to get it. She cursed a few times, then slammed the phone down.

"You know I am convinced when Alonzo was born, somebody dropped him on his head," Lorraine said, scowling. "He said he was going to kick your ass for something or another."

Ayana's face contorted into some form of disgust and she sat back on the sofa as if she were a teenager and her father had just called and told her to come home.

"Earth to Ayana," Lorraine said, waving her hands.

Ayana sighed. "He's gonna drive me crazy."

Lorraine sat down beside her young friend and placed a hand on her knee. "You can always stay here."

"Thanks, but I can't do that. You're his family, and I know you guys have your moments but you're still family."

"What about your mother?"

As far as Lorraine knew, Marcy was her real mom.

"That's not an option. Tried that and it was worse than staying with Alonzo."

"Damn."

"Damn is right. Plus she's a druggie."

"Why don't you get her some help? Tell Mr. Money Bags to write the check and send her to a rehab center."

"I tried that. She doesn't want any help. She would rather sit around and wallow in her pity. And don't get me wrong, life has been hard on her but . . ."

"But what?" Lorraine said, catching Ayana. "She has to get over the past and live her life? That sounds like advice you should be taking yourself."

Ayana took a sip of wine and looked away.

"But I hear ya. If there's one thing I learned it's that people deal with their issues in different ways. Some people's vices are just more public," Lorraine said.

"Yeah, but to turn to drugs. What is that going to help? You know I was seriously thinking about not letting Brandy go over there anymore but then I realized that Brandy was probably the one person who kept her from jumping off a bridge or something."

Lorraine stared at Ayana, then looked down at her hands. She fingered her wedding finger and shook her head.

"Can I tell you a story?"

"Go right ahead."

"Do you know why I live in this big house all alone?"

"No," Ayana said.

"I was married once."

"Really?" Ayana asked, surprised. In all these years neither Lorraine nor Alonzo had ever mentioned that.

"Yeah, and we had a daughter. Her name was Naja and she was God's angel, beautiful inside and out. We got her the best education money could buy even though we could barely afford to eat at the time. We enrolled her in etiquette classes at the church and every other little thing we could think of to make her the best child she could be. But things got real tight. My husband lost his job and my hours were cut back so we had to move Naja over to a public school. She had just hit the ninth grade. Naja was always proper, she was a little lady and she acted like one. Well . . ." Lorraine closed her eyes to stop the tears but they came anyway.

Now it was Ayana's turn to lend a hand.

"These little bitches," Lorraine continued. "Called themselves the 'Project Chicks,' like that's something to be proud of. Well, they thought Naja wasn't acting 'black' enough. Why? Because she spoke proper English and didn't dress like some video ho. So they jumped my baby. Ten of 'em took turns beating my baby like she was the devil himself. And they killed her." Lorraine wiped her eyes and tried to recover. "And for what? Because she refused to act like a nigga."

"Oh, Lorraine," Ayana said, her own eyes full of tears.

"After Naja died, my husband came to me one day and said he was leaving. Said he couldn't look at me without seeing Naja. Could you imagine the man you love leaving you because every time he looks at you he breaks down and cries?" Lorraine said, closing her eyes.

"Now I can sit here and talk until we're old and gray about the pain a mother feels when she loses a child, but I can only imagine the pain a mother must feel when her child chooses not to talk to her. That has to feel worse than death itself. If your mother is using drugs then she needs you more than you'll ever know."

Ayana nodded her head and wiped her eyes.

"Lorraine, I'm so sorry to hear about your daughter," Ayana said, reaching over to hug Lorraine.

"Yeah, me too," Lorraine said.

Pulling away from their embrace, Lorraine turned her goblet up to her mouth and drained it.

Once she was done she took Ayana's glass and gulped that down too. "Sorry, girl, I'll pour you another one."

Lorraine stood, steadied herself, and made her way to the bathroom and Ayana sat there thinking about what she had just heard. Life wasn't great for her but she still had Brandy and that made it worth living. She thought about what Marcy must be going through. She didn't deserve the treatment Ayana was giving her. *She's the only woman I ever called Mom,* she thought to herself.

The phone rang again and Lorraine checked the caller ID. "Girl, it's Alonzo again. Damn, he's aggravating."

"Don't answer it. Let's go and grab lunch."

5

DADDY'S GIRL

*N*asir held his daughter's hand as they walked out of his mother's house. Once outside, it seemed as if the entire projects were standing on his mother's front yard.

"Come on, Nasir, let me hold a twenty like you gave Monroe?" someone asked.

"Man, you gave old drunk-ass Monroe some money? Let me borrow fifty until the fifteenth."

Nasir held up his hand. "Hey, hey, hey. I gave Monroe five dollars. What do I look like, Bank of America? Move," Nasir said, lifting his new love into his arms and walking through the throng of people.

"Oh, there you go getting all uppity again," someone said.

Nasir ignored them and kept walking until they made it to his car.

"Man, when you gonna let me drive this thing?" said one of the youngsters who was still seated behind the wheel.

"How old are you?"

"Ten."

"I'll let you drive when you get a driver's license," Nasir said.

"You don't need no driver's license to drive. You need a license to show the police," the boy said.

Nasir chuckled and shook his head. "I guess you're right about that. Now get your little knotty head out of my seat."

"Man, you better lock this thing up when you leave it," the little boy said, still seated. "You don't wanna get got."

"You plan on stealing it?"

"Nah, I don't steal. I was watching it for you."

"Well, thank you very much. Now get up."

"Brandy, that's your daddy?" the boy said, still seated.

"Yes," she said, smiling.

"He rich?" the little boy asked.

"Boy, if I have to ask you one more time to get your narrow behind out of that car, I swear I'm gonna take my belt off," Nasir said, halfway joking.

"Aight, aight. No need to get violent."

Nasir was beside himself at the little boy's wit.

"What's your name?"

"It's Chaziel but you can call me Chaz. Where y'all going?"

"Chaz, we're going to see a man about a mule."

"I guess that means none of my business, huh?"

"You catch on quick."

"Of course," Chaz said, backing away from the car. "I'm hungry. Can I have a few bucks to grab a bite to eat?"

"Chaz, what's going on with your hair?" Nasir said, nodding toward the boy's half afro, half braided hair.

"I can't afford a haircut so I rock it like this. Won't you let me clean your rims for you for a few bucks?"

Nasir walked around to open Brandy's door. Then walked back around to the driver side and slapped Chaz five before getting in.

"I need money not a handshake," Chaz said.

Nasir slipped him a five-dollar bill before turning the ignition. The car roared to life and all of the other little kids slapped each other high fives, all claiming "That's my car."

"That little boy is something else, ain't he?"

"He's always nice to me."

Boys! Nasir thought. *I'm not ready for this.*

"Do you spend a lot of time with your great-grandmother?" Nasir asked when they pulled away from The "U."

"Granny," Brandy said, her smile telling him that she had already felt the warmth of the sweetest lady on the planet.

WHILE NASIR was incarcerated his grandmother was the only one who refused to leave when he wouldn't come out for his visit.

Finally the warden himself came down and talked to Granny. She still wouldn't leave. The warden came to Nasir and threatened him with solitary confinement if he didn't come out and make his visit with his grandmother.

Nasir reluctantly walked into the visiting room and was met by Granny's hand across his face. Twice.

"Have you lost your mind? I'm your grandmother and I don't care if you got triple life, I'm coming to see about you whenever I get good and doggone ready," she fussed. "You understand?"

Nasir didn't respond. A look of defiance across his face.

Slap.

"Yes, ma'am," Nasir said, holding the side of his face.

"Good," she said, then she sat down and pulled homemade fried chicken and a few Tupperware dishes from a brown paper bag and fed half of the visiting room.

"I'm sorry, Granny, it's just I . . ."

"Hush your mouth." She waved Nasir off with her chubby hand. "I done said my peace. You 'round here feeling sorry for yourself and got everybody up in arms. Now eat and the next time I come here you better be shaved and clean-looking. Just because you in here don't mean you lose your dignity. You look like a bear with all that crap on your face."

Agreeing to visit with Granny was the best thing Nasir could have ever done for himself and his sanity.

She was the only person with whom he could share all the

stresses of incarceration and she proved to be a wonderful wartime consigliere as well.

"Put a foot to his ass," she would say when Nasir alerted her to an inmate's threat.

"You gots to show 'em what you made of. When in Rome do as the Romans do. Since you in prison, you're going to have to act a fool every now and then. Even if you don't win the fight, you got to let him know you were there. Let 'em know whenever they decide to fool with Nasir Lassiter it ain't gone be no walk in the park."

For as long as he could remember his father's mother wasn't your typical southern grandmother. She didn't sit around sewing or sitting on the porch minding other folks' business. She took karate classes, coached an all-boys swim team, and all kinds of other so-called young folks' activities.

But Granny proved to be even more down for the cause when she agreed to Nasir's request to not mention anything about the outside world to him. He didn't want any updates on what his family or friends were doing. Not even a death in the family was good enough to break the rule. As far as Nasir was concerned, with the exception of Granny, life outside of those walls didn't exist. If she couldn't abide by those guidelines he'd gladly spend the rest of his life in solitary. She agreed and hadn't missed a visit since. Well, other than that one time Nasir was in lockup for following Granny's advice and putting some foot to a little ass. Granny brought him two books a week, one nonfiction and one fiction. The nonfiction ranged from the autobiography of Frederick Douglass to simple things like *How to Make Glass*. She wrote him long letters filled with stories of his own father's childhood that kept him glued to the pages, and to make the time a little more bearable, she kept money on his prison account. In other words, she kept him alive.

"WHEN WAS the last time you seen her?" Nasir asked his daughter.

"Hmmmm," Brandy said, furrowing her brows just like her father did when he was deep in thought. "Probably last week. She comes to Grandma Marcy's house and gets me."

His daughter was proper, no signs of Ebonics. Obviously Ayana had her in a good school. He liked that, although he wasn't too thrilled about Ayana's decision to let her stay with his mother, at least not while she was dealing with her drug addiction.

"Well, before we head to the restaurant, we're going to run by there so Daddy can change clothes."

"Daddy," Brandy said, "you know my mom is getting married?"

Nasir's heart felt as if it were going to fall out of his chest.

"I didn't know that."

"She's marrying Mr. Alonzo."

"Is that right? Do you like Mr. Alonzo?"

"He's okay. He fusses all the time but he's hardly ever there. He says we're moving to Africa."

"Africa?" Nasir almost screamed before calming himself. "Africa?"

"I don't want to go. Can I stay with you and Grandma Marcy? Please?"

Nasir could tell he wasn't going to be a very good father. Telling her no would be a very difficult task indeed. Hearing her beg made him want to give her the world.

"I'm going to have to talk to your mom about that. But I'll tell you this. No matter what happens, your daddy will never ever be far away from you again," he said with a smile.

"So you're going to move to Africa too?" she asked, excited.

"If I have to," Nasir said, reaching over and pinching her cheek. "Whatever it takes."

"I love you, Daddy."

Nasir swallowed hard. Those four words hit him like a ton of bricks. He loved his grandmother even more for not telling him about his daughter. Had he known about her there would've been no way he could've survived inside prison and away from her.

"And I love you too."

Nasir turned onto Granny's street and noticed a police car idling in front of the house. His palms began to sweat, and he became nervous. This happened every time he saw anything remotely resembling the so-called Justice Department: highway patrol cars, inmate transportation vans with wire mesh over the windows, and buildings that resembled jails, all sent his heart into overdrive. He kept having these visions of twenty or so police officers swarming him with guns and handcuffs, screaming that his release was a mistake and he was headed back to prison.

His fears were unwarranted because before he could unbuckle his seat beat, the police cruiser drove away.

6

TROUBLE MAN

*A*yana sat in the passenger seat of Lorraine's Jaguar half listening to her trade love talk on her cell phone with her married boyfriend and half trying to block out thoughts of what she had allowed her life to become. She thought back to the days when she and Nasir would sit on the yard at Georgia Tech and talk about what their lives would be like when they graduated.

"Ayana, George is bringing a friend to lunch," Lorraine said, snapping Ayana back to the here and now.

"How convenient," Ayana scoffed, wishing Lorraine would stop trying to play matchmaker. *This lady's not going to stop until she gets me killed,* Ayana thought.

They pulled up in front of the C'est Bon restaurant in Lithonia.

Standing in the waiting area of the restaurant was Lorraine's fiftyish-looking friend George and some man who looked old enough to be George's older brother.

"Didn't I tell you she was the finest thing the Good Lord ever created?" George nudged his friend.

"Thank you, George. Now you know I don't like you gushing all over me like that in public," Lorraine said.

"You know damn well I ain't talking about you. I'm talking about Ayana."

"Well, fuck you too," Lorraine said.

"A little later. I gotta give this Viagra time to kick in," George said.

"You keep it up and you'll be playing with yourself."

"Ayana, this is my buddy Quincy," George said, fanning Lorraine off. "Quincy, this is God's gift to the male eye," George said, sweeping his arm in an exaggerated motion. "Ayana, the Goddess of Beauty."

Quincy grabbed Ayana's hand and kissed it. She could smell alcohol on his breath.

"The pleasure is all mine," Quincy said, holding on to her hand while he salivated all over it.

Ayana snatched her hand back and wiped it on his shirt.

George, who had Lorraine in some kind of bear hug, spoke over her shoulder. "How's life been treating you, Ayana?"

"I'm good. You guys should get a room."

"That's not a bad idea," George said as he spun Lorraine around and kissed her neck.

"Let's eat first. Then we can all go get a room," Quincy said.

Ayana looked at him like he had lost his mind but she didn't say anything. The hostess led them to their table and Quincy pulled out Ayana's chair for her.

"Let me tell you right now, Ayana, all that chivalry crap is gonna stop the minute you give him some. Look at this fool," Lorraine said, standing with her arms folded looking at George, who had already taken his seat.

"Hey, don't you look at me all crazy. I never started any of that bull 'cuz that ain't me. If a woman is healthy enough to talk all the shit you talk, Lorraine, then she can get her own door, chair, and pick up the tab if she wanna."

Quincy walked over but Lorraine shooed him away.

"Ah, I got it," she said, taking her own seat. "You're only good for one thing, you know that, George?"

"Yep," George said, looking at the menu. "But I do my job so well."

"Not all that well. You're nothing to brag about."

"Order your food and shut your trap," George shot back. "Before I decide not to . . ." George made a snaking action with his tongue.

"Ohh," Lorraine said, making a lustful face, then quickly picked up her menu.

Ayana looked at both of the perverted pre-senior citizens and shook her head.

"It's going to be hard for me to eat. Being that I already seen my dessert," Quincy said, lusting at Ayana.

Ayana wanted to throw up at the thought of being touched by this filthy old man. She couldn't believe Lorraine had set her up for this.

"Ayana, Quincy is a doctor," Lorraine said quickly before Ayana could read him the riot act.

"Just like the guy from the TV show," Quincy said.

"Never heard of it," Ayana said. "Must be before my time."

"How old are ya if you don't mind me asking."

"Twenty-five."

Quincy's eyes almost popped out of his head and he licked his lips.

"George," Quincy said, holding his heart. "I'm going to have to borrow a few of those Viagras from you. Ain't no sense in me fooling myself. I know I can't hang with a young stallion like that without some help."

Ayana smiled. "Are you drunk?"

"Drunk off your beauty."

"You have to be under the influence of some kind of mind-altering substance if you even think you're going to be touching me. I don't know what you heard, old man, but it ain't that kind of party."

"Feisty," Quincy said, nodding his head. "I likes. I likes."

Ayana fought the urge to get up and walk out.

The waiter came and they ordered their food. After a few drinks, Ayana went from being angry to just plain amused at the fact that these old men had it in their heads that they were about to jump off into a raunchy sex scene out of some freaky pornographic movie.

"Hey," a loud voice said from all the way over by the door.

Everyone turned in the direction of the outburst.

Ayana couldn't believe her eyes. Alonzo was headed straight for her. He stopped at the table and stared at her. He looked at every one of them before pulling a chair from a nearby table and taking a seat.

"Wait a minute, brother . . ." George began, but stopped when Alonzo slammed a pistol on the table.

"What?" he asked, rubbing his shiny pistol as if it were his pet. "What in the hell were you about to say? Were you just speaking to me?"

"No, sir," George stammered, eyes wide watching the gun.

"Now, you," Alonzo said, turning to Quincy. "You fucking my lady?"

"No," Quincy said. "We just met."

"That don't mean shit. You got your arm all wrapped around her like y'all been knowing each other for ages. Don't move it now. Y'all look cute together. Maybe I should send y'all asses to hell together?"

"We're just having lunch," Quincy stuttered. "And my arm is on the chair. Not your lady."

"Yeah, I see that but I asked you a question. Are you fucking this little"—he looked at Ayana like he wanted to spit in her face—"tramp."

"Alonzo, is that called for?" Lorraine said.

"Yes, the hell it is called for, Lorraine. You see this one here got a lot of growing up to do. See, you don't know her like I do. She's a bitch. I was being too kind when I called her a tramp. A bitch. Yeah, that's more like it. A damn dog that just runs around letting any stud with a dick jump all on her."

"Alonzo," Lorraine snapped.

"Shut up, Rain. 'Cuz you just like her. Did you take your medication? Crazy ass!"

"Fuck you."

"Fuck you too. But let me tell you about this one here. See, I rescued her from her previous owner."

"Alonzo," Lorraine snapped. "That's enough."

"Didn't I tell you to shut the hell up? I should've known better than to let her hang out with you in the first place. I'm surprised your old-ass coochie still works."

Lorraine grabbed her glass of wine and threw it on Alonzo and stood up to go after him but was restrained by George.

"Hang out with that, you li'l ugly bastard. I don't give a damn about your little gun."

"If you weren't family I'd make you regret that," Alonzo said calmly as he picked up his gun.

"You ain't family to me. You may have the same blood running through you but you ain't my family. You miserable piece of—"

"Okay." Ayana stood. "Let's go, Alonzo."

"Whoa," Alonzo said, spreading his arms out. "You mean to tell me you want to leave with me? I mean, you were sitting cute over here with your grandfather," Alonzo said, carelessly pointing his gun in Quincy's direction.

"Alonzo, let's go," Ayana said, a little more sternly.

Alonzo sat there for a few more seconds, then stood.

He grabbed the tablecloth from the table, knocking over glasses and plates in the process, and wiped his face.

"I'll leave you three to do whatever it is y'all do. Don't look so sad, old man; I'm sure that one over there will take care of you. Word is that li'l ho likes that double whammy stuff."

"Screw you, you crooked-eyed son of a bitch," Lorraine barked.

Alonzo slid his gun down in the front of his pants and turned to Quincy.

"If I ever see you around my woman again, I'll kill you."

"Hey, man. It's not like that," Quincy said, almost begging. "We were just having a few drinks."

"Stop bitching and take heed," Alonzo threatened before turning and following Ayana out of the restaurant.

7

DANGER

*A*yana sat in the passenger seat of Alonzo's black Mercedes-Benz staring out the window at a hawk soaring in the friendly skies. Oh, how she wished she could join it.

That scolded-child feeling came rushing back as she listened to Alonzo's rant, which had been going on nonstop since they left the restaurant.

"You know I went to a breeder a few weeks back because I was looking to buy a puppy for Brandy. And do you know the one thing he said to watch out for? I mean he was real adamant about this."

Ayana didn't answer and kept her eyes on the hawk, but even it had seemed to tire of being around Alonzo and flew away.

"He said to make sure I got a full breed. And do you know why?"

Ayana didn't respond. Whatever he had to say no longer mattered, their time together had come to an end.

"Because crossbreeds are unpredictable. That's what you are, Ayana—a crossbreed. I don't know what the hell you are but your momma should've never screwed your daddy. She should have sucked him off and spit your trifling ass out."

Ayana looked at Alonzo, who was driving with his left hand and waving the gun around with his right hand.

"After everything I've done for you, this how you repay me?"

No answer from Ayana.

"Oh, you not talking now? You were mighty talkative with your new sugar daddy."

"It was just lunch, Alonzo. You act like you caught me in bed with somebody."

"Oh, I'm sure that's where it was headed. I mean y'all all wrapped in each other's arms and things."

"Nobody was wrapped in anybody's arms. You're tripping."

"I saw y'all with my own two eyes."

You mean that one good eye? she thought.

"I don't want you hanging out with Lorraine no more. Her old horny ass is bad business and there's no need for a woman who is in a relationship to hang out with a woman who's always looking for the next dick to hop on. Pretty soon you'll be hopping on one too. That's if you haven't already. Plus, she's crazy. Takes more medicine than the law should allow."

What the hell was I thinking staying with this man?

"You hear me talking to you?" Alonzo said. Then out of nowhere, he placed his gun to Ayana's temple.

Ayana froze. "Alonzo," she said, trying to remain calm, "will you please take that gun away from my head?"

Alonzo snatched the gun back and placed it up to his own temple.

"Is this what you want?" he said, closing his eyes and swerving all over the road.

"Alonzo," Ayana screamed as they barely missed an oncoming eighteen-wheeler that was blaring down on its horn. "What is wrong with you?" she yelled.

Alonzo dropped the gun on the seat and regained control of the vehicle. Ayana wanted to pick it up so bad but something told her not to.

"You're what's wrong with me!" he screamed.

"Alonzo, you're scaring me."

"Do you take me for some kind of fool?"

"No, I don't," Ayana said, trying to soften her tone. "And I do understand how things may have appeared to you but it was just lunch. I didn't even know they were going to be there. Those are Lorraine's friends."

"What was his name?"

"Who?"

"The man you were sitting with?"

Ayana had to think for a second.

"Quincy."

"Oh," Alonzo said, shaking his head. "Now I see. And how long have you known this Quincy fella."

"I just met him. Come on, Alonzo, that man was a hundred years old."

"So. I'm forty-four. You like that sugar daddy shit."

Ayana threw up her hands.

"Don't dismiss me," Alonzo snapped. He reached down and picked up the gun. "So what do you wanna do, Ayana? I mean, is this the man you want to be with? If so, then let me know, and I'm cool."

If Ayana thought for one second he was telling the truth she would've lied just to walk away, but she knew better. He had threatened her enough times for her to know that leaving wouldn't be an easy task. Besides, the reality was, she didn't have a pot to pee in or a window to throw it out of.

"I told you, I don't know that man."

"So you're saying you're happy with me?"

Ayana took a deep breath. Now was not the time. She had to come up with a plan. She nodded her head.

"You know if I find out you're running around on me, it ain't gonna be pretty for you."

Ayana felt trapped and she hated herself now more than ever for allowing herself to be in this situation.

"I tried to do right by you but all I get in return is disrespect. Why?"

Ayana sighed. Then as if the God of truth took over her body she blurted it out.

"I don't love you. I don't even like you."

"What?" Alonzo asked. He couldn't have looked more shocked than if he had just caught his mother at a swingers' party.

"I've never loved you."

"You . . . you said you did," Alonzo said. "Why'd you lie?"

"Alonzo, I don't know. I don't know much of anything any-more."

"So you just use people up and toss 'em away when you don't wanna be bothered? Is that how you handle yours?"

"No."

"Well, what is it then?"

"I don't know but I'm tired of playing this game."

"So it was all a game, huh? Well, let me give you a quick lesson in this game called 'grown folks' business.' I don't give a rat's ass what you are tired of. I won't be disrespected and used. And I'll tell you another thing: you ain't shit, so any man who's trying to holla at you only wants to have sex with you. I mean what else you bringing to the table other than a pretty face? And on the path you are going with me, I'mma cut that up before the night is over."

"What do you want me to do, Alonzo? Stay miserable? I'm try-ing to be honest with you."

"I'm not forcing you to stay. I don't lock you up in the house when I leave. You're free to haul ass whenever you want but do you do that? Nope. You stay and try to suck the life out of me."

"You were very adamant about me not working. Every time I tried to get a job you had a fit. And I knew what you were doing. You were trying to keep me dependent on you. But as long as Brandy was happy I put up with it."

Alonzo was silent. Then out of nowhere he reached over and backhanded Ayana with so much force her head hit the headrest and snapped back. Ayana shook her head to clear the cobwebs.

"There's a price to pay for fucking with people's emotions. You could've just asked me to help you with Brandy and I would've done everything I'm doing now but no, you had to act like you wanted me. Well, playing games is costly," Alonzo said, banging his fist on the steering wheel.

Ayana covered her mouth and tried to stop the flow of blood oozing from her lip. She willed her tears to stay put.

"I should've left your ass in the street where I found you, you worthless bitch."

"You feel better now?" Ayana said. She didn't know where the words came from or if she was being foolish or brave. "You feel like a real man now? I got news for you, Alonzo: you'll never be a real man. That's why you always running with a gun. Because you ain't man enough to—"

Slap!

Alonzo let off another backhand.

Ayana reached over and tried to claw out his eyes. She no

longer cared about her own safety because she made a vow to herself that night in Lucky's apartment that no man would ever hit her and get away with it.

The car swerved back and forth as Alonzo tried to keep his eyes on the road and hold off Ayana, who had obviously become possessed. He finally pulled the car over, barely missing a neighbor's mailbox. He placed his gun under Ayana's chin, his face covered in blood and scratches.

"Have you completely lost your cotton-picking mind?" Alonzo said, breathing hard and holding his eye. "Who the hell you think you are, Tina Turner?"

"You keep your hands off of me!" Ayana screamed and opened the car door.

"You dead, Ayana. You're a dead bitch."

"Go to hell," she yelled.

"That's where I'mma send yo ass."

8

MR. POLICEMAN

*N*asir noticed a black Ford F-150 truck parked in the driveway next door to Granny's house, and he wondered whose it was. The house had been vacant since he graduated from high school. He grabbed his daughter's hand and walked toward his grandmother's yard.

"Boy, I didn't know you could gain any weight," Priest said from the rocking chair on the screened-in porch.

"Looks good on 'im though," Granny chimed in proudly.

"But he still got that rock head," Mario "Baldhead" Jackson, Priest's best friend, said.

Priest Dupree was a neighborhood police officer

who took an interest in all the kids of the West End area of Atlanta when Nasir was growing up. For young Nasir and his mother, Priest was a godsend. It was nothing for him to show up at their house with a truckload of groceries to get them through another month or to pay an electric bill to get the lights turned back on. He did this for a lot of other families too, but he seemed to take a special interest in Nasir.

Nasir was a quiet child and his soft features seemed to make him the target of the neighborhood thugs who were always on the prowl for their next victim. Nasir's timid nature made him a lamb in a land full of wolves. That was until Priest came along and showed him how to keep the predators at bay. A few boxing lessons later, Nasir was knocking guys out right and left.

No one ever knew why Priest took such an interest in Nasir. Maybe it was because he was a friend of Nasir's father and felt obligated out of friendship to a fallen comrade. Or maybe it was simply because Nasir latched on to him so tightly. Whatever the reason, Nasir couldn't imagine life without the soft-spoken man who had the fear and respect of the entire city.

Not only did Priest impart a lot of life wisdom over the years, but he also wrote those big checks so that Nasir could attend AAU, Nike, and Adidas basketball camps all throughout the state that ultimately got him national attention.

Nasir smiled and walked over to the man he missed the most while he was away and gave him a brotherly hug.

"Hey, man," Nasir said.

"Priest the only person you see?" Baldhead said.

Mario "Baldhead" Jackson was a sort of big brother to Nasir. Baldhead was a complex character but loyal to the end. He once played the role of a crackhead for two years while Priest was undercover working to take down the largest drug dealer in the state of Georgia.

"What's up, Baldhead?"

"Why do they call you Baldhead? You have hair," Brandy asked.

Baldhead touched his hair and jumped back, looking at his hand with a shocked expression on his face. His eyes got big and he let out a short scream. "How did hair get up there?"

Brandy laughed and leaned on her father's leg.

"Who is this pretty lady?" Priest said, reaching out for Brandy.

"My daughter," Nasir said with a smile.

"Daughter?" Priest turned to Granny. "Granny. You mean to tell me you've been holding out?"

"Oh, boy, hush. I don't see you but once a year and even then you just drop by to get something to eat," Granny said, fanning Priest away. "Mario the only one come 'round here with any regularity."

Baldhead puffed out his chest. "See, I knew this was Nasir's daughter," Baldhead said.

"Why didn't you tell me then," Priest snapped.

"Thought you knew."

"Come 'round here more often and you won't be so surprised when things happen," Granny said.

"Now, Granny, you know I come by here more than that," Priest said, lifting Brandy up and giving her a big smile.

"No you don't," Granny snapped.

"Well, I mean to," Priest said.

"Well, meaning ain't doing. How 'bout I tell you I meant to give you that sweet potato pie you begged for instead of doing it?"

"I guess you got a point there. I'mma have to do better," Priest said.

"Granny, you cooked a pie?" Nasir asked, his mouth already watering.

"Yeah, but that old bigheaded scoundrel right there done took it."

Priest used his free hand to point his remote control key at his truck. *Beep. Beep.*

"If the door wasn't locked I'd give you a li'l piece," he said before putting the key back into his pocket.

Nasir frowned and looked at Granny as if he couldn't believe she could do such a thing.

"Now look here, pretty lady, I'm your uncle Priest and if you ever need anything in this whole wide world, you call me. 'Cuz I'm the man 'round here."

"Don't believe that, Brandy. If you ever need anything, then you call me. As you just heard, this knucklehead don't even come around," Baldhead said.

"Okay," Brandy said with a smile.

"Were you in the army with my daddy?" she asked.

"Yeah, but they kicked me out 'cause I don't like getting up too early in the morning," Baldhead said, making a funny face and not missing a beat on the cover-up.

"Brandy, come on in here with me. I gotta bake another pie for your daddy or I'm sure I'll never hear the end of it," Granny said.

"I can't believe you took my pie," Nasir said.

Priest put Brandy down and waved bye to her.

"You better start believing." Priest clicked the lock again.

"Priest, you make sure you bring your butt by here a little more often and tell your brother and your sister I said, unless they done fell down and broke both their legs, I wanna see them too. Mario, come on in here and help me put a box in the attic," Granny said, walking in the house not waiting on a response.

Baldhead frowned but he followed her into the house.

"Yes, ma'am," Baldhead said.

"How's life treating you?" Nasir asked.

"I can't complain."

"That's good to hear," Nasir said, feeling a hint of shame for not allowing Priest to visit him either while he was in jail. "And what about your brother and sister?"

"They're hanging in there. Carmen just got married. You won't believe who she married."

"Who?"

"Mario."

"Baldhead?"

"Yeah. They jumped the broom about six months ago and if that ain't a marriage of misfits, I don't know one. She's a world-renowned physician, highly respected in her field, and he's a local nutcase."

"Baldhead still crazy?"

"As a mutha . . ." Priest said, catching himself after he noticed the front door was still open.

"Priest!" Granny called from inside the house. "Do you need me to come back out there and wash your mouth out?"

"No, ma'am," Priest said with a serious face. "That woman is a firecracker, ain't she? Hasn't lost a step. How old is she?"

"I'm eighty, and I'll still put a strap to your butt," Granny yelled from inside of the house.

"And that's why I ain't saying nothing else," Priest said, motioning for Nasir to follow him out of Granny's hearing range. "So what's up with those drops of blood on your shoes?"

Nasir looked down. He didn't even notice the little specks that Priest easily caught with his cop's eyes.

"Had a little altercation with this cat that I got into that trouble behind."

"Savion?"

"Yeah."

"I thought he was dead," Priest asked, confused.

"Nah, he's still running around here."

"For real? Somebody shot him up pretty good behind that thing with you or maybe it was something else his sorry a . . . butt did." Priest snuck a peek at the door. "Ah, man, I thought he was pushing up daisies."

Nasir mulled over who could've shot Savion, then let it go when the list got too long.

He was waiting for Priest to give him a long speech about how he had told him to stay away from Savion.

"So what happened? How did you get out?"

"Don't know. I've been asking myself that same question over and over." Nasir reached in his back pocket and pulled out the papers he got from the Department of Corrections. "I feel like a slave walking around with my freedom papers."

Priest looked at the papers.

"Looks like they overturned the case," Priest said, hunching his shoulders. "Happens every now and then. You should've never been in there in the first place. Why didn't you call me when this thing went down? I mean, I didn't find out about it until you were already convicted."

Nasir looked away.

"I was undercover at the time so I wasn't privy to a lot of what was going on at the courthouse or in the city."

"Well, it's over now. At least I hope so."

"What do you mean 'you hope so'?"

"I guess I'm still getting used to it. I keep thinking they're going to come back and take me away."

"Nah, that's not gonna happen, man. Enjoy yourself. You're free."

"I'll feel better when I know what happened. You know, make sure this isn't some kind of clerical error. I know the prison system didn't do an audit and realize they made a mistake. Hell would freeze over before the State admits to a mistake. They would rather let an innocent man rot. I'm just another nigga to them."

"You right about that," Priest said, shaking his head. "That's a nice car. Where'd you get it from?"

"A friend of mine from the Tech squad. He's a sports agent now and he's trying to get me to sign with him. He might be the one who got me out but he's not admitting to it."

"Nice friend. That's a quarter-million-dollar car."

"I guess he's doing well."

"I'd say. So you gonna play ball?"

"Nah, man. I'm done with that. The thrill is gone."

Priest frowned.

"So what are your plans, Nasir?"

"I don't know, man. I wanna go back to school and finish my degree. I always wanted to be a teacher. Your brother Dallas is a teacher, right?"

"Yeah. He has his hands full trying to open up a school. Damn do-gooder. Gets on my nerves."

"Wonder where he got it from?"

"I don't know 'cause I'mma nasty summabitch. You should

give that ball some more thought. Lord knows Tech could use you with they sorry asses."

"I haven't played since I caught that case. Skills are probably shot."

"You know I tried to visit you a few times."

"I know," Nasir said, his voice just above a whisper. "I'm sorry about that."

"Yeah, well, I figured you were going through it. I had folks in there looking out for you though." Just then Priest's cell phone rang and he looked at the number but didn't answer it. "Listen. I gotta run. Working with the FBI now and they're worse than my wife."

"Wife?"

"Yeah, man, got married too. I'll fill you in on everything soon. Maybe I'll have a cookout or something at the house. I know everyone would love to see you."

"Yeah, I'd love to see them too."

"You look good, Nasir."

"Likewise." Nasir put his hand on Priest's shoulder. "I really appreciate everything you did for me, and I feel like I let you down ending up in prison anyway."

"You didn't let me down. You were just in the wrong place at the wrong time. How's your mother?"

"Don't ask."

"Why? What's up? I'm a little out of the loop. I hardly ever come around this way anymore."

"Drugs."

"Ah no." Priest frowned and looked away. He shook his head.

"Yeah."

"Man, I'm sorry to hear that. You're going to have to get her some help. She's too smart for that life."

"I'mma do everything I can."

"I know you will. Look here. I gotta boogie. I'll do a little checking around to see who got you out," Priest said.

"Thanks, man."

"Oh and, Nasir, didn't I tell you to stay away from that li'l bad-ass Savion?"

"I knew it was coming," Nasir said, closing his eyes.

"You damn right it's coming. I hate to see a good kid mess his life up trying to be down with a bunch of lowlifes. I told you from the jump that boy was going to be your downfall. He had you hiding your good grades just so you could fit in with him and his dumb-ass friends."

Nasir chuckled. "I remember you and Baldhead slapping me upside my head about that one."

"That's right. I never did like that li'l dirty-ass Savion. Everybody could see he was jealous of you except you."

Nasir took the lashing without a comment.

Nasir and Priest hugged again.

"Aww, damn. Y'all having a group hug without me," Baldhead said, running down the steps to join in. "Nasir, it's good to see you, boy."

"You too, Baldhead."

"Okay, man, we gotta get out of here," Priest said.

Nasir watched as Priest and Baldhead walked over to Priest's truck and got in.

Priest rolled his window down and brought the sweet potato pie to his nose.

"Granny got skills, boy," he said. "And I wish I had time to cut you a slice, but I gotta go, gotta go," he said, backing out of the driveway.

Nasir smiled, shook his head, and walked into the house.

9

TIME TO RIDE

*A*yana ran into the house and straight into the bathroom. She locked the door behind her and walked over to the wall-length mirror. She saw that her upper lip had already begun to swell.

She took a few deep breaths to calm her nerves because all sorts of evil thoughts were starting to take shape, so she forced herself to think about her daughter. Brandy's father was already in prison, and Ayana couldn't live with herself if she allowed her anger to get the best of her and send her on that same ride.

Ayana ran cold water over a washcloth, then placed it on her lip. Standing there staring at herself, she didn't like what she saw. She had overcome too much in her life to be where she was. It was time to move on. Her anger subsided a little when she had the thought that this was God's way of forcing her to take control of her destiny.

As she stood there staring at herself she realized Alonzo was right about one thing—she shouldn't have played with his emotions. She felt sorry for him. Even with all of his financial trappings, he would never amount to anything more than a miserable little man.

She turned the water off and took a deep breath. Calmness washed over her entire body.

She didn't have the slightest idea where she would go or how she would survive but living with the jealous tyrant was no longer an option.

She picked up the bathroom phone and dialed Marcy's number. The line rang about twenty times before she heard the operator's voice say: *"Your party does not answer. Please hang up and try your call again later."*

She hung up and called again. This time Marcy picked up but she sounded a little out of it. Ayana immediately regretted leaving Brandy over there today. Ayana hung up the phone and walked back out into the bedroom. She looked at the clock on the nightstand; it was 4:00 P.M., she planned on being gone by five.

What was she going to do? She only had a little over a thousand dollars in her checking account. She thought about Lorraine's offer to stay with her but quickly dismissed it. If she was going to cut all ties with Alonzo, then she couldn't be staying with his cousin. She decided she'd rent a weekly hotel room until she could figure out her next move. She walked into her closet and grabbed two of the largest suitcases she could find. She scanned the shelves for the necessities and started tossing them into the bag.

"So you leaving me now?" Alonzo said from the doorway.

Ayana didn't hear him come in, and he startled her. She checked to see if he was still on some Ike Turner stuff, then went back to her packing.

"Don't wanna talk? That's cool. I can handle that," Alonzo said in a calm voice. "Where you gonna go, Ayana? Back to the ghetto? You don't have any money."

Ayana remained silent.

Alonzo walked into the closet and knelt down beside her.

"Listen, I'm sorry for hitting you," he said. "And I'm sorry I pulled my gun on you."

"I'm sorry too. Sorry any of this ever happened. I'm sorry we ever met. I'm sorry I lied and told you I loved you. I'm sorry I got my daughter caught up in this fairy tale of a life but you know what I'm most sorry about, Alonzo?"

"What," he asked calmly.

"I'm sorry that I'm to the point of wanting you dead. I really really want to see you die a slow and painful death and that's not good," Ayana said, shaking her head from side to side.

"You don't mean that. You're just upset."

"No, I mean it and that's why I have to leave. You're not safe," Ayana said.

A nervous chuckle escaped his lips as he read her face. The mask of hate she wore made him uneasy.

Alonzo stood. "Now, I'm not some pimp who'll jump on his knees just because you said so. Be careful who you run up against. I'm no play toy."

Ayana zipped up the first bag and started on the second.

"How did we get here, Ayana?" Alonzo asked.

"I don't know, but right now all I'm interested in is getting away from here."

Alonzo grunted as if he was coming to some resolution within himself. "You know you and I aren't that different. I always wanted a family and I guess I tried to make you and Brandy something that you weren't meant to be. And you . . . well, you only wanted the best for your daughter and who could blame you for that. So I'll tell you what," Alonzo said, walking out of Ayana's closet and into his own. When he returned he tossed a brown paper bag at Ayana and rolls of money fell out on the floor. "That's yours. It'll help you get on your feet. And just to let you know I'm not the bad guy you think I am, you can keep your car. I know you'll need to get Brandy around," he said.

Ayana wasn't falling for this nice guy treatment but she wasn't dumb either. She picked up the money and tossed it in her suitcase. After filling both of the bags, she headed into Brandy's room and started packing her things. She made sure to grab her favorite teddy bear and her dolls.

Ayana struggled with the bags down the stairs and Alonzo ran over and took them from her.

"I can help you with that," he said.

"I got it," she replied.

"Ayana, we don't have to act all indignant. We can go our separate ways without all of the hostilities."

Ayana allowed him to take the bags. Carrying two bags at a time, Alonzo loaded them into Ayana's Lexus SUV. Once all of the bags were secure and Ayana said she had everything she needed, Alonzo held out his hand.

"No hard feelings?"

Ayana ignored his hand and got into her truck. As she backed out of the driveway she looked at the large house with all of its beauty and splendor and realized she never wanted to see the place again. Just as she put her truck in drive she turned and took what she hoped would be her last look at Alonzo, but there was something sinister beneath his fake smile and she knew she would see him again.

*M*arcy pulled herself out of bed and tried to gather her thoughts.

Was she dreaming or had she just received a call from Ayana?

For the last few months she had been having these hellish nightmares about all sorts of things and Ayana had been showing up in more and more of them.

Just last night she woke up shivering in a cold sweat after seeing Nasir hanging from a sheet in his prison cell. The night before that she woke up screaming when she had visions of Ayana being nailed to a cross and stoned. Then there were the dreams where both of them were living happily ever after in a nice home in the suburbs but didn't want anything to do with her. That one scared her more than any of the others.

Marcy stared at the phone for a moment, then chalked the call up to her paranoia. She stood and walked into the kitchen to get a drink of orange juice when she noticed a cuff link on the floor.

She reached down and picked up the little gold basketball and held it close to her heart. She closed her eyes and thanked God for sending her son back home.

"I was beginning to lose faith in You," she said.

Marcy opened the refrigerator, which was empty as usual, and picked up the empty orange carton. "That doggone Brandy," she said, shaking the carton before tossing it into the trash can. She shook her head at the thought of how many times she had to get on Nasir about the same thing when he was her age.

She started scratching her arm and the heroin monkey started calling her name.

Marcy, I'm getting hungry, the monkey said.

With her son being home, it was time to turn over a new leaf and leave those drugs alone.

Who you think you fooling? the monkey said.

It seemed her cravings got stronger at the thought of quitting. It was like they were telling her not to even think about it anymore. She started scratching and she knew what that meant. It was time to feed the monkey.

The thought of the potent morphine sent her scrambling to her bedroom. She almost threw her worn-out mattress on the floor in search of her "medicine." The sight of the clear plastic vial was beautiful. She picked it up, and the spoon that sat beside it. She opened up her drawer and grabbed the lighter. Then she picked up her pillow.

"SHIT! SHIT! SHIT!" Marcy said, realizing that Nasir had thrown her needle away.

Marcy tried to think of a place where she had another needle. Her mind drew a blank. Without any shoes on her feet she ran through her house and out the back door. The alley behind her house was like a shooters' gallery and she knew someone had to have dropped a needle.

"Marcy, what you got?" Wiley, another heroin addict, said. "Don't hold out on me now."

"Hey, Wiley. I'm just out here walking."

"Yeah, but what ya got? I'm doing bad right about now."

Marcy saw a needle that was still in the plastic. She couldn't believe her luck. She reached down but Wiley was too fast.

"Wiley, what are you doing?"

"No, what you doing?"

"I'm trying to clean up this mess behind my house. Do you mind?"

"You gonna share with me or not? Don't forget about that time I looked out for you."

"What time?"

"You remember?"

"No I don't."

"Well, hook me up and I'll look out for you next time."

A police siren wailed in the distance, distracting Wiley. Marcy took advantage of the opportunity and snatched the needle from Wiley's hand and took off running back toward her house.

It took Wiley a few seconds to realize what happened to him before he gave chase.

Marcy jumped over debris and broken glass like a seasoned ghetto child. She made it to her back porch just as Wiley was gaining on her. She slammed the door and locked it.

"Now get away from here, you fool."

"I'mma remember that, Marcy. You'll need me before I need you."

Marcy went into her house no longer thinking about Wiley.

She went back into her bedroom and sat on the floor. She looked around as if someone might be watching, then tied her arm with a belt. She located her favorite vein, then poured the Mexican mud into her already black spoon and put the lighter to the bottom. After the poison turned to liquid Marcy stuck the needle in the spoon and withdrew the stem on the syringe. The needle found its spot in her bony arm and she pushed the stem, allowing the drugs to take her to a high where nothing mattered anymore. As the heroin made its way through her system, her head snapped back and her face turned into a contorted mask of pleasure and pain. Her chin hit her chest and she stayed in that nod for three full minutes.

The ringing phone startled her. She looked at it but couldn't move. Didn't want to move. She wanted to hold on to her high for as long as possible. The phone stopped but soon rang again. She pulled herself up and went over to the phone.

"Hello?" Marcy asked.

"Hey, Ma," Nasir said.

Marcy smiled at the sweet sound on the other end of the phone. She felt good. Life couldn't be better.

"We're on our way back and I wanted to know if you needed anything."

"Oh, thank you, son. No, I'm fine. Did you enjoy your time with Brandy?"

"Ah, I can't get enough of her. Don't know if I would've ever made it to see freedom if I'd known about her."

"Say what?"

"Nothing. I'm just glad to have her."

His voice sounded rough, no-nonsense, but she could still find a hint of her little boy in there.

"Where is she?"

"In the bathroom. I tried to take her in there with me but she said, 'Daddy, I'm a girl.' So I had to ask a waitress to go in there with her." Nasir laughed. "I'm getting a crash course in this fatherhood thing."

Marcy laughed but she was really too high to fully understand.

"Well, I'm lying down. I'll see you when you get here."

"Okay, Ma. You okay? You don't sound right."

"I'm good. Just a little tired."

"Okay, well get some rest."

"Hey, are you staying here with me tonight?" she asked.

"Nah."

"Why?" Marcy whined.

Nasir didn't answer.

"You hate me, don't you?" Marcy said. "I knew you hated me."

"Ma," Nasir cut her off before she could start ridiculing herself. "I already told you to stop saying that. But I have some plans. You won't be there either."

"What are you talking about?"

"You're staying at the Ritz-Carlton in Buckhead."

"Buckhead?"

"Yes. Your room's already taken care of. Massage package and everything."

"Oh, son, you know I don't like all that fancy-schmancy stuff."

"Yeah, but you need it, so consider this a gift from me. I know you know better than to turn down gifts. That would be rude."

"Nasir," Marcy huffed.

"Don't wanna hear it. I'll see you in a few."

"But I wanted to ride out and check Ayana. I've been having bad dreams about her."

Nasir laughed.

"No, for real. Something is going on with her. I can feel it."

"I'm sure she's fine. Are you sure you're not hungry?"

"I'm sure but thanks anyway."

"Okay, get dressed. We'll be there in about fifteen minutes."

"I guess I don't have a choice in this matter, huh?"

"Not at all," Nasir said, hanging up the phone.

Marcy pressed the talk button, then pressed it again. She got a dial tone and phoned Ayana.

"Hello."

"How are you, Alonzo? This is Marcy."

"I'm good, Mrs. L. What about you?"

"I'm doing okay. Is Ayana around?"

"No, she's just left. She should be back shortly though."

"Okay, well, tell her I called."

"I will. But you been doing all right?"

"Yeah, I'm fine," Marcy said, baffled. Alonzo almost never talked to her, especially small talk.

"Good to hear it. You know I was sitting here thinking about how bad Ayana gets on my case for being gone so long, but the minute I come home she takes off," he said with a laugh.

"Well maybe she just wanted to get out of the house," Marcy said.

"I guess so."

"Alonzo, do you know if she called me about twenty or thirty minutes ago?"

"Hmmm. I don't know. Did she call you from her cell phone?"

"I'm not sure. I don't have that caller ID stuff."

"Oh, come on, Mrs. L., you gotta step into the new millennium," he said with a laugh.

"I guess you're right. Well, good talking to you but I better get off of this phone."

"Okay, it was good talking to you too."

"Tell Ayana to give me a call once she gets in?"

"I'll do it."

Marcy hung up the phone. Now she knew something wasn't right. Alonzo was being way too nice. Normally he would rush off the phone or just not answer it if Ayana wasn't home. In all the time she had known him he had never said more than two words to her. Something was definitely wrong.

Marcy stood up staring at the phone as if it could tell her what Alonzo was up to. Then she heard a knock on the door.

She walked over to peek out of the window, hoping it wasn't one of the neighborhood drug addicts with a fresh lie.

It was worse. It was Edna.

"Girl, open this damn door," Edna, Marcy's raunchy friend, said.

"Hey, Edna," Marcy said, opening the door.

"Where he at? And don't try to lie."

Marcy shook her head at the old woman who refused to give up her past. Edna had to be at least sixty years old but dressed like a twenty-year-old. Her miniskirts were just plain wrong. Even the freakiest men would turn their heads in disgust when she walked by with half of her butt cheek hanging out showing more cellulite than fabric.

"Girl, I heard he done got fine as wine. I wanna see 'im," Edna said, walking from room to room.

"He's not here. He took Brandy to get something to eat."

"And I heard he done got muscles all over the damn place. I hope you don't mind being my mother-in-law." Edna laughed so hard her wig shifted. She fixed it and kept on talking. "How old is you, Marcy? 'Cuz if it's against the law for me to be older than my own mother-in-law then they gone just have to lock me up. What you got to drink up in here?" Edna said, opening the refrigerator. "Damn, girl, this thing stays empty," she said, slamming the door shut.

"Edna, stay out of my refrigerator."

"Rich and good-looking. I'll be a rat's ass in the wintertime if that ain't a good combination," Edna said, flopping her large frame down in the chair. "Now that's something I was never able to come up with. Either mine was always fine and broke, or ugly and broke. I keep missing that rich part. When you moving?"

"What are you talking about, Edna?"

"Don't you sit up here and act like you ain't getting the hell on. I know I would. Shit, I'd move if I had an extra twenty dollars, nonetheless twenty million."

"Twenty million?"

"That's what they saying."

"Well, I don't know where 'they' are getting their information. If you don't know, Nasir just came home from prison."

"Well, he must've hit the lottery on the bus ride home. 'Cause they say he got twenty million dollars and he's out there throwing it around like it's conchetti."

"You mean confetti?"

"Whatever," Edna said. "I'm sho gone miss ya li'l white-acting ass."

"You're being a little presumptuous, don't you think?"

"They you go with them big words again. Now what in the hell does that mean? Are you high?"

"No. And if I was, you done blew it."

Marcy heard another tap on the door. She walked over and looked out the living-room window and smiled when she saw her son playing some kind of hand game with her grand-child.

"Hello there, you two," Marcy said, opening the door.

"Hey, Ma," Nasir said, handing her a plastic bag from Dave and Buster's restaurant.

"Hey, Grandma. Hey, Mrs. Edna," Brandy said, running by both of them to get to the television in the living room.

Edna almost ran Nasir over when she rushed up to him, putting her rather large bosom in his chest.

"You don't remember me, do you?"

Frowning and backing up against the wall as much as he could, Nasir shook his head.

"Well, say something. Cat gotcha tongue?" Edna said, fixing her wig again.

"No, ma'am. I think it's still here." Nasir stuck his tongue out.

"Ohh," Edna said, lusting after the young tongue. "Do that again."

"Edna, will you leave my baby alone," Marcy said, shaking her head and trying not to laugh.

"Baby? This ain't no baby. This here a man," Edna said, grunting like a bull on Cialis.

Nasir reached up and straightened out her wig for her. "It was a little crooked," he said, snatching his hand back before she could grab it.

"I got something else that needs straightening out," she said, taking a bite at Nasir.

"Edna, don't make me hurt you," Marcy said.

Edna finally backed off.

"Mrs. Edna, how have you been?" Nasir said to the old woman who unknowingly gave him and his little horny friends their first peek at what real sex looked like when they would climb a ladder and peek in on her and her male friend on several occasions.

"I'll be better if you let me hold a li'l something," Edna said, rubbing her thumb and index fingers together.

"Just plain old rude," Marcy said. "I'm glad you brought me something to eat. I was about to starve in here."

Nasir shifted his eyes.

"I could've sworn I just called and asked if you were hungry. Those are just some leftovers but you're more than welcome to them."

"I didn't want you to go out of your way. I'll just eat this."

"Did you pack?" Nasir asked, noticing his mother in the same clothes she wore when he left.

"Not yet but it won't take me long."

"Pack? Where you going, Marcy?" Edna asked.

"None of your business, Edna."

"What time does Ayana normally get here to pick up Brandy?" Nasir asked.

"Oh, she normally gets here around seven or eight," Marcy said. "Do you think you guys will get back together?"

"I hope not," Edna said.

"Edna, don't you have somewhere to be?"

"Not that I know of."

Marcy threw her hands up and turned her attention back to her son.

"What are you going to do about Ayana?" Marcy asked.

"I just got home."

"I know, but I liked you guys together."

"That's old news, Ma."

"Oh," Marcy said, the wind gone from her sails. "Now explain to me again why I'm going to a hotel?"

"A hotel," Edna said. "Where?"

"The Ritz," Nasir said to Edna, then turned back to his

mother. "Because you could use a change of scenery. And pack enough for a few days."

Marcy stopped in her tracks.

"Wait a minute. Have you been talking to Ayana?"

"Huh?" Nasir asked, confused.

"She thinks she's slick. I'm not going to any drug place and if you think I'm that dumb to fall for you taking me to some hotel, you have another think coming."

Edna stood behind Marcy and started nodding her head feverishly, making all sorts of drugged-up faces, then abruptly stopped when Marcy turned around.

"Get out, Edna!"

"I'm going, I'm going. Hell, I done been kicked outta places better than this raggedy-ass house," Edna said, stopping in front of Nasir.

She held out her hand again.

He slapped it.

She frowned and tried to lick his face before walking out the door.

"I'll tell you right now, Nasir, I'm not going to any rehabilitation place," Marcy protested.

"Who said anything about rehab?"

"Well, just so you know, I'm fine."

"Calm down. It's nothing like that. Just pack a little bag so we can get out of here."

Marcy stared at her son, took a deep breath, then finally

relented. "Are you sure this is just a hotel? No funny business."

"I promise," Nasir said, raising his right hand. "No funny business."

Marcy shot him a look, then retreated into her bedroom.

NASIR PUT Brandy in a backseat that was so small she had to sit with her feet across the seat. His mom looked at the car, then back at him, her eyes begging for an explanation.

"It belongs to a friend, Mom."

Marcy grunted and strapped herself in.

When they pulled up to the Ritz-Carlton, Nasir handed the parking attendant a ten-dollar bill and told him to keep the car close by. Then he and his daughter escorted his mother up to the nicest suite she'd ever seen. A California king-size bed sat on a raised platform in front of a wall-size window overlooking the beautiful Atlanta skyline. There was a plasma-screen television set hanging from the wall over the fireplace. Soft leather sofas and ottomans were everywhere and there was a dining-room table long enough to seat twenty people.

"Oh, Daddy, can I stay with Grandma?" Brandy gushed.

Nasir smiled as his daughter ran around from room to room. His mom stood there speechless.

"I think Grandma could use a little quiet time. Maybe you can stay with her another night."

Marcy looked at Nasir with raised brows.

"Wait a minute, Nasir. Where are you getting money from for all this?"

"I already told you. I have friends," he said, fanning her away.

"There's a swimming pool in the bathroom," Brandy said, waving her grandmother over.

"Oh my. That is a rather large tub," Marcy said, still stunned. "Nasir, this must've cost a fortune."

"Not really. As a matter of fact it didn't cost me a dime. One of my old teammates runs this place."

"I wonder if they have any good books up here," Marcy said, walking over to the glassed-in bookshelf. "I don't remember the last time I cuddled up with a good book."

"Why don't you do that tonight?" Nasir said, grabbing the remote control and turning on the fireplace. "It's all ambiance. No heat comes from this thing."

"That's nice," Marcy said, sitting down at the desk. She willed herself not to cry.

Nasir noticed his mother was overwhelmed and wanted to give her time to adjust to her surroundings. He looked at his watch.

"Come on, precious. We need to get back over to Grandma's so we can meet your mom."

"Awww. I wanted to stay with Grandma."

"I'm hurt." Nasir made a pouting face. "You wanna leave me already?"

"Okay, I'll stay with you," Brandy said, hugging her father. "Bye, Grandma."

Marcy reached out for a hug and Brandy walked over.

Nasir reached down and hugged his mother.

"I want you to enjoy yourself this evening. Order all the room service you want. And just enjoy the evening, okay?"

"Okay," Marcy said, nodding her head. "So I'll see you in the morning?"

"First thing. Sleep well, Mom," Nasir said. He paused and looked back at his mom before walking out.

THE GHETTO GOSPEL

$\mathcal{N}$ asir sat on the steps of his mother's home listening to Sammy deliver the ghetto gospel. He got the run-down on what was happening in their neighborhood: who was doing what, who was doing whom, who had fallen victim to the perils of the ever-so-present crack cocaine, who was locked up, who was about to get locked up, who was doing good, and who was doing bad.

"You know Savion's punk ass came 'round here a few hours ago, drunk as hell, talking about what he gone do to you. Shooting his gun up in the air like he in Dodge City or some damn where."

"Priest told me somebody shot him up while I was in prison."

"Priest was right," Sammy said, smiling.

Nasir looked at his cousin and squinted his eyes.

"Yes, sir, I tried to kill his punk ass. Thought I was gonna be joining you, playboy, but he's so damn sorry not one cop came around here to investigate."

"Doesn't surprise me, but they are always Johnny-on-the-spot to lock up the wrong person."

"Man, I couldn't stand to look at that boy after what he did to you. He stayed on the low for a while but one night I caught him slipping. He was in Magic City throwing money around on strippers like he was Usher or some damn body. I couldn't believe it. I mean, seems like something inside of him shouldn't let him get his party on like that, knowing he just sold you out. Bastard ain't got no conscience, man. So I followed his drunk ass all the way home. Soon as he stumbled out of the car, I let him have it. *Pow. Pow. Pow.* I let all sixteen go on his ass and he still didn't die," Sammy said, shaking his head in disbelief.

"Maybe you need to take some target practice."

"You ain't lying about that." Sammy pulled up his pants leg and revealed a dark scar. "Trynna hold my gun like them damn rappers. All crooked. That shit don't work. Man, I almost killed myself."

"You shot yourself?" Nasir laughed as he pictured Sammy trying to be an assassin.

"Man, I'm trynna shoot this fool in the head. Ya know, make

sure he dead, and a bullet ricocheted off the pavement and went right into my leg. Burned like a summabitch."

Nasir laughed and reached over to lift Sammy's pants leg again.

"Back up offa me, homie," Sammy said, slapping his cousin's hand away. "I guess that was God telling me that He'll deal with Savion."

"Now how did God get involved in y'all drama?"

"Somebody saved his pathetic ass."

"So how many times did you actually shoot him?"

"I don't know. I didn't see him for a few months after that. Then one day, here his bony ass comes driving down the street like nothing happened. I almost started to shoot him again."

"It's probably best you left it alone. You might've killed yourself for sure the second time."

"Go to hell, Knock."

"Just got back."

"Man, have you been to Magic City yet?" Sammy said, changing the subject. "Those hos fine as hell. They got this one up in there name Hurricane. And I'm telling you she's the finest thing the good Lord ever created. Body like BAM! I know she done got me for about two g's."

"You be up in there tricking all of your little ferret money away."

"Hell yeah."

"Nah, I haven't been up in there yet. I need to go 'cuz I sure could use me a woman right about now," Nasir said, thinking about his many lonely nights surrounded by nothing but hard-head dudes.

"I know you can."

"They don't make coed prisons and I don't get down with the gumps."

"Gumps?"

"Faggots, gay boys, transvestites, whatever you call men with titties."

"Ah, hell no," Sammy said, making a disgusted face.

"Yeah, they got 'em running around there with Kool-Aid on their lips. Sheets wrapped around them like dresses. It's all bad, dog."

Sammy scrunched up his face.

"You feel that way hearing about it. How you think I felt seeing it?"

"I'm sorry you had to go through that, cuz."

"Me too."

"I bet yo pretty ass had to fight all the time."

"Had to do what I had to do. I only got into a few fights though."

"I'm glad you didn't end up like Allen."

"Who is Allen?"

"You remember Allen with them big-ass ears. Used to run out on the court at your games trynna fight the refs."

"Oh yeah, he got locked up when I was a kid, didn't he?"

"Yeah and he just came home about a month ago. That fool is institutionalized to the tenth power. Man, we were walking down the street about a week ago and all of a sudden, this nut stops and turns to face the wall. He puts his hands up like he's being frisked. I'm like, man, what is your problem? Do you know what he said?"

"What," Nasir said, already visualizing the hilarious scene.

"The CO's 'bout to do the search."

"I'm looking around the damn street like a fool myself. I'm like what CO. He's like shut up, man, they gonna put you in the hole. You can't talk during a shakedown. That cat's throwed off. Then his sister told me he stands by his bed at night waiting on count time. They got to go and tell this fool that he's free."

"Boy, you crazy," Nasir said, holding his side laughing.

"I'm telling the truth, Knock, he's out there, boy. All he talks about is prison. Be walking around with khakis and flip-flops on like he's still locked up."

"Sounds like he's pretty far gone."

"I'm glad you didn't come home with all that prison talk. 'I overstand.' And 'black man this, black man that.' I be like fool, you probably shot a black man to get locked up in the first place."

"Oh yeah, they get real disciplined when they inside. But, I can't be mad at 'em. Whatever it takes to keep the clock ticking."

"Allen told me he was in there with you and how you damn near killed this dude in the mess hall one day."

"I don't remember being locked up with Allen but who knows? I was on some serious shutdown when I was there."

The cousins enjoyed the peacefulness of the night for a moment. Then a Lexus SUV pulled into the lot and Sammy stood up.

"Well, that's Ayana. Holla at me tomorrow, cuz," Sammy said, slapping his cousin's hand.

"Where's your li'l stud friend?" The sight of Ayana caused his emotions to go out of whack and Nasir said the first thing that popped into his mind, trying to control whatever was going on inside of him.

"He's working," Sammy said, imitating a ferret humping.

Nasir laughed and gave his cousin a quick tap of the fist. His laughter stopped when he saw the mother of his child.

Ayana looked gorgeous. He couldn't take his eyes off of her. She wore a navy blue pantsuit with a white shirt beneath it. Her dark skin looked like it had a glow, making it even more flawless. And those eyes. Those eyes caused him plenty of sleepless nights when he was first sent away.

"What's up, Ayana?" Sammy said, holding out his hand for a high five.

"Hi," Ayana said, oblivious to Sammy's hand. Her eyes were on Nasir.

Nasir didn't move. It seemed like an eternity before either of them took a step toward the other. They just stood there staring at each other.

"Well, I'll leave you two lovebirds to y'all staring contest," Sammy said before walking off. "Let me know who wins tomorrow, cuz."

"When did you get home?" Ayana said, her voice cracking.

"Friday," Nasir said. He was more nervous now than he could ever remember being.

Ayana looked down because she didn't know what else to do. You could almost see her heart beating through her blouse.

"You look good," Nasir said.

"So do you," she said, still looking down.

"Brandy fell asleep. I guess I should go and wake her up."

"So I see you met your daughter."

"Yeah, she's . . ." Nasir shook his head. He was at a loss for words.

Nasir walked over to Ayana and grabbed her shoulders. She didn't resist as he pulled her into him.

They held each other without talking for a long time.

NASIR'S MIND flashed back to prison.

After being incarcerated for about three months he found a spot in the recreation room and cracked open the book he was reading. Then some guy with muscles everywhere walked up to him with a picture of Ayana.

Nasir figured the guy found one of the letters that he tossed in the trash can without even opening.

"I'm about to go and tear this ass up, homie. You don't mind, do ya?" the guy said, rubbing his genitals.

Nasir knew he would be tested at some point and it was pretty obvious that this was the day. All eyes were on him. The entire rec room wanted to see what the new fish was all about. Nasir could feel the stares but he ignored the guy and continued reading.

"Tell me, brah, does she like it in the ass?" the man said. " 'Cause I'm a little partial to putting pain on cute hos."

Nasir looked up and calmly closed the book. The guy smiled and set the picture down. He put his hands in a boxer's stance.

"Come on, li'l ho, let me see what you got," the guy said, circling Nasir. "You better bring it or I'mma make you mine."

Nasir was never much of a fighter but he grew up in The "U," so fighting was par for the course.

Never show fear. The minute they see it they will own you. You might as well lie on your stomach and beg for mercy. It's not about being the baddest, it's about being a man, an old convict schooled him on his first night behind bars.

Nasir stood up and shot a quick jab to the guy's windpipe. He stood back and watched the cock-diesel man's eyes roll around in his head as he struggled to catch his breath. After about thirty seconds, the man finally caught his wind and ran at Nasir. Nasir stepped to the side and caught the man in the same spot, this time with a lot more force. The man leaned over, holding his throat and stomping his feet. Anything to help the wind back into his lungs. Nasir grabbed the now helpless man up by his hair and slapped him hard across his face.

"Apologize?" he asked calmly.

It seemed the entire rec room was now laughing at the man who was doing some funky little dance, still trying to catch his breath. Nasir made a move to hit the man again but the man held up his hand, mouthing the words "I'm sorry."

"The next time you see me, walk the other way or I'll make sure you never breathe again," Nasir said and sat back down. He picked up his book and continued reading.

The whistle blew, calling the inmates for the evening lineup. Nasir stood and started for the line when he looked down and saw Ayana's pretty face. He picked up the picture when rec time was over and used it as a bookmark for the rest of his prison days. Before he went to sleep at night he would open whatever book he was reading and kiss the picture before calling it a night.

AYANA TRIED to pull away from their embrace but Nasir wasn't ready to let go. He held on and she wrapped her arms back around him and laid her head on his chest.

Nasir could hear her sniffling. He wasn't sure how he felt.

"I never thought I would see you again," she said.

"I know the feeling." He closed his eyes and savored a moment he never thought he'd experience again.

Ayana's sobs became more intense. Then she pulled away and started pummeling his chest with both fists.

"Why wouldn't you talk to us?" she said, pounding away.

Nasir withstood the barrage of punches. He tried to pull her close but took a right to his lip for his efforts.

"Why, Nasir?"

"I'm sorry."

"Sorry? You're sorry?" Ayana stepped back and closed her eyes. "Nasir, do you know what you did to us? Do you know how hard it was carrying your child and not knowing if you were dead or alive? Do you know what I've gone through? The sacrifices I've made for our child? It was bad enough that you were sent away but for you to cut everybody off was totally uncalled for. It was wrong, it was selfish, and just plain stupid."

"I know. God knows I know."

"No you don't know," Ayana said, shaking her head. "I basically committed suicide because from the time Brandy was born, I gave up my life, because I had to make sure she didn't experience one iota of what I went through as a child. Not to mention all the sleepless nights worrying about you. And do you know what her first word was? Daddy. It was daddy. And I swear to God from that day on, it was Daddy this, Daddy that. Mommy, where is my daddy?" Ayana balled her fists and tried to control her emotions. "But you know the sad part, Nasir? It wasn't her asking for her father that bothered me. It was that her father never asked about her."

"I didn't know about her," Nasir said softly.

"What?"

"Ayana, I didn't know I had a daughter. Our last conversation you said you were having an abortion. Then I got arrested and things got real stressful for me."

"What are you talking about? I sent you pictures, Nasir. I sent pictures to you by Granny. And I know she gave them to you."

Guilt washed over him. "Ayana, hear me out. That judge gave me life. Now you can call it what you want but I just couldn't deal. I never read your letters, never read anybody's letters."

Ayana was stunned.

"Are you serious? Why?" she snapped.

Nasir grabbed her hand but she snatched it away.

"No, talk to me. Tell me why you never read my letters. Tell me why you left me and your daughter sitting in that stink-ass visiting room."

Nasir felt a tear hit his cheek when he visualized his little girl and the woman he loved sitting in the prison's cold visiting room.

"I was dealing with a lot," was all Nasir could manage to say.

"And did you think you were the only one?"

"No," Nasir said. "But at the time, I thought it was the best thing for everyone." He had never felt lower.

Ayana threw up her hands in surrender. "You mean the best thing for you. But, what's done is done," Ayana said as if she no longer wanted to talk about it. She didn't agree with his logic but nothing good was going to come from her standing out there arguing. She walked toward the house.

"Wait," Nasir said, grabbing her arm. "I know my actions were wrong seeing how things turned out. But that judge gave me life. L-I-F-E," he barked. "Now I know things were hard for you but just try to imagine for one second never seeing your loved ones again as a free man. And for something I didn't even do. So yeah, I made a choice to cut everyone off. I thought it was the best thing to do. This wasn't about me. I did what I did for y'all. I didn't want y'all doing my time. I didn't want you to have a life of Saturday morning visits to the prison. I preferred that you guys looked at me as if I was dead."

"News flash to Nasir. Love isn't just about you being there physically. It's about you being here." Ayana touched her chest. "And how could you do that to your mother? She doesn't only love the part of you she can see. Do you think for one moment that you made her plight easier by shutting her out? You made it harder, Nasir. And I know, because it was me who sat up with her until daybreak listening to her heart break until it was completely broken," Ayana said, tears streaming down her face.

Nasir felt tears welling up in his own eyes.

"I took her to the hospital when she tried to kill herself by taking a whole bottle of pills when the pain of losing you was just too much.

"Brandy was her saving grace. You talk about that judge giving you life; well, he gave her life too. I was going to get an abortion but after seeing your mother like that, I couldn't do it. She had already lost too much, and you know what? I thank her every day."

Silence took over as they were both caught up in their own emotions.

"Ayana, I can't change what's done but I'm sorry. All I can do is promise you that I'll be the best father I can be."

Ayana took a deep breath.

"I believe that you will. And as much as I want to punish you for doing what you did, I prayed to God that He would send you back to her. So I'm not going to sit here and make you jump through all kinds of hoops, but you must know that you'll have to earn her trust. You'll have to earn a place in her heart. I haven't seen you in a long time and I don't know if you are the same person who left here but we can take it day by day."

Nasir nodded.

"Is your mother asleep too?" she asked.

"She's at the Ritz."

"The Ritz? Why is she at the Ritz?"

"We dropped her off a little while ago. I figured a change in scenery would do her some good."

Ayana nodded. "I see. So all of a sudden you are worried about what is good for her?"

"Ayana, I can't do this. I can't keep apologizing for my mistakes. Like I said, I didn't do that for me. I did that because I thought it was best for y'all. So to answer your question, yes I am worried about what is good for her."

Ayana nodded her head.

"A lot has changed. My first order of business is to get to know my daughter, then get my mom into some kind of rehab. She looks bad, which makes me ask . . ." Nasir said, not sure how to approach this subject. "I know you may feel that I don't have a right to ask this, but why did you leave Brandy over here with her? My mother's not in any condition to take care of herself, nevertheless my child."

Ayana chuckled.

"What?"

"Nasir, I'm not blind. I see what's going on with your mother but trust me, Brandy's fine."

"What do you mean 'trust you, Brandy's fine'? When I came here today Brandy was here by herself. Anything could've happened. She's only four."

"Okay, you're her father so I'll allow you to question me, but I've done a good job raising Brandy so far and would never do anything to endanger her. You can trust that Brandy is in good hands when she's here. I have several people watching her when she's here, which is only on Sundays. Like I said, she's good for your mother. They are good for each other. And your mother would never let anything happen to Brandy."

"Well, she wasn't so good for her today. I knocked on the door and Brandy just opened it up. Now, what if I was a pedophile or something? I mean she asked me a few questions but she's not big enough to stop me from pushing my way in the door."

Ayana frowned at the thought.

"I didn't know she left Brandy alone, but like I said, somebody was watching."

"I can't trust that. Not with my daughter."

"She's my daughter too, Nasir. I've raised her and I know what is best for her. Marcy probably ran next door to Mrs. Edna's. Was she gone long?"

"Too long for a child to be alone. I don't want her out here at all. Look." Nasir pointed at two scantily clad girls who were waving at cars. Neither of them could've been a day over fifteen. "Fuck that. I can't take those kinds of chances."

"I see we've started cursing," Ayana said.

"Yeah, well, you can pick up a few bad habits where I've been."

"No need to worry, Brandy is fine. You've been gone a long time. It's probably easier to harm one of George Bush's daughters than it is for someone to lay a finger on Brandy around here," Ayana said.

"How you figure?"

"You may have forgotten what you meant to these people. You

were their hero and all they did was transfer that same love to Brandy. She's safer here than any other place I could think of."

Nasir shook his head.

"Nah. You got it all wrong. People around here talk a good game but that's all it is, is talk. The love they have for me is just fluff. They only like the hype. It's not real love."

"Okay, Nasir. If you say so," Ayana said.

"What happened to your lip?"

Ayana looked up at Nasir and then away.

"Is it none of my business?"

"I hurt it working out."

"What were you working out with? A fist?"

"No," Ayana lied.

Nasir realized with the exception of Granny, none of his women were being taken care of. His mom was a wreck, his old girlfriend was obviously in some kind of abusive relationship, and Brandy wasn't always in the best conditions whether it was in the hood or wherever Ayana and her abusive boyfriend lived.

"Mr. Alonzo, huh?"

Ayana cringed at the mention of his name.

"That's over."

"Since when?"

"Since today."

Nasir nodded. Then he reached out and pulled her close. She resisted at first but then didn't pull away. He leaned down and placed his lips on hers and they shared a long passionate kiss. She wrapped her arms around his slim waist.

"I missed you," she said, coming up for air.

Nasir wanted more. He pressed his lips against hers again as their tongues got reacquainted with each other. He slid his hand down over her round butt and felt himself growing inside his pants.

"I missed you so much," she said, reaching up and grabbing the back of his head.

"I missed you too," Nasir said. "You have no idea."

Ayana pulled away when she noticed they weren't alone.

Mrs. Edna was standing behind her with her hands on her hips.

"Get it, girl. I ain't mad at cha," she said, walking up to her own house next door.

Nasir and Ayana laughed at the same time.

"That lady is crazy," Ayana said.

"She tried to rape me today."

"That's Edna," Ayana said before turning to face Nasir. "What was that all about?"

"What was what about?" he asked.

"The kiss."

"It was about us."

Ayana sighed before speaking.

"Nasir, I'm a mess right now. Can we take it one day at a time? Let's focus on Brandy, then we'll see about us."

Nasir nodded his head. "I can respect that. But you fooling yourself if you think we're not getting back together. Mr. Alonzo was temporary."

"What are your plans?" Ayana said, trying to change the subject.

"I really don't know. Gotta get a job. I have a child to take care of. So that's the first priority."

Ayana smiled.

"What?"

"Nothing."

"You're smiling about something."

"Just happy you're home."

"Yeah okay."

"Well, it's getting late and I need to get home. I have a long day tomorrow."

"Are you bringing Brandy by tomorrow?"

"I can do that. She gets out of school around three."

"Maybe I can meet you guys up there. I would like to meet her teachers, if you don't mind?"

"I don't mind."

"Since we're gonna do that, she might as well spend the night with me and I just meet you in the morning?" Nasir pushed.

"This may sound a little selfish being that today is your first day with her but I really need her tonight."

Reading her face, Nasir nodded his head. After all, he had the rest of his life to spend with his little girl.

"Are you sure everything's okay?"

"Yeah. But I better get going."

Ayana grabbed Nasir's hand and squeezed it before walking up the steps to the house.

"Don't look so sad. You'll get to spend plenty of time with her," she said, turning around before walking in.

JUST THE TWO OF US

*a*yana checked into a Marriott Hotel in the small town of Covington, Georgia.

"Mommy, why are we going to a hotel?"

"We're going to be staying here for a while."

"Why?"

"Because it's time for a change," Ayana told her daughter.

Short and to the point Ayana kept telling herself. Don't get into too many details with her—she's too young to be weighed down with grown folks' problems.

"But I don't have my clothes," Brandy whined.

"I have all of your clothes, sweetheart. What I didn't bring we'll replace."

"Are you mad with Mr. Alonzo?"

At this moment, Ayana couldn't be happier that she had stood her ground in not allowing Brandy to call Alonzo daddy.

"No, I'm not mad at him. It's just time for us to get our own place. It's time for Mommy to get a job and act like a grown-up."

"You are a grown-up."

"Well, it's time I started acting like one. Did you enjoy your time with your father today?"

"Yes," Brandy said, wild-eyed with excitement. "He's the best dad in the whole wide world. He bought me candy, he let me ride on his back, and he said we're going to Six Flags this weekend," Brandy said, bubbling over with joy. "Mommy?"

"Yes."

"People at Grandma Marcy's house say my daddy was in prison. They said he wasn't in the army like you told me."

Ayana's heart ached. She knew one day she would have to come clean with her daughter.

"Did you talk to your daddy about that?"

"No."

"Well, don't worry about where he's been. He's home now."

"Hey, Mommy, are we going to stay in this hotel forever?" Brandy said, over it and on to the next question already.

"No, we're going to get our own place. It won't be as big as Mr. Alonzo's house but it'll be ours. Just you and me. And we're going to make it look real pretty."

"Can my daddy come and live with us?" she asked.

"You know what I need?"

"What?"

"I need for you to give me a big kiss and a big hug, and then I want you to cuddle up in that bed and go to sleep. You have school tomorrow, little lady."

"Okay," Brandy said.

Ayana got her hug and kiss, then they got down on their knees and said their prayers. Ayana lay beside her daughter until she could hear her light snoring.

Her cell phone rang. She reached into her purse and grabbed it. She looked at the number on the caller ID. It was Alonzo. She hit the END button and sent the call to her voice mail. Two minutes later the phone rang again. This time she turned the ringer off and placed the phone on the nightstand. She didn't have time to deal with Alonzo. Her mind was filled with thoughts of Nasir. God, she was happy he was home. She never realized how much he meant to her until he was taken away. He was so much more than just the father of her child. He was the best friend she ever had, the brother she always wanted, and the only man she ever needed.

Ayana leaned over and kissed Brandy's sleeping face. She stood and walked into the bathroom to wash away a long and stressful day. She needed a hot bath but she didn't trust the cleanliness of hotel tubs so a shower would have to do. As she disrobed she couldn't help but fantasize about Nasir. She turned on the shower, grabbed the removable showerhead, and moved it down her body.

She could actually see his face. He was standing right behind her. He turned her around and she watched his long slender muscular body emerge from his clothes. She couldn't take her eyes off of him. He reached out to her, grabbing the sides of her face and pulling her lips to his. She felt his tongue enter her mouth and she took it. As they kissed he slid her blouse from her shoulders, dropping it to the floor. He slowly reached around her and unzipped her pants, allowing them to fall from her body.

Nasir held both of her hands in his as she stepped out of her pants. Then he knelt down and removed her thong with his teeth.

"Oh," she heard herself say as his tongue made its way to her softest spot. He nibbled on her cookie while she ran her fingers through his wavy hair.

Nasir stood up, his face wet with her lust. He removed her bra and massaged her breasts. She moaned as she grabbed his ass, pulling him closer. He turned her around so that her back was against his chest and slowly kissed her neck. As always, he took his time, his mouth traveling from her neck down to her shoulder. She closed her eyes, enjoying every moment of their foreplay. She felt herself becoming wetter and a moan escaped her lips.

Nasir slid his hand down between her legs and slowly slid his finger inside of her.

Then he shoved her forward, not too rough but rough enough to let her know he was in control. She leaned over the bathtub and reached behind her and guided Nasir's manhood inside of her. She gasped as his thickness stretched her to her limit. It didn't take long for them to find their stride. Ayana rocked back and forth as Nasir slid his length in and out of her. Harder. Faster. Then her knees buckled and as she felt herself about to climax he pulled out. Another moan escaped her lips as he sat on the edge of the tub and pulled her onto him. Ayana straddled Nasir and slid down on his throbbing manhood. She sucked on his neck as he wrapped his massive arms around her waist.

I'm coming, baby!

Come on.

I love you, Nasir.

I love you too.

"Oh, ahh, ohhhh damn, Nasir," she heard herself say as she reached her final destination.

"Whew," Ayana said, leaning against the shower walls. She looked around for Nasir but he wasn't there.

She turned off the shower, wrapped a towel around herself, and sat on the edge of the tub trying to regain her composure.

Her fantasy felt so real that she found herself still looking around for Nasir. She took another deep breath and smiled.

"Boy, I sure did miss you."

ON THE MOVE

It was 4:30 A.M. when Nasir's cell phone rang. He reached over and looked at the caller ID screen. *Ritz-Carlton.*

"Hello," he said, sleep still in his voice.

"Mr. Lassiter, my name is Kamala and I'm really sorry to call you at this hour but there's been a problem."

Nasir popped up and sat on the edge of the bed.

"What kind of problem?"

"Night security was making his rounds and he noticed your mother's room door open. He called her but didn't get an answer so he entered the room. She wasn't there but he noticed the CD clock and a lamp was missing."

"Are you serious?"

"Sorry, sir, but . . ."

"No problem. I'll replace the lamp and clock if we can't find it."

"Thank you. Like I said, I'm sorry to call you but my manager, I guess he's a friend of yours, and he told me to call you rather than go through our usual procedures."

"Don't sweat it. Thanks for your call. I'm on my way down there."

"Okay. Take care."

Nasir flipped the phone closed and ran his hands through his hair. He massaged his temples as he wondered where his mother could've gone. First he reasoned that maybe she went out for some fresh air but there were two balconies in her suite. He wanted to believe she had decided to take an early morning stroll but he knew that was wishful thinking.

Nasir stood and put on a pair of sweatpants and a long-sleeved T-shirt. He slipped his feet into his white Air Force Ones and walked into the bathroom to wash his face and brush his teeth.

When he walked out into the kitchen he noticed his grand-mother sitting at the table, hands folded and meditating. He tapped on the door frame so he didn't startle her.

"Hey there, lady," he said.

Granny opened her eyes and smiled.

"Up kind of late, huh?" Nasir asked.

"Quite the contrary," Granny said as she took a sip of her steaming coffee. "Up early. This is my favorite part of the day.

Quiet and peaceful. I figure this is the best time to talk to God. Catch Him before everyone else gets up and starts bombarding Him with their gripes and issues." Granny smiled as she sipped her coffee.

"So you get up early so your requests are first on His list, huh?" Nasir smiled.

"No requests. I only thank Him for what He's already done. I know He'll take care of my needs. Always has and I believe He always will."

"How do you stay so faithful? You only had two children and both of them died young. Why are you still singing God's praises?"

"Because I don't question Him. I know where my children are. Besides, they're just ours on loan anyway. They all belong to Him."

"So, do you believe that it was your prayers to God that got me out of prison?"

Granny shook her head. "I never prayed for that. I told you, I don't ask for anything. I only thank Him. He knows what's best."

"I hear ya," Nasir said, walking over to the stove. "Mind if I have a cup of this coffee?"

"Not at all, let me get you a cup."

"I'll get it," he said, waving her down.

"What has you up before the crack of dawn?" she asked.

Nasir poured his coffee and took a seat across from his grandmother.

"I got my mother a hotel room earlier and they just called to tell me she left the room with the clock and a lamp."

Granny moaned.

"I feel so bad for that child. You know if you hit something long enough, it's bound to break, and God knows she's been hit with enough to make a sane person crazy."

"Yeah, I need to go out there and try to find her. I hope she hasn't gotten herself into any trouble."

"Yeah, I think you should. I know seeing you has been good for her but progress doesn't happen overnight."

"I just hope she's not too far gone."

"No one is ever too far gone. As long as you believe in her, you can help her. Sometimes people need others to believe in them because they forgot how to believe in themselves. That might be the case with Marcy. I love her like she was my own daughter, but once those drugs get ahold of you it's an uphill battle. But she's strong, just hit a weak moment."

Nasir stood and kissed his granny on her forehead.

"I hope so," he said before heading back into his room to get his jacket and car keys.

Nasir hopped on I-20 East, then merged onto I-85 North and headed toward Buckhead.

When he pulled up to the Ritz a doorman who wore a dark green overcoat and top hat rushed over and opened his door.

"Welcome to the Buckhead Ritz-Carlton. Will you be needing help with any bags this evening, sir?"

"Nah," Nasir said, getting out of the car.

"All right. Enjoy your stay here with us. My name is Henry and I'll be here until eight in the morning, so if you need anything don't hesitate to give me a ring."

"I'll do—"

"You know people complain about the graveyard shift but it works for me. I get to sneak a little nap in every now and then plus I still have my whole day to myself," the old gray-haired man rattled off with a wide, give-me-a-tip smile.

"I hear ya, Henry," Nasir said, walking past the man who was obviously hungry for conversation, but then stopped and turned around.

"Hey, Henry, how long have you been out here?"

"Graveyard. Twelve to eight."

"Did you see a woman walk out of here about an hour ago?"

"There must've been some kind of party tonight because I've been seeing beautiful women come and go for the last two, maybe three hours."

"No, this woman wouldn't have been dressed like she was leaving a party," Nasir said, giving the man the eye, hoping he wouldn't have to spell it out for him.

"Oh, yeah, short light-skinned woman 'bout this high." Henry held his hand to about mid-chest. "Looking a little homely?"

"Yeah," Nasir said.

"Oh yeah." Henry's smile turned into a snarl. "She tried to sell me a lamp and a clock."

"What?"

"Yeah. The hotel's clock and lamp at that. I'll tell you these druggies will steal the laces out of your shoes while you're walking," Henry said, shaking his head.

Nasir hated hearing his mother being referred to as such but the truth was the truth.

"Where did she go?"

"I don't know but I told her if she didn't take that stuff back to where she got it I was calling the police. That's when she ran off."

"Which way?"

"Down Peachtree toward Piedmont."

"Thanks, Henry," Nasir said, walking back over and getting in his car.

His tires skidded as he blasted out of the hotel's driveway. He drove down Peachtree Road doing about three miles per hour, scanning the faces of the strangers who staggered out of the many clubs that lined the Buckhead club scene.

"Where are you, woman?" he asked himself.

After about an hour of driving and looking, Nasir decided it was in vain. Because he had no idea where drug addicts hung out he decided to call off the one-man search party and go back to the hotel.

He pulled back into the driveway and Henry hustled over to get the door again.

"Hey, Henry," Nasir said, stepping out.

"Let me get you a ticket," Henry said, running as fast as his sixtyish-year-old legs would take him. "Did you find her?"

"Nah," Nasir said.

"Is she a friend of yours?"

"She's my mother."

"Oh," Henry said, trying to remember if he said anything offensive earlier. "Yeah, well she was nice. Just seemed to be a little distracted is all," he said, handing Nasir the ticket and taking his key.

"If you see her coming back this way, don't tell her I'm here," Nasir said, handing him a ten-dollar bill.

"Okay. I'll put your car in the side lot."

"That's fine."

Nasir walked over to the front desk, got a key card, and took the elevator to the top floor.

Inside the suite, Nasir couldn't sit still. He wished he could just go out onto the balcony and yell out for his mother like she used to do to him when he was a young boy. He walked over to the small refrigerator bar and opened it up. All of the mini bottles of alcohol were gone. He snatched open a bottle of water and drained it. Just as he was walking over to the trash can he heard the door click.

'THE MONKEY

*M*arcy's walk was brisk as she headed down Peachtree Road. She had no idea where she was headed but her cravings would no longer allow her to sit in that hotel room. With no money in her purse, she grabbed the first things she saw that looked to have any semblance of value: the nice brass lamp sitting on the nightstand and the CD clock. She could sell either of them for at least twenty or thirty dollars. After barely escaping that minstrel show of a doorman, she headed for the sights and sounds of the club district.

A carful of teenage girls blew their horn at her and she threw her hand up in the air hoping they would stop but all they did was call her a few names and kept driving.

Another horn sounded and once again her hand shot up. This time the car's brake lights illuminated and Marcy ran up to it before it came to a complete stop.

"Are you a cop?" she asked, rubbing her arm and immediately letting the driver know what she was after.

"No," a pimple-faced kid with red hair said. "Are you?"

"Hey, I got this nice lamp and clock here that I'm trying to get rid of. I'll give them both to you for a good price."

"How much?" Redhead said.

"Give me thirty dollars."

"All I have is a fifty," Redhead said, smiling.

"I'll take that."

Marcy could already feel the high. "You're really getting a deal. This lamp is worth at least two hundred dollars and the clock is at least sixty."

"Oh yeah," Redhead said, rubbing his crotch.

Marcy wasn't slow. She knew what signal Redhead was trying to send and she also knew he wasn't interested in her ill-begotten goods.

The morals she had once had tried to rise to the surface and she was tempted to take that lamp and crack Redhead across his forehead for being disrespectful, but the heroin monkey said, *Get that fifty.*

The battle between the morals and the monkey didn't last long. Marcy looked around for any police activity before snatching at the car's door handle.

Once inside the car, Marcy noticed Redhead had already un-zipped his pants. She looked down at his little pale penis and cringed. After all the years of using heroin she had never had to stoop this low. But that monkey was winning her over.

"Listen, I'm a cut-and-dry kind of guy so I'll let you know right now that I don't want your lamp or your fucking clock. I wanna fuck."

Somewhere in the depths of her spirit, Marcy realized that she still had an ounce of pride left. She couldn't do it.

"Hey, I don't think this is a good idea. Why don't you let me out right up here?" Marcy said.

Redhead ignored her and pulled off of the busy Peachtree to a quiet side street.

"Hey." Marcy waved to get his attention. "Will you let me out?"

"I think I'll take that lamp after all. My mother would love it," Redhead said, smiling.

"Take the lamp and just let me out."

"I can't do that. I have to pay you for it. I'm not a thief."

"It's a gift. Just take it," Marcy said, her voice cracking.

Redhead kept driving.

Sensing danger, Marcy eased her hand over to the door, but just before she could pull it, she heard the automatic door locks engage.

"Listen, you seem like a nice young man. All I was trying to do was get some money so I could buy my son . . ."

"Save the shit, lady. Who are you fooling? You're a junkie. But I'm not here to judge you—I only want to fuck," Redhead said, turning down a cul-de-sac and into the driveway of a colonial-style home.

"Now, what were you saying?" he said, cutting off the ignition.

Marcy's eyes widened with fear.

"Listen, I don't have a lot of time. So why don't you slide those pants off and we can be done with this," Redhead said.

What have I allowed myself to become? she thought.

A tear welled up in the corner of her eye.

"Come on!" Redhead said, banging on the steering wheel. "What's the big deal? Don't act like you've never done this before. You're a dope fiend, for Christ sake. Don't you guys suck dick all day long?"

Marcy covered her face with her hands.

"Okay fine." Redhead popped the locks. "Get out."

The words were music to her ears but something kept her glued to her seat. She needed money, and that heroin monkey did a little dance on her shoulders.

"Maybe we can . . ."

"Save it. Get the fuck out of my car."

"Okay," Marcy said, feeling the money to feed her habit slipping away. "I'll do it. It's just I . . ."

"Listen, lady. Don't play games with me. Either you will or you won't. Which one is it?"

You better suck it and suck it good, the monkey said.

Marcy nodded her head.

Redhead grabbed her by the back of her head and roughly tried to shove her head down to his crotch.

"I need my money first," Marcy said, resisting his harshness.

"Do I look like a fool? I'll put your money here on the dashboard but don't you touch it until we're done." Redhead slammed the fifty-dollar bill on the dash and grabbed her head again.

"Can you at least put on a condom?"

"You are un-fucking-believable. A clean dopehead," Redhead said, pushing her away and pulling a condom out of his armrest. He tore the wrapper and removed the latex. "You put it on," he said, handing it to Marcy.

Marcy shook her head. She wasn't touching that thing. Redhead huffed and growled before sliding the latex down on his small pecker.

"You happy now?" he said. He grabbed Marcy's head again and guided her down. She didn't resist this time but stopped right before the penis touched her lips. She could smell the lubrication.

"Can we . . ." she started.

"If you say one more thing, you are going to get your ass out of my car."

Marcy hushed. She closed her eyes and decided she had to do it. She reached for the boy's penis but she couldn't do it. She couldn't bring herself to touch it. She sat up.

"Get out. That's it. I'm sick of you."

The locks popped and a different kind of fear registered. The fear of not being able to feed that monkey to satisfy her cravings.

Why did I let Nasir take me to that hotel? she thought. *It would be so easy for me to get my stuff at home.*

"Okay," Marcy said, crying now. She reached for the door handle. "Do you still want to buy the lamp? We can go get some change." Redhead snarled and jabbed a finger at the door.

Marcy got out of the car and started walking back toward Peachtree Road. As soon as she turned onto the main street, she noticed a well-dressed man who looked familiar walking away from a Bank of America automatic teller machine. As she approached him she felt something deep inside of her but couldn't put a finger on it, so she quickly tossed the thought from her mind. All she could or wanted to think about was getting some heroin in her veins.

The man stopped and looked at her as if he had never seen a human being in such disarray.

Marcy stopped walking under the man's glare and felt ashamed. She couldn't understand why because she had long grown used to people staring at her since she started using, yet there was something disturbing about this man. She dropped her head and turned the other way, but something told her the man was still staring at her. She looked over her shoulder and sure enough his eyes were glued to her.

She picked up her pace, still stealing glances at the man who was now slowly walking toward his car.

What the hell is his problem? she wondered.

"Hey!" the man called.

"Oh, shit!" Marcy said, dropping the lamp and the clock and running as fast as her skinny legs would take her.

"Hey, excuse me," the man barked, this time with enough authority to stop her in her tracks, but that only lasted a minute. Fear had a death grip on her and she started running again.

"Stop that woman!" the man said to a police officer standing by a club door.

The police officer reached out and grabbed Marcy, slamming her against the wall.

"Hey," the man shouted to the cop. "Was that necessary?"

"What's the problem, sir?" the officer asked, holding Marcy against the wall by her neck.

The man walked over and looked at Marcy. His stare cut right through her. She looked up into his eyes, and once she realized who he was, she took a deep breath then fainted.

A NEW DAY

*A*yana tossed and turned for most of the night. Two days ago, her biggest concern was what to wear to the park; now she had real-life issues. And although she always knew the day would come for her to stand on her own two feet, she was far from prepared for it.

She looked over at Brandy, who was sleeping peacefully beside her. Tears sprang to her eyes as she imagined her daughter going through the loveless childhood she herself had endured. The beatings she took for no other reason than being an inconvenience to the people who swore to the social workers that they would love and protect her as if she was their own. And the shame she felt on the day they returned her as if she were an unruly puppy who wouldn't stop peeing on the carpet. The embarrassment she felt when a man three times her age entered her bed on the night she turned thirteen, whispering to her, "You're a woman now, it's time to do what women do."

Ayana shook the thoughts of her childhood from her mind and kissed Brandy's forehead. None of those things would ever happen to her daughter, she would make sure of it.

She pulled herself up out of the bed and headed to the bathroom to prepare herself for what she knew would be a long day.

"Good morning, Mommy," Brandy said as she staggered into the bathroom.

"Good morning to you, little lady."

"Are we going home today?"

Ayana couldn't bring herself to tell her child that there was no home. "We'll be staying here for a few days. I told you last night that we'll be getting our own place soon."

"I don't want to stay in this hotel, Mommy. It stinks. Can I stay with my daddy?"

Ayana sighed and thought about her daughter's request and figured she could use the time to get herself together. Besides, Nasir's admonishment of her showed that he was a natural at being a father.

"I'll see."

"Yaaaay." Brandy pumped her little fist as if victory was hers.

"You are too much. Get dressed. We're already late."

Brandy chattered away while they drove to her school. Ayana found it amazing that her child could take so much away from spending one day with her father and talk nonstop about him.

"Now remember, don't catch the bus today. I'll be here when school gets out," Ayana said, kissing her daughter before Brandy jumped from the car and caught up to her friends. Brandy turned around right before she walked through the school doors and blew a kiss at her. Ayana blew one right back.

After watching her daughter disappear through the school's doors, Ayana hit the ground running. For the first time in four years, she had a sense of urgency. Alonzo gave her six thousand dollars to add to the grand she had in her checking account, which she estimated to be a little over three months of living expenses.

Her first stop was the library to scan the job listings in the newspapers. The last job she held was in the college admissions office and that was almost five years ago. The first question any employer was going to ask was why such a long gap in employment.

It was time to get creative. She would either have to make up a job and take her chances with the references or be honest and almost certainly be overlooked for a more experienced candidate. She flipped open her phone and called Mary, Alonzo's secretary.

"World Travel, how may I help you?"

"Mary, hey. This is Ayana."

Mary hesitated before speaking. "H-hey."

"How are you?"

"I'm fine, and you?"

"I've been better. Listen, I need a huge favor."

"Sorry, Ayana. Alonzo already told me if you called here to hang up on you."

"Listen, I'm not trying to get you in any trouble but I really need this favor."

"What is it, Ayana?"

Ayana never liked Mary and she was pretty sure the feeling was mutual. Mary looked at Ayana as a spoiled child who was living off of a rich man, and Ayana thought she was a miserable old hoot who needed to mind her own business. But that was neither here nor there. Ayana was in a desperate situation so her feelings would have to take a backseat.

"I'm looking for a job, and I was wondering if you'd mind giving me a reference. That's if they call."

"A reference?" Mary yelled before catching herself and lowering her voice to just above a whisper. "Girl, you let me tell you something. A reference is the least of your worries. Alonzo's been in here all morning ranting and raving about how you did him wrong and how you used him. I've never seen him like this. I'd watch my back if I were you."

"Yeah, well, thanks for the warning but can you do me that favor?" Ayana said, dismissing Mary. Alonzo might scare some people but Ayana was far from worried. She knew the man behind the mask and he was nothing but a bag of hot air.

Mary took a deep breath. "If someone calls, I'll lie and tell them you worked here. And lying is a sin. I'm a woman of God and I don't do that kind of stuff but I'll make an exception this time."

"Thank you, Mary."

"Don't thank me. 'Cuz I don't care two cents for you. I don't know why you didn't have a job anyway. If you didn't have that little girl to look after, I'd hang this phone up so quick I'd get a gold medal, but like I said, I'm a woman of God. Now if you don't need anything else, I'd actually like to get back to doing some real work," Mary said, hanging up without even saying goodbye.

HE DID WHAT?

"Room service," the maid said as she stuck her key in the door. She jumped back and placed a hand over her chest when she noticed Nasir barreling toward her. "Do you need your room cleaned, sir?"

"No," Nasir snapped, realizing that it wasn't his mother. "I'm fine."

"Okay, you have a good day," the maid said quickly before backing out of the door.

Nasir flipped open his cell phone and was surprised to see that it was already nine o'clock.

His cell phone rang and he couldn't open it quick enough.

"Hello."

"Nasir, this is Ayana."

"Hey, Ayana," Nasir said, disappointed.

"Are you okay?"

"Yeah. What's up?"

"I was calling to see what your schedule was like today."

Nasir looked around the empty room. He was hoping his mother would've been back by now. "I'm pretty free," he said.

"Well, I need a favor. I'm trying to get a job and this agency asked me to come in today at two-thirty. Problem is I have to pick Brandy up at two-thirty. So I was wondering . . ."

"It's not a problem. Nor is it a favor. Ayana, that's my child. The past is the past and I can't do anything about that, but going forward I'm going to handle my responsibilities. You can trust me to do that."

"You're right. It's just that I'm used to . . . well, you know."

"Yeah, but I'm home now."

"She wants to stay with you for a few days."

"Sounds great. She can stay forever." Nasir smiled. He needed some good news and his little girl was already brightening up what was sure to be a dreary day.

"Do you still eat soul food?" Ayana asked.

"Yes. Nothing has changed. I didn't become a Muslim, a crip, a blood, or nobody's sex toy. I'm still the same old me."

"Okay, Nasir, calm down," Ayana said. "I didn't mean anything. I was just asking you a question. I wanted to take you to dinner tonight so I could bring you up to speed with Brandy."

Nasir took a deep breath and blew out the tension that was building inside of him.

"Sorry for snapping like that. I've been walking around this hotel since five this morning."

"What's wrong?"

"My mom pulled a disappearing act."

"Oh no."

"Yeah."

"Has she called?"

"Nope. And I don't have the slightest idea where to look."

"Did you call Sammy?"

"No. Why would I call him?"

Ayana was silent.

"Ayana, why would I call Sammy?" Nasir's voice was stern and hard.

"I'm just saying. He might know where she is."

"And why would he know where she would be. And why was his name the first name to leave your lips?"

Silence again.

"Ayana," Nasir barked.

Still nothing from her.

"Ayana, that's my mother. What I did when I went to prison was wrong and it hurt her, but now I'm trying to fix that. So if you know something please tell me."

"He's her supplier," she blurted out.

Nasir's body tensed up and his hand involuntarily started trembling. He started rocking back and forth.

"He's what?"

"He's the one who gives her that stuff she uses."

"I gotta go. I'll pick up Brandy."

"Nasir, wait . . ."

Nasir hung up the phone without saying goodbye.

He grabbed his jacket and ran from the room.

It took forever for the valet to bring Nasir's car around. Just as he thought he couldn't wait another second, he saw the powerful European sports car turn the corner.

"Dude, this Vanquish is a beast," Blondie said, hopping out and holding the door for Nasir. "V-12 kicks ass."

Nasir handed him a five-dollar bill and jumped in the driver seat without so much as a "sure does, dude."

Five minutes later he was ripping down I-85 South at close to a hundred miles per hour.

Nasir couldn't believe what Ayana had just told him.

Not Sammy.

Why?

She always treated him like her own son yet he turns around and feeds her poison.

Maybe Ayana had made a mistake, he thought.

Nasir made it to The "U" in less than fifteen minutes and was literally out of the car before it stopped rolling. He jumped back in, put the car in park, and took the key out.

"Hey, Nasir, let me holla at you for a minute," someone called out.

Nasir ignored the person and headed straight for Sammy's apartment door.

He didn't even knock, just burst through the door like he had a search warrant.

Sammy was sitting at a cheap card table with two white men. One of the men was holding a ferret.

Nasir didn't waste any time bum-rushing his cousin. He snatched Sammy up by his collar and slammed him against the wall.

"Oh my God," one of the men said in a high feminine voice.

"Time to go," the other man said in an equally delicate tone. They both rushed toward the door.

Nasir reared back, then punched Sammy in the face as hard as he could.

Sammy was dazed but he still had his wits about him. Just as Nasir was rearing back for a second lick, Sammy pulled a gun from the small of his back and fired a shot toward the corner. He placed the barrel on Nasir's neck.

"Shit," Nasir yelled as the hot gun scorched his skin.

"I won't miss from this close, cuz," Sammy said in a surprisingly calm voice.

Nasir grimaced, holding his neck.

"Why, Sammy?"

"Why what?"

"Why are you giving my mom that shit?"

Sammy was quiet and he lowered the gun to his side.

"I'm waiting," Nasir said, his chest rising and falling at a rapid pace.

"Knock, I had no choice, man."

"Bullshit," Nasir screamed. "You always have a choice."

"Hey," Sammy yelled. "Don't be running yo ass up here pointing fingers at me, nigga."

"What she ever do to you?"

"You know what, Knock? I did it. And I'd do it again. Because Auntie was out there, cuz. I damn near pulled a dick out of her mouth myself. She was on her knees about to blow some clown for a hit. I wasn't letting her go out like that. So yeah, I said fuck it. If she's willing to go out like that, I'll just get it for her. But it was only because I knew come hell or high water, she was gonna get what she wanted. By any means necessary."

Nasir visualized his mother on her knees in some dark alley performing oral sex on some perverted drug dealer and felt himself getting sick. He ran to the kitchen and barely made it to the trash can before the vomit came pouring out.

Sammy walked into the kitchen holding a towel. He tossed it to Nasir and jumped up to sit on the counter. Nasir wiped his mouth clean.

"You aight?"

Nasir shook his head.

"I didn't have a choice, cuz. I could look the other way or do what I did. I'm not the look-the-other-way type, not when it comes to family."

Nasir walked past his cousin and sat on the same raggedy sofa he had played on as a child.

He couldn't shake the image of his mother as a drug addict.

"Where is she?"

"I thought you took her to the hotel."

"She left. She didn't come back here?"

"Nah. I haven't seen her."

Nasir stood up and walked toward the door. He paused and looked back at Sammy.

"I'm sorry, cuz," Sammy said.

Nasir nodded and walked out of the apartment. The trek across the street to his mother's was dreadful. He felt like a wounded animal. He knocked on the door but nobody answered. He turned the knob and it was locked. He didn't have a key so he walked around to her bedroom window and peeked inside.

Empty.

Nasir checked the rest of the windows and they were all locked and the house showed no signs of life inside.

"Knock," Sammy said, walking up to the front yard. "Let's roll. I think I might know where we can find her."

Nasir and Sammy rode around for hours with very little conversation. They made stops at all of the known drug spots but everyone said they hadn't seen or heard from Marcy.

"She'll show up, cuz," Sammy said.

Nasir groaned. "This is ridiculous," he said, checking the clock on the dash. "Man, I gotta go and pick Brandy up from school."

"Aight. You can drop me off right here," Sammy said as they pulled back in front of The "U."

"Ay, Sam. Sorry about earlier, man, I . . ."

"Don't even sweat it, cuz," Sammy said, opening the door. Once out of the car, he turned around and knelt down by the window.

"She'll be aight."

Nasir nodded and reached over the passenger seat and bumped fists with his cousin.

"We're family and families fight sometimes. But I sure hate that you made them little sweet boys leave. They were buying ten ferrets. But I think they were into some deviant sexual behavior," Sammy said. "So I guess it's a good thing they left. I don't want my babies being molested by freaks."

"I'm sorry about that, cuz."

"No biggie. Give Brandy a kiss for me and tell her I said she better bring my damn yo-yo back to my house."

Nasir grunted out a courtesy chuckle. "I'll tell her."

"I'm just playing. She can have it."

"Let me run before I'm late. I gotta ride all the way out to Lithonia."

"You go ahead. And I'll call you if I see Auntie. Like I said, she'll show up."

"Aight, cuz."

WHERE AM I?

*M*arcy regained consciousness and found herself swimming in a pool of her own sweat. She stared up at the whitest ceiling she'd ever seen. It was a far cry from the water-rusted one she woke up to for the last twenty-some odd years. There was something strangely familiar about her surroundings.

The heroin monkey was back and bouncing up and down on her chest begging for food. She instinctively rubbed her arm to ease the cravings. Her eyes made their way over to a corkboard on the wall. The board had a million and one posted notes stuck to it with little colorful pins.

Where was she?

Marcy sat up and tried to control her anxiety. Was

she where she thought she was or was this just another one of her crazy dreams? She turned to the nightstand and noticed a picture. She stood between her smiling parents on the day she graduated from high school. Marcy smiled. *We were so happy back then,* Marcy thought as she lay back down.

There was a light tap on the door and Marcy jerked her head in the direction of the noise. The door opened and in walked a heavyset woman who looked to be in her late fifties. She was wearing white scrubs.

"Good evening, Marcia. I'm Mrs. Barren and I'm going to be taking care of you for a while."

Marcy hesitated before speaking.

"Did you sleep well?" Mrs. Barren said.

"What do you mean 'taking care of me'?"

"Your father asked me to look after you."

My father!

Marcy tried to get up, but Mrs. Barren placed a firm hand on her shoulder and gently guided her back down.

"Wait a minute. What's going on? What are you doing?"

Marcy looked around wild-eyed.

This was not a dream. This was real.

Damn!

"Relax, honey," Mrs. Barren coaxed. "No one's here to hurt you."

"I need to go," Marcy said, trying to sit up again. "I need my medicine."

"No, honey. The only thing you need right now is rest. Now be still," Mrs. Barren said, holding a little white paper cup with two tiny pills in it and a bottle of water. "Take these; they'll help you."

"I don't want any help. Leave me alone!" Marcy screamed and fought with what little strength she had left.

Mrs. Barren struggled to hold her down and Marcy kicked and pulled. Marcy worked her way onto the floor, and just as Mrs. Barren reached down to try to restrain her, she paused.

Some things never changed. There they were. The two-tone wingtips she used to find so amusing as a child. Her eyes went from the expensive shoes to the nicely tailored slacks, on up past the pudgy middle section to the bronze-complexion skin. Time hadn't changed him much. He had lost a little hair in the front, shaved his beard, and got rid of the thick bifocals and replaced them with a more up-to-date set of eyewear. Other than that he was still the same.

Marcy couldn't take her eyes off of the man who was once her everything. The man who loved her from the time she entered this world to the time he kicked her out of his.

She opened her mouth but nothing came out.

"I can take it from here," Mr. Gold said, walking over to the bed.

Marcy couldn't think straight. The heroin monkey was working overtime as he whispered in her ear. *Feed me. Feed me. Feed me. Feed me.*

Mr. Gold sat in the chair beside Marcy's bed and stared down at his daughter.

"Will you be needing anything else today, Mr. Gold?"

"No, we'll be fine. I'll see you in the morning."

"Are you okay?" Mr. Gold asked his daughter.

Speak up! Tell him I'm hungry, the monkey said, jumping up and down on Marcy's shoulder.

"Daddy, I'm sick," Marcy said, rubbing her arm. "I just need one hit. I mean . . . I need a dose of my medicine and I promise I'll do whatever you want me to do. I don't want to live like this anymore."

Mr. Gold picked up the graduation picture and looked at his daughter. He seemed to be comparing the potential to the reality. He closed his eyes and shook his head.

Reading his mind, Marcy jumped to her feet.

"Don't you dare judge me!" she screamed.

"I'm not here to judge you. I've done enough of that and it's only caused me grief."

Don't you piss him off. We need to eat. I'm hungry, the monkey said.

"Daddy, I'm sick. I'll move back in here and finish school. I can be a doctor just like you wanted me to." Marcy smiled unconvincingly. "But right now I need for you to take me somewhere."

"Where would you like to go?"

Tell him. Tell him now. Feed me, the dancing monkey said.

Marcy went back to her scratching. She took a deep breath and tried her best to act normal.

"If you'll take me back to my house, I'll get my things and come back here with you. There's so much we need to talk about," Marcy rambled. "I . . . I have a son and he has a daughter. Her name is . . . Do you believe it? You're a great-granddaddy," Marcy chuckled as she searched around the room for her shoes.

Mr. Gold tried his best not to break down. He had to be strong for his daughter. He knew his daughter's condition was his doing and it was killing him.

"I think you'll like my son. He's a really good man. I haven't seen him in five years because . . ."

"Because he was in prison," Mr. Gold said.

Marcy stopped her futile search for her footwear and stared at her father.

"Don't you dare take that tone with my son. He's a good boy and he was in prison for something he had absolutely nothing to do with."

"I know. I know all about Nasir and his daughter Brandy. I would love to meet them both."

"How . . . How do you know . . . ?"

Bitch, we don't have time for no family reunion. I'm hungry. Feed me! the monkey screamed at the top of his lungs.

"Will you shut the hell up!" Marcy screamed over her shoulder, startling her father.

"Excuse me? Marcia, who are you talking to?"

"I'm talking to this damn monkey."

"What monkey?" Mr. Gold looked around as if he might have missed something.

"Never mind," Marcy said and went back to her shoe search.

"Honey, will you sit down?"

You better not, the monkey said, making a fist. *I will punch you in the back of your throat if you think about sitting your ass in that chair.*

"Shut up." Marcy covered her ears.

Mr. Gold forced himself to watch his daughter fall apart right in front of his eyes.

"Daddy, I can't sit down right now," Marcy said, scratching her arm and neck.

She tried to flick that monkey off of her shoulder but he jumped over her hand. And then he did a little dance to mock her.

"We have to go and get my medicine."

Mr. Gold took a deep breath before standing.

"Your shoes are in the closet," he said.

Marcy almost ran to the closet. When she opened the door she realized it was just the way she left it over twenty years ago. Nothing had been disturbed. Over fifty pairs of shoes were scattered all over the floor. Her school's letterman jacket from her volleyball and track days was still hanging on the hook by the light switch. She couldn't find the shoes she had on the night before so she snatched the first matching pair she could touch and quickly left the closet.

"Where is Mom?" Marcy asked after walking back over to her father.

Mr. Gold wiped a tear from his eye as he sat back down in the chair. Seeing his daughter like this had a devastating effect on him.

"She's in her office. Why don't you go say hi," Mr. Gold said, tears in his eyes.

Marcy missed her mother but all she could think about was getting some heroin into her veins. She willed herself not to respond to the drug addiction and walked downstairs into the large study. She saw her mother sitting behind the same oak desk that she used to play lawyer with as a child.

Marcy stopped and stared at her mother. Her hair had turned almost completely gray but she was still as beautiful as ever.

"Hi, Mom," Marcy said as she walked over to her mother.

Mrs. Gold sprang to her feet and held out her arms for her daughter. They embraced and cried without words.

"Marcia," Mrs. Gold said. "It's so good to see you."

"It's good to see you too, Mom."

"Please, have a seat."

"I can't, I have to go."

"Nonsense. You just got here."

"I'll be back, it's just I have to get my medicine." Marcy's words were cut short when her eyes glanced down at the desk and noticed a thick manila folder with Nasir's picture paper-clipped to the outside.

"What are you doing with that?"

Mrs. Gold looked down at the folder, then back up at her daughter.

"Why do you have a folder on my son?"

Mrs. Gold dropped her head and sighed.

GRANNY CHECKED the address to make sure she was at the right house before she stepped out of the cab.

"Ma'am, would you like for me to wait?"

"I'll be fine."

These folks out here sure do spend a lot of money on looking the part, don't they? Granny frowned as she handed the driver two twenty-dollar bills. She waited for her change even though it was only one dollar and eighty-five cents.

Granny walked down the walkway to a gated entrance. She looked at the little silver box with the telephone numbers on it and pushed the one that said CALL.

"How may I help you?" a voice said.

She felt weird talking to a box but leaned down and spoke into the speaker.

"I'm here to see Mrs. Anna Gold."

"May I ask who's calling?"

"I ain't calling. I'm out front at the gate. Tell her this is Rose Lassiter."

"Just a second, Mrs. Lassiter." There was a loud click. A few minutes later the same voice came back.

"Mrs. Lassiter, are you sure you have the right address?"

"Yes, I'm sure. You tell her her daughter Marcy was married to my son and you can also tell her that I don't plan on sitting out here all day explaining what she should already know."

"Just a second."

A few minutes later the gate swung open and a young boy who looked to be no more than sixteen years old came out driving a golf cart. He whipped the cart around the driveway and came to an abrupt stop before jumping out.

"Hello, ma'am. Mrs. Gold sent me to pick you up."

"How did Mrs. Gold know I wasn't driving?"

"Cameras, ma'am. They're all over the place."

"I see." Granny looked at the cart, then at the house that sat way back on a hill. Her tired and tested legs would be a hundred before she made it to the front door.

"I'll get on this thing but you better drive like you got some sense. You hear me?"

"Yes, ma'am." The boy smiled as he helped Granny onto the cart. After a nice easy ride through a tree-lined driveway he jumped out again and helped her out. "You can go through that door right there. Mrs. Gold is waiting on you."

Granny walked through the tallest wrought-iron doors she had ever seen. They were pretty, she thought, but not very welcoming.

"Good evening, Mrs. Lassiter." Mrs. Gold said, holding out her hand as she walked toward Granny. "It's nice to meet you."

Granny shook it and nodded her head.

"This is not a social visit. Our grandson needs your help."

"Excuse me?"

"Okay, fine. My grandson needs your help. He's been sent away to prison on false charges and we need to get him out of there."

Mrs. Gold smiled. "Can I get you something to drink, maybe some tea?"

"No thanks. I'm fine."

"Mrs. Lassiter. My daughter came to me when this first happened and it seems the case against him is pretty overwhelming."

"Ma'am, I don't know much about you or your kind."

"And what kind is that?"

"The kind that throws people away just because."

Mrs. Gold pulled her lips in at the jab.

"I'm going to have our driver take you home."

"Thank you. And I'll take you up on that offer after we take care of the business I came here about."

"There's nothing I can do for you."

"Do you mean there's nothing you won't do? You're a lawyer, aren't ya?"

"Good day, Mrs. Lassiter," Mrs. Gold said as she was about to leave the room.

"How can you live with yourself?" Granny said. "Like it or not that boy is your own flesh and blood. And you're willing to let him rot away in a prison because you hate yourself that much. What is it? Does he remind you of everything that's wrong with you? And that's why you're turning your back on him?

"You let me tell you one thing. I didn't raise any crooks or murderers. My grandson would never hurt a fly and he doesn't belong in prison," Granny said, quickly wiping a tear from her eyes.

Mrs. Gold sighed and looked down at her hands. She walked over and sat in a chair. Guilt was eating her alive.

"I don't know what to say."

"Nothing to say. Time for some deeds. Now look here. I done found the one person who can free up my boy." Granny dug into her purse and came out with a business card. "This lady can vouch for my grandbaby's innocence. He was talking to her when them boys started shooting. Said they came out and told him to get in the car. He wouldn't do it because he didn't want any part of their mess. All you gotta do is call her."

Mrs. Gold frowned. "And all of a sudden you have a mystery witness. It's not going to fly."

"There's more." Granny pulled a videotape from her purse. "Somebody sat this on my porch. Now my mind's guess is that it was that boy who got my son caught up in all this mess. On this tape you'll see my boy outside doing exactly what this woman will say he was doing when you hear shots in the background."

"I don't understand why the prosecutor couldn't find this information."

"Obviously they aren't interested in justice. They looking for headlines. Now I'm here asking you for your help to get my boy out of this mess."

"Are you serious about these new findings?"

"Ma'am, I'm too old to play games. Now I'm on a fixed income, but I can sell my house to pay your fees."

Mrs. Gold looked Granny in the eyes. She must've seen the love that she had cheated herself out of all of these years because she dropped her head into her own hands and started sobbing.

Granny took a seat in the far corner and watched the rich woman wither in pain. As far as she was concerned she deserved every tear she could ever shed for disowning her flesh and blood.

"Get out," Mr. Gold said from the doorway. "Get out of my house right this minute."

Granny held her ground. She stared at the man whose skin was darker than hers and felt nothing but pity.

"We will have no part of your conspiracy theory foolishness."

Granny didn't respond. She didn't move either.

"Very well then. I'll have you removed." Mr. Gold walked over and picked up the phone.

"Put it down," Mrs. Gold said, standing up to her husband for the first time in her life.

"What did you say?"

"I said put the phone down."

"Anna, we will talk about this later."

"There's nothing to talk about. Since the day we were married

I played the doting wife. I never went against your wishes, and I lost my only child because of it. But today things change. I will get that boy, my grandson, out of prison if it's the last thing I do."

"Oh my God. That boy is guilty as charged. Now the police don't just make things up."

Mrs. Gold looked at her husband and shook her head.

"Anna, get ahold of yourself."

"You've called the shots for too long. I've said my peace. Now please leave us alone. We have work to do," Mrs. Gold said. "Follow me, Mrs. Lassiter."

Granny smiled and stood. "You can call me Rose."

Mr. Gold stood there with a dumb look on his face as the two women entered Mrs. Gold's study.

MARCY WALKED over to her mother and hugged her.

"Thank you, Mom."

"Getting Nasir out wasn't easy; he wouldn't allow anyone to talk to him. I thought he wanted to stay in there but I was able to work around him. And in the end we prevailed."

"Did he know who you were?"

"No." Mrs. Gold shook her head. "I thought it was best that he didn't know. I didn't want him to let any animosity he may have had for me get in the way."

"You know I prayed that if God would bring my son home, then I would straighten up and fly right," Marcy said.

"Then I suggest you not disappoint God."

A NEW ENEMY

"What do you mean she's not here?"

"Her father picked her up," a white lady with caked-on makeup said to Nasir as he stood in the school's administrative office. "He signed her out about an hour ago."

"Her father?"

"Yes, sir."

Nasir scratched his chin, then whipped out his cell phone. He called Ayana but didn't get an answer.

"Sir?"

He held up a finger to the woman and tried Ayana again.

"Ma'am, are you sure Brandy Lassiter was signed out?"

"Sir, who are you?"

"I'm her father."

"Her father?" the lady asked, confused.

"Yes, her father. Where's her class?"

"Sir, I'm confused. What's your name?"

"Nasir Lassiter."

The lady flipped through the pages of her log.

"I don't see your name on our file."

Nasir tried Ayana again. Nothing.

"Where's her class?" Nasir asked again.

"Sir, I cannot share that information with you."

"Then I need to speak with the principal," Nasir said, hitting the SEND button of the last call again.

"If you'll have a seat I'll go and get her."

Nasir chose to stand. He slammed the phone closed after being sent to voice mail again. Every ten seconds he would try Ayana again but all he kept getting was the voice mail.

"Hello." A pretty black woman with gray streaks in her hair walked up to Nasir with an outstretched hand. "Amanda Winslow. How may I help you?"

"I'm looking for my daughter, Brandy Lassiter, and the lady over there said she was signed out already."

Amanda walked over to the same roster Cake Face had just examined and nodded her head.

"Is it possible for you to take me to her class?"

"Sir, that's against policy."

"But I'm her father."

"But if you're not on our list then our hands are tied."

Nasir grimaced and walked out of the office. Instead of leaving the building, he walked down the hall toward the classrooms, looking into one after the other.

"Call security," Amanda ordered.

Nasir's cell phone rang and he flipped it open.

"Hello."

"What's up?" Ayana said. "I was in an interview and missed your calls."

"Brandy's not here. They said she was checked out already."

"Checked out?" Ayana asked, confused.

"That's what they are saying. They said her father checked her out."

"Oh my God. Oh my God," Ayana yelled.

"What's going on, Ayana? Talk to me!"

"I gotta call the police." Ayana hung up the phone.

"Ayana. Ayana," Nasir called. "Shit!" he said as the line went dead. He turned back around and headed back toward the office. A security guard who looked to be working on his second century on earth walked up to Nasir.

"Ah . . . Ah . . . Ahh . . . sir," the top cop stammered.

Nasir ignored him and barged into the office and right up to Amanda. "I have an emergency. The man that picked up my daughter wasn't supposed to. Ayana is calling the police right now and I really need your help."

Amanda looked to be reading Nasir's face as if she was trying to gauge his sincerity. "I'll have to call Brandy's mother."

Just as she turned to leave, Nasir's phone rang.

"Hello," he said anxiously.

"The police are on the way and he's not answering any of his phones," Ayana said, already crying.

"What's going on, Ayana?"

"I left Alonzo. He knows he's not supposed to pick Brandy up," Ayana said through tears. "I gotta get my baby."

"What's his address?"

Nasir looked around for a pen. There was none lying around so he snatched the one Cake Face had sticking out of her bird's nest of a hairdo. He jotted down the information and tossed the pen on the counter.

"I'm on my way over there," Nasir said, flipping his phone closed. Then he realized that he had no idea which way to turn once he left the school's premises. He tried Ayana again but got her voice mail. He couldn't wait for her to answer so he turned back to Amanda.

"Do you know where this address is?"

"Sir, I don't know what's going on."

Nasir turned a stern face to her. "Ma'am. For the last four and a half years I sat in prison. I had no idea that I even had a daughter until yesterday. I don't want to be away from her again. Brandy's mother was beaten up by the man who signed her out. My daughter may be in trouble. All I'm asking for is directions. Can you help me?"

Amanda looked into Nasir's pleading eyes.

"Take a right out of the parking lot, a left onto Browns Mill Road, and the subdivision is on the right."

"Thank you," Nasir said, nodding before running out of the building.

SERVE AND PROTECT

*N*asir pulled up to the address on the paper and parked one house down from it. His nerves were racing as he opened the car door and hopped out.

What if this guy is packing! What kind of trap am I walking into?

His head told him to be smart but his heart told him to go get his little girl. His heart won.

He walked up to the house and rang the doorbell.

No answer.

He rang the bell again and still no answer. Just as he was about to walk around to the back of the house, Ayana's truck screeched into the driveway. She hit the garage door opener and the door rolled up. She ran past Nasir without even acknowledging him and

fumbled with her keys. She opened the door to the house leading into the kitchen and Nasir followed her in. Ayana ran
through the kitchen and up the stairs but Nasir lingered around
the kitchen feeling uncomfortable in another man's house. As he
stood there on edge, he saw a plain white sheet of paper sitting
on the all-black granite countertop. It was a handwritten to-do
list.

Pack clothes.
Call for transportation.
Choose island.
Pick up Brandy.

Nasir's legs became weak and his heart ached something awful.
He had no idea how so many feelings could develop so quickly
but they were there and he was scared. Scared for his child,
scared for Ayana, and scared for what he knew he would do once
he found the man who was responsible for this pain he felt.

Ayana came back down the stairs huffing and puffing.

"They're not here," she said.

Nasir leaned on the counter trying to control the rage that
threatened to erupt any minute.

Calm down and focus, he told himself.

Ayana read the look on his face and looked down at the note.
She read it twice and screamed at the top of her lungs. Nasir
reached for her and she collapsed in his arms.

Two police officers came to the garage door, a short overweight Caucasian one with a crew cut and a tall black one with a bald head. The screams made them draw their guns.

"Let the lady go and get down on your knees," the black officer said, pointing his nine-millimeter pistol right between Nasir's eyes.

Nasir paused and looked into eyes that said they would love nothing more than to rid this world of another shiftless nigga. The cop's gawp was begging Nasir to make a move. Nasir slowly placed his hands in the air.

"Place your hands behind your head."

Ayana's screams were deafening as she fell into a ball on the floor.

"What's going on here?" the white officer asked as the black one handcuffed Nasir.

"My daughter has been kidnapped. Get the fuck off of me," he growled.

"Whoa, cowboy. Let me find out what's going on," the white officer said.

"Look at the goddamn note and stop jumping to conclusions," Nasir barked.

"Shut up," the black cop said, hatred oozing from his pores.

"Fuck you."

"No, fuck you," the cop said, putting the gun to Nasir's head. "And yo black ass is going to jail."

"Are you gonna look at the note or just stand there jacking off on some power trip?"

"He took my baby," Ayana screamed.

"Let 'im up," the white cop said after reading the note.

Reluctantly the black cop did as he was ordered and removed Nasir's handcuffs.

"Sir, I'm sorry about that but we have to take all precautions," the white cop said.

"Yeah, well I see you keep a house nigga ready to pounce," Nasir said, staring the cop down as he stood.

"Do you wanna go to jail?"

"Do you wanna go to the hospital?"

"Just keep your mouth shut," the black cop spat.

"Fuck you," Nasir spat back.

"One more word and I'm . . ." the cop warned.

"Fuck you." Nasir's distaste for the boys in blue was oozing from his pores.

"That's it. Turn around and place your hands behind your back."

"Wait a minute. Calm down. This man's child is missing. He has the right to be a little upset," the white cop said, dismissing his overzealous partner. "Let's keep our heads here. We're all on the same side."

Nasir fanned them both off and walked over and knelt down beside Ayana.

"Everything is gonna be fine. We'll find her."

"Why?" Ayana cried.

He pulled her to her feet and led her to a chair.

"I'm going to need some information," the white cop said. "So the sooner someone can fill me in, the sooner we can get started, which means the better our chances are of getting your daughter back home safely."

Nasir gave him the details from the time he went to the school to the time a pistol was pointed between his eyes.

"Okay, the first thing we need to do is get you guys down to the station so we can file an official report."

Ayana pulled herself together enough to follow the officers out of the house. She left her truck in the driveway and rode with Nasir.

They walked into the station and gave the police officers all the information they could on Alonzo. An Amber Alert was sent out to the news stations and within minutes Alonzo's car description and license plate was on message boards all over Atlanta's highways. An all-points bulletin was sent out to all surrounding counties and their police departments to check all airports and private airstrips.

Nasir drove Ayana back to the house to get her truck an hour later. When they turned the corner onto Alonzo's street all they saw was a charred mess where her truck had been. Alonzo must have returned and pulled an Angela Bassett and burned it to a crisp.

"I never meant for things to turn out the way they did," Mr. Gold said, fidgeting with his wedding band.

"How did you expect them to turn out, Dad? You disowned me because you hate black people. If you can adjust that rearview mirror and take a look, you'll see that you're black."

"I don't *hate* anybody. It's just that I love you. And I don't make any apologies for that. Any father worth his salt would do whatever it took to make sure his daughter was surrounded by people of a high quality."

"And who are you to judge? No, you wanted to run my life. Did you ever think for one second that maybe I had my own plans for my life?"

Mr. Gold turned into the parking lot of Choices Recovery Center, Atlanta's version of the Betty Ford clinic. He killed the ignition and turned to his daughter.

"All I can say is I'm sorry. But as a father, I couldn't sit back and watch you settle for less."

"Why do you think I was settling for less?"

"Marcia, come on, you have to admit that Moses wasn't the best man for you. Look at how things turned out." Mr. Gold looked at his daughter with pity-filled eyes.

Marcy's face turned red.

"How things turned out had nothing to do with my husband."

Mr. Gold looked away and then back at his daughter.

"I—I—I have something I need to say. This guilt has been eating me alive. Part of the reason I stayed away from you is because I couldn't face you. But I'm an old man now and I don't want to spend the rest of my life living a lie," Mr. Gold stammered.

Marcy's stare could've cut a hole through her father's forehead.

Mr. Gold took a deep breath of his own. He turned and stared at his daughter and swallowed hard. He turned away and looked out of the window.

"It was a mistake. Things got way out of hand."

"Dad, what are you talking about?"

"I . . . um. I had a couple of guys pay Moses a visit. I wanted to talk to him. Get him to leave you alone. But he started fighting with them and well . . ."

"Well what? Finish. Tell me what happened."

"He started fighting and one of the guys pushed him and he fell down a flight of stairs." Mr. Gold frowned at the memory. "He must've hit his head or something because when they went down to get him he wasn't breathing. You have to know that I never meant for things to turn out that way. I just wanted him to leave you alone."

Marcy's chest heaved up and down. As soon as the truth left her father's lips she wondered if she really wanted to know it.

"Do you realize that you were trying to keep me away from a man that was better than you? You're nothing more than a common thug. You're a murderer. You turned into the very thing that you warned me against!" Marcy screamed at her father.

"I've lost everything, Marcia. And all I want to do is love you the way I should've a long time ago. I want to make things right."

Marcy looked at her father, closed her eyes, and grunted. An uneasy smile crossed her lips. "My son told me a story one day and I need to share it with you," Marcy said. "I asked him if he had any memories of his father and he said he did. We had an old car that broke down just about every other day. But on this particular day there was a huge thunderstorm. The rain was coming down and it was very dark. That had to be pretty scary for a three-year-old child. Nasir said he remembered being scared out of his mind until his father picked him up. He said the minute his head hit his father's chest he felt safe. And he remembered falling asleep. In the middle of a thunderstorm, he went to sleep." Marcy shook her head. "Isn't that a beautiful story? My husband was a good man. I didn't settle for less when I married him. He was everything I could've asked for in a man and I believe that you would have agreed if you could've overlooked the fact that he wasn't born with a silver spoon in his mouth. But you decided to play God." Marcy shook her head and pulled the door handle.

Mr. Gold looked at his daughter and turned away.

"There are a few things I want from you. First, I want you to pay these people every dime it's going to cost for me to get myself together. Then I want you to go and find my son and tell him what you did, then I want you to turn yourself in to the authorities. You belong in jail," Marcy said, stepping out of the car.

"Marcia . . ." he said weakly.

Marcy held up a hand and closed her eyes, blocking whatever her father had to say. She turned and walked toward the doors of a new life.

Hey, where you going? Don't you take me into that place! the monkey said, fully aware that his days of being a tyrant were coming to an end.

MAN UP

*N*asir swerved and weaved through traffic like a man on a mission, stealing a peek at Ayana even though he tried desperately not to.

From the moment he walked out of Brandy's school, he felt this worthlessness in the pit of his stomach. As a man and a father, it was his duty to protect the women in his life and on all three of them he fell far short of doing his job. His mother was God knows where, seeking a manufactured reprieve from the pain the men in her life had caused her; his daughter was in the clutches of some sicko; and the woman that five years of prison couldn't stop him from loving was sitting right next to him teetering on the edge of insanity.

Ayana's eyes were bloodshot red, her hair was slick from nervous perspiration, and she kept rocking back and forth, mumbling something he couldn't make out.

Nasir pulled up in front of Granny's house and parked in the driveway. He jumped out and ran around to open Ayana's door. She seemed so helpless, and he made a vow to bring a lot of pain to the man who was responsible for putting her in this condition. He reached in and grabbed her hand and Ayana slowly rose to her feet.

Nasir had called Granny from the police station and she was standing in the doorway waiting on them.

"Heard anything new?" Granny asked, stepping aside so that Nasir could get Ayana in the front door.

"Why'd he take my baby?" Ayana said. "He took my baby."

Granny took Ayana from Nasir and led her over to the sofa in the living room.

"Now, chile, you try to relax. God won't let a thing happen to that baby. You hear me? You gotta believe that."

Ayana buried her head in her hands and continued to cry. Granny sat beside Ayana and wrapped a reassuring arm around her.

Nasir walked into the kitchen and called Sammy. He told him to come over to Granny's. His next call was to Priest.

"Talk to me," Priest said, picking up before Nasir had even heard a ring.

"Priest, this is Nasir. I'm in a bad situation over here, man."

"What's up?"

"This cat Ayana been staying with kidnapped my daughter and the police are acting like it's business as usual," Nasir said. He felt himself losing it and forced himself to remain calm. "We shouldn't have even gotten them involved in the first place. They don't care anything about my daughter. I'mma kill this man."

"Hey, hey. Let's not get reckless. Give me the rundown. Who is this dude?"

"Some guy named Alonzo Benn."

"Oh, damn. I just got that message on the wire," Priest said.

"Okay, there are two ways we can handle this. We can go by procedure and I can help out or I can do it my way. Now keep in mind my way might have all our asses in prison."

"Man, I'm ready for whatever."

"Okay, I'm on my way to you right now."

"Thanks, man."

"You got it. And, Nasir, don't worry. We'll get your baby back."

Nasir closed his phone and started pacing. He couldn't sit still knowing his daughter was out there unprotected. He heard a tap on the front door and in walked Sammy.

The sadness in the room was overwhelming and Sammy went over and hugged his grandmother. He put a hand on Ayana's shoulder, then looked up at Nasir.

"What's going on, cuzzo?"

"Outside." Nasir motioned toward the front door. Sammy turned around and Nasir followed him out to the front porch.

"I need a gun," Nasir said the minute the door was closed.

"I can do that but you need to holla at your boy. I mean guns ain't you. What's going on?"

"Brandy's been kidnapped. We went by the crib and the man Ayana had been staying with been acting crazy. He checked her out of school. Burned up Ayana's car and everything."

"Oh, he clowning," Sammy said.

"Yeah, I'mma clown his ass when I get him."

"I heard something about a little girl being kidnapped on the way over here on the radio." Sammy frowned. "I never thought it was Brandy."

Nasir made an ugly face. "Funky-ass police."

"They seem to be on it with this one, Knock."

"Whatever, my little girl doesn't have blond hair and blue eyes so you know they going half speed. We don't have the complexion for the connection. So we gotta get my baby back," Nasir said.

"What's the plan? You know I'm down for whatever."

"I don't know," Nasir said, grimacing at the thought of not knowing.

"Nasir," Granny called.

Nasir ran back in the house and saw his little girl's picture plastered across the television screen.

An Amber Alert has been issued for a four-year-old little girl. Last seen with this man, Alonzo Benn.

Alonzo's picture replaced Brandy's.

Authorities believe they are traveling in a black six hundred series Mercedes-Benz, license plate NHF 322. Now on to those Atlanta Braves.

Seeing his little girl's picture made Nasir's hand shake involuntarily. He wanted nothing more than to kill Alonzo Benn. He turned and walked back out to the porch.

"I gotta figure something out, man. Time is not on my side," Nasir said.

"We gotta come up with something quick."

"Priest is on his way over here."

"Priest! You sure that's the route you wanna take?"

"What other route is there to take. This is my daughter. I've already lost four years of her life, I'm not losing any more."

Priest pulled up and jumped out of his truck and walked over to them.

"Gentlemen," Priest said, knocking fists with Nasir and then Sammy.

"Priest, how's everything on the force?"

"Yo, this ain't no social call," Nasir cut in. "Y'all can get reacquainted when Brandy gets home."

"Okay," Priest said. "Let's get to it. I got some intel on our guy. Found a cousin of his and she informed me that when he flies, he charters jets. Anyway, I called around and found out that he has one on standby. The plane is parked at a private airstrip off of Buford Highway, so if he's gonna get ghost that's most likely the route he'll take. That way he doesn't have to deal with the security and prying eyes at the airports. So the first thing we need to do is get to that strip."

"And then what? We just sit and wait? Meanwhile, my daughter is going through whatever? This dude could be a pedophile," Nasir yelled.

"Listen, man," Priest said in a stern voice. "If you're gonna roll with me, you're gonna have to check your emotions. Nothing wrong with it if you can't do it. I can get a few guys together and holla back at you when I get your daughter."

"Nah, I'm good," Nasir said, realizing that he was just one outburst away from being left standing right where he was.

"Yo, Priest," Sammy said. "I know you a cop and all but I'm packing. And I was about to go and get Nasir a little something to keep his hands warm."

"Hey, do what you gotta do. Meet me at the strip in thirty minutes. I got some people watching out for him until we get there." Priest tapped fists again and walked away. "We'll get her back, homie. This dude's an amateur. He's made too many mistakes already."

"Let's roll," Nasir said, heading to his car.

"You ain't gonna tell Granny you leaving?"

"Nah. Let's go."

Nasir and Sammy made the five-minute drive over to University Homes. He pulled up in his mother's driveway and noticed a tall well-dressed black man standing on the steps.

"You lost?" Nasir asked as he stepped out of his car.

The man stared at him. Then as if he couldn't take it anymore he looked away.

Nasir returned the old man's stare.

"Yo, cuz. You aight?" Sammy asked.

"Yeah," Nasir said. "I'm cool."

"Okay," Sammy said, eyeing the man suspiciously. "I'mma go grab that and I'll be right back," Sammy said, getting out of the car and running across the street.

"I take it that you are Nasir."

"Who's asking?"

"My name is Michael Gold and I'm your . . ." Mr. Gold's voice trailed off.

"Excuse me?"

"I'm Marcia's father. Your grandfather."

"I see," Nasir said, scanning the frail-looking man from head to toe. "Are you looking for my mother?"

"No. I was hoping to talk to you."

"You gonna have to make it quick."

"This is not a social call. I realize the time for that has long passed." Mr. Gold handed Nasir a thick manila envelope.

"What's that?" Nasir said, not reaching for the envelope.

"I'm not sure. My wife asked me to give it to you."

"She couldn't bring it herself?"

"She asked me to bring it."

Nasir nodded. He didn't know this man or his wife and he wasn't about to sit up here and pretend to be happy to see him. He frowned and tried to block out the sound of some dummy blasting his music with busted speakers. The noise came closer until all you could hear was a loud rumble. Then he heard a familiar voice.

"Playboy."

Nasir turned toward the voice and saw Savion hanging out the passenger-side window with an automatic weapon in his hand.

"You ready to let me drive that car?" Chaz, the little boy from earlier, said as he rode his bicycle up the block.

"It's time to pay the piper," Savion yelled as he sprayed a hail of bullets. They sounded like a string of firecrackers on the Fourth of July. Mr. Gold's crisp white shirt instantly became a deep burgundy as he went down like a rag doll. Nasir leaped chest-first in front of the car and tried to stay down. He saw Chaz's bike lying on its side. The wheel still spinning.

A different kind of gun sound entered the picture and Nasir saw Sammy running toward him shooting at Savion. But then he fell to the ground and rolled to get out of harm's way. The gun flew from his hand right by Mr. Gold's feet. Nasir wanted to reach for it but Savion was spraying bullets like he was in the Wild Wild West. Nasir stayed low and kept his eyes on his cousin. He could see Sammy's lips form into some kind of curse word and he figured he was okay. He turned his head and tried to see Chaz. All he could see was the little boy's dirty sneaker twitching. He knew he had to do something but what?

Nasir prayed he would hear Savion's car riding away but the music was still blasting too close for comfort. Then he heard a car door slam shut.

"Playboy, you trynna hide," Savion said, walking closer to Nasir.

"They say tech nines jam a lot but mine's smooth as a baby's ass," Savion said. He was no more than five feet away from Nasir. "Didn't I tell you you were safer inside? Nobody fucks with me and lives to tell about it. And I'll tell you another thing, you pretty bitch, I'm the reason you in the streets now. I told that old prissy bitch of a lawyer, you ain't had nothing to do with the capping, but you wanna sneak me."

Nasir saw the tips of Savion's Air Force Ones, then he looked up into the drunken eyes of a man he once called a friend.

"You were right about one thing, homeboy, ain't no we. 'Cuz we ain't about to die. You are."

BAM!

AFRICA

*T*he engine roared to life.

"Mr. Benn, we are all set," the captain said over the intercom.

Alonzo pushed the button on his captain's chair and said, "Yeah, let's get the hell outta here."

The plane eased forward, then picked up speed. Less than a minute later they were airborne.

"Mr. Benn, if you'll keep your seat belt on for a few more minutes, I'd appreciate it," the pilot said.

"No problem."

Alonzo pushed a button on the arm of his captain's chair and asked, "Karen, will you bring me a Scotch on the rocks the minute we smooth out."

Alonzo laid his head back, finally able to relax.

Ayana had him stressed out but he was going to leave that alone. A trip to the motherland would do him some good. Just as he closed his eyes he heard the doors of the cabin swing open.

When he opened his eyes he got the shock of his life. Instead of looking up and seeing his curvy stewardess, he looked into six pairs of menacing eyes.

Nasir looked at Alonzo with a stare that could break steel.

"What the fuck, homie?" Baldhead said. "How you just gonna take somebody's child?"

Alonzo was speechless. He looked like he'd seen a ghost.

Priest walked over and took a seat beside Alonzo. He grabbed the remote control. "How you work this thing," he asked calmly as if they were old pals.

"Wait a minute." Baldhead leaned in for a closer look at Alonzo. "Who in the hell are you looking at? Me or him?"

Priest laughed and turned the channel.

"If you can afford a private plane, I know you can pay somebody to fix that fucked-up eye. Which one am I supposed to look at?" Baldhead asked.

Alonzo couldn't come up with any words. He just stared at the strange men, wondering how they got on his plane.

Priest turned and stared at Alonzo. "It's the left one."

"No, 'cuz that's the one that keeps moving all over the damn place. The right one is . . . wait a damn minute. That one is moving too."

Alonzo made a move for his gun but he was too slow.

"Oh no," Baldhead said, placing his own gun up to Alonzo's forehead. He took Alonzo's gun from him. "Don't you know I'm unstable? Please don't try no more dumb shit in here today."

"Wait a minute. What are you guys doing on my plane?" Alonzo said, finding his voice.

"Looka here, Baldhead. It speaks," Priest said. "Where's the little girl?"

"What?"

"I think I was clear but just in case your ears are as fucked up as that eye, I'll repeat the question. Where is Brandy?" Priest said.

"Brandy?" Alonzo looked around. "She's at school."

"So now you wanna play games."

"What are you talking about?" Alonzo asked and he appeared to be genuinely confused, but Priest had been dealing with criminals for a long time and he found them to be better actors than some of Hollywood's finest.

"She *was* in school but you checked her out. Now I'll ask you again. Where is Brandy?"

"I don't know what you are talking about. I did sign her out but only to take her to lunch and then I took her right back to school."

"Okay, have it your way," Priest said, sitting back with the remote. "But we will find her because you will talk."

"Listen, man," Nasir spoke. "I don't want things to go down the way they are about to. So please tell me where my daughter is?" Alonzo looked up at Nasir with fear and curiosity. *So this was the man who took his woman away,* his eyes seemed to say.

"I swear I'm telling the truth," Alonzo said.

"As you probably know, I just left prison. But what you can't know is that I'm ready to go back. Now the question is, are you ready to die?"

Alonzo closed his eyes and rammed his face into his hands over and over. "I'm not hiding anything. I'm telling you guys the truth. If she's missing I want to help you guys. I love that little girl more than anybody. Including you," he said to Nasir.

"Hey, man"—Baldhead held up a hand as if he were in a classroom—"which one of them eyeballs I'm supposed to look at?"

"Please, guys. I'm a businessman. I'm sure we can work this out."

"Guess what?" Priest asked.

Alonzo turned to Priest.

"I know what you did."

"What I did?" Alonzo asked, confused.

"You know what I'm talking about, Mr. Benn. Don't play dumb."

"I have no idea what you are talking about."

"I'm talking about your half-ass plan. You've been watching too many gangster movies, little man." Priest threw his leg over the arm of the chair and flipped the channel again. "Your first mistake was getting too emotional about a woman who never loved you in the first place. Your second one was hiring an amateur to do a professional's job. Baldhead, you won't believe who he sent at Nasir."

"Who?"

"Savion."

"Savion?" Baldhead frowned. "That li'l skinny bastard couldn't bust a grape with Welch's permission."

"Whatchu do, ask around until you found the one person who had a problem with Nasir?" Priest asked.

Alonzo was stone-faced.

"Are you guys cops?"

"Yep," Baldhead said. "That's Wyatt Earp and I'm Doc Holliday."

"I need to see my lawyer before I say another word."

"I'm not finished," Priest said. "Your little shooter got shot. Bullet landed about an eighth of an inch from his heart. Paramedics said if he would've sneezed he would've died."

"Damn, I wish it was allergy season," Baldhead said.

"No, 'cuz then he wouldn't have been able to tell us what Crooked I over here did. Yeah, through all his screaming and begging he managed to tell us some li'l short cockeyed dude paid him ten G's to take Nasir out."

"Ten G's? Damn, that's all you think my homie is worth?" Baldhead said, taking the remote from Priest. He slapped Alonzo across the head with it before plopping down on the sofa behind the captain's chairs. "This is a nice plane, man. How much one of these cost?"

Nasir never took his eyes off of Alonzo. He walked over to Alonzo and unbuckled his seat belt.

"Stand up," Nasir said.

Alonzo looked around but realized he was outnumbered and outgunned. He stood.

"Damn, he said stand up," Baldhead said. "What are you? Four-six. What's the height requirement to be an official midget?"

"Why did I bring you?" Priest said, shaking his head.

Nasir was all business.

"So you kidnap my daughter and try to have me killed. What I ever do to you?"

"I don't know where these guys got that information from. I'm a businessman, not a criminal."

"I see. You know a little ten-year-old boy was shot because of your little scheme? They said he might not make it. You better hope he does."

"I'm not saying anything else until I speak to my lawyer," Alonzo said defiantly.

"Homie, it ain't that kind of party. You won't be talking to any kind of lawyers. You 'bout to die," Baldhead said.

"Please, man. Okay, I got a little caught up. You gotta understand that I did everything for Ayana. I took her in when she had no place to go. I was there when your daughter was born and when you came home she just dropped me like I was nothing. So yeah, I was a little pissed, but I didn't do anything to Brandy. I swear on my life."

"If you were me what would you do?"

"I'd give me a chance to make this right. Let me help you find your daughter."

"I hope you don't look like O. J. Simpson," Baldhead said. "Did O. J. find those killers yet, Priest?"

"Shut up, man," Priest said.

"The way I see it. I'm due a body," Nasir said.

"What?" Alonzo asked.

"I was sent to prison for a murder I didn't commit. So the way I see it, I'm due a body, being that I already served time for killing one. Isn't that how this society works, Priest? If you pay for something, you should get what you paid for, right?"

"I never looked at it like that but I guess you're right," Priest said, handing Nasir a gun.

Nasir shook his head. "Nah, I don't wanna shoot him. That's too easy. He needs to suffer."

"Whatever you want, I got your back," Priest said.

"Hey, I got an idea," Baldhead said. "Let's sew his asshole shut and feed him grits till he swells up and pops."

"Baldhead, watch TV," Priest said. "I can't believe some of the things that come out of your mouth."

Baldhead hunched his shoulders and turned the channel.

"That's not a bad idea, Baldhead, but I think I got something better than that," Nasir said.

"Whatchu got?"

"How long before we land?"

Priest pushed the button and called out to the captain.

"How long before we make it back home, Captain?"

"I can land anytime you want. I was just circling the city like you asked me to."

"Then take us on down and thanks for your cooperation," Priest said before releasing the button.

"When you woke up this morning did you realize that today might be your last day on this earth?" Nasir asked Alonzo as he took a seat in the chair he had just made him get out of.

"Hey, man, I'll give you money. Just please don't kill me," Alonzo pleaded, sensing his time on earth getting shorter and shorter.

"Nah, I don't want your money. I want your life."

"Please, man," Alonzo said, and he looked so pitiful.

"So your grandfather put one in Savion, hunh?" asked Priest.

"Yeah," Nasir said. "The first time I saw the man, he ended up dying, but I guess he can meet his maker knowing he was there for me when I really needed him."

"We all need something to die for," Priest said.

Nasir looked over at Alonzo, who was biting his fingernails.

"Please, man, don't kill me." Alonzo shook his head. "I've been nothing but good to Ayana. And if anything happened to Brandy, it wasn't me."

"Oh, damn," Baldhead said, sitting up from the sofa. "You mean to tell me it's two li'l short muthafuckas with crooked eyes walking around here checking kids out of school that don't belong to them?"

"I guess so, Baldhead," Nasir said, nodding his head. "I guess so."

The pilot came across the intercom advising everyone to buckle up for landing. Alonzo didn't move. He looked at Nasir for permission.

"Go ahead and take a seat," Nasir said. "Wouldn't want you to get hurt now."

A WASTED SIN

*A*yana couldn't sit still and wait on Brandy to miraculously pop up. She called Lorraine to see if she had seen or heard from Alonzo but she didn't get an answer. She borrowed Granny's old 1961 Bonneville. It took the car fifteen minutes to start. Once she got the engine running she headed back over to Sandstone.

She went back to Alonzo's house and parked. She jumped out of the car and ran up to the house. She hit the code to the garage door and ran inside. She knew she wouldn't find her daughter there but she had to look all over the house at least one more time. She searched every nook and cranny but came up empty. She kept visualizing her little girl in some wet basement tied to a chair. The tears in her eyes would not stop flowing.

She ran from the house and decided she couldn't wait on Granny's beater to start. She cut across the yard and ran around the pond to Lorraine's house. She rang the doorbell, but nothing. She banged on the door, still nothing. She walked around to the back of the house and peered inside. Her heart hit the ground. She saw Brandy's doll on the floor. She banged on the door like a madwoman, screaming out her daughter's name the entire time. She fumbled with her cell phone and dialed 911.

"This is Ayana Zion and I have an emergency. I think I found my daughter," Ayana said, surprisingly calm. She gave them the info they asked for and hung up the phone.

Ayana circled the house looking up at the windows hoping to get a glimpse of Brandy.

Where are the police? What is taking them so long? she wondered, even though she had only called them less than two minutes ago.

Ayana's heart threatened to explode as she paced back and forth. She heard the police pull up and she ran over to them. "I think my daughter's inside this house."

"Just a second, ma'am. What makes you think that?"

Ayana pulled the man to the back of the house and peeked through the window again. She looked at the same spot but the doll was gone.

"It was there a minute ago."

"What was there?"

"My daughter's doll."

"Ma'am, maybe you were mistaken?"

"No! Don't you even try that with me," Ayana screamed. "Kick this door down and get my baby."

The officer walked around to the front of the house and rang the doorbell.

"Don't you think I did that already? Sir, will you please kick this door down."

"Ma'am, I can't just go kicking people's doors down. Now if she's in there we'll get her," the officer said. He clicked the radio on his shoulder and said some police code.

Ayana sat on the steps and rocked back and forth. She looked at the officer's gun and wanted to take it from him but knew that wasn't going to happen. She saw a stone in Lorraine's landscaping and went for it. She picked up the rock and threw it through the large garden window. There was a loud explosion like a gun going off. The house alarm went off as the entire window shattered into a million little pieces. Ayana didn't think twice, she ran and jumped through the window as the officer yelled for her to stop.

Ayana ran through the house calling out Brandy's name. She ran up the stairs and went straight for the first closed door she saw.

Ayana walked into the room and saw Brandy sitting on Lorraine's lap. Lorraine was hugging her daughter tightly. Her eyes appeared unfocused. She seemed to be drugged up. Ayana forced herself to calm down.

"What are you doing here?" Lorraine asked as if nothing was out of the ordinary.

"Lorraine, give me my baby!"

Brandy was sitting on Lorraine's lap looking terrified. Her eyes broke Ayana's heart.

"Naja's staying home," Lorraine said, rubbing Brandy's hair back. "Now you should go so she can get her homework done."

"Lorraine," Ayana spoke as calmly as she could, "that's not Naja. That's Brandy. Let her go."

The police officer came into the room with his gun drawn.

Ayana waved him off.

"I want you to leave my house. Naja has to do her homework, damn it," Lorraine screamed.

"Ma'am, step away from the child," the officer said.

"Why are you trying to take my child? She needs to be home with her mother," Lorraine said.

Ayana looked Brandy over for signs of abuse but she didn't see any from where she stood. She wanted to go over and snatch her child away from her crazy friend but didn't want to traumatize her any more than she had already been.

Lorraine looked up at the officer as if she'd seen a ghost. She loosened her arms from around Brandy and the little girl jumped up and ran to her mother.

Ayana knelt down and scooped up her daughter and almost ran with her from the house. Once they were outside of the house Ayana took a closer look at her. "Are you all right?" Ayana said, hugging her tight.

"Yes," Brandy said. "Mommy, what's wrong with Miss Lorraine? She kept calling me Naja."

"Miss Lorraine is not feeling well. Did she hurt you? How did you get here?"

"Mr. Alonzo took me to lunch but Miss Lorraine was in the hallway at my school and she wouldn't let me go back to class."

"It's okay, baby. You're safe now." Ayana hugged her child again.

The police officer walked out of the house with Lorraine. Her hands were cuffed behind her and as she walked past Ayana she simply nodded her head. She looked down at Brandy and said, "Mommy will be back shortly."

THE BEST MAN

*N*asir followed Priest and Baldhead to a warehouse out in the middle of nowhere. He was told to wait in the car for ten minutes before coming in. Ten minutes later he walked into the building and saw nothing but boxes upon more boxes, but then he heard Alonzo begging for his life. He followed the sound.

He walked toward the back and looked up and saw that Alonzo was hanging from a rafter by his feet. From the looks of things Priest and Baldhead had worked him over pretty good already.

"Whatchu wanna do with him, homie?" Priest asked. "You the quarterback on this one. Call the play and we'll execute."

Nasir stood there watching Alonzo swing back and forth.

"You wanna tell me where my daughter is?"

"I told you, I don't know. God knows I don't know," Alonzo said through slobber and blood.

Baldhead tossed Nasir a baseball bat, and just as he lifted it up to cock back for the home run hit, his cell phone rang. Nasir took a deep breath and lowered the slugger.

"Hello," he said. A minute later he smiled and visibly relaxed. "Is she aight? How are you doing? Okay. I'll see you soon." Nasir flipped his phone closed and looked up at Alonzo.

"I guess he was telling the truth. Let him down."

Baldhead cut the rope that held Alonzo and the short man fell to the concrete floor headfirst. There was a loud splat and a grunt.

"Oops," Baldhead said.

Alonzo rolled on the floor, holding his head.

"Get up," Nasir commanded.

Alonzo hobbled to his feet. His swollen eyes begged for mercy.

"You don't look so well," Nasir said.

Alonzo looked toward Priest.

"I had to get him one time just for trying to have you taken out," Priest said.

"I had some pretty nice plans for you, my man, but I'm not a gangster. I'm not a killer and I'm not a thug. My little girl is safe and that's all that matters. She's at home where she belongs so I'mma give you a pass." Nasir moved to the side.

"Are you sure, Nasir? This cat tried to put you with the fishes," Baldhead said.

"Let the cops do what they will with him."

"All shit. He got some cheese. You might as well let him walk away."

"Then let him walk away," Nasir said. "I'm sure he'll keep his distance."

"Okay," Priest said. "You are under arrest. You have the right to remain silent."

"Wait a minute. What are you arresting me for?" Alonzo asked as if he really believed he didn't commit any crimes.

"Conspiracy to commit murder, carrying a concealed weapon, trynna flee the damn country. Ah shit, you got a laundry list."

"And you have the right to use the prison medical staff to get that goddamn eye fixed," Baldhead said.

Priest finished reading Alonzo his Miranda rights, then slipped on the handcuffs.

Nasir smiled. "I appreciate y'all coming through for me."

"It's all good, li'l brother," Priest said. "Glad to have you home."

"Glad to be home." Nasir smiled.

"So what's next for you?" Baldhead asked.

Nasir sighed. "I don't know. Spend some time with my girls. Enjoy being home for a minute, then I'll decide."

"Don't be a stranger," Priest said.

They all hugged and said their goodbyes.

Nasir watched as Priest led Alonzo away. He looked at Alonzo's blood on the concrete and shook his head. It felt good to take the high road. As he walked back to his car his cell phone rang again.

"Hello," Nasir said.

"How's my favorite ballplayer doing?" Eric, Nasir's college roommate and owner of the Aston Martin he was driving, said.

Eric used to be Georgia Tech's very own white chocolate. He got that nickname because he played ball with the swagger of a guy who grew up in the heart of the ghetto even though he was raised up in an Amish community in Pennsylvania.

"Awww, I'm still in one piece," Nasir said, peeking at all of the bullet holes in the back window. "How's the life of a super agent?"

"Good. It would be better if I had you on as a client."

"Forgot how a basketball looks. I'm a family man now."

"Family man? That was quick."

"Yeah. I got a daughter and a soon-to-be-wife."

"A daughter? A wife? Did I miss something?"

"You remember Ayana?"

"Yeah. How could I forget the woman who had your nose wide as Texas."

"She had my baby while I was in prison."

"Now I know you gotta come aboard. You have bills, baby. I got you a spot on a team in Spain. All you gotta do is say the word, and I'll have a first-class ticket in your hands."

"Boy, you haven't changed a bit. Still the same ol' E."

"Gotta keep hustling, baby. How's the ride treating you? You like it. You can have it if you sign the line."

"Yo, man, some clown shot out the back window of your car. I gotta get it fixed."

"Are you serious? Are you okay?"

"Yeah, I'm aight. I'll get it fixed for you as soon as they have a replacement."

"Don't sweat it."

"Thanks, E."

"How did your mother enjoy her stay at the Ritz?"

Nasir slammed on the brakes. His mind had been so preoccupied with Brandy and Alonzo that he had almost forgotten about his mother.

"E, let me call you back, man."

"No problem."

"Peace."

Nasir closed the phone, then opened it back up. He called Granny.

"Granny, have you heard from my mother?"

"Lord," Granny said. "My mind is getting just as bad. She called. Checked herself into a clinic. Good thing she did too 'cuz the police been swarming 'round here about her father. Somebody shot him."

"I know."

"How you know?"

"Long story, I'll tell you about it when I see you."

"Okay, but you ain't caught up in no mess, are ya?"

"No, ma'am. Brandy and Ayana doing okay?"

"Yeah, they doing fine. Sitting round here hugging each other."

"Okay," Nasir said. "I'll see you shortly."

"Bye."

Nasir hung up the phone and turned onto the interstate. He rolled the window down and stuck his arm out just because he could. The wind blew in his face and he felt free for the first time in what seemed like forever. Even after everything that had happened, he felt like the luckiest man alive. He thought about his grandfather and made a cross with his hand over his chest. He remembered Priest's words. *We all need something to die for.*

*I*t's amazing the changes a year can make. Savion was sentenced to ten years in prison, but worse than that, he's confined to a wheelchair for the rest of his life. Alonzo got six months in the pokey for his failed attempt on my life. I'm not sure how I feel about that one. I mean, he did take care of my girls for me, but then again he also tried to have me killed. I guess things worked out the way they were supposed to on that one. Lorraine is on medication for her depression, and surprisingly, Ayana still talks to her. And me, well, I'm right where I need to be.

We were down by eight with forty seconds on the clock. The ball was in my hands. Just where it belonged. I crossed one defender over and pulled up to hit the three-pointer.

Thirty seconds. Down by five.

Our power forward, a six-eleven dude named Roderick Sellers, blocked a shot that landed about five feet away from me. I raced over and grabbed the ball. I took a few dribbles and headed for the same spot I'd just scored from. Pulled up and nailed another three.

Fourteen seconds left. Down by two.

Enrique Martinez, our Spanish version of Steve Nash, stole the inbound pass and slung it to me on the wing. I knew right away that I wasn't going for the tie. That's me, Mr. All or Nothing. So I stopped right behind the three-point line and let it go. The ball seemed to sail in the air for an eternity before it landed way short of the rim. Damn!

Foul.

The referee caught my opponent hitting my elbow just as I released my shot.

"Three shots," the ref said, pointing at the free-throw line.

Seven seconds.

I walked over to the free-throw line. The ref passed me the ball and I looked over to see my entire family in the stands.

Ayana had her hands over her eyes, unable to look. Some things never changed. She used to do that same thing when we were in college. Brandy blew me a kiss. Man, I love that little girl. My mom looked like she was praying and Grandma Gold was looking up at the clock. Granny was fussing at Chaz about something. Damn that little boy was bad but he was mine. Yeah,

Ayana and I decided to adopt him after we found out his mother was out in the streets fighting the same battle my mom seemed to have licked. She hates when I say that so I'll take it back. She's taking it one day at a time and she looks great. Four months in rehab and she's almost back to her old self. Her skin is flawless and she's just as chipper as a chipmunk. She's even taking college classes again.

Sammy was trying to talk to some woman who was ignoring him. Probably because she couldn't understand his ebonics.

I put the tip of my toe on the line and dropped the first free throw with ease. Now we were down by one.

I dribbled the ball three times and let the second one fly. It rolled around the rim and fell off to the side. Well at least we'll get the tie and I'll kill 'em in overtime. I dribbled the ball three more times and let it go. *Clank.* Damn it. I missed again.

Portugal got the ball on our baseline and tried to throw it the length of the court but Pedro stole it and hit me in the corner for the last-second shot.

Swish.

My coach ran onto the floor screaming something in Spanish about how happy he was I came to Spain. He had no idea how happy I was to be here. After the game I ran to the locker room, showered, and chatted with my teammates, then made my way out to the lobby where my family was waiting.

"I'm so glad you missed that shot," Granny said. "I'm tired. Plus I gotta meet with Sanchez or whatever his name is. We picking out furniture for my room. I don't know why you had to buy that big ol' house," Granny fussed.

"You know you love it," I said, winking at my old girl.

"Baby, I'm so proud of you," my mom said.

She looked good. Gained weight. Her face cleared up and to put the cherry on top of everything, she had agreed to come and live with me and Ayana and the kids over here in Spain.

Grandma Gold, as she now likes to be called, handed me an envelope and kissed my cheek.

"What's this?"

"Read it," she said.

"Alone or now?"

"Whenever," she said, hunching her shoulders. She looked at her watch. She was leaving today to get back to some high-profile case in Atlanta. I really enjoyed spending time with her and we agreed not to let the past affect our future as a family.

"Since you're leaving today," I said, making the sad face, "I better read it now."

"I'm hungry," Chaz said. He was always hungry. I guess it hadn't sunk in yet that he would never be hungry again.

"Hush," I said before opening the envelope.

Dear Nasir,

It was such a pleasure spending time with you and your beautiful children. I can't say how sorry I am with the way things turned out for our family. But I'm glad that we have each other now. The loss was truly mine, and I don't know if I'll ever forgive myself for missing out on all those years.

I found out about your legal troubles right after you were arrested but decided to turn a blind eye to them. God only knows how I'm paying for that decision. But one day I was visited by an angel masquerading on this earth as a woman named Rose Lassiter. She made me see the light.

So I tossed everything else aside and worked tirelessly to get your case overturned, and by the grace of God we were successful. I also took the liberty of suing the state for false imprisonment, and pending your cooperation, we are very close to what I predict could be a million-dollar settlement. I'm sure the district attorney doesn't want the embarrassment of having every case he ever prosecuted exposed. I'm going to expose him anyway. ☺

I really wish I could stay longer but there are too many innocent men and women who could use my services. Don't worry. Now that we are a family you'll never get rid of me. I do realize we must all forgive past sins in order to move on. Based on my actions, I don't have a right to say this but I will anyway, I love you.

I'll end this now but remember: to forgive is to truly be free. I'm trying to forgive myself and I hope you will find it in your heart to forgive me too.

With Love,

Anna

I folded the letter up and reached over to give my other grandmother the biggest hug she could stand.

"Thank you. And I don't blame you for anything. If it wasn't for you, then I would still be rotting away in prison. You gave me another life and . . ." I swept my arms around for her to see the many blessings I had. "I couldn't be more thankful."

"Baby, I have to go," Ayana said, reaching up to kiss me. She was working at a local English-language elementary school. Said she never wanted to live off another man again. Ain't that something, I'm the man who wants to take care of her but she's not having it. But whatever makes her happy is fine with me.

"Okay, sweetie," I said, kissing her back. "Hey, before you go . . ." I said, pulling her back.

"What's up?" she said, stopping and turning around to face me.

Yeah, I had to do the corny thing, y'all. I dropped down on one knee and pulled out the three-carat marquise-cut diamond ring. I was going to do the romantic horse and carriage over in Paris but what could be better than in front of all my loved ones.

"Will you marry me?" I said.

Brandy had it all wrong because she ran and jumped on me, screaming "Yes!" and knocking me down.

Ayana walked over and stood over me and my daughter. She covered her mouth with both hands. Tears were in her eyes. She nodded her head up and down.

I sat up on my elbow and looked up into those pretty eyes and smiled.

"What am I gonna do with you," she said, kneeling down to kiss me to seal the deal.

SOMETHING
TO DIE FOR

Travis Hunter

A READER'S GUIDE

READING GROUP QUESTIONS AND TOPICS FOR DISCUSSION

1. Hunter opens this novel with a description of the disparity between communities ("a blatant barrier constructed to separate the ghettofied residents of The "U" from the good-paying students across Fair Street"). What other communities, individuals, or ideologies are kept apart throughout the story, and what barriers are used to accomplish that segregation?

2. What is it about a neighborhood like The "U" that allows for a sense of familiarity and closeness between its stars (Nasir), its rejects (Monroe), and its authorities (Priest)? Do you think this is true in real communities?

3. What causes the woman at the gas station to initially respond so negatively toward Nasir? And what do you think of her shift in attitude once she recognized who he was? Does this happen often? Have you ever judged someone too quickly?

4. How is it that Savion, a degenerate and seedy character, is able to retain a top-dollar attorney and Nasir, a local star with a national profile, is left with a "public pretender"?

5. Priest lashes out at Nasir for being "a good kid [messing] his life up trying to be down with a bunch of lowlifes." Why do you think Nasir continued such destructive friendships for so long?

6. Do you believe Nasir's explanation that he didn't keep in touch with anyone in his family while in prison because it would have made it too hard for them to do his time? Do you think that decision was honorable or selfish?

7. How could Nasir's mother, "one of them suburban black folks [who talks] all proper," fall into a heroin addiction?

8. God is primarily referred to as a judge and ever-present force throughout the story. Is this an aspect of the characters' environment? Who are the "people of faith" in this story, and what is their contribution? How do different characters acknowledge God in their lives?

9. "Alonzo wasn't [Ayana's] type, but at the time he was her only choice." Is this really true, or is there something else limiting Ayana's abilities to see all of her available options?

10. Marcy's father, admonishing her choice to move into the middle of the ghetto, asks her, "Why do you want to help those people who don't even want to help themselves?" and "Those ghetto people turn to crime because they are lazy." What factors and ideologies do you think contributed to his response?

11. In considering Lorraine's familial ties to Alonzo, was it naive of Ayana to trust her with her distress? Why did Lorraine try to hook Ayana up with Quentin?

12. Discuss the mentality of the "Project Chicks." What is "acting black enough"? Why would speaking "proper English"

and not dressing "like some video ho" cause girls to beat up one of their peers? How could this rage develop into something so severe it could result in murder?

13. What function does Chaz—the boy who tells Nasir, "You don't need no driver's license to drive. You need a license to show the police"—play in this story? What elements of his community does he reflect?

14. Lorraine tells Ayana, "All that chivalry crap is gonna stop the minute you give him some." What does this say about the kind of men Lorraine is accustomed to dating? Have you seen this happen in your relationships?

15. Sammy describes his flawed shooting technique as "Trynna hold my gun like them damn rappers. All crooked." What does this suggest about the glorification of violence in rap music?

16. What would cause Lorraine to say that Ayana "doesn't deserve that baby"?

17. Would Nasir have gotten out of prison without his grandparents' influential involvement?

ABOUT THE AUTHOR

TRAVIS HUNTER, a native South Carolinian, is a novelist, songwriter, and playwright. In 2003 he was named Author of the Year by readers of the *Atlanta Daily World*. He is the founder of the Hearts of Men Foundation, which mentors underprivileged youth. Hunter recently created the Travis Hunter Theater Company to adapt his novels into stage plays. Hunter lives in an Atlanta suburb with his son Rashaad. Visit Hunter's website at www.travishunter.com.

Other bestsellers by Travis Hunter

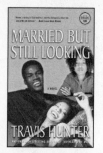

Married but Still Looking

Genesis Styles has a problem: He has never been satisfied with just one woman. Then he meets Terri and everything changes. Sort of.

Trouble Man

Almost thirty years old, Jermaine Banks realizes it's time to change. But can he step up to the challenge?

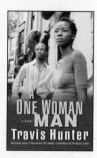

One Woman Man

Dallas Dupree was a one woman man, but the love of his life is gone forever. Back in the dating game, he ends up playing with the wrong woman, who may cost him much more than he can afford.

Name _____ Date _____

Short Vowels *a, i*

Henry and Mudge
Phonics: Short Vowels *a, i*

Write labels on the groceries. Use words from the Word Bank.

Word Bank

milk	bran	mints
jam	yams	ham

© Houghton Mifflin Harcourt Publishing Company. All rights reserved.

Short Vowels *a, i*

Sort the Spelling Words. Put words with short *a* in one column and words with short *i* in the other column.

Spelling Words
Basic Words
1. sad
2. dig
3. jam
4. glad
5. list
6. win
7. flat
8. if
9. fix
10. rip
11. kit
12. mask
Review Words
13. as
14. his

Short *a*

1. _____

2. _____

3. _____

4. _____

5. _____

6. _____

Short *i*

7. _____

8. _____

9. _____

10. _____

11. _____

12. _____

13. _____

14. _____

Write two more words that have the short *a* and short *i* sounds.
Write the words on the lines.

Short *a*

15. _____

16. _____

Short *i*

17. _____

18. _____

Name __Royce__   Date _____

Predicates

Henry and Mudge
Grammar: Subjects and Predicates

> - A **predicate** is the action part of a sentence.
> - A predicate tells what the subject in a sentence does or did.
> - The action part of a sentence uses words that show action.
>
> David (hides toys.)

Thinking Question
What does someone or something in the sentence do?

✏️ **Circle the word or words to finish each sentence.**

1. Sydney _____looks for clues_____

   (looks for clues)   for clues

2. Tara _____.

   house   (goes into the house)

3. The children _____.

   (act like spies)   spies

4. The kids _____.

   clues   (follow their clues)

5. Everyone _____.

   the toys   (finds the toys)

Focus Trait: Elaboration
Adding Details

Without Details	With Details
Jackie's dog liked to play.	Jackie's dog liked to chase sticks and play catch.

Read each sentence without details added. Then rewrite the sentence, using the details in ( ).

1. It was rainy. (morning, with a cold wind)

_____

2. I took my dog for a walk. (in the park, Duke)

_____

3. I got dressed. (in boots, a raincoat, a big hat)

_____

4. We walked to a place. (near my school, in the park)

_____

5. Duke jumped. (big, into a mud puddle)

_____

Name _____ Date _____

Lesson 1
READER'S NOTEBOOK

Henry and Mudge
Phonics: CVC Syllable Pattern

CVC Words

Finish writing the name of the picture. One syllable is
written for you.

1.

pic _____

2.

_____ bit

3.

_____ zag

4.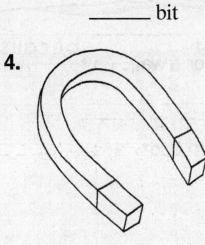

mag _____

5.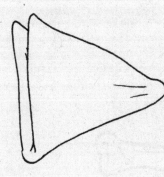

ban _____

6.

_____ kin

Reader's Guide

Henry and Mudge

Henry's Journal

Hi, I'm Henry. I started a journal about getting a dog.
Help me finish each entry. Use examples from the text
and illustrations to help show how I felt.

Read pages 16–17. How did I feel at the beginning of the story?

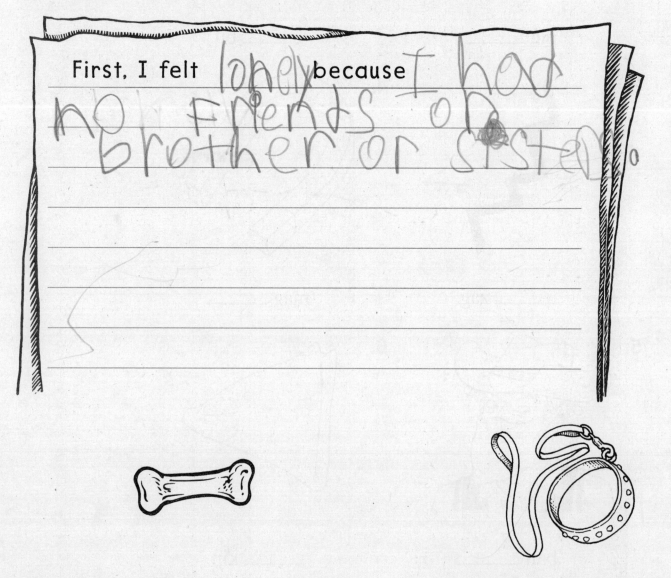

First, I felt lonely because I had no friends or a brother or sister.

Read page 19. How did I feel after my parents said I could get a dog?

Next, I felt HaPAY because We getting a Dog.

Read pages 22–25. How did I feel after Mudge grew up?

Last, I felt excitd because Mudge is the best Dog ever.

Henry and Mudge
Spelling: Short Vowels *a, i*

Short Vowels *a, i*

Write the Spelling Word that answers each question.

1. What do you put on bread? _____

2. What do you do with a shovel? _____

3. What do you wear to look like someone else?

_____

4. What do all teams like to do? _____

5. What word tells that something belongs to a boy?

_____

6. What is a tire with no air in it? _____

7. What do you write before you go to the store?

_____

8. What do you do when something is broken? _____

9. What is a word that means *happy*? _____

10. What is a word that means *not happy*? _____

Spelling Words

Basic Words
1. sad
2. dig
3. jam
4. glad
5. list
6. win
7. flat
8. if
9. fix
10. rip
11. kit
12. mask

Review Words
13. as
14. his

Proofread for Spelling

Henry and Mudge
Spelling: Short Vowels *a, i*

Proofread the sign below. Cross out the four misspelled words. Then write the correct spellings on the lines below.

Welcome to Our Berry Patch!

We're glid to have you! You can pick your own.
Buy our canning cit, and make your
own jamm. Just ask iff you need help.

Basic Words
1. sad
2. dig
3. jam
4. glad
5. list
6. win
7. flat
8. if
9. fix
10. rip
11. kit
12. mask

1. _____   3. _____

2. _____   4. _____

Change the first letter in each word to make a Basic Word.

5. mix _____

6. sip _____

7. slat _____

8. tin _____

Articles

Write the correct article to complete each sentence.

1. Her dog is _____ beagle.

   a, an

2. They fed my horse _____ carrots.

   the, an

3. My favorite pet is _____ cat.

   a, an

4. We saw _____ alligator at the zoo.

   a, an

5. Did you see _____ parrots?

   the, a

Connect to Writing

Short Sentences

Pedro collected toys. Janie collected toys.

New Sentence with Joined Subjects

Pedro and Janie collected toys.

Read each pair of sentences. Use *and* to join the two subjects. Write the new sentence.

1. Miguel wanted to help kids.

   Anna wanted to help kids.

   _____

2. Mom picked up toys.

   Dad picked up toys.

   _____

3. Tyler wrapped toys.

   Max wrapped toys.

   _____

4. Emma took the toys to the shelter.

   Jack took the toys to the shelter.

   _____

5. The children clapped.

   The parents clapped.

   _____

Short Vowels *o, u, e*

Word Bank

tent	skunk	nest	stem
hump	frog	spot	

Write the picture names in the puzzle.

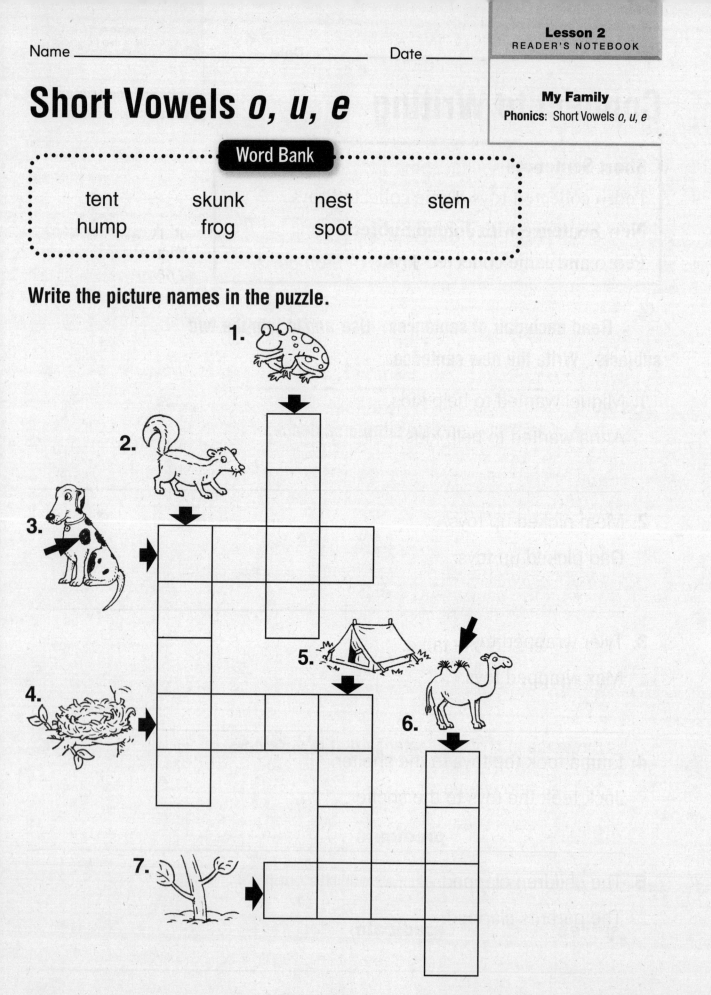

Is It a Sentence?

- A sentence tells what someone or something does or did.
- A **complete simple sentence** has a subject (naming part) and a predicate (action part).

Grandma makes a soup.

Subject: Grandma

Predicate: makes a soup

Thinking Question
What is the subject, or naming part, and what is the predicate, or action part?

Underline each complete simple sentence.

1. Chops peppers.

Harry chops peppers.

2. Stirs the soup.

Nan stirs the soup.

3. My brother sets the table.

My brother.

Circle the part of the sentence that is missing.

4. Grandma and Mama _____.

subject   **predicate**

5. _____ eat the soup.

subject   **predicate**

Name _____ Date _____

Short Vowels *o, u, e*

Word Bank

stop   bump   left
plug   step   up

Write the words on the correct signs.

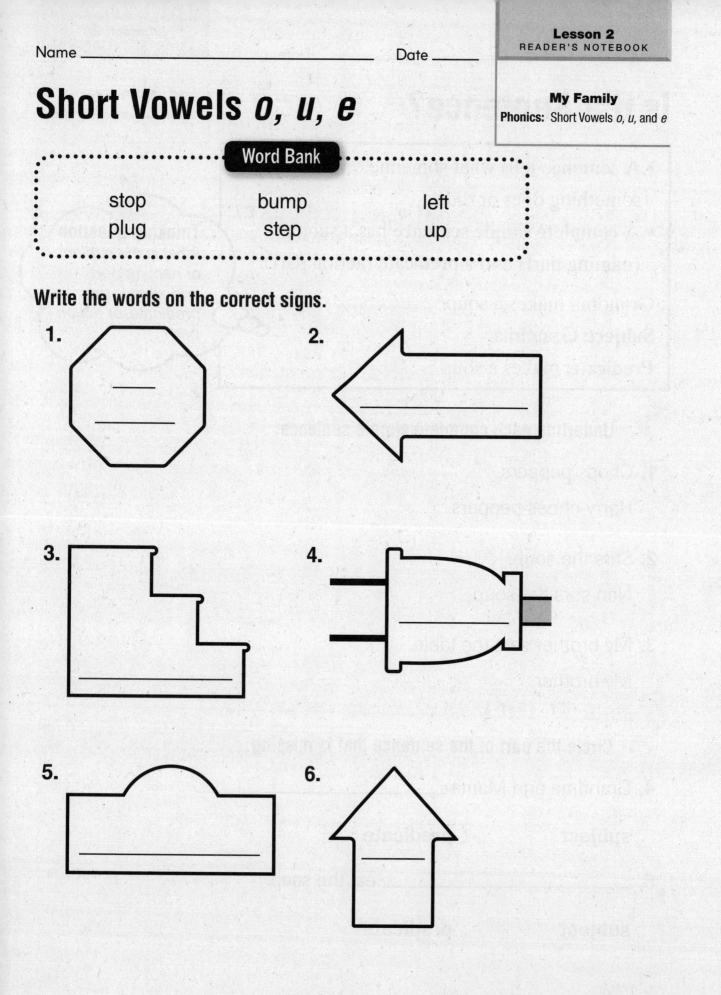

1.

2.

3.

4.

5.

6.

Short Vowels *o, u, e*

Short *o*   Short *u*   Short *e*

Sort the Spelling Words by the short vowel sounds *o, u, e*.

Short *o*	Short *u*	Short *e*
1. _____	5. _____	9. _____
2. _____	6. _____	10. _____
3. _____	7. _____	11. _____
4. _____	8. _____	12. _____
		13. _____
		14. _____

Write two more short vowel sound words that you know.

15. short *o* _____ _____

16. short *u* _____ _____

17. short *e* _____ _____

Spelling Words

Basic Words
1. wet
2. job
3. hug
4. rest
5. spot
6. mud
7. left
8. help
9. plum
10. nut
11. net
12. hot

Review Words
13. get
14. not

Word Order in Sentences

My Family
Grammar: Simple Sentences

- When a sentence tells something, the subject comes first.
- The predicate of a sentence comes next.

Thinking Question
Is the first part of the sentence the naming part?

Incorrect Word Order	Correct Word Order
Told stories we.	We told stories.

✏️ **Draw a line under each sentence that has the correct word order.**

1. The family eats snacks.

2. Louisa baked a cake.

3. Blows out candles Nick.

4. The children play games.

5. All eat together we.

6. Papa opened gifts.

7. So much he enjoyed them.

8. They ate dessert later.

My Family
Writing: Narrative Writing

Focus Trait: Development
Expressing Feelings

Without Feelings	With Feelings
My grandma comes to visit on weekends.	**It's always so much fun when** my grandma comes to visit on weekends.

A. Read each sentence. Add words and details to show feelings.

Without Feelings	Feelings Added
1. I liked to help cook dinner.	_____ to help cook dinner.
2. We talk and work hard.	We _____ and work hard.

B. Read each sentence. Then rewrite it to add feelings.

Without Feelings	Feelings Added
3. I live with my family.	
4. I write stories.	
5. I had dinner at my friend Adam's house.	

Review CVC Words

Say the picture name. Draw a line between the syllables.

1.

d e n t i s t

2.

b o b c a t

3.

p e n c i l

4.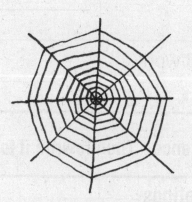

c o b w e b

5.

m a s c o t

6.

l a p t o p

Reader's Guide

My Family

Thank You Notes to My Family

I am Camila. I want to write notes to thank my family. You can help me write the notes. Use examples from the text and photographs to show how each family member is special to me.

Read page 45. Think about what makes Mom special to me.

Dear Mom,

_____

_____

Love, Camila

Read page 46. Think about what makes Grandma Marta special to me.

Dear Grandma Marta,

_____

_____

Love, Camila

Read page 52. Think about what makes Aunt Martica special to me.

Dear Aunt Martica,

_____

_____

_____

_____

Love, Camila

Read page 57. Think about what makes Papi special to me.

Dear Papi,

_____

_____

_____

_____

Love, Camila

Name _____ Date _____

Short Vowels *o, u, e*

**Read the first sentence. Then write the correct
Spelling Word to complete the second sentence.**

1. The day was very sunny. It was _____.

2. The dirt was wet. We stepped in _____.

3. I often eat a purple fruit. I eat a _____.

4. My mom wrapped her arms around me. She gave

   me a _____.

5. I forgot my umbrella. I got all _____.

Write the Spelling Word that matches each clue.

6. A working word that starts with *j.* _____

7. You eat this word that rhymes with *shut.* _____

8. This is another word for *stain.* _____

9. It is the opposite of *right,* but is not wrong. _____

10. This sleepy word rhymes with *test.* _____

Spelling Words

**Basic
Words**
1. wet
2. job
3. hug
4. rest
5. spot
6. mud
7. left
8. help
9. plum
10. nut
11. net
12. hot

**Review
Words**
13. get
14. not

Run-On Sentences

Read each sentence. Decide if it is one run-on sentence or two complete simple sentences. Circle the correct answer.

1. My cousins played soccer. Then they went swimming.

   run-on sentence   complete simple sentences

2. We play in the backyard we dug holes.

   run-on sentence   complete simple sentences

3. Angel and I like to play together we are best friends.

   run-on sentence   complete simple sentences

4. Uncle Manuel works long hours. He is a doctor.

   run-on sentence   complete simple sentences

Rewrite each run-on sentence as two simple complete sentences.

5. My sister learned to dance she took a class.

   _____

6. She practices a lot every day she goes to the gym.

   _____

7. Sometimes I like to watch her I go with her to class.

   _____

Name _____ Date _____

Lesson 2
READER'S NOTEBOOK

My Family
Vocabulary Strategies:
Using a Glossary

Using a Glossary

**Read each glossary entry. Then use the definitions
to write an example sentence for each word.**

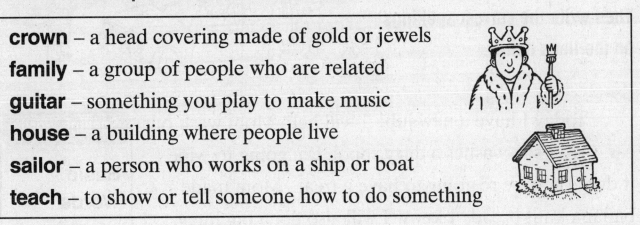

crown – a head covering made of gold or jewels

family – a group of people who are related

guitar – something you play to make music

house – a building where people live

sailor – a person who works on a ship or boat

teach – to show or tell someone how to do something

1. sailor

_____

2. house

_____

3. guitar

_____

4. crown

_____

5. teach

_____

6. family

_____

Proofread for Spelling

Proofread the journal entry.
Circle the four misspelled words.
Then write the correct spellings
on the lines below.

Today I have a new jub! I will help Mom wash our
car. After she washes a dirty sppot, I'm going to wipe
it dry. Then we're going to have a treat. Mom made
banana knut bread. I know I will also get a big hugg.

1. _____   3. _____

2. _____   4. _____

Spelling Words

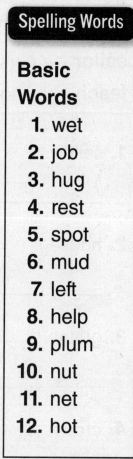

Basic Words

1. wet
2. job
3. hug
4. rest
5. spot
6. mud
7. left
8. help
9. plum
10. nut
11. net
12. hot

Use the code to spell the Spelling Words.

1 = a	2 = b	3 = c	4 = d	5 = e
6 = f	7 = g	8 = h	9 = i	10 = j
11 = k	12 = l	13 = m	14 = n	15 = o
16 = p	17 = q	18 = r	19 = s	20 = t
21 = u	22 = v	23 = w	24 = x	25 = y	26 = z

5. 16, 12 , 21, 13 _____

6. 13, 21, 4 _____

7. 8, 5, 12, 16 _____

8. 12, 5, 6, 20 _____

Subjects

✏️ **Draw a line under the subject in each sentence.**

1. Grandma and Grandpa came to visit.

2. The whole family went on a picnic.

3. The park was crowded.

4. The day was warm and sunny.

✏️ **Write a subject to complete each sentence.**

5. _____ was friendly.

6. _____ took the bus.

Connect to Writing

Not Complete Sentences

Walks me to school. Uncle Luis.

Complete Sentences

My brother walks me to school.

Uncle Luis picks me up.

Read each word group. Add a subject or a predicate to each group to make a complete sentence. Use the words in the box.

Mom	Aunt Rose
brings us gifts	My sister
makes me laugh	

1. Uncle Luis _____.

2. _____ helps me do homework.

3. _____ sings to me.

4. Papa _____.

5. _____ cooks me dinner.

Name _____ Date _____

Long Vowels *a, i*

Dogs
Phonics: Long Vowels *a, i*

Word Bank

time	nice	like
slice	cake	bake

Write the word from the Word Bank that completes the sentence.

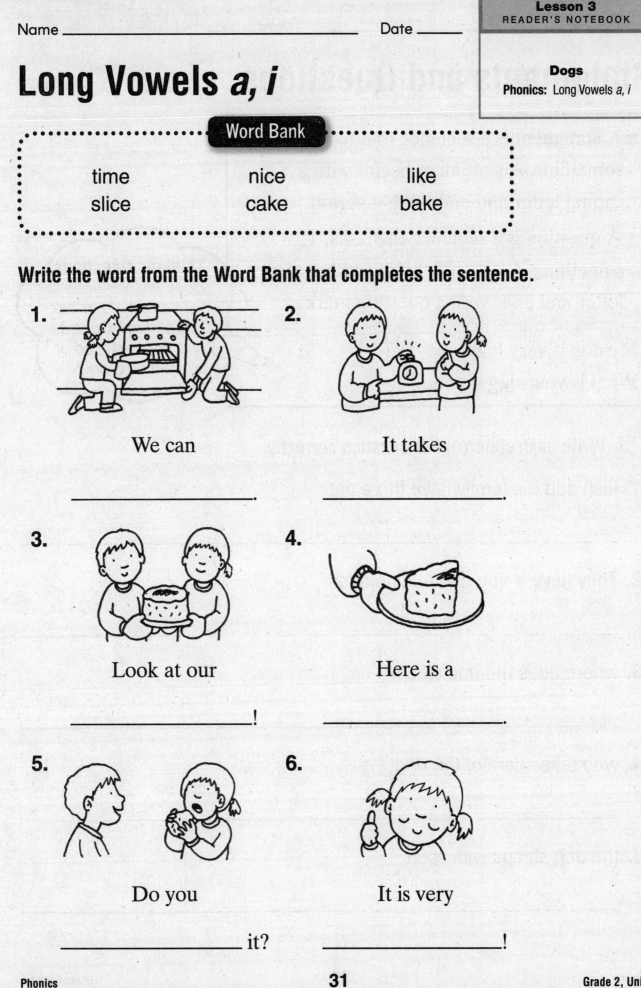

1. We can

_____.

2. It takes

_____.

3. Look at our

_____!

4. Here is a

_____.

5. Do you

_____ it?

6. It is very

_____!

Statements and Questions

Dogs
Grammar: Types of Sentences

- A **statement** is a sentence that tells something. A statement begins with a capital letter and ends with a period.

- A **question** is a sentence that asks something. A question begins with a capital letter and ends with a question mark.

My dog is very big.
What is your dog's name?

Thinking Questions
Does the sentence tell something or ask something? Does it end with a period or a question mark?

✎ **Write each statement or question correctly.**

1. josh and his family have three pets

_____

2. They have a dog and two goldfish

_____

3. where does the dog sleep

_____

4. who takes care of the dog

_____

5. the dog sleeps with Josh

_____

Long Vowels *a, i*

Write the words where they belong. Then write four
more words of your own in each column.

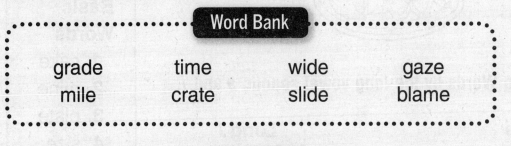

Word Bank

grade	time	wide	gaze
mile	crate	slide	blame

a_e as in *skate*   **i_e as in *pride***

1. _____   9. _____

2. _____   10. _____

3. _____   11. _____

4. _____   12. _____

5. _____   13. _____

6. _____   14. _____

7. _____   15. _____

8. _____   16. _____

Long Vowels *a, i*

Spelling Words

Basic Words
1. cake
2. mine
3. plate
4. size
5. ate
6. grape
7. prize
8. wipe
9. race
10. line
11. pile
12. rake

Review Words
13. gave
14. bike

Sort the Spelling Words by the long vowel sounds *a* and *i*.

Long *a*

1. _____
2. _____
3. _____
4. _____
5. _____
6. _____
7. _____

Long *i*

8. _____
9. _____
10. _____
11. _____
12. _____
13. _____
14. _____

Write the spelling pattern that answers each question.

15. What spelling pattern do you see in words with the

long *a* sound? _____

16. What spelling pattern do you see in words with the

long *i* sound? _____

Commands

- A **command** is a sentence that gives an order.

- A command begins with a capital letter and ends with a period.

Bring your dog to school.

Thinking Question
Does the sentence give an order, begin with a capital letter, and end with a period?

✏ **Write each command correctly.**

1. give the dog a treat

_____

2. take your dog to the park

_____

3. teach your dog a trick

_____

4. find a collar for the dog

_____

5. keep your dog quiet

_____

Focus Trait: Elaboration
Sense Words

Without Sense Words	Sense Words Added
I run across the grass.	I run across the <u>wet</u> grass and <u>feel the hot sun.</u>

Read each sentence below. Rewrite each sentence to include sense words.

Without Sense Words	Sense Words Added
1. <u>Outside my window there is a flag.</u>	
2. <u>The bat hits the baseball.</u>	
3. <u>The snow lies on the ground.</u>	
4. <u>The wind blows.</u>	
5. <u>We ate a good dinner.</u>	

Name _____ Date _____

Lesson 3
READER'S NOTEBOOK

Dogs
Phonics: Hard and Soft Sounds
for *c*

Sounds for *c*

Complete the sentences about Cal and Cindy. Use words from the box.

Use words with the /k/ sound for *c* for Cal. Use words with the /s/ sound for *c* for Cindy.

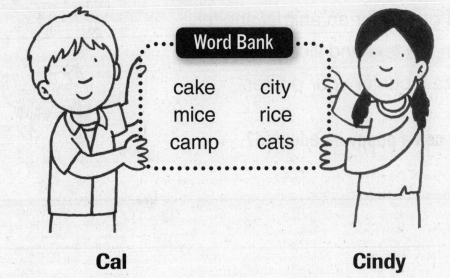

Word Bank

cake	city
mice	rice
camp	cats

Cal

1. Cal has two pet

_____.

2. Cal likes to eat

_____.

3. Cal went to a big

_____.

Cindy

4. Cindy has two pet

_____.

5. Cindy likes to eat

_____.

6. Cindy went to a big

_____.

Dogs

Create an Adopt-a-Dog Poster

Did you like learning about dogs? Use what you
learned to create a poster for an animal shelter.
Use examples from the text and illustrations
to help you organize facts for your poster.

Read page 79. When can a puppy be adopted?

_____

_____

Read page 85. What do dogs eat?

_____

_____

Read page 86. What do you need to care for a dog?

_____

_____

Read page 88. How do you take care of a dog?

_____

Use the four questions and answers to complete each box in the poster. Remember to write a title for your poster.

Name _____   Date _____

Long Vowels *a, i*

Dogs
Spelling: Long Vowels *a, i*

Write a Spelling Word for each picture.

1. _____

2. _____

3. _____

4. _____

5. _____

6. _____

Basic Words
1. cake
2. mine
3. plate
4. size
5. ate
6. grape
7. prize
8. wipe
9. race
10. line
11. pile
12. rake

Review Words
13. gave
14. bike

Write the Spelling Word that best completes each sentence.

7. Jed won first place in the _____.

8. The mail is in a _____ on the table.

9. Is that your coat or _____?

10. I think I _____ too much pasta.

Exclamations

- An **exclamation** is a sentence that shows strong feeling.
- An exclamation begins with a capital letter and ends with an exclamation point.

That dog saved the day!

Thinking Questions
Does the sentence show strong feeling? Does it end with an exclamation point?

Write each exclamation correctly.

1. People like my dog

_____

2. he is the smartest dog I know

_____

3. My dog chewed my friend's shoe to bits

_____

4. her dog had puppies

_____

5. Those dogs run so fast

_____

Multiple-Meaning Words

Read both definitions of each word. Then read the sentence. Put a checkmark next to the definition that best matches the meaning of the underlined word.

1. **pet** 1 an animal kept at home ☐
       2 stroke or pat gently ☐

Which do you think makes a better <u>pet</u>, a cat or a dog?

2. **pick** 1 take something with your hands ☐
        2 choose something or someone ☐

Joe will <u>pick</u> four people to be on his team.

3. **cool** 1 cold ☐
        2 neat and interesting ☐

The winter air was <u>cool</u> and windy.

4. **kid** 1 a child or young person ☐
      2 a young goat ☐

I have liked to read since I was a <u>kid</u>.

5. **raise** 1 move or lift something higher ☐
         2 make an amount or number bigger ☐

Mr. Jones goes outside to <u>raise</u> the flag at school each morning.

Name _____ Date _____

Proofread for Spelling

**Proofread the story. Circle the six misspelled words.
Then write the correct spellings on the lines below.**

I was working in the yard when Jake and Ken stopped by with a new byke.

"Is it yours?" I asked Ken.

"No," Jake said. "It's mien. Do you want to rase?"

"Yeah, let's!" I answered. I took my rak and made a starting lyne in the dirt. "Ken, you be the judge and give the winner a prise!"

1. _____   4. _____

2. _____   5. _____

3. _____   6. _____

Change one letter in each word to make a Spelling Word.

7. ripe _____   10. ape _____

8. slate _____   11. lake _____

9. side _____   12. tile _____

Spelling Words

Basic Words
1. cake
2. mine
3. plate
4. size
5. ate
6. grape
7. prize
8. wipe
9. race
10. line
11. pile
12. rake

Review Words
13. gave
14. bike

Predicates

Draw a line under the predicate in each sentence.

1. Her dog ran to greet her.

2. They raised three dogs.

3. We feed our dog eggs.

4. I took my dog for a walk.

Write a predicate to complete each sentence.

5. The vet _____.

6. The puppies _____.

Connect to Writing

> **Statement:** Dave is happy walking his dog.
> **Question:** Is Dave walking his dog?
> **Command:** Walk the dog.
> **Exclamation:** Dave loves walking his dog!

Change each sentence to another kind of sentence.
The word in ( ) tells what kind of sentence to write.

1. Carlo's dog likes to play catch. (question)

_____

2. Does her dog know how to sit up? (statement)

_____

3. Feed the dog. (question)

_____

4. My dog is a good pet. (exclamation)

_____

5. You need to give the dog a bath. (command)

_____

6. Call your dog. (statement)

_____

Long Vowels *o, u, e*

Read the words in the box. Cross out the words with short vowels. Use the words that are left to complete the jokes.

mole	home	stamp
Luke	blond	rust
hunt	Ken	mask
rose	stone	nose
nest	broke	

What do you get if you toss a big

s_____ into a little lake?

A wet stone!

What smells best at

Jen's h_____?

Jen's n_____!

What did the m_____

say to the r_____?

Hi Bud!

What did L_____ say

when he b_____ his leg

in two spots?

I will never go back
to those two spots!

Nouns for People and Animals

> A **noun** is a word that names a person or animal. A noun can name one or more than one.
> A <u>spider</u> spins a web.

Thinking Question
Which word names a person or animal?

✏ **Read each sentence. Write the noun that names a person or animal.**

1. The bee plays on the swings.

_____

2. The girls run away.

_____

3. An ant walks on the picnic blanket.

_____

4. The boy eats his lunch.

_____

5. The butterfly has a birthday.

_____

6. The leaf fell on two caterpillars.

_____

Long Vowels *o, u, e*

Add *e* to finish each word.

Then use the words in the puzzle.

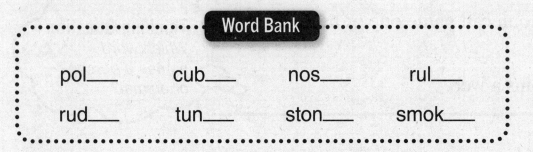

Word Bank

pol___   cub___   nos___   rul___

rud___   tun___   ston___   smok___

Across

2. what to do or not do

4. rock

5. a flag is on it

7. can be made of ice

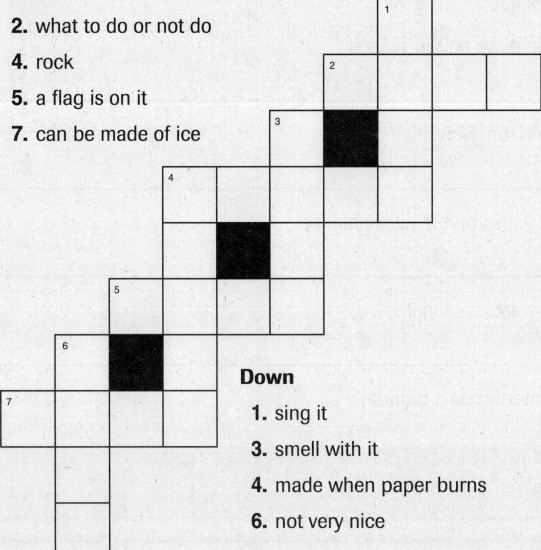

Down

1. sing it

3. smell with it

4. made when paper burns

6. not very nice

Name _____ Date _____

Long Vowels *o, u*

Sort the Spelling Words by the long vowel sounds *o* and *u*.

Spelling Words
Basic Words
1. doze
2. nose
3. use
4. rose
5. pole
6. close
7. cute
8. woke
9. mule
10. rode
11. role
12. tune
Review Words
13. home
14. joke

Long *o*

1. _____

2. _____

3. _____

4. _____

5. _____

6. _____

7. _____

8. _____

9. _____

10. _____

11. _____

12. _____

Long *u*

13. _____

14. _____

15. _____

16. _____

17. _____

18. _____

Add two words you know with the long *o* sound to the list. Then add two words you know with the long *u* sound.

Nouns for Places and Things

- Not all nouns name people and animals.

- Nouns also name **places** and **things**.

Spider went to a <u>party</u>.

Thinking Question
Which word names a place or thing?

✏ **Write the noun that names the place or thing.**

1. Ladybug ate a cookie.

_____

2. Beetle baked a pie.

_____

3. Ant went to the store.

_____

4. Butterfly writes a song.

_____

5. The soup spilled on the bees.

_____

6. Fly loves a party.

_____

Focus Trait: Development
Main Idea

All of the sentences in a paragraph should be about the main idea. Below, the writer crossed out a sentence because it was not about the main idea.

Main idea: I went to the park with my sister today.

     I went to the park with my sister today. We tried the seesaw. It didn't work. ~~Grampa says that in his day, flies and spiders did not get along.~~ We tried the tire swing. It didn't work, either.

Read the main idea and the details below it. Cross out the detail sentence that does not tell more about the main idea.

1. **Main idea:** I'm sleeping over at my friend's house.

   After dinner, we will watch a movie.

   We will stay up late.

   I forgot my homework today.

   We will tell scary stories.

2. **Main idea:** A big storm is coming this way.

   The wind is blowing things around.

   My friends like to swim in a pool.

   The sky is getting dark.

   Cold rain has already started.

Hard and Soft Sounds for *g*

Complete the sentences. Use words from the box.

Word Bank

garden	magic	dig	gave
gate	huge	giant	

1. Today Granny _____ me some
seeds.

2. Now we can start a _____.

3. We start work next to the _____.

4. We will _____ before we plant the seeds.

5. Granny says seeds are like _____.

6. A little seed grows into a _____ plant.

7. I hope our plants grow as big as a _____!

Name _____ Date _____

Diary of a Spider

An Interview with Fly

Hello. I'm Fly. I am best friends with Spider. Do you
want to know what it is like to have a spider for a
friend? Find examples from the text and illustrations
to learn about my friendship with Spider.

Read page 109. What do you learn about the friendship on this page?

Spider and Fly _____

_____

Read pages 108 and 118. Look at the illustrations.
What do you learn about spiders and flies on this page?

Spiders eat _____ and flies eat with _____

Read pages 118 and 119. What do you learn about the friendship on this page?

Spider _____

Read page 128. What do you learn about the friendship on this page?

Spider and Fly are friends, because _____

_____

Name _____ Date _____

A newspaper is interviewing me about my friendship with Spider. Use what you learned to answer their questions.

What do you and Spider like to do?

Spider and I like to _____

_____

What problems do you and Spider have?

Spider and I _____

_____

Why is it nice to have a spider as a friend?

Spider helps me _____

_____

What is the secret to your friendship?

Spider and I take time _____

_____

Long Vowels *o, u*

Write the Spelling Word that belongs in each group.

1. horse, donkey, _____

2. music, song, _____

3. daisy, sunflower, _____

4. actor, play, _____

5. ears, eyes, _____

6. house, apartment, _____

7. funny, laugh, _____

8. stick, rod, _____

9. sleep, nap, _____

Read the word or words. Write the Spelling Word that means the opposite.

10. throw away _____

11. open _____

12. slept _____

Spelling Words

Basic Words

1. doze
2. nose
3. use
4. rose
5. pole
6. close
7. cute
8. woke
9. mule
10. rode
11. role
12. tune

Review Words

13. home
14. joke

Name _____ Date _____

Kinds of Nouns

✏️ **Write the noun that names a person or animal in each sentence.**

1. The girl sees a web.

_____

2. The boy screams!

_____

3. The spider scurries away.

_____

4. The grass tickled the dog.

_____

✏️ **Write the noun that names a place or thing.**

5. Spider carries a suitcase.

_____

6. Beetle puts on his hat.

_____

7. The snow fell on the bugs.

_____

8. The bugs move inside the garage.

_____

Lesson 4
READER'S NOTEBOOK

Diary of a Spider
Vocabulary Strategies:
Context Clues

Context Clues

Read the sentences. Use context clues to figure out the meaning of the underlined words. Circle the definition that best matches the meaning of the word.

1. We <u>travel</u> to many countries. Sometimes we travel by plane. Sometimes we travel by ship.

   a. to eat

   b. to go on a trip

   c. to grow

2. I want to <u>learn</u> how to play the piano. A piano teacher can teach me to play.

   a. to get knowledge

   b. to read about something

   c. to see

3. Cats run away when dogs <u>scare</u> them.

   a. to yell loudly

   b. to jump or skip

   c. to make someone feel afraid

4. Julio <u>brought</u> his folder home in his backpack.

   a. forgot something

   b. carried something

   c. hid something

Proofread for Spelling

Diary of a Spider
Spelling: Long Vowels *o, u*

Proofread the announcement. Cross out the four misspelled words. Then write them correctly in the margin.

Classmates! Can you carry a toone? Do you have a noze for talent? Try out for a roll in this year's play. We can youse you!

Circle the six Spelling Words in the Word Search. Then write the words below.

X	P	E	W	U	M	V	S	R
H	R	Q	A	C	U	T	E	O
C	L	O	S	E	L	V	D	S
E	X	U	Z	S	E	W	F	E
Z	W	Y	P	B	Q	F	R	J
W	O	K	E	V	P	O	L	E

1. _____   4. _____

2. _____   5. _____

3. _____   6. _____

Spelling Words

1. doze
2. nose
3. use
4. rose
5. pole
6. close
7. cute
8. woke
9. mule
10. rode
11. role
12. tune

Review Words
13. home
14. joke

Statements and Questions

Write Statement or Question to identify each sentence.

1. The web is in my tree. _____

2. Did Mom say the web is hers? _____

3. Who said the next bug is mine? _____

4. You can share my tasty treat. _____

Write each statement or question correctly.

5. who likes the spider's web

_____

6. it looks like my web

_____

Connect to Writing

Noun	Exact Noun
animal	spider
place	park

Replace each underlined word with an exact noun from the Word Box below.

The spiders have a picnic. Every bug at the picnic brings some food. Beetle brings <u>food</u>. Caterpillar brings
1

<u>drink</u>. The party is near the <u>flowers</u>. The bugs all sing
2   3

and dance. They have a great time. <u>Insect</u> must leave
4

early. Baby Bee has flying lessons. <u>Bird</u> is the teacher.
5

Crow	roses	Bee	pasta	juice

1. _____

2. _____

3. _____

4. _____

5. _____

Name _____ Date _____

Consonant Blends with *r, l, s*

Read the words in the box. Underline the blends.
Then use the words to complete Greta's letter.

Word Bank

skate	best	cold	plane
Clare	stripes	smile	froze

Dear _____,

   Soon I will be on a

_____ to your house. I

_____ when I think of it!

How _____ is it there? I

will bring my _____ mittens.

They have _____ on them.

I hope the pond _____!

Then we can _____ on it.

              Your friend,
              Greta

One and More Than One

- A **singular** noun names one person, animal, place, or thing.
- A **plural** noun names more than one person, animal, place, or thing.
- Add **-s** to most nouns to make them plural.

She has a <u>pet</u>.   Two <u>pets</u> play.

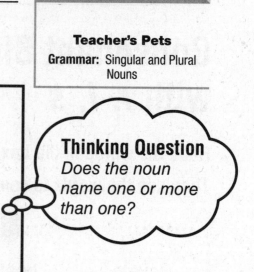

Thinking Question
Does the noun name one or more than one?

✏️ **Decide if the underlined noun is singular or plural.**

1. Many <u>students</u> have pets.

   singular   **plural**

2. One <u>cat</u> purrs softly.

   singular   **plural**

3. Some <u>crickets</u> are noisy.

   singular   **plural**

4. A <u>hamster</u> is furry.

   singular   **plural**

5. Three <u>kittens</u> play happily.

   singular   **plural**

6. The <u>teacher</u> watches quietly.

   singular   **plural**

Name _____ Date _____

Consonant Blends
with *r, l, s*

Matt can't decide! Help him by writing words from the box.
Compare your advice to a classmate's advice.

Word Bank

plums	milk	slides	sprint
frog	skate	snake	Wild West
swings	Space Trek	grin	brag

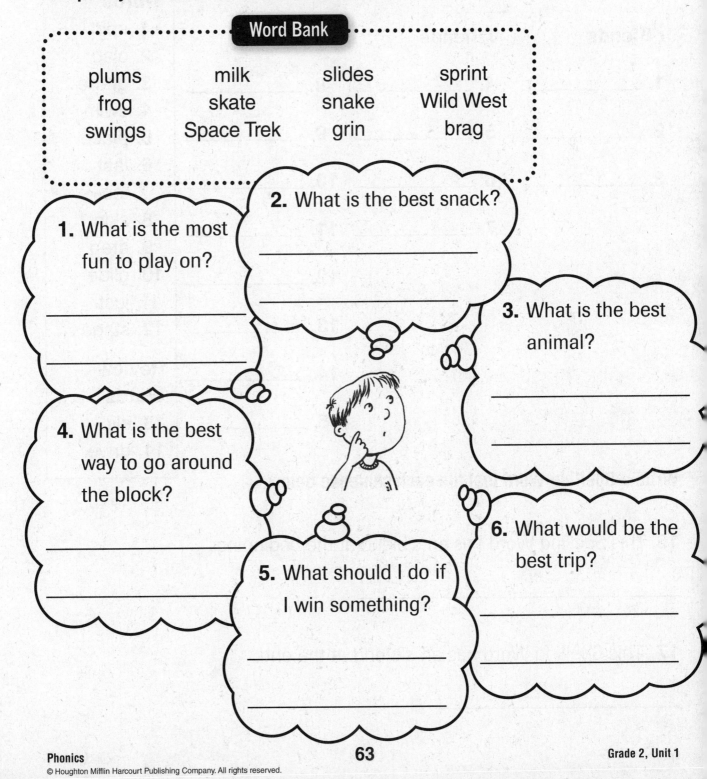

1. What is the most fun to play on?

_____

_____

2. What is the best snack?

_____

_____

3. What is the best animal?

_____

4. What is the best way to go around the block?

_____

_____

5. What should I do if I win something?

_____

_____

6. What would be the best trip?

_____

_____

Consonant Blends with *r*, *l*, *s*

Sort the Spelling Words by the consonant blends. One of the words belongs in two groups.

r Blends	*l* Blends	*s* Blends
1. _____	4. _____	8. _____
2. _____	5. _____	9. _____
3. _____	6. _____	10. _____
	7. _____	11. _____
		12. _____
		13. _____
		14. _____
		15. _____

Spelling Words

Basic Words
1. spin
2. clap
3. grade
4. swim
5. place
6. last
7. test
8. skin
9. drag
10. glide
11. just
12. stage

Review Words
13. slip
14. drive

Write a Spelling Word that fits each sentence below.

16. This Spelling Word has an *s* blend at the beginning.

_____

17. This Spelling Word has an *s* blend at the end.

_____

Making Nouns Plural

- Use **plural** nouns when you are talking about more than one.
- Add -*s* to most nouns to name more than one.

Singular	Plural
My cat drank milk.	My cats drank milk.

Thinking Question
Does the noun name one or more than one?

Change the underlined noun into a plural noun.
Write the new sentence.

1. The <u>pie</u> sat on the table.

_____

2. The <u>smell</u> filled the classroom.

_____

3. The <u>cat</u> jumped.

_____

4. The <u>plate</u> fell to the floor.

_____

5. The <u>girl</u> looked surprised.

_____

6. The <u>pet</u> ran away.

_____

Focus Trait: Organization
Time-Order Words

Time-Order Words
first, then, last, soon, next, tomorrow, later, last night, today

Read each pair of sentences. Rewrite the sentences by adding the time-order word given.

1. The puppy was tired. It sat down. (Then)

_____

2. It was getting dark outside. It would be time to go home. (Soon)

_____

_____

3. The puppy stood up. It ran home. (Next,)

_____

_____

Write two sentences. Use at least one time-order word in each sentence.

4. _____

_____

66

Cumulative Review

Read the clues. Write the correct word on the line.

1. It starts like **plan**.

   It rhymes with **lane**.

   It goes fast and high.

   What is it?

   _____

2. It starts like **slid**.

   It rhymes with **side**.

   You play on it.

   What is it?

   _____

3. It starts like **cat**.

   It rhymes with **page**.

   A pet bird can live in it.

   What is it?

   _____

4. It starts like **stop**.

   It has a long **o** sound.

   Dad makes dinner
   with it.

   What is it?

   _____

5. It starts like **gas**.

   It rhymes with **same**.

   It is fun to play.

   What is it?

   _____

6. It starts like **flag**.

   It rhymes with **cute**.

   You play a tune on it.

   What is it?

   _____

Word Bank

gold
stove
slide
game
plane
scrape
flute
cage

Reader's Guide

Teacher's Pets

Friend to Animals Award

The animal shelter gives an award called "Friend to Animals." Roger thinks Miss Fry should win the award this year. Use examples from the text and illustrations to help show why she should win.

Read page 153 to see how Miss Fry cares for the pets.

Miss Fry cares for the pets by _____

_____

Read page 156 to see how Miss Fry treats the pets.

Miss Fry _____ when Vincent does a trick.

Read page 163 to see how Miss Fry treats the pets.

Miss Fry thinks about _____.

Read page 167 to see how Miss Fry feels about her new pet.

Miss Fry feels _____ when Roger gives her Moe.

Name _____ Date _____

Design a "Friend of Pets Award" for Miss Fry.
Use what you learned from the story. On each end
of the ribbon, write a reason that Miss Fry is a friend to pets.

Friends
of Pets
Award

Miss Fry   **Miss Fry**   **Miss Fry**

_____   _____   _____

_____   _____   _____

_____   _____   _____

_____   _____   _____

_____   _____

Name _____ Date _____

Consonant Blends with *r, l, s*

Write a Spelling Word for each clue.

1. opposite of *first* _____

2. to go around fast _____

3. It covers your body. _____

4. to pull hard _____

5. to steer a car _____

6. to slide or fall _____

7. pat hands together _____

Write the Spelling Word that makes sense.

8. This word is used by actors. _____

9. This word rhymes with *rust*. _____

10. This word may be used when giving directions.

    _____

11. This word is what you do when you ice skate. _____

12. This word is something a teacher might give you in

    school. _____

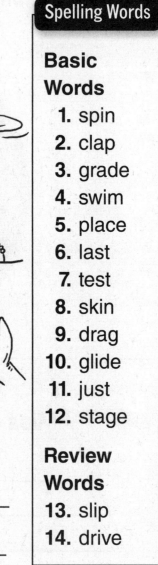

Spelling Words

Basic Words

1. spin
2. clap
3. grade
4. swim
5. place
6. last
7. test
8. skin
9. drag
10. glide
11. just
12. stage

Review Words

13. slip
14. drive

Singular and Plural Nouns

Write the sentences. Use the plural nouns.

1. Two (rabbit, rabbits) run a race.

_____

2. The (turtle, turtles) join in.

_____

3. Many (student, students) laugh.

_____

4. The (pet, pets) run as fast as they can.

_____

Change the underlined noun into a plural noun.
Write the new sentence.

5. The bird flew in the window.

_____

6. The frog jumped around the room.

_____

7. The snake hissed loudly.

_____

8. The student walked outside.

_____

Name _____ Date _____

Lesson 5
READER'S NOTEBOOK

Teacher's Pets
Vocabulary Strategies:
Word Endings -ed, -ing

Word Endings -ed, -ing

Choose the word that best completes each sentence.
Write the word on the line.

1. Troy and Chad _____ to school yesterday.

walked   **walking**

2. Vicky is _____ Tina on the phone now.

called   **calling**

3. I see two dogs _____ at that cat.

barked   **barking**

4. My grandma _____ with us last summer.

stayed   **staying**

5. Yesterday the teacher _____ us a question.

asked   **asking**

6. Dad took the key and _____ the gate.

locked   **locking**

Proofread for Spelling

Proofread the paragraph. Circle the six misspelled words. Then write the words correctly on the lines below.

> I like sports. I like to swimm, but my favorite sport is ice skating. My sister is a great skater. I juhst like to watch her glid around the ice. She is so good that people clapp when she skates. The ice is her stagge. If I had to give her a graide, it would be an *A*.

1. _____   4. _____

2. _____   5. _____

3. _____   6. _____

Make a word chain by adding to the words below. Use as many Spelling Words as you can.

S

T

A

G R A D E

E

Spelling Words

Basic Words

1. spin
2. clap
3. grade
4. swim
5. place
6. last
7. test
8. skin
9. drag
10. glide
11. just
12. stage

Review Words

13. slip
14. drive

Commands and Exclamations

Write **Command** or **Exclamation** to identify each sentence.

1. Take good care of our pet. _____

2. Tell us about your pet. _____

3. I can't believe how slow that snail is! _____

4. Our pet is the greatest pet in the school! _____

Write each command or exclamation correctly.

5. help me feed the pets

_____

6. our new pet is terrific

_____

Connect to Writing

Singular Nouns	Plural Nouns
one lizard	two lizards
a student	many students

Rewrite each sentence. Use the plural for each underlined noun.

1. We saw many <u>pet</u> at school.

_____

2. Two <u>rabbit</u> lived with the first graders.

_____

3. Some <u>duck</u> quacked in the second grade class.

_____

4. Three <u>snake</u> hissed in the third grade class.

_____

5. The fourth graders fed some <u>spider</u>.

_____

6. Many <u>animal</u> lived at the school.

_____

Common Final Blends
nd, ng, nk, nt, ft, xt, mp

Write the name of each picture. Then circle the final consonant blend.

1. _____

2. _____

3. _____

4. _____

5. _____

6. _____

7. _____

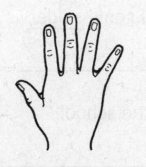

8. _____

9. _____

Adding -*es* to Nouns

- Add -*s* to most nouns to name more than one.
- Add -*es* to nouns that end with *s, x, ch,* and *sh* to name more than one.

one fox   two foxes

Two (fox, <u>foxes</u>) live in a den.

Thinking Question
Do I need a noun that names one, or a noun that names more than one?

✏️ **Write the correct noun in each sentence. Reread each sentence to make sure that the noun makes sense.**

1. The fox den is next to a _____.

(bush, bushes)

2. Mama Fox wears her _____.

(glass, glasses)

3. She makes three _____.

(lunch, lunches)

4. Papa Fox eats one _____.

(sandwich, sandwiches)

5. Baby Fox eats two _____.

(peach, peaches)

Common Final Blends
nd, ng, nk, nt, ft, xt, mp

Answer each pair of clues using the words below them.

1. Coming after: _____

Went away: _____

next   **left**

2. A small lake: _____

To be on your feet: _____

stand   **pond**

3. To take a sip: _____

Sleep in a tent: _____

camp   **drink**

4. Write letters on a page: _____

Look for something that is lost: _____

print   **hunt**

5. A tune you can sing: _____

The sound a horn makes: _____

honk   **song**

Name _____ Date _____

Final Blends *nd, ng, nk, nt, ft, xt, mp*

Animals Building Homes
Spelling: Common Final Blends
nd, ng, nk, nt, ft, xt, mp

Sort the Spelling Words by their final blends.

nd blends _____

ng blends _____

nk blends _____

nt blends _____

ft blends _____

xt blends _____

mp blends _____

Now add two words that you know to any of the lists.

Spelling

Basic Words
1. next
2. end
3. camp
4. sank
5. sing
6. drink
7. hunt
8. stand
9. long
10. stamp
11. pond
12. bring

Review Words
13. jump
14. left

Nouns That Change Spelling

Some nouns change their spelling to name more than one.

one child   two children

Two (child, <u>children</u>) find a nest.

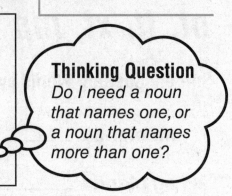

Thinking Question
Do I need a noun that names one, or a noun that names more than one?

✏ **Write the correct noun to finish each sentence. Reread each sentence to make sure that it makes sense.**

1. Two _____ take a walk.

   (child, children)

2. I soaked both my _____ .

   (foot, feet)

3. One _____ is in the pond.

   (goose, geese)

4. Many _____ stand near the hole.

   (man, men)

5. Two _____ ran into the hole.

   (mouse, mice)

Focus Trait: Purpose
Main Idea and Supporting Details

Main Idea	Supporting Details
Animals need homes.	Keep them safe from enemies. Protect them from weather. Help them raise babies.

Read each set of sentences. Underline the sentence that contains the main idea.

1. Snakes also live in holes.

   Rabbits live underground in warrens.

   Many kinds of animals live in holes.

2. Some people live in apartments.

   People live in different kinds of houses.

   Some people live in ice houses called igloos.

3. They can protect you from harm.

   Dogs make good pets.

   They are loyal.

4. Some mammals live in the water.

   Dolphins look like fish, but they are mammals.

   Sea otters are mammals that live in the Pacific Ocean.

Name _____ Date _____

Cumulative Review

Read the words in the box. Write the word that completes each sentence.

Word Bank

nest	twigs	end
spring	play	branches

1. The _____ of winter is near.

2. It is a sunny day in the _____.

3. Squirrels run and _____.

4. Buds on the _____ will open soon.

5. Two robins build a _____ in the tree.

6. They use _____ and grass to make it strong.

On the lines below, write a word that begins with the beginning blends shown.

7. br _____ 9. fr _____ 11. st _____

8. pr _____ 10. cl _____ 12. tr _____

Name _____ Date _____

Lesson 6
READER'S NOTEBOOK

Animals Building
Homes
Independent Reading

Animals Building Homes

Research Notebook

You are a scientist studying animal homes. Take notes and make sketches in your research log about the different animal homes.

Read page 196. Draw the home you read about. Then write the animal's name and answer the questions.

Animal: _____ How does this animal make its home?

_____

_____

How is the home used?

_____

_____

Read page 202. Draw the home you read about.

Write the animal's name under the drawing.

Then answer the questions.

HOME SWEET HOME

Animal: _____

How does this animal make its home?

_____

_____

How is the home used?

_____

_____

Think with a partner about what you learned. Use your notes to answer the questions.

Why do animals build homes?

_____

_____

Where do animals find materials for building? _____

_____

Final Blends *nd, ng, nk, nt, ft, xt, mp*

Use the Spelling Words to complete the story.

My dad and I like to (1) _____
out. This year, Dad let me (2) _____
my friend Jason. It was a (3) _____
drive. Dad stopped near a clear
(4) _____ .

We don't (5) _____ animals,
but we do like to fish. It was hot, so we
brought a lot of water to (6) _____ .
Dad taught us to (7) _____ old songs.
We had a great time! At the (8) _____ of
the weekend, we didn't want to go home. Jason and
I hope to go again (9) _____ year.

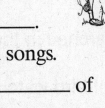

Use the Spelling Words to fill in the blanks.

10. Instead of sitting, you should _____ .

11. I need a _____ to mail my letter.

12. The ship _____ .

Spelling Words
Basic Words
1. next
2. end
3. camp
4. sank
5. sing
6. drink
7. hunt
8. stand
9. long
10. stamp
11. pond
12. bring

Collective Nouns

A **collective noun** names a group of people or things.

Our <u>class</u> reads about beavers.

 Draw a line under the collective noun in each sentence.

1. Some animals work as a team to build their homes.

2. I have a collection of feathers.

3. An army of ants marched in the sand.

4. She joined a club of bird watchers.

5. We saw a flock of birds at the pond.

Name _____ Date _____

Prefixes *un-* and *re-*

Choose the word from the box that best completes each sentence. Write the word on the line.

Word Bank

rehang	untie	rebuild	unreal
unfold	remake	unload	

1. I _____ my shoes before I take them off.

2. Please _____ the blanket and put it on the bed.

3. I know that story is true, but it is so strange that it

   seems _____!

4. The picture fell off the wall, so I have to

   _____ it.

5. My little brother messed up my bed, so I had to

   _____ it.

6. The birds used twigs to _____ their nest after it fell out of the tree.

7. I helped Mom _____ all the food from the car.

Name _____   Date _____

Proofread for Spelling

Animals Building Homes
Spelling: Common Final Blends
nd, ng, nk, nt, ft, xt, mp

Proofread the story. Circle the six misspelled words.
Then write the correct spellings on the lines below.

Spelling Words
Basic Words
1. next
2. end
3. camp
4. sank
5. sing
6. drink
7. hunt
8. stand
9. long
10. stamp
11. pond
12. bring

I needed to buy a stampe to mail my letter. I was at the end of a log line at the post office. One person in line started to sang. Another took a drenk from a water bottle. A grandpa tugged at a child and scolded, "Stad still!" I was about to give up and go home when I heard, "Nextt!" The line was finally moving.

1. _____   4. _____

2. _____   5. _____

3. _____   6. _____

Write in the letters to spell the Basic Words.

7. bri + ___ ___   9. ca + ___ ___

8. po + ___ ___   10. sa + ___ ___

Parts of a Sentence

Read each sentence. The action part has one line underneath it. Draw two lines under the naming part.

1. The cat and dog <u>live</u> in the house.

2. The puppy and kitten <u>play</u> together.

3. A man and woman <u>feed</u> them.

4. A boy and girl <u>pet</u> them.

5. An aunt and uncle <u>visit</u>.

Read each sentence. The naming part has two lines underneath it. Draw one line under the action part.

6. <u>Tigers and bears</u> sleep in caves.

7. <u>Turtles and snails</u> live in shells.

8. <u>Bees and wasps</u> make hives.

9. <u>Birds and mice</u> build nests.

10. <u>Gophers</u> dig burrows.

Connect to Writing

Short Sentences	New Sentence with Joined Subjects
Foxes live in dens. Bears live in dens.	Foxes and bears live in dens.

Short Sentences	New Sentence with Joined Subjects
Mice make their own nests. Birds make their own nests.	Mice and birds make their own nests.

Read the sentences below. Use *and* to combine their subjects. Write the new sentence on the line.

1. Geese fly to warm places in winter.
   Ducks fly to warm places in winter.

   _____

2. Seals live in cold places.
   Penguins live in cold places.

   _____

3. Squirrels use the branches of trees.
   Crows use the branches of trees.

   _____

4. Baby finches are fed in nests.
   Baby cardinals are fed in nests.

   _____

Name _____ Date _____

Lesson 7
READER'S NOTEBOOK

The Ugly Vegetables
Phonics: Double Consonants
and *ck*

Double Consonants and *ck*

Read the words below. Think about how the words in each group are alike. Write the missing word that fits in each group.

Word Bank

quack	fluff	dress	duck
mitt	kick	spill	neck

1. pants, shirt, _____

2. fish, frog, _____

3. bat, ball, _____

4. arm, leg, _____

5. tip, splash, _____

6. moo, meow, _____

7. fur, fuzz, _____

8. run, jump, _____

Write a word that rhymes with each word below.

9. stall _____   **11.** back _____

10. mess _____   **12.** will _____

The Ugly Vegetables
Grammar: Proper Nouns

Names for People, Animals, Places, and Things

Some **nouns** name special people, animals, places, or things.. These special nouns are **proper nouns**. Proper nouns begin with capital letters.

Today <u>Lanie Lin</u> plants a garden.

Thinking Question
Which word names a special person, animal, place, or thing?

Write the proper nouns correctly.

1. She gets help from maggie.

_____

2. We took a field trip to the grand canyon.

_____

3. They plant peas for eric barker.

_____

4. They eat wacky crunch crackers in the garden.

_____

5. They plant carrots for their rabbit hoppy.

_____

Name _____ Date _____

Double Consonants and *ck*

Put these letters together to write words that end with double consonants.

1. m + i + t + t = _____

2. g + l + a + s + s = _____

3. s + t + u + f + f = _____

4. b + e + l + l = _____

5. a + d + d = _____

$2 + 2 = 4$

Now use the words you made above to complete the sentences below.

6. I will fill my _____ with milk.

7. The _____ rings for class to start.

8. Pam wants to _____ all her things into one bag.

9. We will _____ your name to the list.

10. Get your bat and _____.

Name _____ Date _____

Double Consonants and *ck*

The Ugly Vegetables
Spelling: Double Consonants
and *ck*

Sort the Spelling Words. Put words that end in *ck* in one list.
Put words that end in double consonants in the other list.

Spelling Words

Basic Words

1. dress
2. spell
3. class
4. full
5. add
6. neck
7. stuck
8. kick
9. rock
10. black
11. trick
12. doll

Review Words

13. will
14. off

ck Words

1. _____
2. _____
3. _____
4. _____
5. _____
6. _____
7. _____

Double Consonant Words

8. _____
9. _____
10. _____
11. _____
12. _____
13. _____
14. _____
15. _____
16. _____

Add one more word that you know to each list.

Names for Special People and Animals

Some **nouns** name special people or animals. These are **proper nouns**. Names for people and animals begin with capital letters.

<u>Grace</u> fed her cat <u>Fluffy</u>.

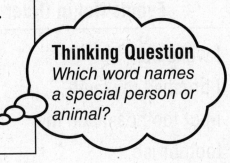

Thinking Question
Which word names a special person or animal?

✏️ **Rewrite each sentence. Write the name for each special person or animal correctly.**

1. The fitzgeralds grow flowers in their garden.

_____

2. My dog woofy is really loud.

_____

3. Our cat sandy likes to sit in the garden.

_____

4. We brought soup to mrs. crumerine.

_____

5. I like playing catch with mickey.

_____

Focus Trait: Organization
Retelling Events in Order

Events Not in Order	Events in Order
I woke up. I brushed my teeth. I put toothpaste on my toothbrush.	1. I woke up. 2. I put toothpaste on my toothbrush. 3. I brushed my teeth.

Work with a partner. Number each set of sentences in the order that makes the most sense.

1. ___ I put on my shoes.   2. ___ I had dinner.

   ___ I put on my socks.   ___ I had breakfast.

   ___ I tied my shoes.   ___ I had lunch.

Work on your own. Number each set of sentences in an order that makes sense.

3. ___ The plants started to grow.   5. ___ I went to school.

   ___ We planted seeds.   ___ I woke up.

   ___ We dug up the soil.   ___ I grabbed my lunch.

4. ___ I took out a glass.

   ___ I poured milk.

   ___ I drank the milk.

Double Consonants (CVC)

Write a word from the box to complete each sentence below.

> **Word Bank**
>
> happen   bottom   button   cotton   puppet

1. The dress is made of _____.

2. What will _____ if it starts to rain?

3. The children had fun at the _____ show.

4. The rag doll has a _____ for a nose.

5. The prize is at the _____ of the sack.

Answer each clue using a word from the box.

> **Word Bank**
>
> rabbit   kitten   hidden   mitten   muffin

6. Something good to eat _____

7. Another name for a bunny _____

8. It keeps your hand warm. _____

9. A baby cat _____

10. Hard to find _____

Reader's Guide

The Ugly Vegetables

E-mails to Grandma

Hi. I am e-mailing my Grandma to tell her about the garden. Help me finish each e-mail. Use examples from the text and illustrations to show how I feel about the garden.

Read page 233. What can I tell Grandma about the garden?

⊗ ⊖ ⊕   ✉ re: Garden

How is your garden looking?
Love, Grandma

I am _____ because our plants _____

_____

Read page 237. Now, what can I tell Grandma about the garden?

⊗ ⊖ ⊕   ✉ re: Garden

How is your garden looking today?
Love, Grandma

I am _____ because our garden _____

_____

Read page 237. What can I tell Grandma about the garden?

⊗ ⊖ ⊕   ✉ re: Garden

Now, are you excited about your garden?
Love, Grandma

I am _____ because our garden _____

_____

Read page 242. What can I tell Grandma about the garden?

⊗ ⊖ ⊕   ✉ re: Garden

How is your garden looking now?
Love, Grandma

I am _____ because our garden _____

_____

Read page 243. What can I tell Grandma about the garden?

⊗ ⊖ ⊕   ✉ re: Garden

How are you feeling about your garden?
Love, Grandma

I am _____ because _____

_____

Lesson 7
READER'S NOTEBOOK

The Ugly Vegetables
Spelling: Double Consonants
and *ck*

Double Consonants and *ck*

Write the Spelling Word for each picture.

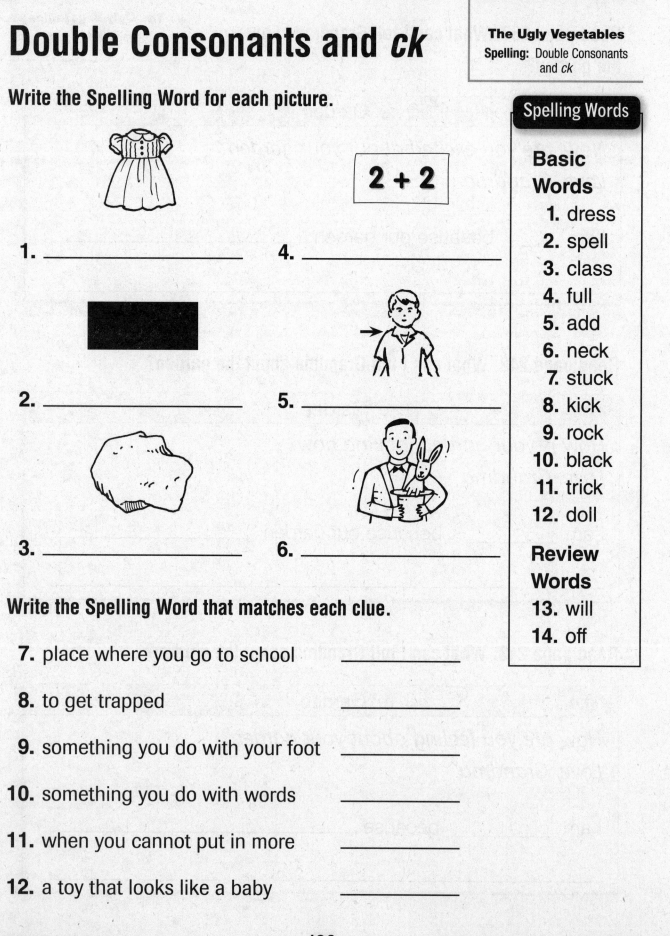

1. _____   4. _____

2. _____   5. _____

3. _____   6. _____

Spelling Words

Basic Words
1. dress
2. spell
3. class
4. full
5. add
6. neck
7. stuck
8. kick
9. rock
10. black
11. trick
12. doll

Review Words
13. will
14. off

Write the Spelling Word that matches each clue.

7. place where you go to school _____

8. to get trapped _____

9. something you do with your foot _____

10. something you do with words _____

11. when you cannot put in more _____

12. a toy that looks like a baby _____

Writing Proper Nouns

Rewrite each sentence. Write the name for each special thing correctly.

1. Sue gardens with her deep digger shovel.

_____

2. I gave my dad happy day raisins.

_____

3. I drink giggly grape juice.

_____

Rewrite each sentence. Write the name for each special place correctly.

4. Grapes grow on franklin road.

_____

5. Olives grow in italy.

_____

6. Apples grow in portland.

_____

Homophones

Word Bank

too	won	wear	plain
two	one	where	plane

Choose the word from the box that best completes the sentence. Write the word on the line.

1. The farmer has _____ shovels.

2. _____ did you put my keys?

3. I don't like stripes or spots. I only like to wear _____ clothes.

4. I am happy because my team _____ the game.

5. My sister is going to the movies. I want to go, _____!

6. I have only _____ flower in the vase.

7. What are you going to _____ to the party?

8. We will take a car to the airport, and then we will get on a _____.

Name _____ Date _____

Proofread for Spelling

**Proofread the journal entry. Circle the five misspelled words.
Then spell the words correctly on the lines below.**

Today we went on a clas trip. The first bus was
ful, so we waited for the next one. After about a block,
the bus ran over a big rouck. There was a loud noise
and then the bus stopped. The driver said that we were
stukk. He had to ad air to the tire before we could go.

1. _____

2. _____

3. _____

4. _____

5. _____

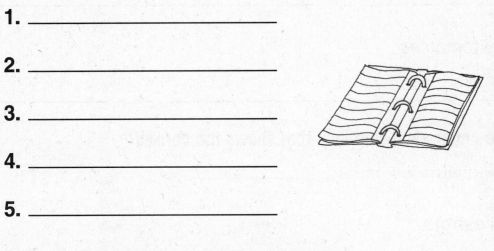

Spelling Words
Basic Words
1. dress
2. spell
3. class
4. full
5. add
6. neck
7. stuck
8. kick
9. rock
10. black
11. trick
12. doll

Unscramble the letters in each Spelling Word.

6. olld   _____

7. cablk   _____

8. ustck   _____

9. eknc   _____

10. kkic   _____

11. lwil   _____

12. elpsl   _____

Name _____ Date _____

Complete Sentences

✏️ Add a naming part or action part to each word group to make a complete sentence. Write the new sentence.

1. likes to grow pumpkins

_____

2. the farmer

_____

3. plants many tomatoes

_____

✏️ Draw a line under each sentence that shows the correct word order.

4. John grows carrots.

Grows carrots John.

5. Lori needs more seeds.

More seeds Lori needs.

6. Beans she wants to plant.

She wants to plant beans.

Connect to Writing

Sentence Without Exact Nouns	Sentence With Exact Nouns
A man plants cherry trees along a street.	Jim Brown plants cherry trees along Sweet Street.

Read the paragraph. Replace the underlined words with exact words from the word box. Write the exact words on the lines below.

Carol Ach	Magic Garden Grow	Ohio
Columbus	Sparky	Jack

A woman has a big garden. She grows the best lettuce and tomatoes in the state. She plants her garden with dirt. Her son, Jack, helps. Every summer, people come from the city to her farm stand. The son sets everything up. His dog, Sparky, looks on. The dog wags his tail every time a new customer comes by.

1. A woman _____

2. dirt _____

3. the state _____

4. the city _____

5. The son _____

6. The dog _____

Name _____ Date _____

Lesson 8
READER'S NOTEBOOK

Super Storms
Phonics: Consonant Digraphs
th, sh, wh, ch, tch, ph

Words with *th, sh, wh, ch, tch, ph*

Write a word from the box to answer each riddle.

Word Bank

math	white	fish	bath	ship
watch	chick	phone	dish	wheel

1. It can swim. It has a big fin. It is a _____.

2. It is a class in school. It uses numbers. It is

_____.

3. It comes from an egg. It has soft fluff. It is a

_____.

4. It has two hands. It tells you the time. It is a

_____.

5. It floats in the sea. Many people ride on it. It is a

_____.

6. It is on a car. It helps the car move. It is a

_____.

7. It can ring. You use it to chat with a pal. It is a

_____.

Action Verbs

A **verb** names an action that someone or something does or did.

The wind <u>blows</u> hard.

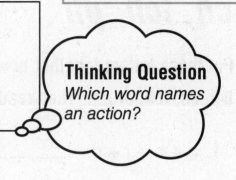

Thinking Question
Which word names an action?

Read each sentence. Underline the verb in each sentence.

1. The clouds cover the sky.

2. The rain pours down.

3. People open umbrellas.

4. Water flows down the street.

5. Soon the sun shines.

6. The children play.

7. Children splash in puddles.

8. It rains again after dinner.

9. This time everyone stays dry.

10. Everyone sits inside.

107

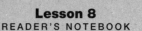

Words with *th, sh, wh, ch, tch, ph*

Put these letters together to write words with *th, sh, wh, ch, tch,* or *ph*. Then read each word.

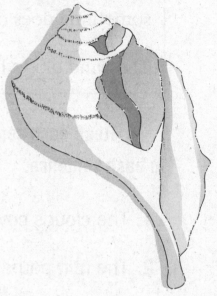

1. c + h + i + p = _____

2. s + h + e + l + l = _____

3. g + r + a + p + h = _____

4. t + h + i + n = _____

5. w + i + s + h = _____

6. w + h + i + t + e = _____

7. m + a + t + c + h = _____

8. p + a + t + h = _____

Write a word you know that begins with each pair of letters.

9. ch _____   11. sh _____

10. th _____   12. ph _____

Spelling Word Sort

Super Storms
Spelling: Consonant Digraphs *th, sh, wh, ch, tch*

Sort the Spelling Words under the headings below. If a word can sort into more than one place, choose one.

Spelling Words

Basic Words
1. dish
2. than
3. chest
4. such
5. thin
6. push
7. shine
8. chase
9. white
10. while
11. these
12. flash

Review Words
13. which
14. then

th   *sh*   *wh*

_____   _____   _____

_____   _____   _____

_____   _____   _____

_____   _____

ch

_____

_____

_____

Think about the letters *th, sh, wh,* and *ch*. Which Spelling Word could go under two of the headings above?

_____

Action Verbs and Subjects

A **verb** tells what someone or something does or did. The **subject** tells who or what is doing the action.

The hail <u>pounds</u> on the roof.

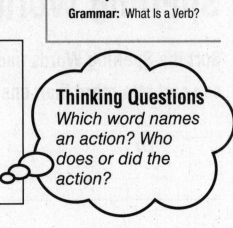

Thinking Questions
Which word names an action? Who does or did the action?

✏ **Read each sentence. The verb is underlined. Circle the subject.**

1. Jan <u>hears</u> the sounds.

2. The cat <u>hides</u> under the bed.

3. The hail <u>bounces</u> on the ground.

4. The clouds <u>turn</u> gray.

✏ **Read each sentence. The subject is circled. Underline the verb.**

5. The (air) gets cold.

6. (Dan) feels the rain.

7. The (dog) runs through puddles.

8. The (mail) stays dry.

Focus Trait: Evidence Definitions

Read each sentence. Draw a line under the definition of the word in dark type.

1. The rain shower became a **thunderstorm**, a storm with heavy rain, thunder, and lightning.

2. They were in the **eye**, or calm center, of the storm.

3. A **blizzard** is a storm with fast winds and heavy snow.

4. The ship was caught in a **hurricane**, a severe tropical storm with winds of more than seventy-five miles per hour.

5. Scientists who follow the path of a storm to study it are called **storm chasers**.

Base Words and Endings
-s, -ed, -ing

Read each word pair. Use the words to answer the clues.

1. prints   **jumps**

Hops up and down   _____

Writes words on paper   _____

2. lifting   **camping**

Pulling something up   _____

Living outside and sleeping in a tent   _____

3. packed   **checked**

Looked at something again to be sure   _____

Put things in a box or a bag   _____

4. passing   **helping**

Doing part of the work   _____

Walking by a person or place   _____

5. rested   **hunted**

Took a nap   _____

Looked for something   _____

Name _____ Date _____

Super Storms

Write a Storm Poem

Let's look at types of storms. Read the text and study the illustrations. Find details to describe the storms. Then, use those details to write a poem.

Read page 271. Describe a thunderstorm in your own words.

_____

_____

Read page 273. Describe a tornado in your own words.

_____

_____

Read pages 276–278. Describe a hurricane in your own words.

_____

_____

Read page 279. Describe a blizzard in your own words.

_____

_____

Use your notes to write a poem. Choose a storm that interests you. Answer the questions on the lines. Your answers will make a poem. When you are done, read your poem to a friend.

Which storm did you choose?	_____
What are 2 words to describe the storm?	_____, _____
What are 3 words to describe the storm's actions?	_____, _____, _____
What are 2 words that describe how you would feel in the storm?	_____, _____
What is the name of the storm?	_____

Super Storms
Spelling: Consonant Digraphs *th, sh, wh, ch, tch*

Words with *th, sh, wh, ch, tch*

Write the Spelling Word that is the opposite of each word.

1. black _____   3. now _____

2. thick _____   4. pull _____

Complete each Spelling Word with a consonant digraph.

5. di __ __   10. __ __ ile

6. su __ __   11. __ __ ase

7. __ __ est   12. __ __ ese

8. __ __ an   13. __ __ i __ __

9. fla __ __   14. __ __ ine

Spelling Words

Basic Words

1. dish
2. than
3. chest
4. such
5. thin
6. push
7. shine
8. chase
9. white
10. while
11. these
12. flash

Review Words

13. which
14. then

Action Verbs

✎ **Read each sentence. Underline the verb.**

1. The wind ended.

2. The thunder started.

3. We cover our ears.

4. We sit in the house

✎ **Read each sentence. The action verb is underlined.**
Circle the subject that is doing the action.

5. Jerry <u>peeks</u> out the window.

6. The rain <u>floods</u> the street.

7. The water <u>flows</u> down the hill.

8. The storm <u>stops</u> the next day.

Name _____   Date _____

Lesson 8
READER'S NOTEBOOK

Super Storms
Vocabulary Strategies:
Compound Words

Compound Words

Choose the word from the box that completes the compound word in each sentence. Write the word on the line.

Word Bank

light	time	fly	house
writing	shine	book	print

1. We built a dog + _____ for our new puppy to live in.

2. I have a flash + _____ in case it gets dark.

3. Please use neat hand + _____ when you do your homework.

4. Dee saw an orange butter + _____ fluttering in the garden.

5. Mark read his favorite story + _____ before bed.

6. Please don't touch the window with dirty hands. You'll leave a thumb + _____.

7. I can go out and play in the sun + _____.

8. In the summer + _____ we like to go to the pool.

Proofread for Spelling

Super Storms
Spelling: Consonant Digraphs *th,*
sh, wh, ch, tch

**Proofread the note. Circle the six misspelled words.
Then write the correct spellings on the lines below.**

Dear Mom,

    I want you to know that I broke the whitte dishe.

Whil I was trying to pulsh the door of the

chast closed, it slipped out of my hands. Spike was

covered in mud, and I was in a hurry to chese him

outside. I am sorry.

    Love,

    Matt

Spelling Words
Basic Words
1. dish
2. than
3. chest
4. such
5. thin
6. push
7. shine
8. chase
9. white
10. while
11. these
12. flash

1. _____ 4. _____

2. _____ 5. _____

3. _____ 6. _____

Unscramble the letters to make a Spelling Word.

7. cshu _____   10. shfla _____

8. ehtes _____   11. inshe _____

9. htna _____   12. nthi _____

Statements and Questions

✏️ **Read each sentence. Circle the kind of sentence it is.
Then rewrite the sentence correctly.**

1. will it rain today   statement   question

_____

2. i think it will snow   statement   question

_____

3. did you see the clouds   statement   question

_____

✏️ **Read the paragraph below. Then rewrite the
paragraph correctly. Use question marks at the end of
questions. Use periods at the end of statements. Remember
to use capital letters.**

A storm hits our town we stay in the house. What
else can we do. mom gives us popcorn Dad reads to us
When will the storm end

_____

_____

_____

_____

Connect to Writing

Sentence without Exact Verbs	Sentence with Exact Verbs
The wind <u>blew</u> the door closed.	The wind <u>slammed</u> the door closed.

Sentence without Exact Verbs	Sentence with Exact Verbs
The storm <u>goes</u> through town.	The storm <u>races</u> through town.

Read the paragraph. Replace each underlined word with an exact word from the box. Write the exact words on the lines.

pounded	stared	hid
howled	swirled	

The town was quiet. Then the wind <u>blew</u> loudly. Leaves <u>went</u> in circles. Rain <u>fell</u> on the streets. We <u>put</u> our bags under our coats. We stayed dry inside the bus stop. Then the rain stopped. We <u>looked</u> at a rainbow for a long time.

1. blew _____

2. went _____

3. fell _____

4. put _____

5. looked _____

Base Words and Endings -ed, -ing

Read the sentences. Draw a circle around each word that has the ending *-ed* or *-ing*.

1. Mom is baking a cake for dinner.

2. Dad closed the window when it started to rain.

3. The apple tasted cold and sweet.

4. Jen hoped that her cat was hiding under the bed.

5. The children went hiking last summer.

6. Todd raked the leaves into piles.

Now write each word you circled under the word that has the same ending.

chased   riding

_____   _____

_____   _____

_____   _____

_____

Adding -*s* to Verbs

A **verb** can name an action that is happening now. Add -*s* to this kind of verb when it tells about a noun that names one.

The <u>chipmunk</u> eat<u>s</u>.
The <u>chipmunks</u> eat.

Thinking Question
Does the subject, or naming part, of the sentence name one or more than one?

✏️ **Read each sentence. Then write it correctly.**

1. The squirrels (see, sees) the chipmunk.

   _____

2. The chipmunk (share, shares) food.

   _____

3. A squirrel (run, runs) down the tree.

   _____

4. More chipmunks (help, helps) the squirrels.

   _____

5. The animals (eat, eats) together.

   _____

Base Words and Endings *-ed, -ing*

Read each word. Then write the base word and ending on the lines.

1. hoped _____ + _____

2. skating _____ + _____

3. spilled _____ + _____

4. chasing _____ + _____

5. saving _____ + _____

Now complete the sentences below with the words from above.

6. Ling _____ she would get a puppy.

7. Jack is _____ his money to
   get a new mitt.

8. Maria _____ milk on her
   pink dress.

9. The boys like _____ on the
   frozen lake.

10. My cat was _____
    a mouse, but he didn't catch it.

Lesson 9
READER'S NOTEBOOK

Base Words with Endings -*ed* and -*ing*

How Chipmunk Got His Stripes
Spelling: Base Words with Endings -*ed* and -*ing*

Sort the Spelling Words by -*ed* and -*ing* endings.

-*ed* Endings

_____

_____

_____

_____

_____

_____

_____

-*ing* Endings

_____

_____

_____

_____

_____

_____

_____

Spelling Words

Basic Words
1. liked
2. using
3. riding
4. chased
5. spilled
6. making
7. closed
8. hoping
9. baked
10. hiding
11. standing
12. asked

Review Words
13. mixed
14. sleeping

Add a word you know to each list. Do you need to drop the final *e* before you add -*ed* or -*ing*?

Name _____ Date _____

Lesson 9
READER'S NOTEBOOK

Adding -*es* to Verbs

How Chipmunk Got
His Stripes
Grammar: Verbs in the Present

A **verb** can tell about an action that is happening now. Add -*es* to this kind of verb if it ends with *s, x, z, ch,* or *sh* and if it tells about a naming part that names one.

The <u>bear</u> mess<u>es</u> the leaf pile.
The <u>bears</u> mess the leaf pile.

Thinking Question
Does the subject name one or more than one?

Read each sentence. Then write it correctly.

1. The mice (fix, fixes) the pile.

_____

2. The bear (watch, watches) the mice.

_____

3. The bear (push, pushes) the pile down again.

_____

4. The mice (wish, wishes) the bear would stop.

_____

5. The bear (relax, relaxes) on the pile.

_____

Name _____ Date _____

Lesson 9
READER'S NOTEBOOK

How Chipmunk Got
His Stripes
Writing: Informative Writing

Focus Trait: Purpose
Include All Important Steps

Good instructions include all the important steps. Writers leave out steps that are not important.

Read the steps for each set of instructions. What step do you think is missing? Write the missing step.

Pouring a Glass of Milk

Put a glass on a table.

Go to the refrigerator.

Open the refrigerator door.

_____

Pour the milk carefully.

Making Toast

Get a piece of bread.

Put the bread in the toaster.

Start the toaster.

_____

_____

Spread the butter on the toast.

Name _____ Date _____

Lesson 9
READER'S NOTEBOOK

How Chipmunk Got
His Stripes
Phonics: CV Syllable Pattern

CV Syllable Pattern

Read each word. Then write the word and draw a
slash (/) between the two syllables.

1. pilot _____

2. later _____

3. lemon _____

4. hotel _____

5. tiger _____

Now use the words you wrote above to complete the
sentences below.

6. A _____ has orange fur with

black stripes.

7. Stan will add _____

to his tea.

8. The _____ sits in the front of

the plane.

9. We stayed at a big _____ by

the beach last summer.

10. Mom likes to stay up _____

than Dad does.

Name _____   Date _____

Lesson 9
READER'S NOTEBOOK

How Chipmunk Got
His Stripes
Independent Reading

Reader's Guide

How Chipmunk Got His Stripes

Write a Newspaper Article

Newspapers have many different parts. One part
is the advice column. In this part, you can write a
letter telling your problem. Other people write
back telling you what they think you should do.
Use examples from the text to help these kids
solve their problems.

Read page 311. What would Grandmother tell the writer?

Dear Grandmother,
I told my brother that I run faster than he
does. We had a race. I won. I jumped up and
down and yelled, "I told you I was faster."
Now he is mad. What should I do?
Dash

_____

Dear Dash,
You should remember _____
_____ I would _____
_____

Love, Grandmother

Name _____   Date _____

Read page 313. What would Bear tell the writer?

Dear Bear,
Last year, I got all A's on my report card.
I won a prize for reading the most books.
I am the best swimmer on my team. My
coach told me I should not brag, but I am
good at everything. What should I do?
Champ

_____

Dear Champ,
You should remember _____

_____

I would _____

_____

_____

_____

Good luck,
Bear

Name _____ Date _____

Lesson 9
READER'S NOTEBOOK

How Chipmunk Got
His Stripes
Spelling: *-ed* and *-ing* Endings

-ed and *-ing* Endings

Use a Spelling Word to complete each sentence.

1. We _____ the ball down the street.

2. You _____ the play, didn't you?

3. We always keep that door _____ .

4. Matt was _____ he could go to the game.

5. On the first day of school, Ms. Bell _____ us our names.

6. The game is over, but Ivan is still _____ in the closet.

7. My dog enjoys _____ near my bed at night.

Write the Spelling Word that best matches each set of clues.

8. bike, horse, bus _____

9. leak, drip, tip over _____

10. bread, pie, muffins _____

11. sit, walk, dance _____

12. doze, nap, dream _____

Spelling Words

Basic Words
1. liked
2. using
3. riding
4. chased
5. spilled
6. making
7. closed
8. hoping
9. baked
10. hiding
11. standing
12. asked

Review Words
13. mixed
14. sleeping

Name _____ Date _____

Lesson 9
READER'S NOTEBOOK

How Chipmunk Got
His Stripes
Grammar: Verbs in the Present

Verbs with -s and -es

Draw a line under the verb that completes each sentence correctly.

1. The bear (walk, walks) through the woods.

2. The snake (slide, slides) on the ground.

3. The rabbit (hop, hops) though the grass.

4. The mouse (run, runs) through the field.

Write the verb correctly to go with the naming part of the sentence.

5. Chipmunk _____ the stew. (mix)

6. Squirrel _____ for a spoon. (reach)

7. Bear _____ to eat. (rush)

8. Bear _____ he had more. (wish)

Name _____ Date _____

Lesson 9
READER'S NOTEBOOK

How Chipmunk Got
His Stripes
Vocabulary Strategies:
Synonyms

Synonyms

Read the sentences. Choose the word from the box that means almost the same as the underlined word and write it on the line.

Word Bank

boast	happy	fast
biggest	small	fall

1. In <u>autumn</u>, the leaves change colors.

_____

2. The elephant is the <u>largest</u> animal at the zoo.

_____

3. The mouse is very <u>little</u>.

_____

4. Anita was <u>glad</u> to see her best friend.

_____

5. The runner was <u>quick</u>, so he won the race.

_____

6. Hans likes to <u>brag</u> when he wins a game.

_____

Name ______________________________ Date ______

How Chipmunk Got His Stripes
Spelling: *-ed* and *-ing* Endings

Proofread for Spelling

Spelling Words

Basic Words

1. liked
2. using
3. riding
4. chased
5. spilled
6. making
7. closed
8. hoping
9. baked
10. hiding
11. standing
12. asked

Proofread the story. Cross out the six misspelled words. Spell it correctly above the word you crossed out.

Tomorrow school will be klosed, so we are going bike ridin along the lake to the next town. All of us have been makeing plans for a long time. My brother bakked some cookies to take along. I am useing my dad's backpack to carry sandwiches and juice, but I haven't aksed him yet!

Use the code to spell the Spelling Words.

1 = e	2 = s	3 = i	4 = n	5 = d	6 = a	7 = k
8 = p	9 = m	10 = o	11 = 5	12 = b	13 = t	14 = u
15 = c	16 = j	17 = h	18 = f	19 = r	20 = l	21 = g
22 = x	23 = z	24 = y	25 = q	26 = w		

1. 6-2-7-1-5 ____________

2. 17-3-5-3-4-21 ____________

3. 15-17-6-2-1-5 ____________

4. 20-3-7-1-5 ____________

Name _____ Date _____

Lesson 9
READER'S NOTEBOOK

How Chipmunk Got
His Stripes
Grammar: Spiral Review

Kinds of Nouns

Draw a line under the noun in each sentence.
Write whether it names a person, place, thing, or animal.

1. The dog growls. _____

2. The tree stands tall. _____

3. Sally looks out. _____

4. The yard is busy. _____

Read the paragraph. Write a noun from the box in
place of each underlined noun.

| forest   mouse   owl   rock |

The place is dark. An owl looks for food to eat. It
sees a mouse near a big thing. The owl swoops down
and lands on the rock. It wants to catch the animal.
The mouse quickly scurries into a small space under the
rock. It is safe! The animal flies back up to its nest.

5. place _____   7. animal _____

6. thing _____   8. animal _____

Name _____ Date _____

Lesson 9
READER'S NOTEBOOK

How Chipmunk Got
His Stripes
Grammar: Connect to Writing

Connect to Writing

Short Sentences	New Sentence with Joined Predicates
The bear sees honey. The bear eats it all.	The bear sees honey and eats it all.

Join each pair of sentences. Use *and* between the predicates. Then write the new sentence.

1. The squirrels climb the tree.

   The squirrels eat some nuts.

   _____

2. The deer eats leaves.

   The deer drinks from the pond.

   _____

3. Chipmunks rest on rocks.

   Chipmunks sleep on leaves.

   _____

4. The lion runs fast.

   The lion looks for food.

   _____

Contractions

Put the words together to write contractions. Then read each contraction.

1. you + are = _____

2. is + not = _____

3. we + will = _____

4. it + is = _____

5. do + not = _____

6. I + am = _____

Use the contractions you wrote above to complete the sentences below.

7. The sun _____ going to
shine today.

8. I think _____ going to rain all day.

9. _____ have to stay inside.

10. I hope _____ planning to
come over to my house.

11. I _____ know what we can play.

12. _____ sure we can think of
something to do.

Name _____ Date _____

Lesson 10
READER'S NOTEBOOK

Jellies: The Life of
Jellyfish
Grammar: Verbs in the Present,
Past, and Future

Past Tense Verbs with -ed

Some **verbs** name actions that are happening now. Other **verbs** name actions that happened before now, or in the past. Add -ed to most verbs to show that the action happened in the past.

Yesterday the jellyfish (float, <u>floated</u>) in the water.

Thinking Question
When does or did the action happen?

✎ **Read each sentence. Choose the verb that tells about the past. Then rewrite the sentence.**

1. Fish (pass, passed) by the jellyfish.

_____

2. Sea turtles (splashed, splash) near the fish.

_____

3. Whales (leap, leaped) over the sea turtles.

_____

4. The sharks (watched, watch) the animals move.

_____

Name _____ Date _____

Contractions

Jellies: The Life of Jellyfish
Phonics: Contractions

Use the two words below the line to make a contraction. Write the contraction on the line. Then read each completed sentence.

1. I _____ know how to skate.
   do not

2. _____ more fun to ride my bike.
   It is

3. I _____ find my knee pads.
   did not

4. _____ try to find my helmet.
   I will

5. Then _____ have fun on our bikes.
   we will

Draw a circle around the contraction in each sentence.
Then write the two words for each contraction.

6. I'm going to the store. _____

7. If you're ready, you can go, too. _____

8. The store isn't too far away. _____

9. We'll need to buy milk and meat. _____

10. I don't think I can carry it on my bike! _____

Name _____ Date _____

Contractions

Jellies: The Life of Jellyfish
Spelling: Contractions

Sort the Spelling Words by the word that is shortened to make each contraction. The first one is done for you.

with *not*   **with *is***   **with *have***

don't _____   _____   _____

_____   _____   _____

_____   _____   _____

_____

_____

with *am*   **with *will***   **with *are***

_____   _____   _____

_____   _____   _____

_____   _____   _____

Then add three contractions that you know to any of the lists.

Spelling Words

Basic Words
1. I'm
2. don't
3. isn't
4. can't
5. we'll
6. it's
7. I've
8. didn't
9. you're
10. that's
11. wasn't
12. you've

Review Words
13. us
14. them

Verbs in Future Tense

Some **verbs** name actions that are going to happen. Add *will* before a verb to show that the action is going to happen in the future.

The sea turtles <u>want</u> food.   **Present**
The sea turtles <u>will want</u> food.   **Future**

Thinking Question
How can I make the verb tell about a future action?

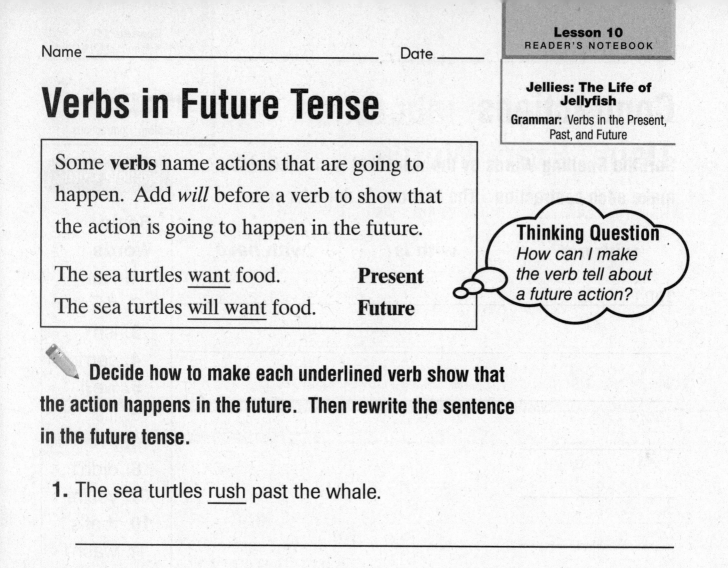

Decide how to make each underlined verb show that the action happens in the future. Then rewrite the sentence in the future tense.

1. The sea turtles <u>rush</u> past the whale.

_____

2. The waves <u>wash</u> over the beach.

_____

3. The jellyfish <u>drift</u> out to sea.

_____

4. Sea birds <u>swoop</u> down.

_____

Focus Trait: Elaboration Using Exact Words

Using exact words can make your writing clear and interesting.

Some jellyfish have a sting that is <u>strong</u>.	Some jellyfish have a sting that is <u>powerful</u>.

Read each sentence. Replace each underlined word with a more exact word.

1. The ocean is a <u>big</u> place.	
2. There are many <u>things</u> in the ocean.	
3. Getting stung by a jellyfish is <u>bad</u>.	
4. Jellyfish are <u>pretty</u>.	
5. Special plants <u>live</u> underwater in the ocean.	

Cumulative Review

Read each sentence. Choose the word from the box that completes each sentence and write the word on the line. Then read each completed sentence.

Word Bank

fishing	phone	white	then
wished	chasing	watched	path

1. Dale called jack on the _____.

2. Dale asked if Jack wanted to go _____.

3. The boys walked along a _____.

4. Jack _____ they would get to

   the lake soon.

5. Just _____, a rabbit ran by.

6. The bunny flashed its _____ tail.

7. Dale _____ it run by.

8. Was someone _____ it?

Now write on the line a word you know that begins with each letter pair.

9. ch _____   10. sh _____

Name _____ Date _____

Lesson 10
READER'S NOTEBOOK

Jellies: The Life
of Jellyfish
Independent Reading

Reader's Guide

Jellies: The Life of Jellyfish

Draw and Label a Jellyfish Picture

Let's review some facts about jellyfish. Then, you can use these facts to help you draw a picture of a jellyfish.

Read pages 338–339. What do jellyfish do?

_____

_____

Read page 346. What are some parts of a jellyfish? What are jellyfish shaped like?

_____

_____

Read page 347. What does the author think jellyfish look like when they wash up on the beach?

_____

Read page 348. What does the author think jellyfish look like in the sea?

_____

Name _____ Date _____

Lesson 10
READER'S NOTEBOOK

Jellies: The Life
of Jellyfish
Independent Reading

Did you see a jellyfish that you thought was really interesting? Draw a picture of the jellyfish below. Make labels near parts of the jellyfish and tell how the jellyfish looks and acts.

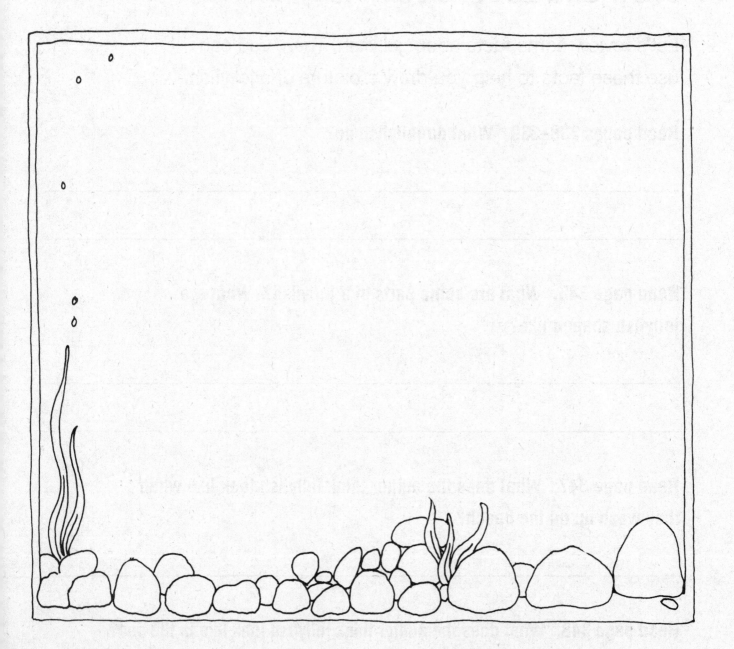

Contractions

Write the Spelling Word that has the same meaning.

1. you are _____

2. cannot _____

3. I am _____

4. is not _____

5. we will _____

6. you have _____

7. it is _____

8. I have _____

Spelling Words
Basic Words
1. I'm
2. don't
3. isn't
4. can't
5. we'll
6. it's
7. I've
8. didn't
9. you're
10. that's
11. wasn't
12. you've
Review Words
13. us
14. them

Read each sentence. Think about the underlined word or words. Then write the Spelling Word that makes the sentence say the opposite.

9. I <u>did</u> make my bed. _____

10. <u>That is</u> <u>not</u> my book. _____

11. Sara <u>was</u> late to school. _____

12. <u>You are</u> <u>not</u> my friends. _____

13. <u>I am not</u> asking Miguel. _____

14. I <u>do</u> have time to spend with you. _____

Present, Past, and Future Tense

Rewrite each sentence. Change the verb so it is tense shown in parentheses.

1. The sea animals <u>want</u> food. (past tense)

   _____

2. The crabs <u>searched</u> for small fish. (present tense)

   _____

3. The jellyfish <u>look</u> under a big rock. (past tense)

   _____

4. Waves <u>wash</u> away the sand castle. (future tense)

   _____

5. Max and Beth <u>play</u> in the water. (future tense)

   _____

6. They <u>peek</u> inside a shell. (future tense)

   _____

Suffixes *-er*, *-est*

Circle the comparing word that completes each sentence.

1. A mouse is **smaller smallest** than a cat.

2. I am going to exercise so I can get **stronger   strongest**.

3. That is the **bigger biggest** spider I have ever seen!

4. Being sick made me feel **weaker   weakest** than I did before.

5. Juan wants to be the **smarter   smartest** student in the class.

6. That side of the pool is **shallower   shallowest** than this side.

7. Chocolate is the **sweeter   sweetest** kind of ice cream.

Proofread for Spelling

Rewrite each sentence. Use two contractions in each sentence.

1. I am sure he did not see me.

   _____

2. That is where you are going.

   _____

3. It is our class picnic, so we will go early.

   _____

Proofread the note. Cross out the six misspelled contractions. Spell each word correctly in the margin.

Dear Pam,

    I kan't go tomorrow because I'ave got too much homework. I know yo'uve been counting on me. Maybe I can come over later in the evening. Then wi'll have time to talk. I hope its' OK. I'am going to start my math problems right now.

                      Sincerely,

                      Carmen

Spelling Words

Basic Words

1. I'm
2. don't
3. isn't
4. can't
5. we'll
6. it's
7. I've
8. didn't
9. you're
10. that's
11. wasn't
12. you've

Name _____ Date _____

Lesson 10
READER'S NOTEBOOK

Jellies: The Life of
Jellyfish
Grammar: Spiral Review

Singular and Plural Nouns

Draw a line under the noun in each sentence.
If the noun names one, write *S* for *singular*. If the noun
names more than one, write *P* for *plural*.

1. The sharks swim fast. _____

2. Four girls watch. _____

3. One boy points. _____

4. A girl looks again. _____

5. The animals are gone now. _____

Read each sentence. Then rewrite each underlined
noun in the correct plural form.

6. Look at the crab. _____

7. Do not touch the claw. _____

8. Tell the adult to come quickly. _____

9. The boy can use help. _____

10. The crabs crawled in the bag. _____

Connect to Writing

Verbs Telling About Different Times	Verbs Telling the Same Time
Last week Jill and Jake <u>walked</u> on the beach. They <u>play</u> in the water.	Last week Jill and Jake <u>walked</u> on the beach. They <u>played</u> in the water.

Read this story. It tells about something that happened in the past. Five verbs do not tell about the past. Fix these five verbs. Then write the story correctly on the lines below.

Jill and Jake skipped along the shore. Jake saw two large shells. Jake point to them. Jill rush over to see them. Jill and Jake look closely. Jill pick up one shell. Jill and Jake wash the shells and took them home.

_____

_____

_____

_____

_____

_____

Name _____ Date _____

Unit 2
READER'S NOTEBOOK

Poppleton in Winter
Segment 1
Independent Reading

Reader's Guide

Poppleton in Winter

Interview with Patrick

Read pages 11–15. If news reporters interviewed Patrick about his day, what would he say? Read the questions below. Write the answers Patrick would give. Include details from the text and illustrations.

Interview with Patrick

1. What problem did you have at Poppleton's house today?

_____

_____

_____

2. When did you have this problem?

_____

_____

_____

Name _____ Date _____

Unit 2
READER'S NOTEBOOK

Poppleton in Winter
Segment 1
Independent Reading

Now answer questions about the events from Poppleton's point of view. Include details from the text and illustrations on pages 11–15.

Interview with Poppleton

1. Why was it a good thing that the icicles were still frozen?

_____

_____

_____

2. Patrick told us that you built a fence. How did you do that?

_____

_____

_____

Name _____ Date _____

Reader's Guide

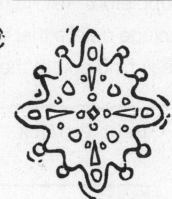

Poppleton in Winter

Letters to a Friend

In Chapter 1, Poppleton met Patrick. Now Poppleton wants to write letters to his friend Patrick.

Read pages 18–35. Imagine you are Poppleton. Write a letter to Patrick. Tell him how you made the bust of Cherry Sue. Use details from the text and illustrations.

Dear Patrick,

_____

_____

_____

_____

_____

_____

Your friend,
Poppleton

Name _____ Date _____

Unit 2
READER'S NOTEBOOK

Poppleton in Winter
Segment 2
Independent Reading

Read pages 36–48. Write another letter from Poppleton. Tell Patrick about your birthday. Include details that tell how you felt at the beginning and at the end of the day.

Dear Patrick,

_____

_____

_____

_____

_____

_____

_____

_____

Your friend,
Poppleton

Base Words and Endings
-s, -es

**Click, Clack, Moo:
Cows That Type**

Phonics: Base Words and
Endings *-s, -es*

Put the letters together to write a base word.

Then add the ending *-s* or *-es*.

1. m + a + t + c + h = _____

2. b + u + z + z = _____

3. g + l + a + s + s = _____

4. b + u + s + h = _____

5. h + a + m + m + e + r = _____

Now use the words you wrote above to complete the sentences below.

6. Dad _____ the nails into
   the wall.

7. I drank two _____ of milk
   for dinner.

8. Today my jacket _____ my hat.

9. My dog likes to hide in the _____.

10. The bee _____ near the hive.

Name _____ Date _____

Compound Sentences

- A **compound sentence** is made up of two shorter sentences joined by <u>and</u>, <u>but</u>, or <u>or</u>.

The cows got blankets, but Duck kept the typewriter.

- A comma is used before the joining word.

Thinking Question
Is the sentence made up of two shorter sentences joined by and, but, or or?

 Draw a line under each shorter sentence in the compound sentences.

1. The cows wanted blankets, and Farmer Brown said, "No way."

2. The cows went on strike, and Farmer Brown was upset.

3. The hens had nests, but they were still cold.

4. Farmer Brown needs milk and eggs, or he can't run his farm.

5. Duck took the typewriter, and he decided to keep it.

Name _____ Date _____

Lesson 11
READER'S NOTEBOOK

Base Words and Endings -s, -es

Click, Clack, Moo:
Cows That Type
Phonics: Base Words and
Endings -s, -es

Write the words from the box under the word that has the same ending. Then write two more words of your own in each column.

```
····················· Word Bank ·····················

      eggs        trucks      brushes       fixes
      wishes      tigers      pinches       rafts
```

lunches   **chicks**

_____   _____

_____   _____

_____   _____

_____   _____

_____   _____

Base Words with Endings
-s, -es

Sort the Spelling Words by -s and -es endings. Then draw a line under each word ending that changed the word from meaning one to meaning more than one.

Words with -s Endings   **Words with -es Endings**

1. _____   11. _____

2. _____   12. _____

3. _____   13. _____

4. _____   14. _____

5. _____

6. _____

7. _____

8. _____

9. _____

10. _____

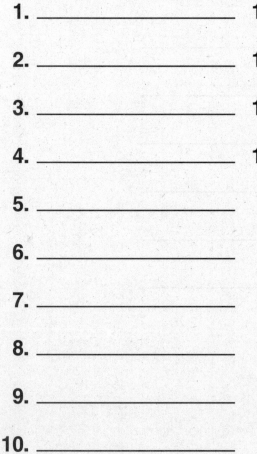

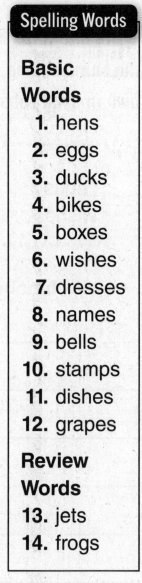

Spelling Words

Basic Words

1. hens
2. eggs
3. ducks
4. bikes
5. boxes
6. wishes
7. dresses
8. names
9. bells
10. stamps
11. dishes
12. grapes

Review Words

13. jets
14. frogs

Click, Clack, Moo:
Cows That Type
Grammar: Compound Sentences

Compound Sentences

- A **compound sentence** is made up of two shorter sentences joined by <u>and</u>, <u>but</u>, or <u>or</u>.
- A comma is used before the joining word.

The cows found an old typewriter.

The cows learned to type.

The cows found an old typewriter, and they learned to type.

Thinking Question
How can sentences be combined to make writing less choppy?

Write each pair of sentences as a compound sentence. Use a comma and a joining word.

1. The ducks need a diving board. The ducks will be bored.

_____

_____

2. The ducks liked to swim. The ducks preferred to dive.

_____

_____

3. Duck knocked on the door. Duck handed Farmer Brown a note.

_____

_____

Focus Trait: Purpose
Stating a Clear Goal

Not a Clear Goal	Clear Goal
I would like you to <u>do something.</u>	I would like you to **take me to the park next weekend.**

A. Read each goal that is not clear. Fill in the blanks to state each goal more clearly.

Not a Clear Goal	Clear Goal
1. I would like you to buy <u>something</u> for our computer lab.	I would like you to buy _____ for our computer lab.
2. I want you to send me <u>stuff</u> for a project.	I want you to send me _____ for a project.

B. Read each goal that is not clear. Add a word or words to make the goal more clear. Write your new sentences.

Not a Clear Goal	Clear Goal
3. We would like you to <u>do us a favor</u>.	
4. I am writing to ask you <u>to do something</u> for the music room.	

Name _____ Date _____

Lesson 11
READER'S NOTEBOOK

**Click, Clack, Moo:
Cows That Type**
Phonics: Cumulative Review

Cumulative Review

Write the word that goes in each sentence.

> **Word Bank**
>
> cider   fever   later   virus

1. Jack has a _____ that makes him sick.

2. Mom says his _____ is very high.

3. "You can sit with Jack _____ today," said Mom.

4. "I'll warm up some _____ for both of you," said Mom.

Write the words that make up each underlined contraction.

5. "I <u>won't</u> have lunch with Sam today," said Jack.

   _____.

6. "<u>I'll</u> tell Sam you miss him, Jack," I said.

   _____.

7. "<u>You're</u> a good sister," said Jack.

   _____

Name _____ Date _____

Lesson 11
READER'S NOTEBOOK

Click, Clack, Moo:
Cows That Type
Independent Reading

Reader's Guide

Click, Clack, Moo: Cows That Type

Make a Cartoon

The animals used the typewriter to tell Farmer Brown what they wanted. Read the text to find out what each animal said.

Read pages 379–381. What did the cows tell Farmer Brown?

_____

_____

Read pages 383–384. What did the hens want Farmer Brown to know?

_____

_____

Read page 391. What did the ducks tell Farmer Brown?

_____

_____

Name _____ Date _____

Lesson 11
READER'S NOTEBOOK

Click, Clack, Moo:
Cows That Type
Independent Reading

Which was your favorite animal? What if Farmer Brown and that animal could talk to each other? What would they say? Use the examples from the text and illustrations you found to make a cartoon. Use speech bubbles to show what Farmer Brown and the animal might say.

Name _____ Date _____

Base Words with Endings -s, -es

Write the Spelling Word or Spelling Words that match each clue.

Spelling Words

Basic Words

1. hens
2. eggs
3. ducks
4. bikes
5. boxes
6. wishes
7. dresses
8. names
9. bells
10. stamps
11. dishes
12. grapes

Review Words

13. jets
14. frogs

1. These are animals. _____

_____ _____

2. You can eat these. _____

_____

3. Put things inside these. _____

4. Put food on these. _____

5. Ride on these. _____

6. These ring. _____

7. These are airplanes. _____

8. You hope these come true. _____

9. Girls sometimes wear these. _____

10. Put these on letters. _____

11. We give pets these. _____

Name _____ Date _____

Lesson 11
READER'S NOTEBOOK

**Click, Clack, Moo:
Cows That Type**
Grammar: Compound Sentences

Compound Sentences

> - A **compound sentence** is made up of two shorter sentences.
> - The two shorter sentences are joined by <u>and</u>, <u>but</u>, or <u>or</u>.
> - A comma is used before the joining word.
>
> Farmer Brown was angry. Farmer Brown finally made a deal with the cows.
>
> Farmer Brown was angry, but he finally made a deal with the cows.

Write each pair of sentences as a compound sentence.

1. The animals tried to listen. The animals couldn't understand Moo.

_____

_____

2. The cows had a meeting. The cows decided what to do.

_____

_____

3. The cows needed to be happy. The cows wouldn't give milk.

_____

_____

Name _____ Date _____

Lesson 11
READER'S NOTEBOOK

Click, Clack, Moo:
Cows That Type
Vocabulary Strategies: Prefixes
pre- and mis-

Prefixes *pre-* and *mis-*

Read each definition below. Add *mis-* or *pre-* to a
word in the box to make a new word that matches each
definition.

Word Bank

heard	judge	read
order	heat	

1. to order before _____

2. to judge badly _____

3. to heat before _____

4. did not read right _____

5. did not hear right _____

Write a sentence for each word.

6. **misdial** _____

_____

7. **precut** _____

_____

Proofread for Spelling

Proofread the newspaper story. Circle the nine
misspelled words. Then write the correct spellings.

Wishs Come True

Mr. and Mrs. Smith kept birds in a pen. Saturday, they
rode their biks. Then they checked the pen. They found
only empty boxees. "I wanted to ring alarm belz," said Mr.
Smith. "I wish that we would find our birds."

When they went inside the house, they found the
duks sleeping on Mrs. Smith's dreses, and the henz had
laid egs on her new dishis!

Spelling Words
Basic Words
1. hens
2. eggs
3. ducks
4. bikes
5. boxes
6. wishes
7. dresses
8. names
9. bells
10. stamps
11. dishes
12. grapes

1. _____   6. _____

2. _____   7. _____

3. _____   8. _____

4. _____   9. _____

5. _____

Unscramble the letters to spell a Basic Word.

10. pgares _____   12. pmasts _____

11. maens _____

Name _____ Date _____

Lesson 11
READER'S NOTEBOOK

Click, Clack, Moo:
Cows That Type
Grammar: Spiral Review

More Plural Nouns

🖉 **Circle the noun that correctly shows more than one.**

1. We eat (sandwichs, sandwiches) in the barn.

2. Our (dresss, dresses) get dirty.

3. The (mouses, mice) play in the hay.

4. The (horse, horses) stomp their feet.

5. The (cow, cows) stand still.

🖉 **Read each sentence. Then rewrite each sentence to use the correct plural form of the underlined noun.**

6. Two <u>fox</u> visit the farm.

_____

7. Many <u>man</u> help plant seeds.

_____

8. How many <u>child</u> are in your school?

_____

Name _____   Date _____

Connect to Writing

Short, Choppy Sentences	Compound Sentence
Cows give us milk. Hens lay eggs.	Cows give us milk, and hens lay eggs.

✏️ **Write each pair of sentences as a compound sentence.**
Use a comma and a joining word.

1. The cows can type. The cows can't dance.

_____

_____

2. The cows want electric blankets. The ducks want a diving board.

_____

_____

3. The cows will get blankets. The cows will stay cold.

_____

_____

4. The ducks can dive. The ducks need a board.

_____

_____

Words with *ai, ay*

Write a word from the box to complete each sentence.

Word Bank

pail	maybe	say
tail	play	wait

1. I like to _____ games with my

   dog Spot.

2. "Come here, Spot," I _____.

3. Spot jumps up and wags his _____.

4. _____ Spot will run after a ball.

5. I toss the ball, and it lands in a _____.

6. Spot fetches the ball while I _____

   for him.

**Now write each word under the word that has the same
pattern for long *a*.**

m<u>ai</u>l   **d<u>ay</u>**

_____   _____

_____   _____

_____   _____

Compound Sentences

- A **compound sentence** is two simpler sentences joined by a comma and the word <u>and</u>, <u>but</u>, or <u>or</u>.

- Moving words around and adding details in a compound sentence can make the sentence more interesting.

Thinking Question
How does moving words around and adding details make sentences more interesting?

Less interesting

I like to sing, and I like to dance.

More interesting

I like to sing popular songs, and I think dancing is fun.

Move words around and add details to make these compound sentences more interesting.

1. Shawn plays the guitar, or Shawn plays the drum.

_____

_____

2. Kim plays the piano, but Kim wants to play the organ.

_____

_____

3. We like classical music, and we like jazz.

_____

_____

Words with *ai, ay*

Read the letter. Draw a circle around the words with *ai* and *ay*. Then write two sentences to finish the letter. Choose two words from the box to use in your sentences.

Word Bank

rain	hail	day	may
gray	mail	pay	trail

Dear Jay,

    Today my class went on a trip. I could not wait! We saw people make crafts. A man made pots out of clay. One woman wove a braid for a rug. The people sell their crafts and then they get paid. _____

_____

_____

_____

        Your friend,

      _____

Words with *ai, ay*

ai

ay

Sort the Spelling Words by the long *a* sound spelled
ai and the long *a* sound spelled *ay*.

Spelling Words

Basic Words
1. pay
2. wait
3. paint
4. train
5. pail
6. clay
7. tray
8. plain
9. stain
10. hay
11. gray
12. away

Review Words
13. stay
14. day

ai Words	*ay* Words
1. _____	7. _____
2. _____	8. _____
3. _____	9. _____
4. _____	10. _____
5. _____	11. _____
6. _____	12. _____
	13. _____
	14. _____

Underline the letters in each word that make the long *a* sound.

Name _____ Date _____

Compound Sentences

Ah Music!
Grammar: Compound Sentences

- A **compound sentence** is two simple sentences joined by a comma and the word <u>and</u>, <u>but</u>, or <u>or</u>.
- Moving words around and adding details in a compound sentence can make the sentence more interesting.

Thinking Question
How does moving words around and adding details make sentences more interesting?

Less interesting

Lin prefers loud music, but Lin's sister prefers soft music.

More interesting

Loud music is Lin's favorite, but her sister prefers soft music.

🖉 **Move words around and add details to make these compound sentences more interesting.**

1. Some people find headphones comfortable, but some people find headphones uncomfortable.

_____

_____

2. Is your goal to be a singer, or is your goal to be a musician?

_____

_____

3. Do you want to clap, or do you want to tap your feet?

_____

_____

Focus Trait: Organization
Showing Feelings

Ah Music!
Writing: Opinion Writing

Weak Sentence	Strong Sentence
I like movie music.	Movie music is so great to listen to!

A. Read each sentence that has a weak voice. Add or change some words to make the voice stronger.

Weak Sentence	Strong Sentence
1. The guitar is a musical instrument.	The guitar is a _____ musical instrument.
2. I like all music.	Any kind of music _____ _____

B. Read each sentence. Add words to make the sentence stronger. Include a reason for the opinion. Write your new sentences.

Weak Sentence	Strong Sentence
3. Our band played a concert.	_____ _____
4. The trumpet is a good instrument.	_____ _____

Cumulative Review

Write the word that goes in each sentence.

Word Bank

snails   boxes   glasses   bikes

1. "I can't lift these big _____ of books," said Meg.

2. "We'll ride our _____ to school," Rick said.

3. "I've filled three _____ with milk," said Max.

4. "You're moving at the speed of _____ this morning," Mom said.

Now write each word from the Word Bank under the word that has the same ending.

paints   patches

_____   _____

_____   _____

Name _____   Date _____

Ah, Music!

Think Like a Musician

A heading tells you about the text that follows it. For example, the heading on page 412 is "Music Is Sound." That section tells about sounds in music. Write each heading and tell what you learn.

Read page 413. What is the heading on this page?

_____

What did this section teach you about rhythm?

_____

Read page 414. What is the heading on this page?

_____

What did this section teach you about melody?

_____

Read page 416. What is the heading on this page?

_____

What did this section teach you about feeling in music?

_____

Name _____ Date _____

Now teach others. Based on details from the text, think like a musician. Pretend a friend is going to a performance. Give your friend advice about rhythm, melody, and feeling in music. Remember you can find information in the book by using headings.

When you go to a music performance, listen for these things.

1. Rhythm: _____

_____

_____

2. Melody: _____

_____

_____

3. Feeling in music: _____

_____

_____

Words with *ai, ay*

Spelling Words

Basic Words
1. pay
2. wait
3. paint
4. train
5. pail
6. clay
7. tray
8. plain
9. stain
10. hay
11. gray
12. away

Review Words
13. stay
14. day

Read each word aloud. Then write the Spelling Word or Spelling Words that rhyme with the word.

1. main _____ _____

   _____

2. faint _____

3. play _____ _____

   _____ _____

   _____ _____

Compound Sentences

- A **compound sentence** is two simple sentences joined by a comma and the word <u>and</u>, <u>but</u>, or <u>or</u>.

Simple Sentences

The crowd sang along to the music.

The crowd was moved by the music.

Compound Sentence

The crowd sang along to the music, and they were moved by the music.

More Interesting Compound Sentence

The large crowd sang along to the joyful music, and the music moved the crowd to cheer.

Combine each pair of simple sentences into a compound sentence. Move words around and add details to make each sentence more interesting.

1. The teacher listens to the children's singing.

   The teacher is pleased by the children's singing.

   _____

   _____

2. Playing the piano well is hard work for Tasha.

   Playing the piano well is satisfying for Tasha.

   _____

   _____

Idioms

Read the sentence. Choose the idiom from the box that could replace the underlined words. Write the idiom.

> ### Word Bank
>
> | step on it | cry my eyes out | get the picture |
> |---|---|---|
> | shake a leg | run like the wind | hang in there |

1. We were late for school, so Dad told us to <u>hurry up</u>.

_____

2. I kept striking out, but my coach told me to <u>keep trying</u>.

_____

3. Mike explained to Tina how to play the game.

"Do you <u>understand</u>?" he asked.

_____

4. My best friend is moving away. I am so sad I feel like

I could <u>cry forever</u>.

_____

5. We need to leave soon, so <u>get moving</u>!

_____

6. I'm going to <u>run really fast</u> so I can win the race.

_____

Proofread for Spelling

Proofread the journal entry. Circle the ten misspelled words. Then write the correct spellings on the lines below.

Today was fun. I helped paynt my room. I couldn't wate to start. My walls were plane grae. Dad had a payl of blue paint. He showed me how to use a paint brush and trai. We had to be neat so paint would not stane my carpet. We made the gray go awai. Then we drew a trane passing a farm with hae stacks on the wall.

1. _____   6. _____

2. _____   7. _____

3. _____   8. _____

4. _____   9. _____

5. _____   10. _____

Spelling Words

Basic Words

1. pay
2. wait
3. paint
4. train
5. pail
6. clay
7. tray
8. plain
9. stain
10. hay
11. gray
12. away

Review Words

13. stay
14. day

Read the following sentences. Circle each misspelled word. Then write it correctly.

11. We bought modeling claie at the store. _____

12. I had a gift card to pa for it. _____

Writing Proper Nouns

✏️ **Write the proper noun in each sentence correctly on the line.**

1. My friend jessica plays the flute. _____

2. The concert is in chicago. _____

3. She will bring her dog willy. _____

4. After the concert we'll have juicy jelly smoothies.

_____

✏️ **Read each sentence. Choose the correct proper noun to replace the underlined words. Write the new sentence on the line.**

5. The woman loves the piano. (Carmen, Canada)

_____

6. She plays it for her fish. (New Mexico, Bubbles)

_____

7. She feeds her fish its food. (Fin Flakes, Main Street)

_____

8. Carmen and Bubbles live on drake road. (Florida, Drake Road)

_____

183

Connect to Writing

Moving words around and adding details in a compound sentence can make the sentence more interesting.

Less Interesting	**More Interesting**
Do you like vocals, or do you like instrumentals?	So you like vocals, or are instrumentals your favorite?
My brother only listens to pop, and my sister only listens to country.	My brother only listens to popular music, and country music is all my sister wants to hear.

Move words around and add details to each sentence.

1. Mom plays the guitar, and Mom is teaching Manny.

_____

_____

2. Shawn is a singer, but Shawn is not a dancer.

_____

_____

3. Do you enjoy concerts, or do you find concerts too loud?

_____

_____

Words with *ee, ea*

Write a word for each clue.

1. It rhymes with *see.*

It begins like *bat.* _____

2. It rhymes with *beaches.*

It begins like *pig.* _____

3. It rhymes with *sweet.*

It begins like *mail.* _____

4. It rhymes with *sheep.*

It begins like *kitten.* _____

5. It rhymes with *beast.*

It begins like *fox.* _____

6. It rhymes with *clean.*

It begins like *bay.* _____

**Use two of the words you wrote above in sentences of
your own.**

7. _____

8. _____

Name _____ Date _____

Lesson 13
READER'S NOTEBOOK

**Schools Around
the World**
Grammar: Quotation Marks

Using Quotation Marks

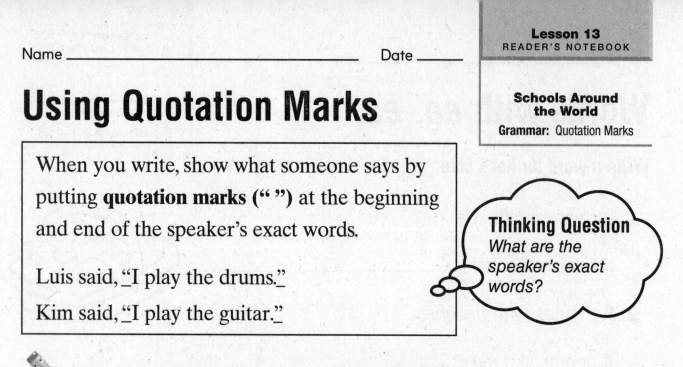

When you write, show what someone says by putting **quotation marks (" ")** at the beginning and end of the speaker's exact words.

Luis said, "I play the drums."

Kim said, "I play the guitar."

Thinking Question
What are the speaker's exact words?

Write each sentence. Put quotation marks around the speaker's exact words.

1. Jamal asked, Will you play for me?

_____

2. Luis said, We will play for you.

_____

3. Kim asked, Do you play, too?

_____

4. Jamal answered, I play the piano.

_____

5. The kids said, Come play with us!

_____

Name _____ Date _____

Lesson 13
READER'S NOTEBOOK

Schools Around
the World
Phonics: Words with *ee, ea*

Words with *ee, ea*

Read the sentences. Draw a circle around each word
that has the long *e* sound spelled *ee* or *ea*.

1. A creek is a small river or stream.

2. We ate roast beef and green beans.

3. The wheels on the car squeak.

4. If you heat a pot of water, you can make steam.

5. We clean our home every week.

Now write each word you circled under the word that has the
same spelling for the long *e* sound.

speed	**beach**
_____	_____
_____	_____
_____	_____
_____	_____
_____	_____
	_____

Words with *ee, ea*

ee   *ea*

Sort the Spelling Words by *ee* and *ea* spellings.

ee Words	*ea* Words
1. _____	6. _____
2. _____	7. _____
3. _____	8. _____
4. _____	9. _____
5. _____	10. _____
	11. _____
	12. _____
	13. _____
	14. _____

Spelling Words

Basic Words
1. free
2. teach
3. teeth
4. please
5. beach
6. wheel
7. team
8. speak
9. sneeze
10. sheep
11. meaning
12. weave

Review Words
13. eat
14. read

Underline the letters in each word that make the long *e* sound.

Quotation Marks

Follow these rules when you use
quotation marks.

1. Put a **comma** after words such as *said* and
   asked.
2. Begin the first word inside the quotation
   marks with a **capital letter**.
3. Put the **end mark** inside the quotation
   marks.

Example: Jenna said, "I wrote a poem."

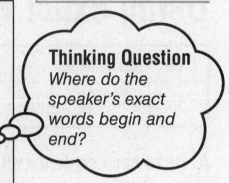

Thinking Question
*Where do the
speaker's exact
words begin and
end?*

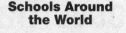

✏ **Draw a line under the sentence that is written correctly.**

1. Maddy asked, "Are you an artist?"

Maddy asked, "are you an artist?"

2. Jenna said "I am a writer."

Jenna said, "I am a writer."

3. Maddy asked, "Are poems hard to write?"

Maddy asked, "Are poems hard to write"

4. Jenna said, "poems are fun to write."

Jenna said, "Poems are fun to write."

Focus Trait: Elaboration Using Exact Words

Overused Words	Exact Words
Painting is a <u>fun</u> <u>thing</u>.	Painting is an **artistic hobby**.

A. Read each sentence on the left side. Add or change words to make them more exact.

Overused Words	Exact Words
1. Lunch is <u>the best</u> part of the day.	Lunch is _____ of the day.
2. At lunch, I can <u>talk</u> with <u>people</u>.	At lunch, I can _____ with _____.

B. Read each sentence with overused words. Add or change words to make them more exact. Write your new sentences.

Few Exact Words	Add Exact Words or Phrases
3. My art teacher is <u>good</u>.	
4. I love <u>making</u> <u>stuff</u>.	

Cumulative Review

Read each word. Add *-s* or *-es* to each base word.
Then write the new word.

1. rain _____

2. peach _____

3. train _____

4. pail _____

5. fox _____

6. wash _____

7. teach _____

8. catch _____

9. glass _____

10. stain _____

11. box _____

12. buzz _____

Name _____ Date _____

Schools Around the World

Create Your Own School

There were many different schools in the story.
Some were like your school, and some were different.

Read page 441. How are all schools the same?

_____

Read page 442. How are school buildings different?

_____

Read page 443. What are some ways students get to school?

_____

Read page 444. How do children dress at school?

_____

Read pages 445–447. What are some things children do at school?

_____

Name _____ Date _____

Lesson 13
READER'S NOTEBOOK

Schools Around
the World
Independent Reading

You are going to open your own school!
Write an announcement telling people what
makes your school special so they will want to
come to your school. Think about the school
building, what children will wear, what children
will learn, and what children will do.

A new school will open soon in our town!

The name of the school is _____

_____

This school is different from other schools in these
three ways:

1. _____

   _____

2. _____

   _____

3. _____

   _____

$\frac{2}{3}$ abc + 5 × $\frac{1}{2}$

Words with *ee, ea*

Write two Spelling Words to complete each sentence.

Spelling Words

**Basic
Words**
1. free
2. teach
3. teeth
4. please
5. beach
6. wheel
7. team
8. speak
9. sneeze
10. sheep
11. meaning
12. weave

**Review
Words**
13. eat
14. read

1. Use your _____ to chew when

you _____ .

2. Will you _____ cover your

mouth when you _____ ?

3. We _____ wool from

_____ to make a sweater.

4. You can _____ the

_____ of a word in a dictionary.

5. The swimming _____ had a

race at the _____ .

6. Ariana will _____ her friend

how to use a pottery _____ .

7. During recess, we are _____ to

_____ about whatever we want.

Quotation Marks

✎ **Write each sentence correctly.**

1. Mrs. Smith said, Artists mix colors.

_____

2. Greg said, I will mix blue and yellow.

_____

3. Annie said, You will make green!

_____

✎ **Draw a line under the sentence that is written correctly.**

4. Jamie said "I made a basket."

   Jamie said, "I made a basket."

5. Robin asked, "how did you do it"?

   Robin asked, "How did you do it?"

6. Jamie answered, "I made it out of straw."

   Jamie answered ",I made it out of straw."

Name _____ Date _____

Using a Dictionary

Read the names for parts of a dictionary entry. Then read the dictionary entry. Write in the boxes the labels for the parts of the dictionary entry.

example sentence   part of speech   pronunciation

word meaning   entry word

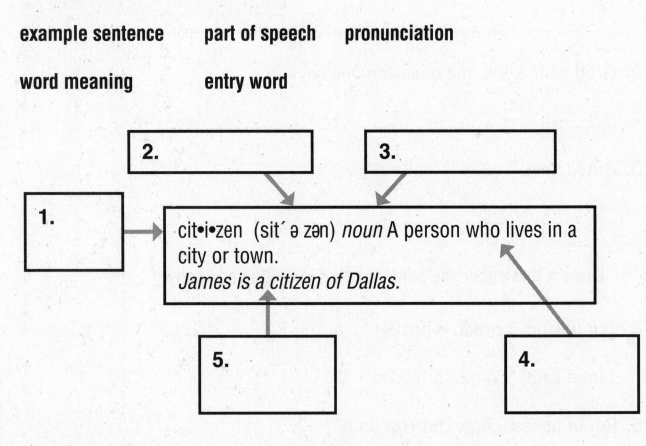

2.

3.

1.

cit•i•zen (sit´ ə zən) *noun* A person who lives in a city or town.
James is a citizen of Dallas.

5.

4.

6. Write two good reasons to use a dictionary.

_____

_____

Proofread for Spelling

**Proofread the letter. Circle the twelve misspelled words.
Then write the correct spellings on the lines below.**

Dear Grandma,

    We had a fun trip. Dad had to fix a weel on our car. Then we went to pet a shepe. The animals made Mom sneaz. We saw a girl weve a colorful rug. She tried to teech us the meening of each color.

    At last we got to the beech. The shells were fre. I learned that some fish don't have any teeeth. We saw a volleyball teem. I got to spek to the players.

    Well, that is all. Pleze write soon.

                 Love,
                 Tori

Spelling Words

Basic Words

1. free
2. teach
3. teeth
4. please
5. beach
6. wheel
7. team
8. speak
9. sneeze
10. sheep
11. meaning
12. weave

1. _____ 7. _____

2. _____ 8. _____

3. _____ 9. _____

4. _____ 10. _____

5. _____ 11. _____

6. _____ 12. _____

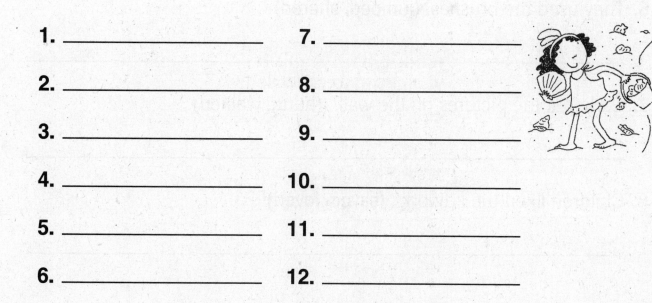

Name _____   Date _____

Lesson 13
READER'S NOTEBOOK

Schools Around
the World
Grammar: Spiral Review

Action Verbs

✏️ Circle the verb. Underline the subject that is doing the action.

1. Bobby jumps to his feet.

2. He dances to the music.

3. Sasha sings out loud.

4. They cheer for the band.

✏️ Underline the verb in the sentence. Circle the verb that makes the action more exact. Then write the new sentence.

5. The class made a picture. (painted, watered)

_____

6. They used the brushes. (jumped, shared)

_____

7. Carla put the pictures on the wall. (hung, walked)

_____

8. Children liked the artwork. (saved, loved)

_____

Name _____ Date _____

Lesson 13
READER'S NOTEBOOK

Schools Around
the World
Grammar: Connect to Writing

Connect to Writing

Sentences Written Incorrectly	Sentences Written Correctly
Jimmy asked "Is that a clay bowl?" Mom said. "yes, I made it in art class."	Jimmy asked, "Is that a clay bowl?" Mom said, "Yes, I made it in art class."

Write each sentence correctly. Fix mistakes in capitalization and punctuation. Put the quotation marks where they belong.

1. Mom asked "Do you want to come to art class?

_____

2. I asked, what will we do?"

_____

3. "mom answered this week we will make puppets"

_____

4. I said "That sounds like fun!

_____

5. She said Next week we will put on a puppet show!"

_____

Long *o* (*o*, *oa*, *ow*)

Write a word for each clue.

> ### Word Bank
>
> | zero | clover | coast |
> |------|--------|-------|
> | groan | gold | glow |

1. It rhymes with **toast.**

It begins like **cap.** _____

2. It rhymes with **loan.**

It begins like **grapes.** _____

3. It rhymes with **fold.**

It begins like **gap.** _____

4. It rhymes with **show.**

It begins like **glad.** _____

5. It rhymes with **hero.**

It begins like **zip.** _____

6. It rhymes with **over.**

It begins like **clip.** _____

Days of the Week

- There are seven days in a week.
- The names of the days of the week begin with **capital letters**.

Monday	Thursday	Saturday
Tuesday	Friday	Sunday
Wednesday		

Bonnie teaches sign language on <u>Tuesday</u>.

Thinking Question
Which word names a day of the week?

Write each sentence correctly.

1. Bonnie teaches Jessica on wednesday.

_____

2. Jessica has a piano lesson on Tuesday.

_____

3. Jessica mails Bonnie a card on Friday.

_____

4. On monday Bonnie gets the card in the mail.

_____

5. On saturday Bonnie sends Jessica a card.

_____

Long *o* (*o, oa, ow*)

Read the sentences. Draw a circle around each word that has the long *o* sound spelled *o, oa,* or *ow*.

1. A crow sat on the branch of the old oak tree.

2. Snow began to fall on a cold winter day.

3. Throw a stick in the water and see if it floats.

4. You can fold your own paper and put it away.

5. I know that the coach has a gold ring.

Now write each word you circled under the word that has the same spelling for long *o*.

told	loan	blow
_____	_____	_____
_____	_____	_____
_____	_____	_____
		_____

Name _____   Date _____

Long *o* (*o, oa, ow*)

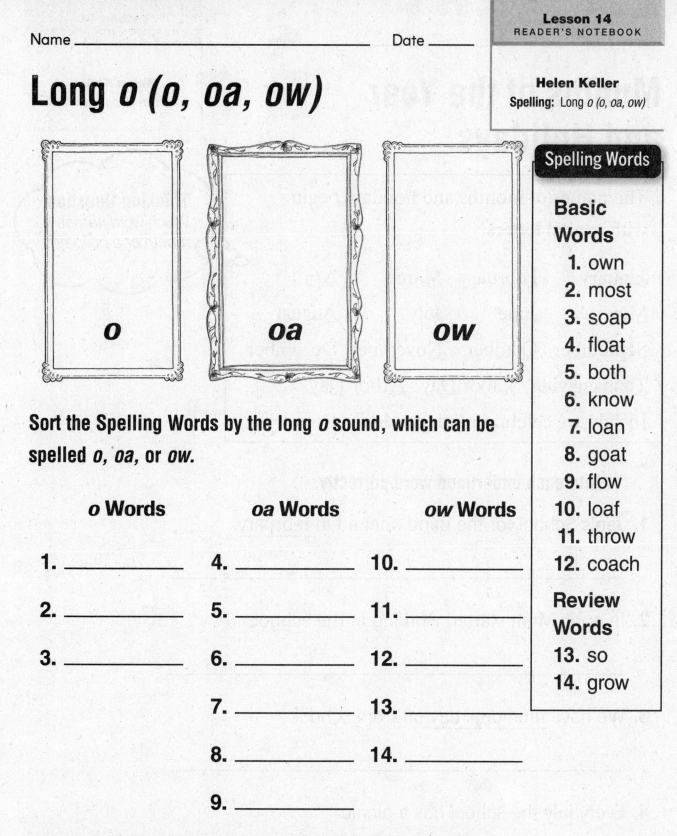

| o | oa | ow |

Spelling Words

**Basic
Words**
1. own
2. most
3. soap
4. float
5. both
6. know
7. loan
8. goat
9. flow
10. loaf
11. throw
12. coach

**Review
Words**
13. so
14. grow

Sort the Spelling Words by the long *o* sound, which can be spelled *o, oa,* or *ow.*

o Words	*oa* Words	*ow* Words
1. _____	4. _____	10. _____
2. _____	5. _____	11. _____
3. _____	6. _____	12. _____
	7. _____	13. _____
	8. _____	14. _____
	9. _____	

Underline the letter or letters in each word that make the long *o* sound.

Months of the Year and Holidays

The names of months and holidays begin with **capital letters**.

January	February	March	April
May	June	July	August
September	October	November	December
Thanksgiving	Labor Day	Arbor Day	

In July, we celebrate Independence Day.

Thinking Question
Which word names a month or a holiday?

Write each underlined word correctly.

1. Jan's School for the Blind opened in february.

_____

2. In april, Mom started working at the school.

_____

3. We have memorial day off from school.

_____

4. Every july the school has a picnic.

_____

5. presidents' day is in February.

_____

204

Focus Trait: Purpose
Facts and Opinions

A **fact** can be proved. An **opinion** cannot be proved. An opinion tells what someone thinks or feels. Words such as <u>I think</u>, <u>I like</u>, or <u>I believe</u> are used to show opinions.

Read the paragraphs below. Write the opinion from each one. Write two facts that support each opinion.

Helen Keller learned to read, write, and speak. I believe she was a remarkable person. She traveled around the world. She spoke to large crowds of people.

Opinion: _____

_____

Facts: _____

_____

Annie Sullivan was Helen Keller's teacher. In the beginning, Helen fought with Annie. She even knocked out one of Annie's teeth. I think Helen was a real challenge for Annie.

Opinion: _____

Facts: _____

_____

Cumulative Review

Answer each pair of clues using the words below the clues.

1. A place with sand by a lake or sea _____

A big meal _____

beach   **feast**

2. Make a trip in a boat _____

The feeling you have when you cut your hand

_____

pain   **sail**

3. Show someone how to do something _____

Stretch out your arm to grab something

_____

teach   **reach**

4. How fast a car or truck is going _____

A long way down under water _____

deep   **speed**

5. To stay in one place until something happens

_____

A path that you hike along _____

trail   **wait**

Helen Keller

Make a Speech

When Helen Keller grew up, she gave
speeches. Now you will write a speech about
Helen Keller's life.

**Read page 475. What was it like for Helen Keller to grow up blind
and deaf?**

_____

Read pages 476–477. What problems did Helen Keller have?

_____

_____

Read pages 482–485. How did Helen learn to communicate?

_____

_____

Read pages 486–487. What other ways did Helen learn?

_____

_____

Name _____ Date _____

After you gave the speech to your friends, they asked you questions. Use details from the text and illustrations to help you answer their questions.

Read page 475. How did Helen become blind and deaf?

1. _____

Read pages 476–478. Could Helen communicate at all before she learned to finger spell?

2. _____

_____

Read pages 481–484. How did Helen learn to spell?

3. _____

_____

_____

Read page 489. How did Helen become so famous?

4. _____

_____

_____

Long *o* (*o, oa, ow*)

Write the Spelling Word that matches each clue.

1. It cleans hands. _____

2. The biggest part _____

3. An animal that eats grass

_____

4. Something you do with a ball

_____

5. This person trains a team.

_____

6. You get taller when you _____

7. Two of something _____

8. A boat can _____.

9. When someone borrows money, it is a _____.

10. Water can _____ through a hose.

Spelling Words

Basic Words

1. own
2. most
3. soap
4. float
5. both
6. know
7. loan
8. goat
9. flow
10. loaf
11. throw
12. coach

Review Words

13. so
14. grow

Book Titles

> The first letter of each important word in a book title is capitalized. The entire title is underlined.

Write each book title correctly.

1. The book diary of a spider made me laugh.

_____

2. I read henry and mudge yesterday.

_____

3. Did you like reading teacher's pets?

_____

Write each sentence correctly.

4. Super storms was a great book.

_____

5. I read the book called my family.

_____

6. We all read schools around the world.

_____

Suffix -*ly*

Add -*ly* to the base word to make a new word. Write the new word on the line.

1. neat _____

2. soft _____

3. slow _____

4. warm _____

Choose the word from the box that completes the sentence. Write the word on the line.

Word Bank

happily	quickly	safely

5. The girl smiled _____ when she got the award.

6. I was _____ buckled into my seat.

7. We were able to clean up _____ because we had lots of help.

Proofread for Spelling

Proofread Dan's report. Circle the twelve misspelled words. Then write the correct spellings on the lines below.

I think baseball is the best game ever. My team is the Rams. A ram is a gote with big horns. Moast of my friends are on my team. Our coche teaches us to hit and throa the ball. You need to kno how to do bothe to play. You can't lofe at practice. We practice throwing until we make the ball floe from base to base.

I have my oan ball and glove. Our hard hats are on lon from the baseball club. I like to run from base to base. I feel like I can flote on air. Sometimes I slide into a base. When I get mud on my team shirt, Mom cleans it with sop.

Spelling Words

Basic Words
1. own
2. most
3. soap
4. float
5. both
6. know
7. loan
8. goat
9. flow
10. loaf
11. throw
12. coach

1. _____   7. _____

2. _____   8. _____

3. _____   9. _____

4. _____   10. _____

5. _____   11. _____

6. _____   12. _____

Present and Future Time

- Add *-s* to the end of the verb when it tells about a noun that names one. Add *-es* to verbs ending with *s, x, ch,* and *sh* when they tell about a noun that names one.

  Examples: The boy <u>jumps</u>. The egg <u>hatches</u>.

- Add *will* before the verb to tell about an action that will happen in the future.

Draw a line under the correct verb.

1. The coach (teach, teaches) the girl.

2. The child (read, reads) in Braille.

3. The man (fix, fixes) their answers.

Write each sentence correctly to show future time.

4. Carlos reach for a pen.

_____

5. Mary wash her hands before dinner.

_____

6. Ben pass the ball to me.

_____

Connect to Writing

Without Words That Tell When	With Words That Tell When
Ben visits me. He hurt his leg. I made a card for him.	Ben visits me every Saturday. He hurt his leg on June 12, 2014. I made a card for him on Valentine's Day.

Read the paragraph. Add phrases from the box to tell when. Write the phrases on the lines.

next Presidents' Day	last Thanksgiving
September 16	every Thursday

Sarah teaches sign language. She started to teach

on _____, 2015. She teaches two

classes at my school _____. She did sign

language for a school play _____.

She will do it again for the play coming up

_____.

Name _____ Date _____

Lesson 15
READER'S NOTEBOOK

Officer Buckle
and Gloria
Phonics: Compound Words

Compound Words

Read the letter. Draw a circle around each compound word.

Dear Grandfather,

   This afternoon I went to the playground with some

kids from my classroom. We played baseball until

sunset. It was so much fun! Then I went inside to do

my homework. I went upstairs and saw the photo of us

at the seashore in the summertime. I still have the

seashell we found there!

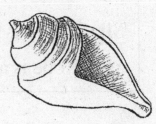

                                        Love,
                                        Julia

Write a compound word you know on each line.

_____   _____   _____

Officer Buckle
and Gloria
Grammar: Abbreviations

Titles for People

- A **title** may be used before a person's name.
- A title begins with a capital letter and usually ends with a period.

Mr. Ramon is a music teacher.

Miss Kobe is a crossing guard.

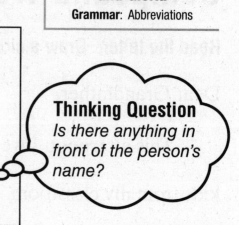

Thinking Question
Is there anything in front of the person's name?

Write each underlined title and name correctly.

1. Our teacher <u>miss Mullen</u> asks a police officer to visit.

   _____

2. On Mondays <u>mr Ramon</u> comes to our class.

   _____

3. He brings his partner, <u>mrs Shay</u>.

   _____

4. They come with <u>dr Lucky</u>.

   _____

5. They talk with the coach, <u>ms Smith</u>.

   _____

Compound Words

Find words in the box that go together to make compound words. Then use the compound words to complete the sentences below. Read each completed sentence.

> **Word Bank**
>
> pop   gold   sun   rain   snow   sail
> flake   boat   corn   bow   fish   shine

1. The _____ melted on my nose.

2. We saw a _____ in the sky

   after it rained.

3. _____ is a good snack to have

   in the afternoon.

4. It is fun to be on the lake in a _____.

5. Kate feeds her _____ twice a day.

6. The _____ felt warm on my face.

Compound Words

**Officer Buckle
and Gloria**
Spelling: Compound Words

Sort the Spelling Words by the number of letters in the
first word in each compound word.

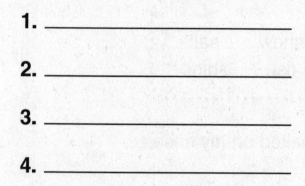

Four Letters or More

1. _____

2. _____

3. _____

4. _____

Three Letters

5. _____

6. _____

7. _____

8. _____

9. _____

Two Letters

10. _____   13. _____

11. _____   14. _____

12. _____

Spelling Words

Basic Words
1. cannot
2. pancake
3. maybe
4. baseball
5. playground
6. someone
7. myself
8. classroom
9. sunshine
10. outside
11. upon
12. nothing

Review Words
13. into
14. inside

Abbreviations for Days and Months

- Each day of the week can be written in a short way, called an **abbreviation**.

Mon. Tues. Wed. Thurs. Fri. Sat. Sun.

- Some months of the year can also be written in a short way. Notice that May, June, and July do not have a shortened form.

Jan.	**May**	**Sept.**
Feb.	**June**	**Oct.**
Mar.	**July**	**Nov.**
Apr.	**Aug.**	**Dec.**

The first Tues. in Mar.

Thinking Question
What does the short form of the word look like?

Write the abbreviation for each word.

1. Wednesday _____

2. December _____

3. Sunday _____

4. January _____

5. Monday _____

6. March _____

7. September _____

8. Tuesday _____

9. November _____

10. Saturday _____

11. February _____

12. July _____

13. June _____

14. October _____

15. Thursday _____

16. August _____

17. Friday _____

18. April _____

Focus Trait: Organization
Topic Sentences

A good persuasive essay has a goal, reasons, facts, and examples. The **goal** is what the writer wants. **Reasons** tell why. **Facts** and **examples** give more information about the reason.

Read the persuasive essay. Write the goal. Circle the reasons. Underline facts and examples.

Why We Need Officer Buckle and Gloria

I have a great idea! Officer Buckle and Gloria should speak at our school.

One reason is that we all need to learn about safety. Safety tips can keep us from hurting ourselves. They can even save lives!

Another reason is that Officer Buckle and Gloria put on a great show! Gloria acts out all the safety tips. Kids love watching Gloria!

So please, let's invite Officer Buckle and Gloria to speak at our school. I think it would be great!

Goal: _____

What reason does the second paragraph tell about?

_____

_____

Schwa Vowel Sound

Write each word. Draw a slash (/) to divide the word between syllables. Then circle the quieter syllable with the schwa sound.

1. happen _____

2. about _____

3. talent _____

4. nickel _____

5. alone _____

6. dragonfly _____

Now use the words you wrote above to complete the sentences below.

7. Luis has a lot of _____ for singing.

8. Sometimes Mia likes to be _____.

9. A _____ flew by.

10. What will _____ if it rains during the game?

11. Stan paid a _____ for a gumball.

12. Tell me _____ the picture you made.

Name _____ Date _____

Lesson 15
READER'S NOTEBOOK

Officer Buckle
and Gloria
Independent Reading

Reader's Guide

Officer Buckle and Gloria

Make a Poster

Use details and pictures from the book. Describe how Officer Buckle and Gloria learn to work together.

Read page 509. What did the children do while Officer Buckle gave talks without Gloria?

_____

Read pages 511–514. Now Officer Buckle has Gloria. How does Gloria help make his speeches better?

_____

_____

Read page 515. How did Officer Buckle change after Gloria joined him?

_____

Read page 523. What did Gloria do when Officer Buckle was not with her?

_____

Name _____ Date _____

Officer Buckle wants you to create a poster. The poster will tell people about his safety speeches. Use details and pictures from the book to help you create your poster.

Safety First
Safety Speeches by Officer Buckle and Gloria

Who We Are

_____

_____

_____

_____

What We Do

_____

_____

_____

_____

How We Make Safety Fun

_____

_____

_____

_____

How to Reach Us

Find us at our website!
SafeSchoolsRFun.org

Compound Words

Draw lines to match the words that form the Spelling
Words. Then write the Spelling Words.

play	self
sun	to
my	ground
in	shine
some	not
can	one
out	side

pan	thing
no	cake
may	on
base	be
class	side
up	ball
in	room

Spelling Words

Basic Words

1. cannot
2. pancake
3. maybe
4. baseball
5. playground
6. someone
7. myself
8. classroom
9. sunshine
10. outside
11. upon
12. nothing

Review Words

13. into
14. inside

1. _____   8. _____

2. _____   9. _____

3. _____   10. _____

4. _____   11. _____

5. _____   12. _____

6. _____   13. _____

7. _____   14. _____

Abbreviations for Places

Write each underlined place correctly. Use abbreviations.

1. I live on <u>Robin Road.</u>

_____

2. The pool is on <u>Shore drive.</u>

_____

3. Where is <u>Third avenue</u>?

_____

Write the name of the underlined words correctly. Write each abbreviation in its long form.

4. Max lives on <u>North St.</u>

_____

5. Gloria visited a school on <u>Elm Ave.</u>

_____

6. <u>Rose Rd.</u> is only two blocks long.

_____

Lesson 15
READER'S NOTEBOOK

**Officer Buckle
and Gloria**
Vocabulary Strategies:
Root Words

Root Words

Underline the root word in each word. Use what you
know about the root word to figure out the word's meaning.
Complete each sentence by writing the word whose
meaning fits the best.

```
····································· Vocabulary ·····································

    timer        unwrap       deepest      retake
    restacked    freezer      reddish      fielder
```

1. Joe didn't pass the math test. He will _____

the test next week.

2. I put the meat in the _____ because

it must stay cold.

3. Sarah used a _____ to see how long she swam.

4. After he ran, his face was a _____ color.

5. You can't _____ your presents until your birthday.

6. Scientists want to learn what lives in the _____

part of the ocean.

7. Maria _____ the books on her desk.

8. Roger was a good _____, so he

played in the outfield.

Proofread for Spelling

**Proofread these sentences. Circle the misspelled words.
Then write the correct spellings on the lines below.**

1. Wear sunscreen when you are owtside in the
   sunsheen.

   _____   _____

2. You canut throw things in your clasroom.

   _____   _____

3. Let somone help you cook a pancak.

   _____   _____

4. To protect miself, I wear a bike helmet uppon my head.

   _____   _____

5. Nutting should be close by when you hit a basbal.

   _____   _____

6. Mayby we can go to the plagrownd on Sunday.

   _____   _____

Spelling Words

Basic Words

1. cannot
2. pancake
3. maybe
4. baseball
5. playground
6. someone
7. myself
8. classroom
9. sunshine
10. outside
11. upon
12. nothing

Past and Future Time

Rewrite each sentence to change when the action happened. Use the word in ( ).

1. The police officers talk about safety. (past)

_____

2. The children listen to them. (future)

_____

3. They follow the rules. (future)

_____

Read the story. Find five verbs that do not tell about the past, and fix them. Write the story correctly on the lines.

The policeman and his dog walked to the school. They wait at the front door. Then the dog bark. The principal open the door. The policeman talk with the children about safety. The children thank him.

_____

_____

_____

_____

Name _____ Date _____

Connect to Writing

Incorrect Abbreviations	Correct Abbreviations
dr levi	Dr. Levi
ms Jones	Ms. Jones
miss Oaks	Miss Oaks
River st	River St.
Tues	Tues.
jan.	Jan.

Proofread the paragraph. Fix any mistakes in abbreviations. Write the paragraph correctly on the lines.

My dad is a teacher. Kids call him mr Gary. On tues Dad read to his class. In mar they studied butterflies. Then on fri they visited a butterfly show. The show was on Main st.

_____

_____

_____

_____

_____

Reading and Writing Glossary

Use this glossary to help you remember and use words that you are learning about reading and writing.

A

....

abbreviation A short way to write a word by taking out some of the letters and adding a period at the end.

adjective A word that describes a noun. An adjective may tell how something looks, tastes, smells, sounds, or feels.

adverb A word that describes a verb. An adverb may tell how, where, when, or how much something is. An adverb may end in -ly.

alphabetical order When words are listed in the same order as the letters of the alphabet.

analyze To look at or study something carefully.

antonym A word that has the opposite, or nearly the opposite, meaning as another word.

apostrophe A punctuation mark (') that takes the place of missing letters in a word.

author's purpose The reason an author has for writing a text.

B

....

bar graph A drawing that uses bars to compare numbers.

base word A word to which endings, prefixes, and suffixes can be added. A base word is also called a root word.

biography A story that tells about the real events that make up a person's life.

boldface print Dark print that stands out from the rest of a text.

C

caption Text that gives more information about a photograph.

categorize To name a group of similar objects.

cause The reason why something happens.

characters The people and animals in a story.

chart A drawing that lists information in a clear way.

classify To group similar objects.

command A type of sentence that gives an order. A command may end with a period (.) or an exclamation mark (!).

compare To tell how things are alike.

compound sentence A sentence made up of two shorter sentences. A compound sentence is connected by words such as *and, but,* and *or.*

compound word A longer word made up of two shorter words.

conclusion An idea or opinion reached after thinking about several facts.

connect To link things that are similar.

context The words and sentences around a word that give readers clues to its meaning.

contraction A short way of writing two words using an apostrophe (').

contrast To tell how things are different.

D

detail A fact or example that tells more about a main idea.

diagram A drawing that shows how something works.

dialogue A conversation between two or more characters in a story.

dictionary entry A book part that lists a word with its correct pronunciation, part of speech, and meaning.

directions Step-by-step instructions for how to do or make something.

E

effect Something that happens as a result of something else.

electronic menu A feature of a website that lists the information that can be found on the website.

ending A word part attached to the end of a base word (or root word) that can change the meaning of the base word.

evaluate To form an opinion or make a judgment about something.

exclamation A sentence that shows a strong feeling. An exclamation begins with a capital letter and ends with an exclamation point (!).

F

fable A short story in which a character learns a lesson.

fact Something that can be proved true.

fairy tale A make-believe story that has been told for many years.

fantasy A story that could not happen in real life.

folktale A type of traditional tale.

formal language The kind of words and sentences that should be used when writing or speaking in school or with someone you do not know well.

future tense The form of a verb that tells about an action that will happen in the future.

G

glossary A list of unfamiliar or specialized words with their definitions, usually found at the back of a book.

graphic features Photographs or drawings, including maps and charts, that stand for ideas or add details to the text.

H

heading The title of part of a text.

homograph A word that has the same spelling as another word but has a different meaning and may be pronounced differently.

homophone A word that sounds the same as another word but is spelled differently and has a different meaning.

humorous fiction A story that includes characters who do or say funny things. Humorous fiction may also include events that would not happen in real life.

I

icon A symbol or picture on a website.

idiom A saying or expression that cannot be understood from the individual meanings of the words that make it up or by its literal meaning.

illustration A drawing that shows important details to help the reader understand more about the story.

informal language A casual way of using words and sentences when writing or speaking to friends or family members.

informational text Text that gives facts about real events and people.

informative writing Writing that gives facts about a topic.

interview A conversation in which a person asks another person questions and records his or her answers.

L

label Text that points out an important part of a diagram or other picture.

M

main idea The most important idea about the topic.

map A drawing of a town, state, or other place.

moral The lesson a character learns in a story.

multiple-meaning word A word that has more than one meaning.

N

narrative nonfiction Text that tells a true story about a topic.

narrative writing Writing that tells a story. A narrative tells about something that happened to a person or a character.

noun A word that names a person, an animal, a place, or a thing.

O

opinion What someone thinks, believes, or feels.

opinion writing Writing that tells what the writer believes and gives reasons.

P

past tense The form of a verb that tells about an action that happened in the past.

photograph A real-life image, taken with a camera, that can help to show ideas in a text.

play A story that people act out.

plot The order of story events, including the problem and how it is solved.

plural noun A noun that names more than one person, animal, place, or thing.

poetry Text that is written in a special way to use rhythm and the sound of the words to show ideas and feelings.

point of view The way a character or person thinks about an event.

possessive noun A noun that shows a person or animal owns or has something.

possessive pronoun A pronoun that shows ownership, such as *my, your, mine, yours, his,* and *hers.*

predicate The part of the sentence where the verb is found. The predicate tells what the subject did or does.

prefix A word part attached at the beginning of a base word (or root word) that changes the meaning of the word.

present tense The form of a verb that tells about an action happening now, in present time.

pronoun A word that can take the place of a noun, such as *I, he, she, it, we,* or *they.*

proper noun A special name of a person, animal, place, or thing. A proper noun begins with a capital letter.

Q

question A type of sentence that asks something and ends with a question mark (?).

quotation marks Punctuation marks that show what someone says. Quotation marks (" ") are placed at the beginning and end of a speaker's exact words.

R

realistic fiction A story that could happen in real life.

reflexive pronoun A special pronoun, such as *myself, himself, herself, themselves,* and *ourselves,* that is used after a verb.

repetition A pattern of writing in which the same words are used more than once.

research report Writing that tells what a writer learned from doing research about a topic.

rhythm A pattern of beats. The musical notes, words, and phrases in a song make up its rhythm.

root word A simple word that is part of another word. It is also known as a base word. Adding a prefix or suffix to a root word changes its meaning.

S

sequence of events The order in which things happen.

setting When and where a story takes place.

simile A comparison that uses *like* or *as.*

simple sentence A short sentence with a subject and predicate. Two simple sentences joined by a comma and a word such as *and, but,* or *or* make up a compound sentence.

singular noun A noun that names one person, animal, place, or thing.

song Words and music that are sung together.

statement A type of sentence that tells something and ends with a period (.).

story structure The way characters, a setting, and a plot are put together in a story.

subheading A short title that gives more information about a selection. A subheading comes after a selection's heading.

subject The naming part of a sentence, which tells who or what did or does something.

suffix A word part attached to the end of a base word that changes the meaning of the word.

synonym A word that has the same, or almost the same, meaning as another word.

T
....

text and graphic features Photographs, labels, headings, captions, illustrations, dark print, and other special features that add information to a selection.

text evidence Clues in the words and pictures that help you figure things out.

text features Parts of the text, such as headings or boldface print, that help readers recognize important information.

time line A drawing that shows the order in which events happened.

topic What a text is mainly about.

traditional tale A story that has been told for many years.

traits Ways of speaking and acting that show what someone is like.

V

verb A word that names an action that someone or something does or did. A verb can also tell what someone or something is.

W

website An online collection of pages about a topic.

word choice The words and phrases an author uses to make his or her writing interesting and clear.